PENGUIN BOOKS

SHADOW BABY

'Compelling … Forster's complex and moving narrative mirrors our knowledge of the tangle behind that generalized notion, "family feeling"' – Melissa Benn in the *New Statesman*

'The cumulative tension she winds up is extraordinary … Evie and Leah's strange story reads like one of Dickens's darker narratives rewritten by a woman of sense instead of a man of sentiment' – Patrick Gale in the *Daily Telegraph*

'Undeniably gripping … the way Forster demonstrates the way a single act can spawn many fatal consequences is both moving and impressive' – Leo Colston in *Time Out*

'Forster mixes calm historical detail with powerful emotional drama' – Sally Emerson in *The Times*

'Gripping … she lights a crackling firework of emotions, skilfully interweaving the historical with the modern' – Anna-Katharina Peitz in the *Yorkshire Post*

'There is nothing fantastic or implausible about this novel. It is firmly rooted in ordinary human experience: the things that people do to each other and the festering – often secret – suffering which can result … Forster at her finest' – Susan Elkin in the *Literary Review*

'Margaret Forster has the knack of choosing cracking good subjects for her fiction' – Caroline Moore in the *Sunday Telegraph*

ABOUT THE AUTHOR

Margaret Forster was born in Carlisle in 1938. Educated at the County High School, she won an open scholarship to Somerville College, Oxford, where she read history. Her many novels include *Georgy Girl*, *The Seduction of Mrs Pendlebury*, *Private Papers*, *Mother Can You Hear Me?*, *Have the Men Had Enough?*, *Lady's Maid*, *The Battle for Christabel*, *Mothers' Boys* and *Shadow Baby*, all of which are published by Penguin. Margaret Forster has written numerous works of non-fiction, including a biography of Bonnie Prince Charlie, entitled *The Rash Adventurer*; a highly praised 'autobiography' of Thackeray, published in 1978; *Significant Sisters* (1986), which traces the lives and careers of eight pioneering women; a biography of Elizabeth Barrett Browning, which won the Royal Society of Literature's Award for 1988 under the Heinemann bequest; a selection of Elizabeth Barrett Browning's poetry; her critically acclaimed biography *Daphne du Maurier*, which was awarded the 1994 Fawcett Book Prize; and *Hidden Lives*, a family memoir, which was nominated nine times in 1995 as Book of the Year and is also published by Penguin.

Margaret Forster lives in London and the Lake District. She is married to writer and broadcaster Hunter Davies and they have three children.

SHADOW BABY

Margaret Forster

PENGUIN BOOKS

PENGUIN BOOKS

Published by the Penguin Group
Penguin Books Ltd, 27 Wrights Lane, London W8 5TZ, England
Penguin Putnam Inc., 375 Hudson Street, New York, New York 10014, USA
Penguin Books Australia Ltd, Ringwood, Victoria, Australia
Penguin Books Canada Ltd, 10 Alcorn Avenue, Toronto, Ontario, Canada M4V 3B2
Penguin Books (NZ) Ltd, 182–190 Wairau Road, Auckland 10, New Zealand

Penguin Books Ltd, Registered Offices: Harmondsworth, Middlesex, England

First published by Chatto & Windus 1996
Published in Penguin Books 1997
7 9 10 8

Printed in England by Clays Ltd, St Ives plc

IN LOVING MEMORY OF
MY SISTER-IN-LAW
MARION
1939–1995

Prologue

LEAH STOOD still. The stairs were narrow and steep, the whole flight, fourteen steps in all, quite straight. The light was not on in the vestibule, nor in the parlour opening off it to the right, but there was a dim glow seeping from under the door to the kitchen at the end of the passage. Without that one feeble band of light there would have been no shadow to torment her. It was five o'clock on a dark and wet December afternoon. All was black in the street outside. The street lamp was broken, destroyed by boys throwing stones, and was now without glass except for some shards still clinging to the casing.

She couldn't move until the shadow moved, and it was quite frighteningly motionless. It was so familiar, the outline, hardly a shadow at all. There was nothing blank or flat about it, nothing insubstantial. Solid, it was to Leah, solid, hard, especially the head, like a lump of iron behind the glass of the door. Over and over again she had told herself to change that front door, to have the two glass panels removed and replaced with wood. Then there could never be any shadow. But a greater fear always stopped her. If there were no shadow, there would be reality to face. She might be caught unawares, she might answer a knock some innocent-feeling afternoon, and be confronted. In daylight, of course, she could always see more, though the glass was not plain. It was tinted green, pretty glass, with a pink rose engraved at the bottom of each panel. But it allowed a good deal of vision, especially on a sunny day. It gave her warning of who was there and she could not bear to do without this.

The shadow moved, the knocker rang out, the brass ring lifted and lowered three times, as always. She was so regular, the shadow. Twice more she did it, always three slow, deliberate knocks. Then she would go, the ritual complete. Leah went on standing there, clutching the handrail, waiting. She never moved first, never left her position. She could have gone into her bedroom and closed the door and the curtains. But she never did, she had to bear witness: it was her duty, part of her punishment. There. It was gone. Nothing at all to be seen now, except the door itself, wood and glass, harmless once more. Sometimes she had visions of the door being broken down, of her visitor becoming so demented, so incensed with grief or anger that she smashed the glass and thrust her strong hand through to open it. She imagined violence all the time but the shadow was never violent. Henry had always said she had the wrong idea, that she had nothing to fear in that respect, but she had never believed him. He was a man, he did not understand. All the time, all these years, she had asked herself what she would want if she had been the shadow and she had no doubt of her answer. Henry said if only she would agree to a meeting ... but the idea threw her into paroxysms of terror. Let Henry meet her (as indeed he had done).

How tired she felt, an awful exhaustion quite different from any other she had ever experienced. She could hardly get herself into the bedroom, even the act of levering herself on to the bed, sitting first, swinging her legs up afterwards but failing, having to lift each one on to the slippery blue eiderdown, was almost beyond her. She did not expect to sleep. Nobody as guilty as she knew herself to be could ever sleep after such visitations. Sleep would come later and the bliss now, as she lay aching inside and out, was to know that. Soon, she would fall into such a deep sleep it was as if she entered another state of being altogether. Often, she wondered if this kind of sleep was akin to death, a sleep quite dreamless, slipped into with such unconcern, without struggle. She could always feel it about to happen, and she would feel herself smile as she went eagerly over and into the welcoming oblivion. Even waking, a long satisfying time later, was pleasant. She felt calm and sensible. She was thoroughly refreshed, restored by this sleep of relief.

She ordered herself to be still, to let time pass, to endure the fear and misery with fortitude. This was always how it was and how it would be until one of them died.

*

It would have been the perfect crime except no crime was committed. Hazel knew she had done wrong but she had learned to live with this awkward knowledge quite quickly. It always seemed to her when she looked back, though this was something she tried (rather successfully) not to do, that her mother had conspired to make her feel she had done no wrong except to herself. And yet she had tried, always, to be honest and to make no excuses. 'It was my fault,' she had said, without weeping, though not entirely dry-eyed, 'it was my fault, not his, don't blame him, please.' But she had no need to beg that he should not be accused in any way. Her mother didn't even want to know his name. From the very beginning, after her confession, her mother had made it plain that only one thing was vital: absolute secrecy. She and her mother would share this secret. Nobody else. Certainly not her father or her two brothers and never, *never*, the man in question. All would be well if this was kept absolutely secret. It could be managed, and, eventually, obliterated.

Managed it was. Her mother excelled at such management. Hazel felt herself so soothed by her mother's efficiency that she was in danger for a while of thinking she had done something of which to be proud rather than ashamed. What she remembered most vividly from that time was not the moment of confession but the moment of realisation which came much later, the day when it had finally penetrated her consciousness, that what lay ahead was going to be painful and distressing. Her mother had gone. She had brought her to this bleak place and now she had gone, leaving her in the care of people she did not know but who, she was told, were 'utterly dependable'. Two women, quite elderly. One had been a nurse, one a teacher. How her mother had found this couple Hazel never knew. They were part of what her mother called 'a network of women who help other women'. Once, when Hazel had asked if these two women were paid for looking after her those five months, her mother had laughed in astonishment and said of course they were paid, why else would they have done it, how else could they have been trusted? Confused, as she often was by her mother's strange logic, Hazel had said nothing more but it had upset her, this late evidence that the care of her had amounted to a job, a financial transaction.

The pretence was that she was learning Norwegian. 'Norwegian?' her father had exclaimed. 'Good God, why on earth does the girl want to learn Norwegian, nobody wants to learn that language, why on earth would they?' Her mother had thought it all out, her thoughts so complicated and devious they had the peculiarity of apparent truth. Hazel had always been 'fascinated by the Vikings', had she not? From a tiny child, loved tales about them. And she loved snow and ice. She never wanted to go to Mediterranean countries, did she, always begging to go to Scandinavia, so extraordinary. And now she wanted to go to university and read the Norse languages, so what better than actually to go and live in Norway and learn the language, or try to, for a few months? Her father had been exasperated but he had been amused too. 'This is my daughter Hazel,' he said to people when he introduced her, 'going to live in Norway to learn their ridiculous language, can you believe it?' Mostly people couldn't. Hazel grew tired of their bewilderment, even sometimes their irritation, and could hardly tell them she shared it. Why not France? Why not Italy? she had asked her mother. Why not Spain? 'Catholic countries, darling,' her mother said, 'don't you see?' Hazel hadn't done, not really. It was not as though she were seeking an abortion, so why did it matter whether the country she was hiding in was Catholic? Her mother said, 'Think,' and she did, she thought and thought and still it didn't make sense.

Perhaps the whole success of her mother's plan had depended on its bizarre nature. Told that Hazel was going to Bergen in Norway for a few months to learn Norwegian, people had queried only the oddity of her choice. Nobody had thought there could be any other reason for a seventeen-year-old girl to spend half a year in Norway. Even afterwards, when she didn't go to university to study Norwegian, or any other Norse language, but went to read law, nobody had been suspicious. 'Glad you came to your senses,' her father (a lawyer) had said. It only seemed to prove, somehow, how genuine the Norwegian episode had been. The two women in whose house she had stayed had died soon after she returned, one of a heart attack, the other five years later of Alzheimer's disease. Her mother had been quite triumphant: no one would now remember Hazel or her sojourn there. As if it mattered.

And yet somehow it did matter, especially to her mother. She wanted the whole 'episode', as she referred to it, to have been wiped out. The deaths of the two women were important. Only they had known Hazel's name, though even there Mrs Walmsley had covered her tracks. The women never saw Hazel's passport. They believed her 'real' name was Geraldine White. Her mother relished all these complicated subterfuges, she made the whole 'episode' seem like a game. But she was not there when the playing got rough. She never saw me, Hazel used to reflect, when it came to the end, how battered I was, how suddenly wretched and despairing and *guilty*. By the time her mother had come to collect her, she knew she had looked much as she usually looked only paler (that Norwegian winter) and fatter (that Norwegian food). 'All right, darling?' her mother had asked, admittedly anxious for once, and 'Fine,' she had said, 'fine, thank you, Mummy.'

Fine. She was fine. There was nothing melodramatic about Hazel. Slight in appearance, in character she was as solid as the stock from which her father so proudly told her she came. She got on with her life after this aberration and never made the same mistake again, never took the same risk. She wasn't morbid or sentimental, nor was she given to the kind of flights of fancy in which her mother indulged. This pragmatic outlook saved her, though not entirely. Certain things could trigger off such total recall of pain and loss that she would wonder if she knew herself at all. It was often a question of smells – a particular disinfectant, a brand she had never smelled since that night, and the scent of a drink, a drink with cloves (or something similar) in it, which she had been given to drink afterwards. And of shadows. The room had been all white, startlingly white, floor, ceiling, everywhere sterile and white, but since it was dark outside, the blinds – they were white too, everything white – were drawn and lights were on and she saw huge shadows when she briefly opened her eyes. She had tried not to see them, she had wanted everyone to remain unrecognisable, but her eyes had opened involuntarily at the moments when she lost control and then the shadows had danced on the wall in front of her.

That was what remained in her mind for ever. One shadow. Indistinct, an outline only, quickly whipped away. It swung in front of her appalled gaze and then was gone. Never put into her arms: that had been agreed. She heard the gurgling cry, knew the shadow had a voice, but she never felt the body from which it came. She did not weep, not then, she felt too frozen, hypnotised by the enormity of what she had done. A feeling of outright panic mixed with a new fear in her, the fear of one day being called to account, and her mother not being there to manage everything.

Part One

Evie – Shona

Chapter One

It was a narrow little house in a narrow lane, one of many all squeezed together, leaning on each other in what seemed such a cosy way. The lane ran between the cathedral and the town square and was much frequented. It was not at all a quiet street. Indeed, it was not really a street. It was paved in giant blocks of sandstone, unusual for a lane, but otherwise it had no pretensions to being a proper street. Mr Dobson, taking the census, hated lanes like this. They made his work difficult. Invariably the inhabitants of lanes like this were not at all clear as to how many people lived with them. They were vague or confused, or both, and yet his question was so simple: on the night of 8 April, how many people resided in this house? The householders were meant to have filled in the appropriate form, delivered by his own good self (therefore let there not be any question of a form not having been received), but in these lanes the job had rarely been done. Often, the form had been lost; another had to be produced and then the effort of memory would be mighty, though fewer than twenty-four hours had gone by.

Mr Dobson was patient and understanding, or so he judged himself. He had at least enough imagination to be aware that to many householders he was also alarming. Nobody was ever cheeky; impertinence to an officer of the Crown carried too great a risk. They were on the whole respectful but resentful and he had to cope with this. He was particularly kind to women, especially to the elderly widows who lived in this lane. He wanted the census form filled in correctly: that was of prime importance. When an old woman opened the door of No. 10, Mr Dobson immediately doffed his hat, smiled and identified himself at once, producing his badge of accreditation. The woman, a Miss Mary Messenger, looked feeble.

She was also, he quickly realised, more than slightly deaf. Instead of bawling at her, Mr Dobson flourished a census form, pointed to the date and then to what was required by law and hoped Miss Messenger was not also short-sighted. She stood so long staring at the form that Mr Dobson began to wonder if she were illiterate, not uncommon with these elderly women. Fortunately she was not. After her long perusal, Miss Messenger shuffled off down the passageway and re-emerged clutching the original form delivered days before.

She put it into his hand without a word. Mr Dobson looked at it. To his surprise, it was filled in. The only occupant of No. 10 on the night of 8 April had been Miss Messenger herself. Mr Dobson thanked her and backed away as she shut the door. But he saw, just before it closed, the face of a small girl appear round the corner of the door at the far end of the passage. Only the briefest and most indistinct of glimpses but indisputably real, the face of a young girl, a small white blob of a face framed by a good deal of untidy dark hair. He stood for a moment, thinking. Had the old woman concealed the fact that a child lived with her? But why would she do that? Mr Dobson walked slowly down the lane reflecting that whether there was a child residing at No. 10 or not was of no great importance. She might be only a visitor, a relative there for the day. There was no reason to conclude that she lived there. Residents in lanes like this were forever hiding things from landlords, terrified that rents would be raised if it were discovered they harboured paying lodgers. One little girl living with an elderly woman was neither here nor there. He was not a landlord, thank heaven, nor a policeman. It was not his duty to pry, only to collect. The census form had been collected and that was that, but he went on his way faintly worried.

Mary Messenger, aged eighty (as stated on the census form), was still standing behind her front door, listening. She had her good ear pressed to the wide crack in the door, only recently emptied of the rags which had filled it all winter. She heard the census man's footsteps go off down the lane and was satisfied. But when she turned and saw Evie standing there, she shouted at her. 'Didn't I tell you, eh, didn't I say stay in the kitchen, eh, what you playing at, you want taken away to the poorhouse, eh?' Evie withdrew and Mary muttered her way after her, into the small dark kitchen at the back of the house. 'Nothing but bother, you're nothing but bother, and what thanks do I get these days, eh?' Evie ignored her. She stood on a stool and kneaded the dough on the table, her little firsts barely making any indentation, though she was trying so hard to do what her grandma did. The sight of the child's ineffectual kneading recalled Mary to the task at hand. She picked up the dough and slapped it about, her hands no longer shaking, as they did when they were not busy, but suddenly strong and skilful. Evie watched and admired and, without needing to be told, smeared lard on the inside of the bread pan. There was silence until the dough was shaped and moulded into the pan and then Evie hopped on to another stool and, using an old dishcloth, carefully opened the door of the oven in the range. In went the bread and Mary sighed and sat down and said, 'You're a good girl when all's said and done. We'll have a cup of tea and you can sugar it.'

She watched Evie take the blackened kettle off the hook over the fire. Very careful, the child was, did everything she was told carefully and liked to do it. There was no sulking, no impudence, not yet, but then she was only five, only just turned five. Not pretty, never would be, Mary had seen that from the beginning, but she was healthy, that was the main thing, and strong, and she had a cheerful disposition, so far. The tea was made and they both sat in front of the steaming mugs with a measure of contentment which each could sense in the other. 'Well, Evie,' Mary said, watching the child blow the steam and warm her hands on the mug, 'I don't know what's to be done about you. I haven't said you're here, don't you worry, but it can't go on for ever, can it, eh? Not for ever. I won't live much longer, that's for sure, my time'll be up soon, then what, eh?' Evie said nothing at all in reply. She appeared quite unperturbed by her grandmother's ramblings and only looked up from her tea at the 'eh?' sounds, as though not understanding the rest. Any 'eh?' commanded her attention, as it was meant to. Sometimes Mary said 'eh?' in no context at all, a sudden, harsh querying of nothing.

Evie went on blowing the steam which rose from the tea and stirring the sugar she had been allowed to put in even though it had long since dissolved. She liked the faint tinkle of the spoon on the side of the mug, a sound too faint for her grandmother to catch and object to as she objected, inexplicably, to so many things. Each day, it seemed to Evie, was full of traps, of things she must not do or say. She must not get up until she was told, unless she needed to use the po and even then she was expected to hop back into bed sharpish until given the signal to rise. Her grandmother slept in a double bed which took up most of the room and Evie slept on a mattress at the foot of it. There was room for three of her size in the bed with her grandmother, but she was not allowed to share it. 'I might smother you,' Mary said, and Evie accepted this as she was bound to accept everything.

She knew this old woman was not in fact her grandmother because she had been told so, not long ago. 'Am I your grandmother, eh?' Mary had barked at her, sounding angry. She had nodded dumbly, though aware as ever of verbal traps. 'No, I'm not,' the old woman said. 'Good as, used as, but I'm not, now don't you forget, eh? You haven't got a real grandmother and what do you need one for when you've got me willing, eh? You've got me willing, I dare say I'll get my reward in heaven.' And then, later, equally unexpected and sudden, she had said: 'If anyone asks, mind, I *am* your grandmother, eh? You remember that, don't you forget, it could be more than your life is worth.' Evie's heart had thudded a little at those words. It wasn't the contradiction which frightened her – first she had a grandmother (all she had) and then she didn't and now she did again (only sometimes, only if asked) – but the mention of her life. What was a life? How could anything be worth more? But she merely nodded, as though she had understood, and said nothing.

Evie, just turned five, was an expert at knowing when to say nothing. They were the first words she remembered, the first instruction – 'Say nothing.' She remembered being bundled into shawls and taken by Mary to the market and being told, 'Say nothing, if anyone talks to you, say nothing, eh?' She had obeyed, though it had not been difficult since all that the other butter women said to her was 'Are you cold, pet?' and 'Are you hungry?' and in both cases a shake of the head was sufficient. She sat on a little stool behind the old wooden bench that served as her grandmother's stall and watched the people coming to buy. She was seated so low down, almost on the ground, that what she mostly saw were skirts and feet, an endless procession of long skirts and black boots. Seeking to see something more interesting and of greater variety she gave herself a crick in the neck, peering upwards so hard and earnestly at all the faces looming over her grandmother's eggs. At the end of the morning, when she was carried to the cart and they trundled all the long way back to Wetheral, she fell asleep and never saw anything of the return journey to the village.

Those days, the days of going to market with her grandmother, were already a long way off in her young mind. She could only just recall the green in the village and the big houses round it and the plains above the river where they had lived. But she knew she had preferred it: that country life, and the presence of someone else, some other woman whose face she could not recall. All that had gone. Here, in the city, she stayed in the house almost all her time, with her grandmother. They went out to shop once a week to that same market where once they had sold flowers and eggs. On Sundays, the cathedral bells, so close by, vibrated through the house but she and her grandmother did not go to church. She had never, to her knowledge, in her short memory, been inside a church. She was sure she *should* go to church and did once suggest it but her grandmother told her there was plenty of time for her to be a churchgoer in the future if she wished. 'Any road,' Mary had said, 'you're baptised, you can rest easy, she saw to that at least, baptised, all proper, in Holy Trinity, does that satisfy you, eh?'

It almost did. Evie knew where Holy Trinity was. It was the big church at the junction of the two roads in Caldewgate, outside the west wall of the city. She felt proud to have been baptised there and could see herself being held over the font and almost feel the holy water on her baby forehead. She longed to go into Holy Trinity and she resolved that one day she would indeed get inside the church and see the font. She had pictures and that was all. Her grandmother had a bible, even if she never went to church, and inside was a little illustrated booklet about Holy Trinity. One picture, very grainy, showed the font and a woman holding a baby and the vicar about to baptise it. Maybe the baby was her; she could at least pretend it was. But who, then, was the pleasant young woman holding her? Not her grandmother. There was a man in the picture too, standing a little behind the woman, his hat in his hand. Who was the man? Impossible to know, as most things were.

'You've made a meal of that tea,' Mary said. 'Sup it up, there's work to be done and half the morning gone. Get the tub, get that kettle back on, get the soap.' Evie got everything. She had to drag the heavy tin tub along, it was too heavy to carry, but she managed successfully to position it under the tap in the yard. The yard was tiny, barely three feet wide and five feet long; and at this time on a bleak spring morning it was bitterly cold. The fronts of the houses in the lane were protected from the wind by the high buildings opposite but the backs were not. The east wind, scudding down on to the city direct from the Pennines, hopped and skipped over the walls of the yards and, once inside them, ricocheted from end to end forming a whirlpool of dust. Evie went back inside and found her shawl and fixed it over her head and across her chest, fastening it with a safety-pin. Then she was ready.

She got the washing and put it into the tub and ran cold water on to it, and Mary appeared carrying the big kettle and added its contents to the tub. The water coming out of the spout was boiling but all it did was reduce the freezing cold of the water already in the tub. Mary made it clear that donating this hot water was a matter of being kind and that when she was a girl like Evie she had had to do the washing without its benefit. She stood and watched as Evie took a bar of soap and began soaping the clothes and pummelling them about and she sighed, as she always did, and said, 'I miss my wash-house, I should never have left that wash-house, eh?'

She still had a mangle, though. There was nowhere inside to put it so it stood in the yard, and Mary worried about it constantly. When they were in the house and the rain and wind were lashing the windows she'd groan and say, 'Oh, my mangle, out in this. Oh, that lovely mangle.' It was kept covered with a bit of sacking but many a wind was strong enough to whip this off in the night, no matter how well it had been secured, and then the mangle would be soaked and little by little the soakings were rusting the iron. It took both of them, these days, to turn the handle and it tired Mary. 'Sooner you grow big and strong the better,' she would say. 'This mangle is beating me, it's a devil, I had it tamed once but it's breaking out, it's beating us.' One day, not so long ago, she had said something else while she struggled with the fearful mangle. She said the usual bit about how the mangle was beating her now and there followed the well-worn memory of how once she had mastered it easily, and then she said something new: 'Your mother always promised ...' And then she stopped, abruptly, and turned the handle of the mangle furiously, with a sudden extra vigour, for a while.

Evie had heard the words quite distinctly – 'Your mother.' Her mother. She had a mother, then. Was it a mother who, like Mary, like her so-called grandmother, wasn't a mother at all? She didn't ask, she only registered the crucial word 'mother'. She'd seen little girls with mothers, she heard them saying 'Mam, mam,' she'd seen them belonging together, girls like herself and women called mam. She'd never asked, not yet, why she didn't have a mother but that wasn't because she was not curious, or that she didn't want to know the answer. It was just that she didn't ask questions at all. Questions annoyed Mary, even simple ones. 'Why does the clock tick?' for example produced rage, and a sharp 'It's a *clock*, now stop bothering the life out of me, why do clocks tick indeed, the idea, I don't know what's to become of you, I don't!' Any question at all brought forth this cry – 'I don't know what's to become of you!' and Evie had grown to dread it. It worried her, that and her grandmother's constant refrain that soon she would no longer be around, that her time was nearly up, she had not long to go.

The day after the census man came, Mary was even more short-tempered than usual and muttered all day long in a state of extra agitation. The bread was made, the broth cooked, the washing done, everything went on as normal but Evie knew something was going to happen. Her grandmother was forever telling her to 'Be still, settle yourself,' but now it was she who flitted about, touching things, as though checking them, as though making sure the table and chairs and cupboards were there. She opened and shut drawers all day long and in the afternoon, when she often had forty winks on her bed while Evie was given some task to do quietly – cleaning the cruet, making a fresh paper doily for it, cleaning the six precious silver teaspoons, tidying the larder, polishing the sideboard – she could be heard moving about and dragging something from under the bed. Evie wasn't in the least surprised to be shouted for long before the regular half hour was up and she went willingly, eagerly, up the few narrow stairs into the one bedroom.

Her grandmother was sitting on the edge of the bed with a small suitcase open beside her. It appeared to be full of papers, bundles of what looked like letters and some longer documents tied up with string. Mary was undoing the string on one lot. 'I'm all thumbs,' she complained, 'damned knots. Here, with your little fingers, you do it, Evie, but take care, mind, don't tear anything, eh?' Evie took care. She enjoyed delicately plucking at the knots and gradually working them loose and managing to draw the string free time after time. The knots were knobbly things, hard with age; they had been meant to be as secure as they were proving to be. Mary watched her, breathing hard, but for once ceasing to rant on. When the last vicious knot was undone she pushed Evie's excited hand away and pulled the bundle towards her, protecting the papers with her hands as though Evie might snatch them and run off. 'Now,' she said, staring at the child, 'now, there's something I'd better be telling you before it's too late. I don't know what's going to happen to you when I'm gone but it isn't right you should be left wondering, I never thought it was, you can't blame me for that, eh? It wasn't my fault, not what I wanted, I never thought it right.' She stopped and stared at Evie, who returned the stare. Mary saw what she had always seen, a small pale face, not pretty, and a mass of unbrushed dark hair and eyes that held no challenge, that were accepting of everything before them. She saw a calmness and stillness that pleased her. And Evie saw an old woman who had suddenly changed. All the crossness had momentarily gone, all the power. Mary's face was as creased and pinched, her skin as yellow and coarse as ever, but she looked helpless, all the fight Evie was used to had vanished. It made her nervous, this collapse of her grandmother, it worried her and she twisted her hands together not knowing what to do.

'You can't read,' Mary said, in dismay. 'You should be at school, you'd learn soon enough, eh? I should have seen to it, but there's been enough to do, keeping body and soul together.' She selected an envelope from the papers on her lap and waved it in front of Evie's eyes. 'Now,' she said again, 'see this here? This is yours and don't let anyone tell you otherwise. Look, see this mark?' – and she showed Evie the letter 'E' on the envelope – 'that's you, that's for Evie, I kept it for you and nobody knows. It's in the Holy Trinity register for those who'll bother to look if anyone does and I'll be surprised if they do, though there's no telling what will happen after I'm gone, no knowing the mischief that will be done and me not here to see fair play, but you've got this here and I'm giving it to you now and it's up to you to guard it and keep it and use it when you need to, eh? There'll be questions and you won't know the answers but this will give you something to hang on to, you'll always know who you are if people forget to tell you, eh? Something, it's something; there's only one person knows more and she's never told and there's nothing I can do about that, Evie, and nothing you can do either, no good upsetting yourself, my lass.'

But Evie was not upset. She was confused but too excited to feel real distress. Her attention was completely caught by the envelope with the mark on it that was her, the line down with three straight spokes coming out of it. Her grandmother held it out to her and she took it and loved the feel of the very paper with 'E' written on it so plainly. Whatever was inside the brown envelope was thin. If she didn't hold the envelope tightly it was so flimsy it would slip from her fingers. 'Do you remember that day we stood outside the church, Evie?' her grandmother said, in a whisper. 'When the trees were all orange, eh? We stood well back, nobody could see us, the trees hid us. And that lady and gentleman came out?' She took Evie's wrists and pulled the child, still clutching the envelope, to her and whispered even lower and more urgently, 'Do you remember, Evie, eh?' Slowly, Evie shook her head. She didn't remember standing outside any church with her grandmother nor any orange leaves nor a lady and gentleman coming out. Mary sighed. 'You were too young,' she said, 'too young. Well, it can't be helped, it wouldn't do any good anyway, it's maybe just as well. Now, where will you put that envelope? Where have we got for you to put it?'

'In my pocket?' Evie suggested, feeling inside her apron pocket to see if it was big enough. Instantly, Mary was back to being as irritable as she nearly always was. 'No, no, child, for heaven's sake, an envelope with *that* in it in an apron pocket, the idea, no, you'll need somewhere safer, but it'll have to go with you wherever you go, it'll have to be a box or a bag you never let out of your sight when you leave here, now what can I give you, what'll serve ...?' Mary looked about the bedroom and her eye fell on the mahogany chest of drawers on top of which there was a clutter of different kinds of boxes containing a variety of things, necklaces and brooches, pins and buttons. She pointed and said to Evie, 'Fetch that tin here, the one with the dog on.' Evie reached up – it was a chest a little taller than herself – and pulled the flat tin towards her and lifted it off. She knew what was in it. Nothing important, nothing of value, only some ribbons, all folded neatly and never used. Her grandmother said that when her hair was smooth and tangle-free she could have one of these old, long-preserved ribbons to tie it up with, but Evie had never succeeded in brushing her wild and springy hair into anything like the required state and had never earned a ribbon. 'Nobody will bother about a girl having this,' Mary said, 'a tin of ribbons, they'll think nothing of it when the time comes. Look, we'll lift the ribbons and the envelope will fit snug.' It did. 'Then we'll cover it with ribbons, see?' The coils of ribbon, lilac and yellow and a beautiful red Evie particularly coveted, were laid flat side down together forming a concealing band over the envelope with 'E' on it. 'There, that'll fox them, eh?' said Mary, and seemed pleased. 'You take it now, keep it with you, put it under your mattress.' Evie hurried to do just that, putting the tin under the pillow end, and Mary sighed with satisfaction.

Evie slept on the flat tin of ribbons for almost another year. Every day when she made her bed she peeped inside the tin and gently lifted one of the ribbons to check the envelope was there. She never took it out and she never looked inside it. It was enough to know it was there. Every now and again her grandmother would ask to see it and she'd take it to her and it would be inspected and then returned to its hiding-place. Meanwhile, Evie learned to write not just an 'E' but her whole name and some other words besides the alphabet. A man came round and, though Evie was instructed as usual to hide, the man was persistent and, lurking in the kitchen, Evie could hear him raising his voice to her grandmother and saying, 'I have it on good authority there is a child in this house of school age, madam.' Next time he came her grandmother had prepared her. 'You're sickly, Evie,' she told her, 'remember that if asked, you're sickly and can't go out, you have to stay with me or you get took badly. It might work for a while and there's nothing else will.' It did work. The man stared at Evie, who must have looked as convincingly sickly as she tried to suggest because he said, 'I see,' to her grandmother and then, 'The child needs a doctor.' Mary said she had no money for doctors nor for the medicines they might prescribe. The man addressed Evie directly and asked her how often she went out, how well she ate, whether she slept well – but Evie had been well instructed by Mary and simply stared up at him in bewilderment with her mouth hanging open. He never came again.

Life went on in the same way until one day Mary did not get up. Evie took her tea and toast and got on with what she always did, the household tasks by which she measured time. It was only when it grew dark and her grandmother was still in bed that things began to feel strange. She drew the curtains and lit the lamp and built up the fire but then, sitting alone with the mending, she felt awkward, she missed Mary in her chair talking to herself. She went to bed early, carrying out all the going-to-bed rituals of locking doors and dampening the fire and putting the guard round it to catch stray sparks and checking the wick of the lamp was turned low and the oil extinguished. But even lying on her mattress at the foot of her grand-mother's bed didn't seem right. Twice in the night she was wakened by the rattling of Mary's breathing and twice she got up and went and peered at the old woman, but she was deeply asleep and did not respond to the timid touch on her cheek. The next morning Mary woke up but did not touch her tea and toast nor the soup offered later on, and Evie began to be frightened. She spent most of that day in the bedroom hovering by the bed, longing for some instructions and receiving none, not a word. She wanted somebody to come but nobody ever did. There were people next door, on both sides, and Evie knew their names but not their faces. Even the names seemed to change – 'New folk,' her grandmother occasionally said when somebody had come to their door and Evie had been told to keep herself hidden, 'new folk again next door, I knew that last lot would never stay, but they're nothing to do with us, Evie, eh? Potts they're called, but that's no concern of ours, we keep ourselves to ourselves and ask nothing of nobody, eh?'

There was a smell on the third day that told Evie she must call on the Potts, or someone. She knew the smell of urine but this was worse, it came from her grandmother's mouth and it was foul. Going downstairs, opening the curtains on to the grey dawn light, Evie found herself crying. She didn't want to cry, she hadn't intended to, but the tears rolled down her cheeks and would not stop. She stared out of the window but there was nothing to see, nobody going down the lane at that time of the morning. But she couldn't tear herself away from the window, it offered some sort of hope. She stood motionless for half an hour, an hour, and when the first footsteps sounded on the sandstone flags she pulled the net curtain aside and peered out and tapped hard on the window-pane. A man passed by without so much as a glance but shortly after two women carrying big baskets heard her tapping and stopped and stared at her. But then, stupidly, Evie just stared back and did nothing and the women frowned and looked annoyed and went on their way. Still weeping, and trembling now, she at last left the window and stumbled to the door which she opened with difficulty, it was always so stiff, and then she stood in the doorway and waited, not knowing what she was going to say when someone asked her, as they surely would, what was the matter.

The woman who did ask her was young and she was carrying a baby. She hitched the baby on to her hip and looked at the little girl weeping in the doorway, a pathetic figure, very small and pale and ill-kempt and thin, standing there shaking violently. 'What's the matter, pet?' she asked, and when Evie went on shaking and sobbing the woman peered into the passageway of the house and said, 'Is your mam there? Hello, missus?' The baby, affected by Evie's sobs, began to cry too, though half-heartedly, merely in imitation, and the young mother knew it and paid no attention. 'We can't have this,' she said, putting the baby down on the step, whereupon it began to bawl in earnest, feeling the cold even through its layers of shawls. She drew Evie to her and stroked her hair and said, 'There, there,' over and over again. When Evie was quieter, though her thin body still shook, the woman said, 'Now what is it? What's wrong? What's your name, pet? Can't you talk? Can't you tell me?' Choking, Evie managed to hiccup the words. 'My grandma's sick.' 'Are you on your own then?' asked the woman anxiously, already seeing herself dragged into a mess she'd rather keep out of. 'Isn't there anyone else in the house? Where's your mam? Where's your dad? When will they be coming home? Where are they? Where can they be sent for?'

But Evie was incapable of giving any information and the young woman knew she would have to go into the house and see where this sick grandmother was. Hesitantly, holding her baby with one arm, putting it back on her hip, she took hold of Evie's hand with the other and allowed herself to be led up the stairs. She knew before she saw the old woman that she was dead and she stopped in the doorway of the bedroom and turned round. 'You'll have to come with me,' she said, her tone now sharp and not as caressing as before. 'Have you a key? We can't leave the house open.' Evie did know where the key was, a big iron thing hanging behind the front door and rarely used because they so rarely went out. The woman put it in her pocket. She seemed bad-tempered now, but Evie herself was calmer knowing responsibility had passed from her hands. She followed the woman down the lane eagerly, in her relief hardly noticing the cold. The woman hurried, her skirt flapping and her head bowed against the wind. Furtively, Evie looked about her. It was strange to be moving so fast instead of patiently keeping pace with her grandmother's slow amble. It felt exciting, urgent, and she no longer felt terrified. She wondered where they were going but did not dare ask in case she was cast off.

They passed St Cuthbert's church and came out on to West Walls, hugging the crumbling old wall, keeping out of the narrow road itself. But then, past Dean Tait's cut, the woman veered right and stopped at a door and knocked on it. It opened quickly and another woman, also young, stood there and said, 'You've taken your time, you'll be late.' 'I know I'll be late,' Evie's rescuer snapped. 'It can't be helped, it's this kid, standing crying fit to burst in the lane and saying her grandma's sick.' Here she dropped her voice and whispered in the other woman's ear. 'What could I do?' she went on, 'I couldn't leave her. And now what can I do? Who'll I tell?' They were all still standing on the doorstep but now the two women went inside and Evie followed, though they paid no heed to her. She had never, to her knowledge, been in any other house but her grandma's, first in the village, that dim memory, and then in the lane. She peered about her nervously, feeling it was wrong to stare. The room wasn't much better than her grandma's, it was just as small, but there was a good fire burning, bigger than her grandma ever allowed, and a good smell of some kind of cake cooking. And there was a brightly coloured rag-rug on the stone floor with two small children sitting on it playing with pan lids and pegs, and making a great racket.

'What's your name, pet?' the woman who lived there asked, turning aside from a whispered consultation with her friend.

'Evie.'

'Oh, she has a tongue. Mine's Minnie, and this is Pearl. Now what are we to do with you? Where's your mam?'

Evie didn't know what to say. Did she have a mam? She wasn't sure, she had never been sure. If she did have one then she'd gone. 'Gone,' she said.

'Where?' asked Minnie.

'Don't know.'

'When? When did she go? Early this morning?'

Evie shook her head and twisted her skirt in her hands. Finally, she said, 'I've never seen her, if I have a mam,' and began to cry again. Both women told her to shush, but kindly. Minnie gave her a piece of bread and a small mug of tea, and told her to get them down, she'd feel better. Another whispering session followed and then Minnie, who seemed to be in charge, said, 'Pearl's got to go now, so you can help look after little George. You can help me this morning till we see what's what.'

Evie enjoyed the morning helping. She spent it on the rag-rug playing with George and the other two children. She put the wooden pegs into a pan, a battered old tin thing, and put the lid on and shook it about and then emptied it with a flourish. The babies loved it. She did it again and again and they never seemed to tire of the rattling noise and the surprise, a surprise every time, of the pegs cascading out. 'You've a way with you,' Minnie said approvingly. Later, she fed all three children. Minnie gave her a bowl of porridge and she made a game of feeding it to them. When one of them crawled or rolled off the rug she had to persuade them back on to it and she loved the feeling of the warm, soft, wriggling bodies. She hugged them and they hugged her back, their hands catching in her untidy hair and pulling it but she didn't mind. 'Got little brothers and sisters, have you?' Minnie asked. Evie shook her head. 'Big ones, then?' Evie shook it again. 'Oh dear, you are an odd one,' Minnie said. She watched Evie carefully. It was as clear as crystal what would happen to her, what the situation was. The grandmother was dead, Pearl was sure, the stench in the bedroom alone had told her, and unless some relative stepped forward it would be the orphanage up above the river for poor Evie. It was a shame, she was a pathetic scrap of a thing, she deserved better, but better was unlikely to be available.

Pearl, on her way to work in Carr's factory, reported the situation she had found at 10 St Cuthbert's Lane that morning, and the temporary address of the little girl, Evie. The body of Mary Messenger was removed before noon. A policeman came round to Minnie's house in the afternoon and asked (in front of Evie) if she was willing to keep Evie. Minnie said she was willing but that she couldn't, she had no room. Evie would have to go somewhere else but she hoped the child wasn't to be sent off without her things. The policeman said he'd take Evie back to her grandmother's house first, before handing her over to 'them up above the river' (with a significant look at Minnie) and she could take some clothes and anything else of hers that was small enough to go in a bag. Minnie made each of the babies kiss Evie, then told her she'd see her one day and to try not to take on too much, she would only make it worse.

The policeman took Evie home and made a list of what the child took from the house. It was not a long list. Two dresses, two pinafores, two shawls, a pair of clogs, some woollen stockings and a tin box. These all went easily into a bag with a drawstring which Evie produced from behind the bedroom door. She found a coat, which she put on, a shabby article but thick and warm-looking, and a tam-o'-shanter which hid her hair completely. 'Ready for your travels?' the policeman asked her, but she neither responded nor nodded, she just stood there obediently, evidently quite composed. Knowing nothing of the weeping Evie had already done that day, he thought it odd she didn't shed a single tear. She seemed quite passive and he was glad: it made his job so much easier. She followed him, he thought quite happily, out of the house, never a backward look, and down the lane and across the Town Hall square and up Lowther Street and across the bridge. The noise of carts on the bridge was so loud and the crush of people so great that he took her hand for fear he would lose her. It was a steep hill to climb, up Stanwix Bank, but she managed it without faltering. They came to St Ann's House just as it began to rain and the policeman hurried her into the shelter of the doorway. He knocked on the door several times before it was opened by a stout woman wearing a dark blue apron.

'Here you are,' the policeman said, 'another for you. Her grandma's been found dead and there's nobody to have her, not yet anyway.'

'I haven't been told,' the woman said indignantly. 'There's been no notification.'

'Well, there should've been, it'll come,' the policeman said, and turned and left.

That was how Evie came to St Ann's House. She stayed there six months before she was claimed.

Chapter Two

SHONA'S FATHER was a sea-captain. She was proud of him and boasted about him continually. Nearly every father in the village was a sailor but there was only one a captain and that was her daddy. She was like him in looks, not her mother. She had his red-gold hair, his very pale blue eyes and his full lips, though in his case these were hidden by a moustache and beard. All she had taken from her mother was a certain fragility which belied her true nature. Shona was as tough as her father, every bit as tough as Captain Archie McIndoe both in body and in mind. She only looked frail, 'a delicate wee girl' people said, but they were wrong.

The McIndoes had come to this remote part of north-east Scotland when Shona was a baby, only a month old to be precise. Her mother, Catriona, was still recovering from the birth which every woman in the village quickly learned had been a difficult one. Catriona was so weak afterwards she hadn't been able to breast-feed her baby and the other young mothers, all of whom had ample milk and to spare, had felt sorry for her. But Mrs McIndoe was not young, they noticed, she was surely only just the right side of forty and unlikely to have any more children. Shona, they predicted, would be an only child and they were proved right. She was an only child, greatly adored, who, everyone agreed, ruled the roost. It was an extraordinary sight to see her at the age of four dominating both her parents. Even in the kirk Shona exerted her authority, choosing where to sit and which kneeler to have.

Captain McIndoe was slow and quiet, the sort of man who could, and did, sit for hours over a pint of beer and a whisky without saying a word. Aboard ship he was said to be careful, cautious, a good man to sail with, never panicking in any emergency, always reliable: the women in the village liked their men to sail with him. And Mrs McIndoe was equally lacking in any spark, equally colourless though pleasant enough. She was in the Women's Guild and helped at bazaars but she was not sociable, she kept herself to herself and that self was thought of as a bit dull. So where, everyone given to such curiosity wondered, had Shona got her fire from? 'Is she like her grannie?' women sometimes asked Catriona after witnessing one of Shona's more extravagant displays of temperament and contrasting it with her mother's placidity. 'Is she after following in her grannie's footsteps?' Catriona would smile and say, 'A little, maybe,' but she never went so far as to say, as she was expected to say, that Shona was a throwback, the spitting image of one grannie or another. Another question was a common one put to the Captain himself when Shona's physical resemblance to him was commented on. 'Do you have any sisters, Captain?' But no, he didn't. No sisters whom Shona took after.

The McIndoes lived in a stone house above the harbour, bought outright when they arrived in 1956. The Captain was in the merchant navy by then but was known to have distinguished himself in the war when he had served with the Royal Navy working in X-craft (midget submarines) off the coast of Norway. It was the nature of his job that he was away for long spells throughout Shona's childhood and that his daughter therefore lacked the strong fathering she could be seen to need. But then most fathers in the area were away at sea and it was the mothers who had to do the best they could with the help of the wider family. It was felt to be unfortunate that in the case of the McIndoes that wider family lived so far away.

Shona only became properly acquainted with her grannies when she was seven. She and her mother went to stay with Grannie McIndoe in Stranraer and Shona didn't enjoy the experience one bit (nor, in fact, did Catriona, but she never said so, being much too polite and discreet and much too aware of how dangerous it was to let Shona know). Grannie McIndoe found it hard to tolerate her young granddaughter's tantrums and wondered aloud why anyone else did, particularly her mother. 'Archie was never like this,' she proclaimed. 'His father would have thrashed it out of him. Where does she get it from?' Weakly, Catriona said she didn't know, but she was sure Shona would calm down as she grew older. Things were a little easier when they went on to Glasgow to Grannie

McEndrick, Catriona's mother, but even in that household Shona's energy was a strain. 'Is she never still?' Grannie McEndrick asked. 'You were such a still child.' But though Shona was never still, at least this grannie found her amusing and was briefly entertained by her antics so long as they did not go on too long (though, alas, they often did).

It was at Grannie McEndrick's, however, that Shona disgraced herself and caused the greatest alarm. A neighbour's child, a boy called Gavin, the same age as Shona, had been invited in to play. The two children had seemed to get on tolerably well, once Shona's boasting about her father the Captain was capped by Gavin's pride in his father being Provost (which baffled but impressed Shona), and they had been sent into the garden to run around before tea. It was a big garden and the two children disappeared, not entirely to Catriona's pleasure. 'Och, you fuss too much, Catriona,' her mother said, 'it doesn't do to be fussing. You should be thanking the Lord wee Shona's not a clinger. You were a terrible clinger, so you were, wouldn't let me out of your sight, clung to my skirts all the time.' Catriona remembered, she needed no reminding, and flushed at the contempt in her mother's voice. 'She's a grand wee soul,' her mother said. 'Come and we'll take the chance to put our feet up and have a quiet cup of tea.'

The tea was made, and drunk very quietly indeed. Catriona could never think of anything to say to her mother when they were alone together. She made inquiries about other family members and that was it. It never crossed her mind to share with her mother her true anxieties, knowing, as she did, that since these were all wrapped up with Shona's waywardness her mother would be scornful. There was no one Catriona could talk to about her fears except Archie, and he had little patience with them. She sometimes thought that if she had been able to find the right words to express her unease, then Archie would have listened to her, but as it was, even to her own ears, her sense of there being something not quite normal about Shona sounded silly. They sat and had tea and the weak, wavering shafts of sun came through the open window and warmed them.

The moment Skipper began to bark Catriona was on her feet. 'Whatever's the matter with you?' her mother said, exasperated. 'Look at you, the wee dog barking and you're all of a tremble. It's seen a cat, that's all, sit down, Catriona.' But Catriona could not sit down. She was out of the room and down the steps into the garden before her mother had finished chiding her. Skipper's barking was frantic. Quickly, only just preventing herself from running, she hurried across the lawn and into the rhododendron bushes from where the barking came. Skipper raced out of the undergrowth to meet her and then scurried back at once down a little path leading through the bushes to the wall which marked the boundary of the garden. She scratched her face on some stray gorse growing with the rhododendrons and had to part it to follow the dog, hurting her hands in her haste. Then she stopped abruptly. There was a dip in the ground near the wall, what her mother called a dell, though it was nothing more than a hole, grass-covered and shaded over by the low branches of a beech tree. Shona and Gavin both lay in it, both naked, their clothes in touchingly neat piles either side of them. Shona was examining Gavin's testicles with the greatest interest, first prodding and then holding his tiny scrotum, while Gavin, with his eyes tight shut, held himself like a soldier, rigidly still, his arms straight by his side, his legs clamped together.

'Shona!' Catriona burst out before she could stop herself. 'What do you think you are doing? Leave Gavin alone, leave him!'

Shona looked up, not at all embarrassed, and said, 'We're playing doctors.'

'Put your clothes on, now, this minute, and Gavin, put yours on.'

'Why?' Shona said, but Gavin, red-faced, was already into his shorts. 'What's wrong with playing doctors?'

'Nothing,' her grannie said, appearing from the other side of the dell, arms akimbo and smiling. 'They're only this side of seven, Catriona, have some sense.'

That was how the incident ended, turned into something amusing by Grannie McEndrick, something so funny Shona was quite delighted with herself and Gavin half-hysterical with relief. There was nothing Catriona could say or do to stop the hilarity and she felt humiliated. There she was, a woman in her forties shown how to behave by a woman in her seventies, the older woman a model of commonsense. It was impossible for her to explain that her horror had had nothing to do with the children's nudity nor with what Shona was doing, but everything to do with the atmosphere of what she had seen. It was Shona's intensity, her concentration, her very lack of any sniggering or squealing which had frightened her and made her react so inappropriately and violently.

Putting Shona to bed that night Catriona felt awkward and

though she did all the usual fond things – kissed Shona, hugged her, tucked her up, said her prayers with her – she did it with half her normal enthusiasm, and after all the rituals were over could not quite bring herself to leave. She sat on the end of Shona's bed looking at her. Shona stared back, her big blue eyes not at all sleepy but instead challenging, accusing.

'Shona,' Catriona began, and stopped. What could she say? How could she redeem herself? 'Your Grannie is right,' she said finally, 'there's nothing wrong with playing doctors or with taking your clothes off.'

'You shouted,' Shona said.

'Yes, I did. I shouldn't have. I don't know why I did.'

'It was my turn,' Shona said. 'Gavin had looked at my wee-wee. I was just looking at his.'

'Yes, I know.'

'Did you see it?'

'What?'

'Gavin's wee-wee.'

'Yes.'

'Yuck. It's squidgy. Gavin says his brother says it grows and it makes babies.'

'Yes, it does, in a way. It's late, Shona, time to sleep.'

More cowardice. Catriona despaired. It was not that she was reluctant to describe to Shona how babies were made but that she feared the questions that would surely follow. She wasn't ready to lie so thoroughly yet, even though she had done so before. A new set of lies were needed and she had not got them ready. It was such a long time since she had held Shona, her baby, in her arms and had no doubts or qualms about a single thing – so confident she had been, once she was a mother, once she had been blessed. Archie could have accepted their lot, their destiny to be childless, but she never could have done so, never. She had had to have a baby, it had been vital to her sanity, not merely her happiness. Each time she was pregnant the glory of it transformed her. Each time she miscarried it was a tragedy of epic proportion. And the one stillbirth, the one baby she had carried to term, had made her want to die. She had tried to die. She wanted to be buried with her baby. And then there had been Shona.

One day she would tell Shona everything. When her daughter was of an age to understand, when she had perhaps had children herself, then would be the time to tell her. She would have no fears then, time and Shona's growing-up would have dispersed them and she would be able to speak freely.

*

They did not go again for a long time to stay with Grannie McEndrick. They were invited, in invitations that had an increasing edge to them, that were on the verge of becoming orders, but Catriona managed to be resistant to them. She pleaded her own poor health and there was nothing her mother could do about that except complain her daughter had never been really well since Shona's birth. 'It took it out of you,' Ailsa McEndrick said when, instead of her daughter and granddaughter coming to visit her, she went to visit them (complaining all the way about the difficulties of the journey). 'You were too weak after all those miscarriages, Archie should have had more consideration.' 'I wanted a baby,' Catriona replied. 'Oh. I know *that*,' her mother said, 'we all know that. But not at the cost of your own health. Look at you, stick-thin and no colour at all and think how you once were before.' Catriona smiled. She'd been quite plump, she'd had a good complexion and her mother couldn't forgive her for sacrificing both – as if weight and skin mattered beside the having of a baby. She would have offered up far more vital things to have one, her hair, her teeth, anything. But her mother couldn't be expected to understand that kind of desperation. She had had four children and had often enough in Catriona's childhood come near to implying this had been one, if not two, too many. Her first son had been born when she was only twenty and she had never experienced that craving for a child which had become her daughter's own.

Walking along the beach one rare still August day, Ailsa suddenly said, 'You should have come home, you should have been looked after properly. That's when it all started, when you were carrying Shona. You didn't eat, I know you didn't.'

'Oh, Mother, don't hark back, it was seven years ago for heaven's sake.' She didn't look at her mother at all. They were side by side, keeping an eye on Skipper and on Shona, racing ahead along the edge of the sea. They walked a bit further until, with that violence for which it was famous on this part of the coast, the tide started to rush in over the flat ground forming deep gullies round islands of sand, and they shouted at Shona and the dog and veered sharply inland, into the dunes. Ailsa was panting before she got over them and on to the track behind. 'I'm getting old,' she gasped, 'I must be, I'm puffed after that wee hillock.' But then she looked at Catriona and was so struck by her daughter's pallor she stopped dead. 'You're not well,' she said, her concern as ever coming out as an accusation. 'What is it? What's the matter with you?'

It was tedious, this endless emphasis on how she looked, and Catriona resented it. Every time they met there was this same interrogation, always leading back to the birth of Shona. Catriona had written from Bergen, where Archie was based at the time, and told her that she was pregnant again but said she wanted to keep the expected birth date secret because she was superstitious, after three miscarriages and a stillbirth, and believed that if she revealed it another tragedy would follow. Her mother rang her saying she would come at once. But Catriona had been adamant, no, her mother was not to come. The doctors had declared her perfectly fit and the maternity hospital in Bergen was excellent.

So her mother had been out of it, deprived of the whole experience. She had never seen Catriona pregnant with Shona nor was she anywhere near for Shona's birth. When Catriona rang her and said she had a beautiful, healthy new granddaughter, Ailsa had remained quite silent for a full minute before she had said, 'I can hardly believe it, not without seeing her.' When she did see her, a month later, there was a sharpness in her mother's eyes which Catriona feared. 'Let me look at her properly,' she had said, almost snatching the baby from her cradle. But then the sharpness had disappeared as Shona was minutely inspected. 'She takes after Archie,' Ailsa pronounced. 'Look at the colouring of her. But she has your shape of face, Catriona, heart-shaped, just like your face, and see the way her right ear is a wee bit bigger than the left, that's the same as yours.' The birth weight, 7lb $3\frac{1}{2}$ oz, was exactly the same as Catriona's had been and so was Shona's length, eighteen and a half inches. Once these comparisons were made, Ailsa was happy. 'I never thought you'd do it,' she said. 'I thought it was going to be your cousin all over again, what with the miscarriages and stillbirth, just like her, and then nothing ever again. You've been lucky in the end, Catriona.' 'I know,' Catriona had said, 'I know I have.' 'But,' her mother had added, reverting as she did so to her usual more hectoring tone, 'let that be enough, will you? Don't tempt fate, don't try again, be grateful for what you've got, mind.' 'I'll be grateful,'

Catriona promised, though privately reflecting it was far too late, fate had already been tempted and she had tempted it knowingly.

Without Archie, of course, nothing would have been possible. Another husband might not have been able to bear his wife's obsession, he might have recoiled from the rawness, even the ugliness, of the hunger behind it. But Archie had not. He was patient and understanding and said only, 'If this is what you want' and 'If this will make you happy.' But he had been surprised. He had looked at her and his eyes had been shocked even though he said nothing. Then he had taken her hand – hot, feverish – and squeezed it and said she could have her way if she was quite sure she knew what she was doing. But she felt that she had caused him pain and was sorry for it. She knew that she had forced him into a position of surrender, though she was not entirely sure what she was compelling him to surrender. Control, she supposed. She had taken control away from him. He was not an overbearing man, for all that he commanded a ship, but he liked to do things his way. Now they were doing this thing her way, relegating him to a subservient role at this crucial point in their lives. Fortunately, once Shona was back in Scotland with them, the balance was restored, partly because it became apparent that neither of them controlled her. It amused them both, their little daughter's independent spirit; it helped that they could see nothing of themselves in her. 'She would make her way anywhere,' Archie said, admiringly. He was glad their only child was a girl. A boy would have been more complicated, he felt, he would have worried about Catriona left for such long periods with a son. Leaving mother and daughter felt comfortable and he did not mind at all that he was on the periphery of their relationship for so much of the time. Catriona had what she wanted and he wanted what she wanted, simple as that.

He watched them sometimes without their knowing. Especially at first, when they came to this carefully chosen village on the north-east coast, when they were settling down and he was still anxious about Catriona's mental well-being. He would stand outside the bedroom door, hidden in the shadows, and watch through the gap his wife nursing the baby. She couldn't breast-feed, but she wanted to pretend that she did and so she sat with her blouse undone and the baby nestled close against her empty breast, and the bottle of milk tipped so close to her own nipple that it grazed it and the baby fidgeted, fighting the natural nipple off to get at the satisfying rubber teat. It moved him to see this scene; but it disturbed him, though he was not quite sure why. Catriona carried things too far. She had her baby, why did she need to convince herself she was feeding it? Why was this subterfuge important to her? Was she doing it for the baby's sake or her own, and if for her own what did it mean? But Archie asked none of these questions; he only observed and left his wife to it.

Chapter Three

EVIE WAS a hard worker. It was what everyone remarked on – such a hard and willing worker, for a small child, with a real idea of how jobs should be done. Give her something to clean and she'd go at it as though her life depended on it, scouring dirty old pans as if expecting it to be possible that through her efforts they could be restored to their former shining selves. It was assumed by those who gave her the work to do in the Home that she had had a hard taskmaster, or mistress, that perhaps she had been bullied and beaten into such diligence. But no. When questioned as to her past, and Evie did not speak of it unless she was directly asked, she had only words of affection for her dead grandmother. She had wanted to please her, and hard work was what had given her most pleasure, both the doing of it herself, when she had been able, and seeing Evie being like her, her exact copy.

Except Evie never forgot she was not, could not be, such an exact copy. The woman who had been her grandmother was not her grandmother; nor was Mary the mother of the woman who had been Evie's mother. This was too complicated to explain so she never attempted any explanation. It hurt her even to remember this truth and to find it would not disappear. She had the tin safe, of course. It had gone first into the bag when the policeman stood over her, and when she came to the Home she had managed to hide it inside one of her thick woollen stockings. There was nowhere for her to put her few belongings, except the communal chest of drawers at the end of the dormitory she shared with eleven other girls, but it worried her so much, thinking of other hands finding and handling her precious tin box, that she could not bring herself to place it in any of those capacious drawers without hiding it first inside a stocking. She thought of keeping it under her pillow instead, as she had been used to doing, but that was not safe either. Girls stole things and hid what they had stolen in or under the pillows, and so these were regularly inspected. Nor could she keep it in her apron pocket – it made a bulge and would be remarked on. There was nothing for it but to ask Matron to keep it for her, a solution far from satisfactory and one she had to be driven to after several days of feverishly moving the tin around.

Matron was rarely seen by the girls in the Home, but she was always known to be there, a formidable presence in the background, built up into an ogre by the rest of the staff. It was a big Home, St Ann's, housing at any one time a minimum of sixty and a maximum of a hundred girls between the ages of five and fifteen. It was meant to be a place of safety for orphaned or abandoned girls, but in effect had become a house of correction too. There were girls there who had been convicted of stealing and other minor crimes (though to hear the thundering of the magistrates the theft of a penny bun sounded very major indeed), or of persistent vagrancy. Several were there for soliciting and these inmates took some managing. There was one attendant, referred to by the girls as the Handler, to each dormitory, women of low intelligence and sluttish habits who ruled their own little kingdoms with a mixture of brutality and favouritism. Evie was of no interest to Madge, her Handler, and so she was left mercifully alone except to be made extra use of when her capacity for hard work became noted. 'Proper little worker, are we?' Madge sneered, but soon she left her alone. Evie was first up in the mornings, no lying abed for her, and first to wash in the freezing cold water, without a word of complaint. She laid the tables and washed the dishes and swept the floors with an enthusiasm marvellous to see and was marked out very quickly for future promotion to Monitor when she should be old enough. Madge approved of her and Evie saw that she did, though no word of praise or admiration was forthcoming.

But she could not take her tin box to Madge. She did not trust her. Madge herself, she soon knew, stole, though she was so hard on those girls discovered to be thieves. She took from her charges any sweets or cakes that came their way, on the grounds that they were bad for growing girls, but what was worse was her filching of the small and treasured items they had managed to bring with them. So Evie could not and would not give her tin box to Madge. She would give it to Matron who, for all she knew, might be just as untrustworthy but had not yet proved herself so. The problem was how to gain access to Matron. She was virtually invisible in the Home. Evie had seen her once only, to be checked over (a matter of lice, rashes and sores) and officially registered. She had been taken to Matron's room but was not sure she could find it again.

For a young child the scheming necessary to visit Matron without anyone else knowing was impossible. Evie could not imagine how it could be done. But one morning she was seen hurriedly shifting her box from one stocking to another in the big bottom drawer of the chest and Ruby, the girl who saw her, gave her good advice. Ruby was older, nine to Evie's six, and she had already been in the Home nearly three years. She was quick and clever but, unlike Evie, she was lazy. Madge hated her for the cunning with which she could evade work as surely as Evie welcomed it, and for the intelligence with which she exposed half of Madge's own evasions. Ruby put her hand over Evie's as it struggled to transfer the box and said, 'What you got there?' Evie froze. 'Something you're hiding,' Ruby whispered. 'Show me, I won't tell.' Wordlessly, Evie was obliged to let the little box peep out of its hiding place. ''S only a box,' Ruby said, 'isn't it? What's inside, then? Not money? Sweets? What's inside? I won't tell.' Evie, hoping it would satisfy Ruby, murmured, 'Ribbons, just ribbons,' but Ruby was intrigued. 'Let's see, are they pretty, then? I've never had a ribbon, never.' She looked over her shoulder as she said this, to check that Madge was not bearing down upon them, which comforted Evie. Ruby was evidently disposed to keep her secret. Carefully, she lifted the lid and in a moment of inspiration offered Ruby one of the three ribbons. Ruby's face crinkled into a great smile and she lifted the red ribbon out of its nest. So eager was she to have and hide it that her sharp eyes missed the layer of paper under the ribbons, and Evie was able to put the lid back on before any more questions were asked.

Ruby was so happy with her ribbon. She would never be able to wear it, for fear of Madge, and her hair was shorn so close to her head (she had had nits) that there would have been nowhere to tie a ribbon, but this didn't matter. 'You can't keep on doing this,' she admonished Evie, 'you won't get away with it for ever. Madge'll find it. What you going to do?' Evie shook her head miserably. She didn't dare say she wanted to give her treasure to Matron. But Ruby thought of it herself. 'What you want to do is give it to Mrs Cox, that's what you want to do, give it over to Mrs Cox, Matron, that's her.' Evie confessed she didn't know how to arrange this and Ruby took charge at once.

They finished getting their stockings from the drawer and dressed rapidly. Beds had to be made and then it was breakfast in the huge kitchen and then washing-up, but after that there was a chance. Madge and the other attendants were always preoccupied after breakfast with sorting out the different chores for the day and there was a brief lull for the girls while tasks were disputed and assigned. Ruby took Evie's hand and led her out of the long corridor, where the washing-up was done at a row of stone sinks. She seemed to know exactly where to go, racing up stairs and down passages as though following a trail and bringing her in a minute to a door with MATRON clearly written on it. Ruby even knocked for Evie, who was much too frightened to do so, and when a surprised voice called 'Come in' she opened the door and pushed the terrified Evie in. 'What are you doing here, girl?' Matron said. She was drinking her tea and hated to be disturbed. The effrontery was so appalling she had not yet entirely taken it in. But she could sense already that she would have to react to it with a fine degree of rage so that it would never happen again. Meanwhile she had the most pathetic apparition standing before her, a child literally trembling, utterly ashen-faced and without, it seemed, a tongue in her head, a head Mrs Cox quite failed to recognise, which made this visitation even more outrageous.

Maud Cox was not an unkind woman. She had little of the Madge in her, but she lacked imagination and the feat of empathy was beyond her. 'Now there's no need to take on so, whatever it is,' she said, after she had watched with fascination how Evie trembled. 'What have you done? Who sent you to me?' Evie shook her head. 'Nobody sent you? Then you are very bold, coming to me like this, it is not your place. What is your name?' 'Evie, ma'am.' 'Well, Evie, speak up, or I shall have to look your name up in the register and call for your dormitory monitor to take you away.' Evie closed her eyes and with a great effort thrust the tin box at Mrs Cox. 'What? A box? Is this about a tin box? Did you steal it? Let me look.' Surprised at her own curiosity, Mrs Cox took the box and examined it. It was quite unremarkable, a cheap thing with a gaudy picture of a dog of doubtful breed on the lid. She shook it. It made no sound. Without asking Evie's permission, she opened it. Unlike Ruby, she was aware immediately that there was something under the ribbons.

Watched by Evie, whose eyes were now wide open with apprehension, she went to the table near the window and took the remaining two ribbons out, laying them side by side. 'Now what have we here?' she murmured. 'What is all this fuss about?'

There was a long silence. Evie wanted to cry but she was experienced at withholding the noise of weeping. She saw Mrs Cox smooth out the flimsy piece of paper which had nestled in its envelope under the ribbons and study it. She studied it a long time. Her manner, when finally she put it on the table, also changed. 'Do you know what this is?' she asked, her tone peremptory. Evie shook her head. 'Who gave it to you?' 'My grandmother,' Evie whispered and then was in agony, knowing as ever that her grandmother was not her grandmother and therefore she was telling a lie and would be punished if this was discovered, which it was bound to be. She choked in her agitation, but Mrs Cox ignored this and started looking in a folder. 'Something will have to be done,' she said. 'You belong to a family after all.' Evie felt a little leap of hope, hope not for something grand but for all this to pass over quietly and her box to be protected. She had not yet spoken of why she was here, but now some courage came to her, she blurted out, 'Please, ma'am, will you keep it for me?' 'Keep it for you?' said Mrs Cox, irritated. 'Of course I'll keep it. I have to keep it, and attend to it. Now go away and don't come again until you are told to.'

It was such a long time until Evie was sent for that she was convinced she never would be. Ruby had pleaded to be told what had happened in Matron's room but some innate sense of caution had prevented Evie from telling her. All she had said to her new friend was that Matron had said she would keep the tin box safe and yes, she had been cross and told her not to come again. The two of them were back in the kitchen and were milling about with the other girls before Madge noticed their absence. Evie was grateful for Ruby's cunning and cleverness. She only worried that Ruby would want something in return – everything in the Home, every act of apparent kindness, had its price – but the ribbon seemed to suffice. All Ruby wanted, apart from that, was to be her best friend but Evie was sadly inexperienced in friendship. She did not know how to indulge in cosy, intimate chat, she had no confidences she wished to share, and Ruby was disappointed. There were no larks with the solemn Evie, no possibility of fun at Madge's expense. Evie was too much in awe of authority to become Ruby's true apprentice and was soon abandoned in disgust. 'You've nothing to talk about, so talk to yourself,' Ruby announced one day and that was that.

Evie thought about Ruby's accusation carefully. It was not true, she did have things she wanted to say but she saw no point. She wanted most of all to speculate about what was going to happen to her but she could not bring herself to do so. When she had lived with her grandmother she had never considered the future, she didn't know what it was, but now it loomed frighteningly ahead all the time. She looked at the older girls and wondered if she would live at this place until she was like them, and the thought gave her a strange feeling in her stomach. She wanted also to ask about school, about whether she would get any schooling. Girls went to Lowther Street School from the Home every day but they were all older than she was and she wondered how old she would have to be before she, too, went with them. She and twenty or so others attended lessons in the schoolroom for two hours in the morning, but often the attendant who was supposed to teach them was needed for some other task, and they were set to copying letters on their own. They sat on benches and held bits of slate on their knees and copied the alphabet, which was tedious when you knew it already as Evie did. If only she could become one of the school party she felt she would not fret so much about what was in store for her.

Sometimes she was one of the girls taken into the city and she found this painful. At first it had been exciting to be told by Madge to put her coat on and pick up one of the baskets that hung from nails at the end of the washing-up corridor and wait on the doorstep, because they were going to market. Only the most biddable and docile girls were chosen to go to market and usually they were older than Evie, so she knew she was privileged. Eight of them walked, two by two, behind Madge and one of the other attendants down Stanwix Bank and across the Eden Bridge and up into the market; all the way Evie looked about her, recognising the cathedral and the castle, and her heart beat furiously with a disturbance she did not identify as nostalgia. In the market itself, seeing the butter women, or waiting for Madge to buy eggs and put them in her basket, she could hardly bear the memories. She wanted to leave not by the door they had entered but by the other door, the one at the top of the little cobbled hill in front of the butcher's stalls, the one that led out into Fisher Street and to the Town Hall and across the square to the lane where she had lived. She was pulled fiercely in this opposite direction and was harshly reprimanded by Madge for lagging behind. 'If you're going to be a lagger you won't come again,' Madge admonished her. So Evie controlled herself, as she always did, and marched resolutely back to the Home. So many thoughts she could have spilled out to Ruby but they all stayed in her head, and at the end of each day, especially market days, she went to bed confused, her head aching and heavy with so much suppressed emotion. She fell asleep eventually, convinced she would never escape back into the lane, back into a real house and household, but that there was nothing she could do about it. Fatalism was what her grandmother had dinned into her most successfully of all.

She had been in the Home a few more months after the tin box had been given to Mrs Cox when Madge came into the dormitory one morning and, after yelling at everyone to jump to it and get up, she shouted, for everyone to hear, that Evie was to go to Matron's room straight after breakfast. Madge stood over her while she washed and dressed, and personally brushed her hair, complaining that it was no wonder Evie always looked as if she were pulled through a hedge backwards with hair like hers. It would be a blessing, swore Madge, if Evie got nits and had to have all her dreadful hair shaved off, that would cure it. Satisfied that no more could be done to make Evie fit for inspection, Madge let her go down with the others, but Evie noticed Madge watching her and then the other attendants staring and whispering. This attention was sufficient to alert all the girls to there being suddenly something special about scraggy little Evie, Miss Never-says-a-word. She felt a tension around her which, instead of alarming her as it normally would have done, somehow pleased her. She felt important and it was a rare experience. She ate her porridge slowly and drank her tea (more water than tea and not much of it) and then went to Madge and said she did not know how to find Matron's room. One of the big girls was sent to guide her and Evie trotted dutifully at her heels far more cheerful than on the occasion when she had gone with the breathless Ruby.

There were two people with Mrs Cox, a man and a woman. Neither of them looked comfortable. The man in particular shifted about from foot to foot and was forever turning his cap in his hands. Evie dropped her eyes. It was rude to stare and indeed she had no desire to. She saw only that this man was quite old and bald and had a very red face. The woman was younger but, again, Evie allowed herself only a quick glimpse, enough to take in that she was small and plump, and then looked at the floor.

'This is Evie,' Mrs Cox said. 'She's a good girl, everyone here speaks well of her I'm pleased to tell you. You'll have no trouble. And she's a hard worker for one so young, we'll be sorry to lose her and I can't say that for many of the girls here.'

'She's little,' the man said, 'and thin, desperate thin, not much on her bones. Is she healthy?'

'Perfectly healthy,' Mrs Cox said, sounding quite indignant. 'You can't go by appearances with young girls, let me tell you that.'

'Did she bring anything with her when she came?' the woman asked. 'Any trappings?'

'No, nothing,' Mrs Cox said. 'We took her in what she stood up in and a bag with a change of clothes.' And the tin box, Evie silently added, but Mrs Cox didn't mention it. 'Well then,' the woman said, 'it can't be helped. Will we take her now, is she ready? There won't be a carry-on, will there, there won't be a lot of bawling?'

There was no bawling. Evie was told, there and then, in front of the two strangers, that she was a very lucky girl and thanks to the prodigious efforts of Mrs Cox and the Authorities she would be going to live with her newly located family.

'Do you know what the piece of paper in your ribbon box was, Evie?' Mrs Cox asked. Evie thought it best to shake her head. 'It was your certificate of birth. It showed who your mother was, and where you were born. This, Evie, you will be thankful to know, is your mother's cousin and his wife, and they have kindly agreed to make a home for you. What do you say?'

Evie looked up. Three faces confronted her, all expectant, none wearing a smile. What *should* she say? 'Thank you, ma'am,' she said.

'You'll have to pull your weight, mind,' the man who was her mother's cousin said. 'It won't be a holiday.'

'Go and get your bag,' Mrs Cox said, 'and wait at the front door.' Evie didn't move. 'Evie, did you hear?'

'Yes, ma'am.' Still she stood there, not knowing how to ask for her box but seeing Matron frown she just said, 'My box, please, ma'am,' as a statement rather than the request it should have been.

Fortunately, Mrs Cox was amused and said to the cousin and his wife, 'It's a tin box she had, with ribbons and the certificate in it' – 'No money?' the man interrupted – 'No money. Someone had obviously impressed the child with its importance and she brought it to me for safe-keeping.' The box was produced and handed to Evie, who then did a quick bob of a curtsey and backed towards the door.

The man and woman were waiting for her at the front door when she came down from the empty dormitory with her bag. There had been no one to say goodbye to and indeed she had no desire for farewells. She wanted just to slip away before anyone noticed and before her departure turned out to be a mistake. 'Come on, then,' the man said, 'we've wasted enough time.' She followed him and the woman to a cart outside. 'Get in,' the woman ordered, but however hard she struggled Evie was too small to reach the single step. Hands seized her from behind, strong impatient hands, and dumped her without a word on the wooden plank seat. The woman got in on the other side, with the man in the middle holding the reins of the horse standing patiently in the shafts. 'Settle yourself,' the woman said, 'it's a long ride, hang on to that bar on the corners and going down hills, and if you fall out don't expect us to stop, you'll have to run behind all the way, won't she Ernest, eh?' And they both laughed so heartily Evie wondered how she'd missed the joke. Ernest. Her mother's cousin was called Ernest. She wished she knew the woman's name, but not another word was spoken during the whole long, long journey.

Evie had no idea where she was. The cart turned the other way from the city and was soon in the country. At first it was thrilling to be bouncing along between green fields that stretched far away to the hills on the horizon, but when not a house had been in sight for what seemed hours Evie began to feel uneasy and even afraid. The fields were pretty, there was nothing alarming about them, and the outline of the hills blue and smudgy, not at all grim, but there was no life anywhere. She felt she was being carried away to oblivion and with every mile her sense of herself, never strong, diminished. The woman, who was Cousin Ernest's wife, paid no attention to her but there was at least some little comfort in her squat presence. And Evie was pressed hard by Ernest's flank and though it was uncomfortable it was also reassuring – while someone so solid was next to her she could not disappear. Once, she was handed a piece of cake wrapped in greaseproof paper. She was so surprised she almost dropped it and even when she had unwrapped it from the grubby paper, she still did not eat it for several minutes. She wanted to look at it, at all the raisins and currants embedded in its yellow flesh. There had never been this kind of cake in the Home, only very occasionally a hard, dry kind of gingerbread which left a gritty taste in the mouth. This cake was beautiful. Evie ate it in tiny bites, savouring every last morsel. She would have licked the paper if she had been on her own, but the woman took it from her as soon as she saw the slice of cake was finished.

It was dark before they arrived on the outskirts of a long village. Evie was exhausted and had several times dozed off only to jerk herself awake in case she missed the arrival at wherever the cart was going. Twice she had thought that moment had come but the stops had been to water the horse and for the man, Ernest, to put a coat on. When they stopped for good, Evie was still not certain that they would not trundle off once more, and it needed the woman to lift her down to convince her this journey was over. She was lifted down and set on her feet and her bag was put into her arms, and then the woman opened the door of what Evie could dimly make out was a house of some strange kind. 'Mind the step,' the woman said. 'I only whitened it yesterday, I don't want mucky footprints on it.' Obediently Evie lifted each foot carefully over the white part of the step. She knew about whitening steps and about rudding them too. Her grandmother had whitened her own step once and Evie had loved to help. She thought about offering there and then to whiten this woman's step the next day but as usual the words would not come as spontaneously as she would have liked, and by the time she had thought them out they were in a living-room and the woman was saying, 'Straight to bed, there'll be plenty to do in the morning. Take your shoes off here and follow me, I'm dog-tired myself.'

Evie followed her up one flight of carpeted stairs, the rough carpet feeling scratchy under her thinly stockinged feet, and another, uncarpeted, into the smallest room she had ever seen. It was a slot of a room with a skylight in its sloping roof and the bed filled it so completely that the door had to open outwards. 'You'll be all right here, it's a good bed, too good for a child. You're not frightened of the dark, I hope? No silliness?' Evie shook her head. 'Good. I'll knock you up in the morning and I want no shilly-shallying when I do. There's a chamber-pot under the bed, be careful you aim properly. I'll show you tomorrow where you empty it. Go on then, into bed with you.' Evie hesitated. The only way to get into bed was to climb on to it from the doorway. She clambered up and turned herself round and hesitated again. The woman was still watching her, the lamp she was carrying held high so that Evie was in the shadows of its glow. 'You don't sleep with your clothes on, I hope,' said the woman. 'They haven't brought you that low in that place?' Evie shook her head again and began to unbutton her pinafore at the side and then the neck of her thick woollen frock at the back. The woman put the lamp down on the floor outside the open door and, surprisingly, said, 'Here, come to the end of the bed, I'll help you.' Evie had never been helped to dress or undress in all her life in so far as she was able to remember and was embarrassed, but she did as she was told and the woman unbuttoned her down to her liberty bodice. 'Do you keep this on?' she asked. Evie nodded. In the Home, liberty bodices were only removed once a month for a wash-down of the whole body.

She found her shift in her bag and put it on and got into the bed. The sheets were cold but they were proper sheets and not the bits of bleached sacking used in the Home. The blankets were heavy and she felt trapped, they were tucked in so tightly. 'Goodnight, then,' the woman said, and then, 'I notice you haven't said your prayers, Miss, unless you're being lazy and saying them lying down.' Evie remained still. In the Home, they had all knelt in rows at the foot of their beds, repeating their prayers aloud. But where could she kneel here? On the bed? She began to struggle to get out from between the covers but the woman stopped her. 'Say them in bed,' she said.

Evie slept at once. She slept soundly and deeply but was nevertheless awake before the woman came to knock her up as promised. The light coming through the tiny diamond-shaped skylight directly over her head woke her. She stared up at the dark grey sky, slowly becoming paler, and felt excited. There was no Madge shouting, nobody crying or coughing, none of that cloying smell that hung in the morning air of a dormitory where twelve girls slept with the windows tightly shut. She felt alert and fresh and eager. She got dressed and then with great difficulty made her bed and folded her shift and put it under her pillow – a soft pillow, not stuffed with horsehair as in the Home – and then she sat cross-legged on top of the bed and waited. The moment she heard feet coming up the stairs she was at the end of the bed and had opened the door and presented herself before the woman had got anywhere near knocking upon it. 'Goodness me,' the woman said, startled, 'all dressed without so much as a cat's lick unless you've found your way to a sink which I doubt.' Evie hung her head and stood still. She knew that was always the best way should she be accused of anything. 'I'll show you,' the woman said, 'and we'll say no more about it.' The sink was on the landing, built into a little alcove. 'You're lucky,' the woman said, 'running water on every floor in this house. I bet you haven't had that before, have you, eh?' Evie shook her head. 'And we've a fixed bath but you won't be using that, it's for Ernest.' Evie followed the woman on down the rest of the stairs, relieved that in spite of the evidence of the day before this person was clearly a talker. Life was always better, easier, if a talker was in charge of you. It was those like Madge, glowering and silent except for her sudden spells of shouting, who were dangerous. Madge could be provoked by a returning silence on the part of any of the girls, whereas those Handlers who had been talkers had only needed to be listened to and they were satisfied.

Ernest was having his breakfast already in the kitchen, a great plate of bacon and egg and sausage. He didn't speak to Evie, just went on dipping pieces of fried bread into the yolk of the egg and ramming it into his mouth. She was not invited to sit down and did not presume to do so. 'Here's your porridge,' the woman said, 'and the milk is on the table.' Carefully, Evie took the bowl and carried it nervously to the table, to pour some milk on the top, then stood clutching it, not knowing where to go to eat it. The woman indicated with a nod that she was to go through the door behind Ernest. Evie edged past him, eyes on the bowl she was carrying, and found herself in a small scullery where there was a stool in the corner upon which she perched. It was quite a dark hole of a room but this did not trouble her. She liked being on her own to eat, privately, she enjoyed her food more that way. The porridge was as good as the cake had been, smooth and not glutinous as it had been in the Home, and the milk was rich and creamy. As she ate, slowly and neatly, concentrating on the task, she heard Ernest say, 'Not a scrap like her mother, not a scrap. I'd never have believed she was hers, never.'

'But then you never knew him when he was little,' the woman said. 'She might look like him when he was young.'

'Not like her mother, any road.'

'You said.'

'And I'll say it again, I'd never have believed it.'

There was a pause and then the woman began talking again. 'She's only little, mind, she's time to change.'

'She'll have to change a damned sight more than she's ever likely to if she's going to turn out looking like Leah.'

'You don't know what Leah looked like at this age either, don't let on you do because you don't.'

'I didn't say as I did but I knew her at ten and ten's not that much more than Evie is now, I knew her then, when they brought her from Carlisle. I can see her still, pretty as a picture, the hair on her. Now look at this one's hair and tell me she's Leah's.'

'Her hair hasn't been looked after.'

'Wouldn't make that much difference, it isn't hair like Leah's that I can see.'

'You don't see much. When it's washed regular and brushed regular and braided up it'll improve a treat.'

'You're going to do it, are you, all this messing about with her hair? That's what this is about, is it? That's why you wanted her?'

'It wasn't a case of wanting. I don't know how you dare say it was, it was a case of duty, and *your* duty too, you know it was.'

'Duty? It was a case of training up an extra pair of hands to be useful in the pub, that's what it was, that's what it is, lass. Never mind her hair, there's a pub to run and never enough hands. She'll have to earn her keep pretty soon.'

'She'll have to go to school first, she'll have to learn to read and write and add up.'

'She won't be at school all the time, there's plenty she can be trained to do before school and after school, and on a weekend and in the holidays, or anyways I did when I was her age and so did you, and if you'd had bairns that's what we would have had them doing, so I don't want any soft talk, right?'

There was silence, broken only by the clattering of dishes and the noisy slurping as the man drank his tea. Evie heard a chair pulled back and Ernest saying, 'I'm off.' She had finished her porridge. She decided to wash the bowl in the stone scullery sink but the moment she turned the tap on the woman shouted through at her, 'Don't waste water! There's water standing here, bring it through, you can wash it with the other dishes, now jump to it.'

Evie jumped.

Chapter Four

WHEN SHONA was eight, the McIndoes moved to St Andrews, a move which pleased them all. Shona was much happier. She still had a beach to run on, a wider and longer beach, but now she went to a school which satisfied her more. There were twenty-five girls in a class, all her own age and many of them as lively and energetic as herself as well as equally clever. She had real friends, Kirsty and Iona, for the first time and though she tried to dominate them, as she tried to dominate everyone, she did not always succeed. Kirsty and Iona were equally bossy and the three of them had to learn to give way occasionally to each other. It relieved Catriona to see this happening and she encouraged the friendship. They all lived near enough for the girls to walk to and from school together and visit each other's houses without needing either transport or supervision. Shona gained a new kind of independence and thrived on it.

Of the two houses she preferred Iona's, though Kirsty's was bigger and grander. Iona lived in the Old Town in a narrow close near the ruins of the cathedral. It was quite a small town house, its door opening directly on to the street, and it had no garden, but it had a pretty cobbled yard at the back with an open staircase going up to the door and a pantiled roof and dormer windows, and Shone thought it looked like an illustration from a book of fairy tales she had. She liked Jean, Iona's mother, who was young and attractive and smiled all the time whatever anyone did. She looked exactly like Iona, or rather Iona looked like her, the mirror image as people said, both of them with fine, sleek dark brown hair and large hazel eyes and delicate features.

'Iona's mammy is beautiful,' she said to her own mother, 'and she's young. I wish you were young.'

Catriona for once had the good sense to laugh. 'Well, I was once.'

'When?'

'Don't be silly, Shona – when I was young, of course, when I was Iona's mother's age.'

'When was that though?'

'Oh, about twenty years ago, I suppose, I don't know how old Jean Macpherson is, twenty-eight or nine maybe.'

'Why didn't you have me young?'

'I tried, but you just came when you were ready and that wasn't for a long time.'

Shona frowned. She recognised the tone in her mother's voice without being able to label it and she didn't like it, it made her feel cross, though she couldn't understand why. She felt she wanted to attack Catriona in some way, so she did. 'Why haven't I got brothers or sisters? It's not fair.'

'No, it isn't.'

'It's your fault too.'

'Fault doesn't come into it, Shona. I've explained before, I lost my other babies.'

'Why didn't you find them then?'

'You're being silly now, you know what I mean when I say "lost". I told you all about what happened and how sad it makes me talking about it.'

'Where did you have me?' Shona suddenly asked, in that abrupt, intense the way she had, the way that always disturbed her mother because it seemed as if a much older child was speaking.

'Where?'

'Yes. Was it upstairs?'

'Upstairs? Good heavens, no, it was in hospital.'

'But *where*?'

'Abroad.'

'*Where* abroad?'

'In Norway.'

'*Where* in Norway?' Shona was almost shouting now.

'Really Shona, the name of the town would mean nothing to you.'

'I want to *know*.'

'Bergen. There you are, you see, it means nothing to you.'

'Why did you have me there?'

Once more Catriona told the well-known story of Shona's birth and once more Shona hardly listened. Her mother never seemed to tell her what she really wanted to know, but then she didn't really know what that was. She craved detail, the kind of detail Kirsty boasted about – 'My mammy was making a cake and she'd just cracked an egg on the side of the bowl and she felt me *drop* inside her, and my daddy said she looked funny and he told her to lie down, but she said she had to finish baking the cake and she did and he phoned the doctor and she put the cake in the oven before she went upstairs to have me, and just as I was born two hours later the oven timer pinged and the cake was ready and ...' There was nothing about cakes or ovens pinging in Catriona's account of Shona's birth. Shona didn't want the hospital described, it didn't mean anything to her. The only part of the story of her birth that she liked was the bit at the end, when her father came rushing in to see her and said, 'She's the loveliest thing I ever saw.' She told that bit to Kirsty and Iona only to find it didn't go down at all well. 'Babies aren't lovely when they're born,' Kirsty announced. 'They're ugly wee things, all of them, I've seen them, I saw my sisters just when they were born and they were horrible, screwed up and red and yuck all over their heads.'

'Well,' said Shona, 'I was lovely, that's all.'

To her fury, Kirsty and Iona mimicked her and laughed and she didn't know how to stop them.

Often, when she was walking home from Kirsty's or Iona's house she wished she were going somewhere else, especially when her father was away. She'd walk along the shore road and look out to sea and think first of her father and then of where she had been born. It was like a speck in her mind's eye, fixed far away on the horizon, and she wanted to travel towards it and see it open up into something recognisable, the way lumps of blackness became land the nearer you approached them in a boat. 'One day,' she told her mother, 'I'm going to go and see where I was born.'

'*Where* you're born isn't important,' Catriona said, 'it's just a place. It's where you're brought up that matters and you know all about that, you remember the village, of course you do, and now you're in St Andrews and you won't ever forget this. You're a wee Scottish girl through and through.'

'I didn't mean that,' Shona said.

'What did you mean, then? Sometimes, Shona, I think you talk nonsense, you don't think before you speak – '

'I do so.'

' – and it can be very upsetting.'

'What's upsetting? *I* don't know what *you* mean, *you* talk nonsense, *you* don't – '

'Shona!'

Shona was stopped, for the moment. Her ninth birthday came and went and was tolerably satisfactory, but she preferred the treats her father gave her. He took her all the way to London once, on the sleeper, and showed her Buckingham Palace and the Changing of the Guard and they stayed in a proper hotel and went to Madame Tussaud's, and Shona at last felt in tune with herself, the self that had always wanted to dash about, to be among noise and bustle. She wished, aloud, and passionately, too passionately for a young girl, that she lived in London. Watching her, listening to her, sitting on the train all the long journey home, Archie was touched. It struck him that this was the difference between his own attitude to Shona and his wife's: Catriona was never merely touched by their daughter's restlessness and fierceness. Every flash of defiance, every symptom of some deep-seated rebellious spirit, and Catriona was full of despair and apprehension. She didn't see a clever lively young girl questioning and querying everything and everyone around her, but instead a potential disaster happening when Shona got 'out of hand' as she put it. She thought of the good years being over already, those years when Shona could be treated like a doll, when she could be made to a great extent in her mother's own image, when the force of her own personality had not yet become a real factor in the treatment of her. It wasn't, Archie knew, that Catriona wished to dominate or subdue Shona but that she wanted her daughter to be in step with her. She wanted harmony and intimacy in their relationship and the prospect instead of a growing discord frightened her.

It was supposed to be Archie's job, on these trips he took with Shona, between the ages of nine and twelve, to run the restlessness out of her so that when she came back to her mother she would be a different creature – docile, pleasant, agreeable. But it did not work out like that. Archie saw very well how, on the contrary, being away from her mother and her stable, staid life in St Andrews only made Shona want more of the same. She never wanted to go home, not even after the less successful excursions. It sometimes seemed the girl would rather be anywhere but at home with her mother, and yet Catriona was such a good mother, kind and gentle and absolutely devoted. Remembering his own mother, who had been remote and austere and never once, in so far as he could remember, capable of demonstrating affection, Archie was dismayed at how easily Shona spurned all that was so readily offered to her. But he didn't think anything could be done about this state of affairs. It was natural. Perhaps when Shona was older she would appreciate her mother more, perhaps when she had children herself ... but it was best not to think along those lines. He had always told Catriona to live more in the present, and not to torture herself with anguished speculation about the future, but she was unable to follow his advice.

*

By the time Shona was nearing thirteen and already an adolescent, developing far more rapidly than her friends of the same age, Catriona was overwhelmed by her, helpless in the face of her wilfulness. Motherhood still fascinated and absorbed her but she was increasingly frightened of what it involved. She couldn't talk to Shona about the things that needed to be talked about and felt constantly that she was failing in her own idea of her duty. Her mother was impatient with her. 'For the Lord's sake, Catriona,' said Ailsa McEndrick, exasperated, 'what are you fussing about? The girl's got eyes and ears, she's smart, there's nothing you can tell her she doesn't already know, and I suppose you mean it's sex that is worrying you, is it?' It was. Even hearing her mother refer so openly to sex, as was her defiant habit, made Catriona despair. She had always been so embarrassed by Ailsa's unusually frank attitude to sex. She had never been able to share it and now that there was Shona to instruct this worried her even more than it always had done.

She had not enjoyed sex since she had known she would no longer be able to have children. While she had been fertile, even if her fertility ended in disaster, there had been a feverish excitement to sexual intercourse. All the time Archie was thrusting away she was visualising those little sperm poised ready to swim into her womb and at the moment of climax – Archie's, not hers – she saw the egg pierced and conception happening in a shower of stars. She always lay very still afterwards, holding within herself the life-creating moisture, and as it began to seep out of her she would feel sad. Only the thought of that egg perhaps already fertilised stopped her from weeping. But after Shona arrived, when she was told her tubes were now so damaged that conception would be impossible and that her fertility, on the edge of forty years of age, would be low, she lost the only interest she had had. There was no longer any thrill. But she was a good wife and she loved Archie and so she said nothing. She never turned away from him, never repulsed his advances. It was not distasteful to be made love to, but nor was it pleasurable. It simply no longer had any meaning for her.

Now that Shona was thirteen Catriona was almost fifty-three. She was post-menopausal and glad of it – all those night sweats, all those embarrassing hot flushes, all those symptoms she seemed to have so severely while other women had virtually none. She hadn't spoken to Shona about any of them nor explained her listlessness and general poor health. She didn't want to disgust or depress her with talk of the menopause. But she was obliged to tell Archie, who was equally obliged to notice her general debility and her sudden marked aversion to sex. He was understanding, as he always was. It occurred to Catriona that he might have another woman and though she recognised such a thought as unworthy, since she knew Archie, she found she did not care. It seemed fair enough to her. If she couldn't bear any sexual congress during her menopause and Archie found the lack of it month after month intolerable – well, then. All that worried her was that she, a non-sexual being, was in charge of a nubile thirteen-year-old at exactly the wrong time.

Catriona was not jealous of her daughter but she was afraid of what seemed to her to be Shona's blatant sexuality. She was too young, surely, to give out these signals, to look so sultry and to be perfectly aware of the effect she had on boys and men. She was no longer slight and delicate in build. She had grown tall and developed large breasts and pronounced buttocks – her figure was unfashionably Edwardian, with its tiny waist and exaggerated curves. But there was no fat on her: her stomach was flat, her legs slim. She wore her hair, a deeper auburn now, pulled back from her face, but when she released the hair from the combs which held it, it fell forward in a great mass of waves and curls half obliterating the fine-boned face and lending her an allure Catriona found disturbing. 'Why not have your hair shaped, Shona?' she would say. 'It's so unruly, such a bother for you to wash and brush, why not have it cropped, it would suit you.' But Shona wouldn't. She wouldn't have her hair touched. She took great care of it, indulging in all kinds of shampoos and conditioners and brushing it until it crackled, until it sang with life and all over her head tiny, thread-like tendrils sprang up like a halo.

Shona knew she was attractive and suffered from none of Kirsty's and Iona's teenage angst over their looks. Out of school uniform she looked like an actress, a little like a red-headed Sophia Loren. To her mother's distress she wore clothes completely unsuitable for her, clothes bought not in St Andrews or Edinburgh shopping with her watchful mother but in Carnaby Street on yet another trip to London with Archie. 'Why did you let her buy that ridiculous skirt?' Catriona raged at her husband. 'And those boots, *white* boots, for heaven's sake, Archie, what were you thinking of, look at her, *look* at her.' Archie looked and saw that his wife was right. Shona looked disturbing. The skirt hardly existed and she was the wrong shape for it, and the boots merely drew attention to the barely covered bottom. 'They're all wearing them down there,' he said, lamely, knowing he would be told, as he was, that Shona was not down there, she was here, shocking the whole of North Street and South Street whenever she paraded down them.

Kirsty's and Iona's mothers were suddenly not so fond of Shona. They began to say she was too old 'in her ways' for their daughters to spend so much time with. In Iona's family in particular this new antipathy was marked, but then Iona had a fifteen-year-old brother who could not take his eyes off Shona McIndoe's skirt. Shona, Heather Grant agreed with Jean Macpherson, was even less like her mother than ever and now hardly like her father either. But at least her parents were strict even if they failed to control how she dressed. If Shona stayed the night her mother rang to thank Jean or Heather but they both knew she was ringing to check up that her daughter was really with them.

There was, in fact, no need for her to check up, not then. Shona held hands with the occasional boy but she had not yet been kissed; and though the bolder boys had put an arm round her in the back row of the Old Byre theatre, it was doubtful whether Shona was as interested in boys as they were in her. If there was any sexual response on Shona's part it was well concealed. Her mother suspected, and was relieved to suspect, that Shona was not as mature as she looked – her startling body did not yet know what it was about. And then, having been comforted by this thought, she was thrown into sudden confusion. Had she been like this? Had *she* been like this, the woman she had tried so hard not to imagine all these years? Had she been unaware of her own power and suffered for it? And would Shona do the same, for the same reasons, whatever they had been, in the same way?

Panic filled Catriona. It was time to speak, of course it was, she had been a fool to think that time would never, *need* never, come. It had come, far sooner than she could have anticipated. Yet she stayed silent, eternally vigilant but silent. She simply could not bring herself to destroy what she had come to believe was truth.

Chapter Five

AT THIRTEEN Evie left school but, since she had only managed to be there less than half the time she was supposed to be, it did not make much difference. The transition from schoolgirl to working girl was hardly noticed. Evie had grown very quickly used to being kept from school, never counting on walking the two miles to the schoolhouse until the very moment she was grudgingly told to go. At first, she had minded her poor rate of attendance greatly, but after the first year it had mattered less. School was not the paradise she had once imagined. There were only two rooms, both enormous and divided by partitions, and the noise made her head ache. The partitions were thin and the poetry Class 1 was reciting in unison fought with the recitation of multiplication tables by Class 2 until those sitting in Class 3, as Evie was, found it hard to concentrate on memorising the geographical facts they were required to do.

But Evie, though disillusioned, made the most of her time at Moorhouse Board School. She learned to add and subtract, to multiply and divide. Being a girl she was not expected to master equations, as the boys were, but she struggled with simple fractions and succeeded in understanding them. Ernest was pleased with her. He tested her regularly, sitting with a stick beside him on the table and rapping her knuckles if she got his questions, as to five times nine and the like, wrong. Evie's knuckles were rarely rapped by him; which was fortunate because they had already been rapped by her teacher and were often red raw. Other girls cried when they were taken behind the blackboard by Miss Stoddard and caned with her stick, which was pointed at one end and thick at the other, but Evie did not. Other girls sometimes screamed that they would tell their mams and their mams would come to the school and play war with

Miss, but Evie, of course, never did. She wondered what it would be like to have a mam to tell. She told Ernest's wife Muriel nothing. There was no point. Her heart pounded when Miss called her out because she had got something wrong but she taught herself to endure the punishment which followed without flinching. Miss Stoddard promptly caned her twice as severely in an attempt to make her weaken. But soon there was no cause for caning. Not even Miss Stoddard could fault Evie for anything except her attendance record and since, when the school officer visited the Fox and Hound, Ernest and Muriel gave adequate excuses she could not be blamed for that.

She made no friends during her intermittent years at school. 'Who are you?' she was asked when first she arrived, and 'Where do you live?' When she said she was Evie and lived at the Fox and Hound on the Carlisle road she was asked another question, one she couldn't answer. The question was 'Why?' Evie was obliged to say she didn't know. 'Does your dad work there?' her tormentors persisted, and when she said she had no dad they moved on to inquire about her mam, and then they pronounced her an orphan and sneered. 'She's got no dad, no mam, and she doesn't know who she is,' they sang. Evie listened to this chorus and was puzzled but not upset. What puzzled her was why having no dad or mam made her the object of ridicule, in the first instance, and then indifference. But at least she was left alone and rarely bullied. There was neither fun nor satisfaction in bullying Evie. She was not frightened, she didn't weep or turn red, nor did she attempt retaliation. She slipped in and out of school all those years like a shadow and was hardly remarked on.

Except for her singing. Evie's pretty voice was discovered by accident. She hadn't even known she possessed one since she had never had anything to sing about and had never been invited to. One day, all three classes on the first floor were brought together to sing carols just before the Christmas holidays. The partitions were opened up and all ninety-six pupils were lined up and ordered first to recite the words of 'In the Bleak Mid-winter' which they had been set to learn. Outside, the winter that year was very bleak indeed. Everyone had struggled to school through the snow and more could be seen swirling round the high windows of the vast, cold schoolroom. There was an oil stove at one end, near the teacher and the pianist, but it was making a poor job of heating the further reaches of the room. The coughing was unremitting and the breath coming out of ninety-six mouths into the freezing air caused little clouds to develop all along the rows.

Evie, because she was small, was in the front row and therefore lucky, since she did not feel as cold as those at the back. She was as near to enjoying herself as she had ever been. The teacher, a Miss Hart, was the nicest teacher in the school, young and kind and pretty in her pink frock. Everyone adored her and consequently behaved well for the duration of the time they spent under her gentle instruction. Evie, her eyes fixed on the lovely Miss Hart, felt dreamy and relaxed and not her usual alert, tense, terrier-like self, always on the lookout for trouble, always anticipating persecution or at least disapproval. She swayed slightly in time to the music and hummed the tune of the carol as Miss Gray played it through. 'Now,' said Miss Hart, 'I want each row to sing the first verse, row by row, and then we'll try to sing it together. Ready, the front row?' The front row had ten children in it, eight girls (including Evie) and two boys. 'One, two, three,' said Miss Hart and then dropped her hand as the signal that the front row should begin. Only Evie did. She had closed her eyes as soon as the signal was given and therefore did not see Miss Hart cancel it, with another wave of her hand, because the pianist had dropped her music. Out it came, Evie's sweet, soaring soprano voice and everyone listened spellbound until, realising she sang alone, she faltered and opened her eyes and stopped.

But Miss Hart was charmed. She made Evie sing the whole carol and clapped at the end. In a sense, this appreciation was too much and Evie would rather it had not been given. She didn't like to be the focus of attention. Attention of any kind was dangerous. Yet she could not stop herself feeling a rush of pleasure which continued for days afterwards. She had a voice, she could sing, she wasn't useless. Miss Hart kept her behind and complimented her and asked who she got her voice from. Evie was flummoxed. 'From, Miss?' she managed to ask. 'Yes, who in your family can sing like you? Voices are usually inherited, you know, they tend to run in families. Does your mother sing?' Suddenly, everything was spoiled. She had to begin again on the doleful saga of having no dad, no mam and living at the Fox and Hound with two people whose relationship to her she had never had properly explained. She thought, that day, of asking Muriel if her mother had had a voice but she could not bring herself to the point. She knew by then that a woman referred to as Leah had been, or was, her mother and that she had lived at one time in the same house as Ernest, her cousin, though whether it was in the Fox and Hound or not had never emerged. Neither had any clue as to what had happened to this Leah. Evie listened carefully to every mention of her and sometimes concluded she was dead and sometimes alive.

The strangest things provoked a reference to Leah. Ernest measured Evie each New Year's Day, up against the kitchen doorpost. 'She's still small,' he grumbled, 'she'll never be as tall as Leah, never. She'll be lost behind a bar, she'll never have the strength to draw a pint like Leah could.' And then there was her shyness, still acute after four years at the Fox and Hound. 'Goddamn it, lass,' Ernest shouted at her, 'don't jump like a frightened rabbit just because a stranger speaks to you. What good is that, eh?' And later Evie heard him complain to Muriel that she would never have a way with her, not like Leah who could charm the birds off the trees. Interestingly, Evie then heard Muriel say, 'Maybe just as well, birds weren't all Leah charmed and look what happened to her.' There was a silence. Ernest grunted. 'She'll be safer,' Muriel went on, 'being shy.' 'She'll be useless,' Ernest said, 'no good to us at all at this rate, there's no future to her.' 'She works hard enough,' Muriel said, 'you can't deny that, she's worth her keep.' 'Aye,' Ernest said, 'but I thought she'd be worth more in the long run.'

The work Evie did while she was still of school age was mostly housework, the same kind of cleaning and preparing of food that she had such a dim but happy memory of doing with her grandmother, only altogether harder. Muriel was a stickler for cleanliness and though Evie's own nature approved of her high standards and responded to them, sometimes it would strike her that what she was set to do was after all absurd. Muriel liked pans scoured till you could see your face in the bottoms of them. It was very, very hard to get the bottom of a pan clean enough to act as a mirror, and as she scrubbed and scrubbed, and peered and peered at her own vaguely emerging shadow of a face, Evie ruminated on the lack of sense in this exercise. It was the same with the silver forks, they too had to have faces visible in the handles, but at least that job was easier. Evie quite enjoyed cleaning the silver, spreading it out on the felt cloth kept for the purpose, and applying the paste and then polishing with a soft cloth. It was a restful task and, since she often felt very tired, a welcome one. And so was the sewing Muriel gave her to do, though at first she found it difficult to stitch a seam straight enough to satisfy her teacher. Muriel had the highest standards when it came to plain sewing. She would accept no slipped stitches and they had to run in lines as straight as a ruler.

Muriel sometimes paused from her own labours to talk to her at such times. There was no real affection between the two of them but as Evie had grown older, and proved so obedient, Muriel had become more companionable. She was not exactly kind to her but on the other hand she was not harsh or unfeeling and upon occasion showed a measure of real concern for Evie's welfare which always surprised her and left her somehow nervous. 'It isn't much of a life for a young girl,' she suddenly said one morning as she watched Evie scrubbing the stone floor of the kitchen, 'but then we've all had to do it, all our kind anyway, work, work, work, eh, Evie?' Evie looked up. She wanted the job over, she didn't want interruptions of this sort. 'You've missed a bit of mud there,' said Muriel, pointing with her toe. Relieved, Evie set to and eradicated it. 'Not much of a life,' Muriel repeated. 'You'd be better off behind the bar, where Ernest wants you if only you'd grow.' There was another pause. 'How old are you now, Evie?' 'Eleven,' Evie said, 'next month.' 'Oh yes,' Muriel murmured, 'March, I remember it was in the autumn she left, that would be right, she would just be showing with you.' Evie scrubbed, rhythmically, but she willed Muriel to go on. Something was being said, something of importance if only she could get hold of it. 'But you're small for eleven, that's likely why you haven't come on yet.' Evie paused, only vaguely aware of what was being said. 'That was when the trouble started,' Muriel said, and added with a sigh, 'It usually does, if it's going to. It did for your mother once she was a woman, right from then the men fancied her, though I didn't know her, mind. I saw her often enough later but I didn't know her properly then, it's only rumour, what went on.'

Evie knew it was the perfect opportunity to ask Muriel about Leah, to try to sort out all the enigmatic statements made about her and inquire once and for all if this Leah was indeed her mother and alive or dead, but it was too hard to begin. How should she begin? 'Who is Leah? Was she, is she, my mother?' She realised that she was afraid of the answers and even of there being no answers – it was preferable to have this hazy, shadowy, somehow soothing *idea* of a mother than be perhaps cruelly disappointed. There was such yearning within her for a mother, she so loved her fantasies of having one, that to risk losing them and having to substitute some harsh truth was not to be endured.

But this very failure to ask the questions about her own background, which most girls would have found irresistible, worked in the end in Evie's favour. If she had been openly curious, Muriel was the sort of woman who would have withheld information simply because she loved the power of knowing it when Evie did not. Ernest had told her to say nothing about Leah to the girl. He was quite adamant – 'Best if she knows nothing,' he had said, 'it might give her ideas, it'd lead likely to trouble and there's been enough of that.' But by the time Evie was thirteen, and on the edge of womanhood whatever she still looked like, Muriel knew that she would never be any trouble. She was thoroughly docile, without a flash of temper in her. It was safe to tell Evie anything at all, knowing both that she would never repeat it, because she had no one to repeat it to, and that she would not be unduly shocked or distressed. So Muriel, from then onwards, began to let things slip, little facts about Leah dropped into her monologues ready for Evie to pick up should she so wish. Muriel was not sure whether the girl did wish or not. Her expression betrayed nothing. And yet she thought she detected an extra stillness about Evie at these moments of revelation that alerted her to the girl's deep interest. It became a kind of game, trying to get some reaction from her, and the more Muriel played it the more careless she grew.

Evie, when she arrived at the Fox and Hound, had not appeared to know her surname or indeed that she was bound to have one. It was only when her name was called at registration in school that she realised her other name was Messenger and that she shared it with Ernest and Muriel. This had surprised and pleased her at the time, it had been like receiving a present and made her feel a certain kinship which had been more meaningful than hearing Ernest referred to as a second cousin. When she was older, the shared surname misled people. They assumed she was Ernest and Muriel's daughter and she saw how this irritated Ernest but pleased Muriel. 'She's not ours,' she heard Ernest say, when inquiries were made occasionally, 'she's my cousin's bairn, I've taken her in.' Sometimes, because Messengers had been at the Fox and Hound a long time, the inquirer would ask which cousin and then Ernest would say first of all, 'Leah Messenger, from the Caldewgate lot, kept the Royal Oak, her mam died, came here when they'd had enough of her, but little pitchers have big ears and that's as far as I'll go.' But if the question was asked of Muriel the reply was more detailed and nothing was said about little pitchers. 'No, she's not ours, and she's not my side,' Muriel would say, 'she's Ernest's cousin's bairn, Leah Messenger's, from the Carlisle side. We've taken her in, not that we ever knew she existed till she was six and then we got a letter, they'd traced Leah back to here. She was in a Home, this one, she'd been with another Messenger, old Mary, she lived here once, before my time, and Mary died and this one was put in a Home.'

Suddenly, Evie had a history and, though it remained sparse, she clung on to it. Her grandmother might not really have been her grandmother but at least she had had the same name and there was some connection between her and Leah, the Leah who was her own mother. That thought was precious, that link between Mary, Leah and herself. Bit by bit, Muriel strengthened it. When, at fourteen, Evie finally began her monthlies Muriel told her that now she had come on she must be careful or she'd fall and if she fell she'd share her mother Leah's fate. 'Look what happened to her,' Muriel said, sorting out rags to give Evie and telling her first to wash them well and keep them private. 'Fell, at seventeen, and that was that, that was you, that was her out on her ear and nowhere to go, so you be careful, though you won't have her problem looking as you do.' Another time, when Evie was late back with the milk, it was, 'Where've you been, not dallying with any lad, I hope?' Evie, who knew no lads, shook her head and explained about the late arrival of the milk cart with the churns at the crossroads. 'You be careful,' Muriel said, 'walking that road, that's how your mother got caught, walking that road and him coming up on his horse day after day. Did anyone speak to you? No? Good. Keep yourself to yourself, that's best.'

Evie did now finally help in the bar but only at quiet times when the daytime regulars were in, those with the patience not to mind her hesitations and difficulties with the pumps. Some were kind to her and tried to engage her in banter, but this flustered her – she found it hard to draw beer and take money and talk at the same time. Ernest always had her out from behind the bar long before it filled up and would order her back to the kitchen. 'You're flushed,' Muriel would say, 'your face is right red, Evie, you're more like Leah now, she had a good colour. Of course, she stayed all night in that bar, she drew them like flies, she could have had anyone she wanted, her looks could have been her fortune if she'd played her cards right.' Evie began washing the supper dishes, slipping them very, very quietly through the sinkful of water so as not to disturb Muriel's train of thought. 'But he came along, on his horse, and took a fancy to her and after that nobody could tell her anything, she was daft for him, daft. I told her, I said, "Leah" – I'd just married Ernest then and we were at the Crown, but I saw her often enough – I said, "Leah, lass, give over, he'll make a fool of you, he'll have you and leave you and won't give a damn," and surely she could see it, she'd heard the tales, they were well enough known, but no, she wouldn't have it, she wouldn't listen, not her. If she'd had a mam it might have been different, but her mam was dead and her dad too, and she was brought up in Caldewgate, then sent here. Her mam was Ernest's dad's sister's child and they brought her up as their own like we're bringing up you.' Muriel sipped the brandy and lemon to which she was partial, and looked at Evie's back, bent over the sink. 'She was lovely to look at, your mam, Evie.' And then, what Evie had waited so long for, 'Maybe still is, for all anybody knows, she'll only be in her thirties, wherever she is.'

So. Evie went over and over every one of Muriel's slurred words many times. Her mother might be alive. She was certainly not known definitely to be dead. She had felt quite faint hearing what Muriel said that night, and was glad to be facing away from her or for once in spite of herself her expression might have betrayed her excitement. At first, thinking about what she now knew, it seemed wonderful news but then, after all the hours of mulling it over, it seemed dreadful also. Her mother was not dead. She had therefore given her away. She had not wanted her. She, Evie, had been the cause of betrayal, misery and ruin, if Muriel was to be believed. Her mother had banished her for ever, given her to old Mary Messenger and abandoned her. When Mary died she had not come forward to claim her. She had let her be taken into a Home. But then Evie remembered she had been baptised and had a birth certificate. Did that mean some measure of concern for her and her soul? The thought of that certificate, the piece of paper in the ribbon box which had led to Ernest and Muriel taking her, worried her. She didn't have it any more. She still had the tin box and the ribbons, she still treasured those, but the paper had gone when it had been given back to her by Mrs Cox. Ernest must have it. She wished she had it, now that she understood the full significance of it. Perhaps, if she had it, she could find her mother. But another thought occurred to her: if her mother could have been found why did the people who found Ernest and Muriel not find her first? It could only be because she had disappeared. Unless – and this chilled Evie – her mother had denied Evie belonged to her.

Evie could not remember afterwards when she had decided that her sole purpose in life was to find her mother. She thought probably there was no one time when she had made the decision and doubted if the making of it had been precipitated by any particular thing. It had just grown with her, this strong sense of knowing what she must do, and it had made her curiously happy. She would not remain at the Fox and Hound for ever, working so hard for Ernest and Muriel, her days utterly monotonous and without hope of change. She nurtured her conviction that there would indeed be change and that she would bring it about herself. She would use her brain. She might not be beautiful like her mother but she knew she had a brain and that it must be capable of helping her. Answers came from this admirable secret organ in her head to the questions she put to it and she marvelled at the ease of the process once she got started.

Where and how could she start to look for her mother? Carlisle, of course, where she had lived with Mary once upon a time. And how could she get to Carlisle? By coach. Who would pay? She would have to save the money herself. Very difficult. She had no money except the rare threepence strangers in the bar gave her and the even rarer sixpence Muriel graciously bestowed upon her on market days in a fit of sublime generosity. These miserable pennies would have to be saved and, once accumulated, used for her fare. But in Carlisle where and how would she live during her search? She would have to find work the moment she arrived there, she would have to show a boldness she had never felt she possessed. And if there was no work? If her smallness and slightness and plain features put employers off? What then, brain?

That was too far to go. She stopped her questions at that point and settled for the limited plan of action she had thought up. Meanwhile, as she saved, as she put the small coins into her tin box of ribbons and sighed at how slowly they filled it, she drew from Muriel every last detail she could about Leah merely by forcing herself to say a word of encouragement here and there. 'You'll need a new dress,' Muriel said when, at seventeen, Evie's growth reached its modest limit, resulting in a sudden bursting of the buttons on her bodice. 'We'll make it a different colour, you look bad in navy, we'll try a brown maybe, your mother looked lovely in brown with that hair of hers.' 'Hair?' echoed Evie, timidly. 'Her hair, all gold it was, and masses of it, waves and curls, the lot. You haven't got it, you must've got yours from him, gold hair and hazel eyes, that was Leah, not that it did her any good, she was just the sort he fancied.' 'He?' repeated Evie, only a murmur but enough. 'Mr High-falutin', Mr Smart-as-paint, Mr Here-today-and-gone-tomorrow. Hugo was his name, la-di-da as himself, Hugo Todhunter, but they're ashamed of him now, his family disowned him and not before time, and off he went, to Canada, they said.' Evie stored the name away. It was easy to remember, it thrilled her to say it to herself. But she had no desire to find him, her father, it seemed, no desire at all, he was nothing to her. All she hoped was that through knowing his name she might be aided in her search for her mother when it began.

There were Todhunters in the village but she didn't think they were anything to do with this man on the horse whom Muriel described. There was nothing la-di-da about them, they were blacksmiths. But on the Carlisle road there was a big house, set back from it with a curving driveway, and Muriel passing it once had made some remark to Ernest about the old Todhunters letting it go to waste. 'Look at it,' Muriel had said, 'needs painting, needs the roof mending,' and Ernest had squinted at it in the midday sun as their cart rattled along and pronounced the neglect of this once fine house both a shame and a disgrace. 'Heart went out of them after he left,' Muriel remarked. 'And that other son died. There was only the daughter, and she married and left, remember?' Ernest did, but he wasn't interested. It was Ernest, though, who provided Evie with another clue, one of more importance than much of Muriel's chat. He heard Evie singing to herself one day as she worked in the wash-house, singing a hymn. 'Well,' he said, surprised, 'you've got your mother's voice if nothing else. Proper lark, she was, and she was in the church choir, loved to go to church, did Leah, never mind the rain, never mind the snow, off she'd go to St Kentigern's, came back like a drowned rat many a time, but she didn't care, she loved to sing in church, no stopping her.'

Evie stopped singing at once, struck dumb with the surprise and thrill of it – she had her mother's voice, she had something of hers, something to bring them together, then, to identify her after all as Leah Messenger's daughter. She knew St Kentigern's, though it wasn't the church Muriel had taken her to. Muriel was a Methodist and the Methodist chapel lay in quite the opposite direction to St Kentigern's, which was a dim little church with a broken spire now and cypress trees crowded so closely round it that it was almost obscured. Evie had never been inside it, she had only seen it from the road, but now she resolved to visit it and see where her mother had sung. She walked there, a distance of a mile or so, and all the time she was walking she was thinking about her mother doing the same, feeling as free perhaps as she suddenly felt herself, hurrying out of the village and striking out between the hills until the road curved downwards and a great vista of moorland opened up. It was a fine day, the sky was a watery pale blue with big puffy clouds sent chasing across it by the strong easterly wind. Evie had her head up and her hair blew out in front of her and her skirt billowed around her as the wind pushed her on. Going back would be hard, struggling against it, but for now it was helping her.

It was a Thursday, late afternoon in March, and there was no one near the now ruined St Kentigern's. How black it looked, with its dark trees scowling in front of it and its stone walls encrusted with moss so old the green of it was forgotten. There was an old wrought-iron gate at the entrance to the path leading up to the church itself, wide open, banging in the wind. Evie closed it carefully behind her, rust coming off on to her hand. She was afraid the church door would be locked but, though the handle was stiff to turn, she opened it without much trouble. The smell inside was the smell of all neglected old stone buildings – damp, mould and a whiff of lingering smoke. It was a very small church. Evie counted the rows, only six each side of the narrowest of aisles, room for sixty devout folk at the most. And where could a choir have sung? She was puzzled. There were no choir stalls, only a row of six chairs to the left of the altar with a wooden rail in front.

Her mother would have sat on one of those chairs and stood when it was time to sing. Voices would sound loud in this small space, it would not take much vocal power to fill it with sound. Evie did not dare put it to the test. Softly, she crept down the aisle, tripping once on a piece of the matting which had frayed, and hesitated in front of the one step leading up to the altar. She badly wanted to sit, or at least stand, where her mother had stood, but she lacked the courage to intrude any further. This was enough. Here her mother had come, every Sunday, rain or shine, and she had sung. It occurred to the motionless Evie that she, too, had of course already been here, in her mother's body, and this thought startled her. She was not a stranger here after all. This was where she had begun. Had her mother remembered that every time she stood in a church, after she had parted with her? Did singing hymns bring back the memory of this particular church and of her baby? Lightly, Evie ran her hand along the shelf of the front pew. It was covered in dust. She wrote 'Evie', then she wrote 'Leah', then she drew a heart round the two names, then she pulled her sleeve across and obliterated the names.

Her mother Leah had gone to church, rain or shine, every Sunday. Would that be something she would stop doing? Evie, buffeted by the wind all the way back, did not think so. She would surely find a church wherever she was and sing in it. Visions of Holy Trinity in Caldewgate rose in her head, the church where she had been baptised, a grand, noble church not at all like St Kentigern's. She would go to Holy Trinity when she arrived in Carlisle, when that day came, she would go on a Sunday, to a service, and study the choir. And she would go to St Cuthbert's at the end of the lane where she had been left by her mother, with the woman she'd thought of as her grandmother, and inspect their choir too, and she would not stop there, she would if need be attend services in every church in Carlisle that had a choir. It gave her something solid to cling on to and now that sense of purpose which had been growing within her became so strong she felt she would burst with the desire to start on her quest to find her mother. She had sleepless nights, exhausted though she was, and dark circles developed under her eyes until Muriel was moved to ask, crossly, if she was ill. Evie said she wasn't. 'Then buck up, for heaven's sake,' said Muriel. 'The sight of your miserable face is enough to put men off their beer and then where will we be, eh?'

On 11 March 1905, when Evie became eighteen years of age, she had £6 4s. 6d. in the old tin box which held the ribbons. It had taken more than three years to save, every penny of it screaming hard work and self-denial. She was as ready as she would ever be. Nobody marked her birthday, though Muriel had remarked on its imminence the week before – 'You'll only be a year older than your mother was when she fell for you, so you be careful.' But as she'd issued the entirely unnecessary warning, knowing quite well that no fine men on horses had even so much as stooped to pass the time of day with drab little Evie, Muriel had had the grace to finish with a lame-sounding but quite affectionate, 'But you're a good girl, nobody can say you're not, you've never given us a minute's bother, that's the truth.' There was no reward for this lack of being a bother, not the briefest expression of congratulation on her birthday and no recognition of it in the way of a present. Evie was glad that this was so. It made it easier to leave. Only two things troubled her. Should she or should she not write Muriel a note? She supposed it would be wise, since she did not want a search party sent after her. She made it short: 'Dear Muriel, I am gone off to find other work. I will send you my address when I am settled, Evie.' And where was that precious birth certificate which the matron of St Ann's had given to Ernest? She hated to leave without it but did not dare search further. It hurt to regard the paper as lost for ever but there was no alternative.

She had, after all, more to take with her than she had reckoned. In the twelve years she had been at the Fox and Hound she had been well if not fashionably clothed by Muriel, who did not want her – she had always said – to disgrace the establishment by being in rags. She had had a new dress made every spring for the summer and every autumn for the winter, and always had good boots and shoes, though Ernest complained bitterly about the cost. Of the clothes made for her, four dresses still fitted and she took them all, as she did her new black boots and her Sunday shoes. Her coat had just been renewed and it was a good, heavy tweed and she had two bonnets, both perfectly serviceable. Gloves, stockings, petticoats and chemises, all well worn but not shabby, swelled the pile on her bed enough to panic her. She could not carry all this and yet, if she did not, she knew Muriel would not dispatch these clothes to her in due course. So they must be crammed into a bag somehow and carried to Carlisle. An old carpet bag which a lodger had left behind and which Muriel had told Evie to burn, because it had a hole in it and stank of tobacco, would suffice. Evie patched the hole and wrapped every article in old newspaper in an attempt (vain) to protect it from being impregnated with the smell of stale smoke. She managed to get everything in, though she could not get the clasp to meet so had to tie the two sides together with string.

The weight of her bundle shocked her. She was strong but, even so, the only way she could carry the bag was by wrapping both arms round it as though it were a baby. The problem of getting it out of the Fox and Hound and along to the crossroads where she planned to stop the coach to Carlisle – she'd seen it hailed there even though it was not an official stop – almost defeated her. It was a mile away and half of that journey was lined with cottages from which eyes would peer at her and notice and tell Muriel, or Ernest, perhaps in time to stop her. She had no idea if her mother's cousin and his wife had the right to stop her but in any case could not endure the possibility of any unpleasantness. She must get the bag to the crossroads at night and leave it there, risking its discovery and theft.

Once she'd thought of this plan its execution was not as difficult as she had feared. She did not work in the bar after eight at night, not even now, and it was easy for her to slip out while Ernest and Muriel were hard at it. She took a wheelbarrow from the shed, and taking care to keep in the shadows – which was simple since only one side of the village street had any lamps at all and these gave a feeble light – she trundled her precious bag the mile to the crossroads. The hardest part was seeing her way over the last half mile. Once the village was left behind, it was a pitch-black night, no stars, no moon, no way of distinguishing road from moorland. Again and again she found herself on muddy grass even though she had been sure she was going in a straight line along the road. Only the white signpost helped, when it loomed into view at last, and thankfully she moved more quickly. There was a ditch on the opposite side of the road from where the coach would stop. She'd marked it out the day before and lined a place, about ten yards from the crossroads, with a piece of sacking. She dropped her bag on to this and drew the sacking over it and for good measure dragged some wet leaves across the hiding-place. It was the best she could do.

Her last night in the Fox and Hound was like her first in that she slept deeply and woke very early. She knew off by heart Muriel and Ernest's routine and habits and exactly how to evade their attention. Evie was expected to rise at six, rake out the fire in the kitchen, get it going and boil a kettle ready for tea. This day she rose at five, dressed, made her bed neatly, and crept downstairs. She raked the fire and reset it, as a last service, but did not light it or take any food or drink for herself. She was at the crossroads before six, knowing there was only one early morning coach and that it passed without stopping at the Fox and Hound as it did at other times. She knew it might not stop for her at her crossroads either but had tried to shut such a potential catastrophe out of her mind. She planned to stand in the middle of the road, knowing that though this was dangerous, the coach driver had a long view as he came down the hill and could not possibly miss her. He must stop even if he would not take her and she was determined he would, though she had no idea what form her determination could conceivably take.

It was still not quite fully light as she rounded the last bend and saw the signpost. It hardly seemed possible, but there was someone already there, someone who would have to see her retrieve her bag, someone who would surely guess she was running away. But she had to go on; there was no alternative. It was a man, shivering in the early spring morning air in spite of his thick coat and muffler and cap. He was stamping his feet and blowing on his hands as Evie approached and he looked as startled as she was. Bending her head, Evie walked past and found her bag and began tugging it out of the ditch. The man could not help but see. 'What have you there?' he shouted, and then to her consternation she heard his feet on the road, hurrying to her side. 'Want a hand?' he said, and though Evie shook her head he bent down and swung the bag on to his shoulder. 'Well, well, you'll not want any questions asked, I'll bet, eh?' and he tapped his nose. 'Catching the Carlisle coach, is it?' Evie nodded. 'Then that makes two of us. He'll have to stop now.' They returned to the signpost and stood together, the man in high good humour, chuckling to himself. 'No questions asked,' he kept saying, staring at Evie, who volunteered not a word. 'And you'll ask me none either,' the man said. 'Fair's fair, eh?' Evie nodded. 'Just one thing ...' the man began, but Evie never heard what that one thing was, because the coach came, thundering down the long hill so fast she could not see how it could stop in time.

But it did. The man heaved her bag up and then helped her – she had money only for the outside – and went inside himself. She was all on her own, sitting in state on top of the Newcastle to Carlisle coach, with a fine view all the way.

Chapter Six

THEY WERE going to have a holiday, the three of them, perhaps the last family holiday they would ever have. It was Catriona who thought like that, not Shona. 'Soon you will be gone,' Catriona had been saying for what seemed like years now. 'Soon you will be gone, off on your own.' It sounded such a birdlike plaintive cry, so sorrowful and yet needful, begging for some kind of contradiction. But Shona never did contradict. Yes, soon she would indeed be gone and glad to be gone. She had her own life out there and she meant to have it, and her mother could not tug her back. She was going to go to London, to university, and she was going to read law and then there would be no stopping her. She would have a worthwhile, fulfilling career and be everything her mother had never been.

Knowing she was on the very edge of doing this gave her the deepest satisfaction. All she needed to do was pass her exams, gain the grades requested, and that would be that. London was the only place for her, she had no doubts about this. She felt ready to meet the challenges of crowds and noise and even the violence said to lurk round every corner. Her impatience was great but she was ready to become more tolerant of her mother's distress the nearer she came to her goal. It was sad, after all, she could see that, sad to have your only daughter, your only child, leaving you and being not in the least regretful. She wanted to be kind and so she was gracious about the proposed family holiday to celebrate her eighteenth birthday. Certainly she would go with her mother and her father on holiday in the Easter break. It was only a question of where.

'Somewhere hot?' Catriona suggested. 'The south of France? Spain?' Shona raised her eyebrows. They had never gone abroad. Archie said he got quite enough of abroad and preferred Rothesay and the Isle of Arran. But Shona didn't want to go to the south of France or Spain. She liked snow not heat, skiing and not lolling on beaches. She'd been skiing with the school in the Austrian Alps – that's what she wanted to do for her eighteenth birthday, but she couldn't suggest it. It would not constitute a family holiday because her mother could not ski and hated the cold, and her father, though he had skied in Norway when he was a young man before the war, had arthritis in his knee and couldn't do it any more. Shona thought carefully. March was not an easy month for a family holiday. Perhaps a city would be best. Paris? But she thought longingly of one day being there by herself and not encumbered with parents. Meanwhile her mother's face was contorted with anxiety. Shona wanted so much to please. 'Wherever you like,' she said, trying to sound cheerful, 'you choose.' 'But it's your birthday,' Catriona said, '*you* must choose.'

In the event circumstances dictated the choice, or so Shona thought. Her father came home from six weeks away in the middle of February. He was tired and talking of one last voyage then retirement. In fact, he had committed himself to that voyage and it was to start from Bergen a week after Shona's birthday. 'Oh, Archie!' said Catriona, 'Archie! You knew it was her birthday, you promised we'd have a family holiday, how could you, how can we go anywhere now?' Her father looked stricken. 'Mum!' Shona said in reproach. Often, lately, she had felt she had to protect her father and never more than now when her mother seemed angry out of all proportion. 'I know,' she said brightly, 'let's all go to Bergen, to Norway, and Dad can sail at the end of it and you and I can come home, Mum.'

'No!' Catriona said. Shona stared at her. The violence behind that small word was alarming and her mother's expression disturbing.

'Why ever not?' she said. 'I've always wanted to go to Norway, remember, remember how when I was little I used to want to go and see where I was born? We could go to Oslo and then ...'

'No!' Catriona shouted again.

'Mum!' But Catriona had got up from the table where they were all sitting and begun to clear away their plates, crashing them together in a most uncharacteristically clumsy way. Her hands, Shona saw, were shaking. 'What's wrong with Norway, for heaven's sake?' she asked. 'I mean, I don't care where we go and if it fits in with Dad's plans ...' Catriona had left the room. She turned to her father and said, 'What's wrong with her? What's going on?'

Archie lit his pipe and said nothing. Shona waited, a strange feeling of anticipation banishing the lethargy she usually felt during family meals. She felt curious in a way she so rarely did about anything to do with her mother. There were never any mysteries about Catriona. She was such an obvious person. Once, given 'My Mother' as a title for a school composition, Shona had found her normal fluency deserting her. What of interest could she write? How could she make her mother sound interesting? There were the facts and nothing else, the ordinary story of her birth in Cambuslang in 1916, the youngest of four children, and her perfectly straightforward schooling at Hamilton Academy, before going into the post office as a counter clerk and rising to the heady heights of postmistress of a city post office – it was all boring until she got married to her merchant sea captain. And even then nothing worth recording had happened, just years of being a good little housewife in various parts of Scotland and the occasional temporary few months abroad in places like Bergen where she just went on being a housewife. Nothing, in young Shona's opinion, to write about. Her mother had no hobbies or interests either, unless knitting and sewing counted. It had been embarrassing scratching around for material, whereas if the title had been 'My Father' there would have been an abundance. Her mother was an open and extremely blank book.

But now there was something on the page. Her father might have lit his pipe and appear relaxed but Shona could tell he was not. He was tense, his shoulders hunched, his free hand tapping the table. They both went on waiting for Catriona to reappear and neither spoke. When there had been no sign of her for a full five minutes Shona gathered together the rest of the dishes and went through to the kitchen. Her mother was standing looking out of the window, the kettle beside her steaming away but ignored. Shona heard it click itself off. Her parents always had tea after their evening meal. The teapot stood ready on a tray together with cups and saucers. 'Shall I make the tea?' Shona said, but her mother grabbed the kettle and filled the pot and marched back into the dining-room. Shona followed, feeling more and more like a little dog trotting at its owner's brisk heels, unsure whether it is out of favour or not.

'I thought you had homework?' her mother said.

'I do.'

'Then go and get it done.'

'But I want to know if we're going to Norway or ...'

'No!' her mother said again, just as her father said, 'Yes.' His voice was the quieter but the more commanding. 'I think it's a good idea,' he said. 'We should have gone long ago.'

There was a sudden absolute silence broken only by Archie's puffing of his pipe. Astonished, Shona looked from one to the other barely able to credit that two people could assert themselves in ways they had never done before. They were mild people, her parents. They did not shout or rage, ever. They were hardly even irritable or raised their voices for anything, and exuberance of expression was unknown to them. Living with them was like being steeped in a still pond with nothing to ruffle the surface. And now those waters were broken by an antagonism quite shockingly blatant.

'Look,' Shona said, 'what's going on with you two? This is weird, what's all the fuss about?'

'Go and do your homework,' Catriona said, each word enunciated carefully and distinctly, but her voice at least level once more.

'No,' said Shona. 'You're treating me as if I was eleven, like a child. I won't, I can't, not till you tell me what all this is about. I'm not a child, you can't just shove me off. It's my holiday too, my birthday, I'm entitled to know why you're in such a state just because I suggested Norway to fit in with where Dad has to be.'

'You'll know in good time,' Archie said, 'but not now. We'll go to Norway. We'll go to Oslo, you'll like that, and then maybe explore the Hardanger, stay at Ulvik or Voss, and end up at Bergen. That's what we will do. Now trot off, Shona, there's nothing more to say tonight.'

Shona looked from him, calm but solid and full of an authority she had never been aware of before, to her mother, bent over the tea-tray, hands gripping the table so that the knuckles showed white, face hidden by her hair which had escaped from its small combs and hung dishevelled all around. She had never felt compassion for her mother, only a dry, superior kind of pity for her feebleness, but now she did. Catriona seemed to have been beaten, though in what sort of game, or little private war, she could not fathom. Her good, kind, gentle father had somehow beaten her and she knew it. Uneasily, Shona made for the door, aware, curiously, that she was hoping her mother would revive and retaliate. She did not want to leave her beaten. But there was no retaliation. As she went upstairs to her room Shona heard only the clatter of teaspoons in cups of tea and a cough from her father and then silence.

The silence seemed to go on day after day for the next few weeks, right up to their departure for Norway. Not a literal silence, since all the usual pleasantries were exchanged, all the small talk of basic family communication, but Catriona did not indulge in any chatter and its absence was marked. Shona marvelled that she missed it so, when it had always annoyed her, the accounts of what had been in this shop and that, what someone in a queue had said to someone else, how this price or the other had gone up and that it was scandalous. But now it was not on offer, she missed the security of the monotonous, harmless recital. Meals were awkward in a way she would never have anticipated. There was an onus on her she shied away from. If there was to be any real talk it would have to come from her, in a monologue, and she did not feel equal to it.

It was a relief to be packing to go on the wretched holiday, even if she dreaded the week ahead. At least there was the comfort of knowing it would soon be over and that whatever was wrong between her parents would come to an end, or she supposed and hoped it would. But where was the pleasure in this family trip? Her mother prepared for it as though for a prison sentence, folding clothes and putting them into a suitcase as though she might never take them out again and sighing all the time. 'For God's sake, Mum,' Shona said, 'this is ridiculous, you're so miserable, it's not true.'

'You care, do you?' said Catriona.

'What? What the hell does that mean? Of course I care, it's awful, it's making me miserable too.'

'Oh well, we can't have that.'

'Mum! There you go again, what do you mean, sounding all sarcastic and bitter suddenly?'

'I can be sarcastic and bitter if I want. It isn't your prerogative.'

'Heh, look, I've had enough, you're getting at me and I haven't done a thing wrong.'

'No.'

'Well then. Why the treatment, why are you making me suffer?'

'I don't think you're suffering, Shona. I don't think you know what suffering is.'

'Jesus!'

'Don't blaspheme, it doesn't help.'

'It does actually, it helps a lot, it bloody well does ...'

'I won't listen. I hate swearing.'

'And I hate atmospheres. It's worse than swearing to go around with a long face all mournful and not telling anyone why. Why don't you just swear and get rid of it, whatever's bugging you?'

'It isn't how I am. I don't get rid of things. You, you're the one who never holds back. It's the modern way, tell everyone everything and never mind if it would be better not told.'

'Oh my *God*!'

Exasperated, Shona left her mother and went to pack her own things. At least there were no more rows about clothes or how she looked. Trousers, sweaters, an anorak and all in dark sensible colours, that was her style these days, and the hair, which had caused so much comment, was firmly twisted and plaited and out of the way. She was a serious student and looked it, a cause for parental self-congratulation. Her parents came to open evenings to hear her praises sung by every teacher and were gratified beyond belief. Shona knew she was said to have 'grown out of' her earlier defiance and wilfulness. She enraged her friends now by working so hard and never having fun any more. They did not know what had happened to her. But Shona knew. Ambition had happened and nothing was going to get in its way.

Her mother also knew this, of course. Shona saw she had sensed the reason for her diligence and obedience, for her single-minded application to school work and her entire lack of social life. She'd sensed it and was afraid. Sometimes, on Saturday nights in particular, her mother had taken to saying to her, 'Are you not going out, Shona? All work and no play makes Jill a dull dog, you know.' 'Then I'll be dull,' Shona replied, holding back from adding, 'just like you.' It was ironic. Now her mother had her at home she didn't like it any more than when, at thirteen and fourteen, she had contrived to be out all the time. What Catriona liked was convention, she liked her daughter to do what others did, to be normal and average. It was what she had always wanted – nothing odd, nothing out-of-step in her daughter's behaviour. Pushing her clothes into a bag, Shona wished she could push her mother in with them and then drop the lot in the sea. She couldn't bear all this mournfulness and angst and the thought of having to endure it unrelieved for a whole week was too much – some birthday treat, some happy last-family-holiday this was going to be, probably so awful she would never forget it.

*

They flew to Oslo and spent three days there visiting the Kon-Tiki museum and the Vigeland Park and the Akershus Fortress and all the other sights Archie thought Shona should see. She tried to be enthusiastic but boredom seeped out of every pore. She felt like a small child, following her parents round dutifully while they waited for her reactions. Bedtime was a relief. She went to bed earlier and earlier, pleading exhaustion. It was better on the fourth day when they set off for the Hardanger Fjord, a journey of four hours from Oslo. The snow had begun to melt early and all along the route torrents of water cascaded down the mountains in spectacular waterfalls. But higher up the dark of the fir trees were still heavily snow-covered. It was easy then to exclaim over the beauty of the wild and jagged scenery and even Catriona came out of her sullen silence enough to express awe at the sight of the first fjord.

So they arrived in Ulvik, on Hardanger, in good spirits and booked into the *pensjonat* close to the fjord. The sun shone on the pretty painted houses and on the deep blue waters of the fjord, and Shona was happy merely to be out in the open air and not trapped in buildings looking at things. But the next morning when they drove on to Bergen, her parents had sunk once more into some kind of depression which was mysterious to her. She still could not fathom the atmosphere between them nor work out whether they had quarrelled again. Both had stony faces, Catriona's white and lined, Archie's dark behind his beard as though he were suppressing rage. No one, this time, commented on the beauties of the countryside through which they passed, though it was even more impressive than the day before. The sun was everywhere catching on the white birch twigs mixed with the darker shades of the still-winter landscape and gave a brilliance to the mountains below the snowline. It was impossible not to feel exhilarated by the brightness and clarity of everything, but when Shona said so neither parent said a word. All the way to Bergen, the whole hour, neither of them spoke and she began to feel more and more detached from them.

Bergen delighted her. She had not expected such colour but when they approached the city it was lit by an extraordinary midday sun and seemed all tawny and golden, the many red gabled roofs and ochre-painted houses melding into each other from the angle at which they approached. Shona felt immediately proud that it was here she had been born and even when they were in the middle of the modern part of the city, and she saw it was more ordinary than it had first appeared, she felt drawn to it and excited by it. The seven mountains surrounding it seemed to her so protective and she liked the feeling of being in an amphitheatre. They stayed not in a four-star hotel, as they had done in Oslo, but in a small guesthouse near the fish market, in a hilly street with houses almost touching each other at roof level. Her mother, she noticed, did not seem happy about this, but her father merely said, 'This is where we stayed,' as though that settled the matter. 'It is noisy,' her mother said, 'it was always too noisy,' but he said nothing.

The next morning Archie knocked on her door at seven o'clock when she was still deeply asleep. 'Shona?' he called. 'Get up, please, we need to be off early, before there's too much traffic.' She groaned but got up, thinking at first they were travelling again, but then remembered that no, this was where they were to stay the last two days before she and her mother flew home. Today was the day for visiting where she had been born. Only another day in which to try to be the obedient, dutiful daughter. But she felt irritable when she joined her parents downstairs and even more so when she was told just to have some coffee because they were going at once and could eat later. The sun had not yet warmed the air and it was freezing when they stepped out to go and find their car. Shona shivered as they slipped and slithered across the icy cobbles to the car and she wrapped her scarf more tightly round her. Catriona was buried in scarves and her fur hat was pulled right down over her ears, but Archie showed a careless disregard for the cold and had not even bothered to fasten his coat properly.

It was a short drive and then there they were, outside a building which was obviously a hospital. Shona cleared her throat. She was hungry. All the cold air had made her ravenous. 'Dad?' she said, but Archie was staring straight ahead, his hands still on the wheel of the car, but the engine turned off. 'Dad? This is it, is it, I mean where I was born?' He stayed silent, only shifting in his seat a little. 'Mum? This is it, right?' Catriona nodded. 'Well,' Shona said, trying to laugh, 'groovy place, eh? I'm overcome with emotion but I'm starving, can we go now?' An ambulance turned in, its siren going. 'We can't stay here, Archie,' said Catriona in a hoarse voice, 'we're in the way, we'll have to move.' Archie restarted the engine. 'Do you want to go inside?' he asked Shona, who looked incredulous. 'Inside?' she echoed. 'Dad, please, a hospital is a hospital, why would I want to go inside?' So they drove back to where they had parked the car overnight and trooped once more into the guesthouse and had a late and, in Shona's case, large breakfast. 'Funny,' she said, mouth still half full, 'when I was little I used to think of where I was born as being all romantic. I used to see this sweet little log cabin sort of place, like Heidi lived in, nestling in the snow and smoke coming out of the chimney, and Dad ploughing through the snow to get to it, and you, Mum, in a big wooden bed with a fur cover, having me. Silly, eh?' And she grinned at them and took more butter for her toast.

'Very silly,' Catriona said, 'it wasn't like that at all.'

'No. I've just seen it wasn't, it was just an ordinary hospital, nothing romantic.'

'No,' Catriona said, her voice flat, 'nothing romantic.'

'Except,' Shona said, still munching away, 'all births must be romantic, well, in the thrilling way, I mean they must be exciting wherever they happen. You were thrilled, weren't you, Mum?'

'Yes,' Catriona said, and the tears began to slide down her impassive face. Shona stopped eating. These did not look like tears of remembered joy. Carefully she put down her piece of toast and looked round the room. It was still busy with people finishing breakfast. 'Mum,' she whispered, 'what's wrong?'

Catriona shook her head and to Shona's relief brought out a tissue and applied it to her streaming eyes. 'Archie will tell you,' she whispered back.

'Dad?' Shona said, her stomach suddenly lurching. 'What is it? What's wrong?'

'Not here,' hissed Archie, looking agonised. 'Later, later.'

After that, they left hastily, shuffling out of the room, all three with their heads down, as though apologising for some disgrace. In the street Archie stood for a moment, ahead of the women, as if making some momentous decision only he could make, then set off at a rapid pace without looking back to see if they were following. 'Honestly,' Shona muttered, aggrieved. Catriona clung on to her arm, afraid of falling on the slippery surface along which they were being forced, by Archie's speed, to hurry. He took them to where the cable car started up the mountain and before they had reached him he had paid for their tickets. There was hardly anyone in this early morning car and they all sat in separate seats by the window. At the top, Archie got out. 'Are we staying?' Shona asked. 'Where are we going? Where is there to go?'

'Nowhere,' said Archie, 'we'll just stay here until the next car comes back.'

They were soon alone, the three of them. The sun was out now, growing stronger by the minute, and it was pleasant enough leaning on the rail looking down on the city strung along the seaboard. Without looking either to his left, at Shona, or to his right, at Catriona, Archie began to speak. Shona was hardly listening at first, the words simply did not penetrate. She was expecting her father to launch into a travelogue, a little lecture on the history of Bergen or to begin to wax nostalgic about all the time he had once spent here, or near here. She intended to listen, to take an interest, but found her attention wandering to the ships sailing into the harbour, her mind full of curiosity as to where they had come from and what was in their holds. But then she realised she had heard something odd.

'What?' she said. 'Sorry, I wasn't really listening, sorry, what did you say?' Her father put his head in his hands, leaning his elbows on the rail. 'Dad, I'm sorry, what did you say? Say it again, something about how I was born it was, wasn't it?' She was sure it had been but equally certain there had been something unusual about the familiar story, some mention of the word 'secret'.

'I can't go through it again,' her father said, his voice muffled. Another car was coming up, this one much fuller. Shona waited. Other people, freshly arrived, joined them and began pointing and taking photographs. 'Let's go down,' her father said. He looked awful. 'Dad,' she said, 'what's wrong? What is it?' – but he shook his head and half-smiled, a weary smile that made him look so pathetic.

All day, Shona had intimations of disaster and yet could not think what this catastrophe was going to be. Again and again she scrutinised first the face of her mother and then of her father and tried to imagine the worst. But what was this worst? Their deaths, she supposed. The death of one of them. Was that what this tension was about, this sense of strain which had hung over them now for so long? Was that what her father had been trying to tell her, all mixed up with the well-known tale of her birth? One of them was mortally ill and she had been brought here, where she had been born, to be told the news. It did not make sense, there was no connection to be made and she discarded the notion, annoyed with herself. It must be a different kind of bad news, not so sinister, not so shattering, but serious enough to arouse such anxiety and more likely to be revealed on a last family holiday together. Suddenly, as the three of them wandered in a dazed fashion round Bergen, Shona thought she had it: divorce. That would make a kind of sense – last family holiday – end of *family* – back to the beginning of it to make the breaking of the news not so painful ... A sort of sense but not enough. How weird it would be, to think of her parents apart when they had been together for what seemed an eternity and all that time completely content. Who would it be worse for? Her mother, of course. Her apprehension grew. She would not be able to desert her mother. Her mother would be pitiful and cling. She felt sicker and sicker.

They ate in the evening in a restaurant her father said he knew well. He said it while staring hard at Catriona. 'We used to come here,' he said, 'and talk about you, Shona.'

'Not here,' said Catriona, 'please, Archie, not here, not now.'

Shona turned to her. 'Mum,' she said, 'all day it's been talk of not here, not now. I can't stand this a minute longer. You look terrible, Dad looks terrible, I *feel* terrible. I'm sorry I wasn't listening when you tried to tell me whatever it is I've got to be told, but I'm listening now. Tell me.'

Archie stirred the thick fish soup.

'Not in a public place,' Catriona said. 'It might be better in a public place,' Archie muttered. 'Force us to be sensible.'

'I agree,' Shona said, though wondering if she did. Would she cry? Would her mother cry? Was there going to be a scene? She could hardly sit still, fidgeted about, picked up her napkin and found herself screwing it viciously into a ball and longing to throw it. Sighing, his soup pushed aside, Archie looked straight at her and she saw in his eyes anger, not misery, and knew this was nothing to do with divorce.

'We were very stupid,' he said. 'I especially. Stupid and maybe you'll think wicked. We wanted you so badly, Shona, you cannot imagine how badly. Your mother ...' He stopped.

Shona felt a flash of impatience. 'Yes,' she urged, 'go on, I know Mum had always wanted a baby more than anything and she'd miscarried and there'd been the stillbirth and then I came along, I know all that.'

'No,' said Catriona. She had blushed. Her pale face was a bright and ugly red, Shona saw. 'No, you don't know all of it. You came along differently.'

'Catriona, I thought we'd agreed ...' Archie began.

'I know what we agreed. I've changed my mind. I can manage. It should be me. Oh, God ...' The waitress had come to clear the dishes away and ask what else they wanted. They waited. Shona's heart thumped. Coffee was put on the table and poured. Her mother, she noticed, seemed to find comfort in holding the hot cup. 'It should be me,' Catriona took up again. 'I want to tell her. I ought to. Shona ...' and she turned right round, to Shona sitting beside her, and looked her in the face with such determination that the effort it cost her was touchingly obvious. 'Shona, it's simple really, even if it comes out all complicated. I wanted a baby. I was nearly forty and desperate. We heard about this girl in Bergen, in the care of Miss Østervold, whom your father had known in the war. This girl was going to have a baby and couldn't keep it. We came here and we made inquiries and when you were born we had it all fixed up. It was difficult to arrange, very difficult, but we adopted you. We had you from the moment you were born. I held you in my arms from when you were an hour old and I thought you were mine. You were so much mine I thought you truly were. I begged and pleaded with your father to go along with my plan to pretend I'd given birth to you ...'

'I was stupid,' Archie said.

'No, I was mad,' Catriona said. 'You had to be mine, I believed you were. The moment I saw you and held you I believed you to be mine. You *are* mine. But your father ...'

'It's your right, Shona,' said Archie. 'You're eighteen, we're getting old, you have a right to know the truth and to know it from us.'

'It wasn't necessary, but your father ...'

'It was, it is necessary,' Archie said. 'I believe it to be necessary. But I hope it won't make any difference to us. That's what I hope.'

They were waiting, both of them. How glad she was for the public place, the noise and bustle of the packed restaurant. She could not have coped in a quiet room, just the two of them waiting amid silence. Even more blessed was the arrival of the bill and the offer of more coffee and the ordinariness of the transactions this involved. Had she turned deathly pale? Was the coldness she felt on her skin noticeable? She put a hand up to brush away her hair and her mother flinched. She must say something, quickly. 'I'd like a drink,' she said, her voice embarrassingly croaky. 'Whisky or something, Dad?' Archie ordered three schnapps even though the bill was already paid. He held his glass up, as though in a silent toast. She responded by doing likewise and was pleased her hand did not shake. She cleared her throat. 'It's just amazing,' she said feebly. 'I can't take it all in.' Then she thought a minute. Her mother seemed to have her head bowed so humbly whereas her father had relaxed and seemed once more his old self, at ease, bland and placid. 'Who knows?' she asked finally. 'Does Grannie McEndrick know?'

Catriona shook her head. 'No one knows,' she said, 'no one at all, except Miss Østervold and her friend and they are dead.'

'Imagine,' Shona said, 'pulling it off. It's incredible.'

They couldn't sit all night in the restaurant. At eleven, they left and walked through the dark side streets to the guesthouse. Once there, they stood awkwardly in the tiny snug. 'I'm tired,' Shona said. 'I can't think.' 'Go to bed,' Catriona said. She looked exhausted herself. It seemed wrong to go to bed and leave them, abandoning them to speculation, she was sure, as to how she felt, but Shona could not wait to be alone. She made a point of embracing them both extravagantly, though she could not bring herself to say she loved them. They never said such words, they would sound false and insincere. But she pressed against each of them hard and smiled and it was as if she were telling them nothing had changed. Once in her room, the door locked, the door joining their two rooms, she found she was shaking, but whether with excitement or shock she could not decide. She got into bed and pulled the thick duvet over her and crouched under it, thinking. She felt no inclination to weep. She asked herself if she felt any different and knew she did not. Did she still feel Archie was her father and Catriona her mother? Yes, of course she did, there was no doubt at all in her mind. She should have said this to them at once, it ought to have been instinctive, and she felt ashamed she had not done so. They needed to be reassured, both of them. She would give them reassurance tomorrow, in bucketsful. Nothing had changed. But it had. That bit was not true. She tossed and turned, got up for a glass of water, stood looking out of the window at the sleeping city. Somewhere, in this very place, a girl had lived who had given her away. Who was she? What had happened to her? Somewhere, out there in the wider world, that girl lived with the memory of a baby she had given away. A great pity filled Shona as she thought about her and tears at last came. Poor, poor girl, all the rest of her life spent with this shadow over it. Or had the shadow long since lifted and all memory of that baby gone from her mind? No. Shona told herself she could not believe this. No. She could not have been banished in such a manner.

But in any case it did not matter. She had no choice, none at all. Her need to know her mother was urgent and compelling and she would never be able to deny it. She would find her in no spirit of revenge and not to visit upon her any past sin, but to make sense of herself only. Her mother was her, or rather she, in the literal sense, was made from her mother and she could not resist discovering her own inheritance. I will not harm her, Shona thought, but I must know her, and where is the harm in that?

Part Two

Leah – Hazel

Chapter Seven

LEAH RETURNED every stare with a stare of her own, a look not of defiance but of pride. There was no feeling at all in her mind of shame or embarrassment and this was borne out by her carriage. She had always walked with her head up and her shoulders back, she had never huddled into herself as so many girls did, but now she seemed to emphasise the excellence of her posture. Nor did she attempt to conceal her pregnancy. She let her coat fall open, there were to be no straining buttons, and the child she was carrying already thrust itself forward in the most pronounced way. She saw the stares directed at the bump and then at the ring on her finger and then at her face and she smiled, however accusing or hostile the expression in the eyes. People knew she was not married, that it was impossible for them not to have known if a marriage between Leah Messenger of the Fox and Hound and Hugo Todhunter of Moorhouse Hall had taken place. They were outraged that she wore a ring on her wedding finger and yet no one had directly challenged her, as she half wanted them to.

The ring was a symbol, as all rings are. There was, Hugo had said, no law saying a woman must be lawfully married before she could wear a ring on what was held to be her wedding finger. She must not say she was married because that would be wrong – she was not married according to the laws of either the established church or the country – but there was nothing whatsoever to prevent her wearing a ring if she wished to. And she did wish to. She liked to see it there, a shining reminder of the time Hugo had pledged his undying love and devotion to her, at night, in the little church of St Kentigern lit by the candles he had brought with him. He had repeated all the vows from the wedding service in the prayer book, taking the part of the priest as well as the bridegroom, and she had repeated her own vows, her voice shaking with nerves though there was no one to hear it. There was no music but as they extinguished the candles and walked down the aisle together, their footsteps scraping the stone through the thin torn matting, an owl had hooted outside and then, when it had ceased, a single nightjar sang under the midsummer moon. 'Perfect,' Hugo had sighed, 'perfect.'

Oh, he was such a romantic lover! She had difficulty taking him seriously. Her instant reaction, that first day when he stopped his horse on the road and dismounted, had been derision. She was not a romantic. Her life had been hard and she had faced up to it, never once trying to deny this hard reality by escaping into daydreams. She had not reached sixteen without being aware of how dangerous her own beauty could be, how likely it was to surround her with predators. She scorned flatterers, turned her head away from those who showered her with compliments. There was no barmaid ever as expert at making men feel despised, and yet she was not hated for her aloofness nor did her contempt provoke rage or a desire to see her humbled. She was respected and she knew she was and traded on that respect. Hugo respected her from the beginning. He made no attempt to paw her or to flirt in any way. That first encounter laid the pattern. He walked with her, holding his horse by the bridle, and not one word did he say all the way back to the Fox and Hound beyond 'Would you permit me to walk a little way with you?' to which she merely shrugged. He bowed when they reached the pub and that was all. Again and again he did this, day after day, meeting her on the road, dismounting, asking if he might walk with her, walking, not speaking, bowing, and then going away.

But Leah was not stupid. It was all a means to an end and the more subtle and original the means the more need to watch for the hidden end. She thought she saw his intention when he gave her lilies on Easter Day and hoped he might be allowed to express his unbounded admiration for her loveliness which had bewitched him. She knew she was meant to blush and simper and thank him, and then he would take this as a signal to proceed in what was, after all, likely to be only a common-or-garden seduction. But she did neither. She knew all about him by then. She had heard the tales of his wild living, of how he was back in this bleak part of the world only because he was being hounded for money and had come to get it from his parents who had saved him from prison many times before. He was a rogue and she knew he was and would not be caught. 'Thank you for your lilies,' she had said primly, 'they will look very well upon the altar table if the vicar will accept them, and as for my loveliness, before God we are all lovely.' She had said it quite stern-faced, with due solemnity, but afterwards she had laughed at the astonishment and consternation in his eyes. If he thought her deeply religious, so much the better.

They were observed all the time. A road which looked empty was never empty of eyes watching from somewhere. They looked down from a cottage on a hill or through a hedge where a lone plough was driven in a field. He might not know this but she did and she was glad of it. It governed her behaviour, this certain knowledge that she was being watched. She had a hidden audience and performed for it. They would say of her, those who slyly spied on her, that she never gave Hugo Todhunter an inch, never allowed him anything approaching a liberty, that she showed herself immune to his unwanted advances. But she was not immune and that became the hardest of all things to conceal. She was not immune to his very looks and it made her feel guilty. It was wrong, in her own opinion, to admire a man for his looks. It was foolish, just as foolish as thinking one's own looks of consequence. That was the kind of attraction she feared and of which she was wary. Yet Hugo Todhunter was not generally thought of as handsome. He was not tall enough or broad enough to qualify as a truly handsome man and he did not turn women's heads in the street. But it was his looks she liked, his rough, unkempt hair, the darkness of his hair and eyes, his litheness, his brown complexion, not ruddy but olive-toned, and his air of concentration. He seemed always to be listening as they walked the road silently together and it made her curious.

It became harder and harder to keep silent and it was she who broke the silence in the end, asking him, irritably, why he insisted on accompanying her along the road in such a way. 'Are you tired of it? Shall I leave you in peace?' he said, and she was weak enough to say she did not care, only wondered at the pointlessness of the ritual. He said that to him it was not pointless, that on the contrary it gave him great pleasure and satisfaction, but that each day he met her he was deeply afraid he would be turned off like a dog. 'How could I turn you off?' she exclaimed scornfully. 'It is a free country, this is an open road.' He said she only had to express indignation at his arrival by her side and he would never dare to come again. There and then she should have expressed this indignation but she kept silent, and by her silence betrayed her interest. It made him bolder. He began to talk, though not in the manner she had imagined. He told her things, little bits of history about the area, little anecdotes about when he was a boy. He never asked questions of her or seemed to need any but the most superficial response. And still when they reached the Fox and Hound he bowed and left her, never entering the pub.

Weeks went by, months, and nothing ever changed, except the weather. With the first fall of heavy snow she was not able to walk the road at all and was shocked at her own dismay. She would not see him and it grieved her out of all proportion. The snow lasted a week. She thought he might come in search of her if he missed her as she missed him, but there was no sign of him and she chided herself for expecting him. She dreamed of him every night and woke excited, though all they had done in her dream was walk together as they always did. The moment the snow melted she was out on the road hardly daring to look for him and relieved to the point of faintness when she heard him gallop up behind her. All winter it was the same – the snow, the impossibility of walking, the missing of him, the secret joy when she saw him again.

In the spring, he made a move. She knew it was that, a move: she recognised it as such, but by then she felt he had earned the right to make it. 'Do you only walk here,' he asked her, 'along this road?' She said that mostly, as he knew, she did, but that in the summer, when the evenings were light, she sometimes walked down by the river on Sunday, if it was pleasant weather, if she were not needed at the Fox and Hound. She was fond of the river, she was told she had been born in a house on the banks of a river. He took note and the following Sunday, as she had anticipated, he met her down by the river. It felt strange to see him there. She felt awkward, but he was more at ease. They walked, they parted, she went on to church. But during the week he said there was a river walk he was fond of some miles away and he wondered if he might drive her in his pony trap to it, and they could walk it together. She was quiet for a moment not through any doubt as to the answer she would give, nor out of any desire to tease, but because she knew how significant a moment this was. She had only to accept the first invitation he had issued in almost a year for her interest to be declared. So she accepted.

They were seen, of course they were seen. They did not try to hide, there was no subterfuge. He picked her up in the pony trap at the Fox and Hound. They drove some four miles and walked the river walk and they drove back again, whereupon an avalanche of warnings and advice fell upon her ears. She was not deaf to the dire threats of disaster. She took heed. Hugo Todhunter was said to have been forced by his angry parents to spend this past year at home while they settled his debts, but was now on the brink of being sent by them to a new life in Canada where they had connections. They would not permit him to stay in the country and once more ruin himself, but had made it a condition of their saving him from prison that he would go into business under his uncle in Vancouver. It was to be his last chance. There were even those who told Leah the date he was due to leave and they did not quite believe her when she said she had no interest in knowing it, it was nothing to her.

But Hugo had not mentioned any departure to her, though he had begun to talk about his past life. 'I was spoiled,' he confessed, 'I was overindulged by my parents. Oh, I had the happiest of childhoods and paid the penalty.' Leah, who had known no happiness either as a child or since and barely knew the meaning of the word indulgence, ventured to inquire how there could be any penalty. 'I took my luck for granted,' Hugo said. 'I expected my luck always to be there and so I tried at nothing.' Leah was careful. It struck her as suspicious that a man should so berate himself. What did he expect? That she should protest, that she should not believe such self-depreciation, that she should be charmed by it? She thought hard before she made any comment and then said only, 'How unfortunate.' Hugo nodded. He went on to confess he had caused his parents great pain and if he tried for a thousand years to make amends he could never succeed. Leah thought the 'thousand years' extravagant and coughed. 'You do not know the agony of being ashamed,' Hugo said. 'There is no worse feeling to know that I am to blame for my own misfortune.'

Again, Leah thought hard. Should she point out that he had only just, in fact, placed blame on his parents for spoiling him, from which he alleged all else had followed? Or would he resent this, would he judge her unsympathetic to what he evidently considered a noble confession? He looked so truly sorrowful, she wanted so badly to comfort him. 'You can make a new life,' she finally said, 'and please your parents.' He smiled and said it would take a great deal to please them and, as he had acknowledged, he could never make up for the worry he had already caused them but that he intended to try. He said it had been a hard year. He said he did not know how he would have survived it if it had not been for her. She had given him hope. She, who was so pure and beautiful and modest, who conducted herself with such grace and dignity ... She had stopped him then. She had told him he did not know her and should not speak such nonsense. She was merely a poor girl, an orphan, who worked to live and had no other life and few hopes or aspirations. She did her best and that was all. He said it was for that he admired her – she had nothing and did her best and he had had everything and had done his worst.

So they might have gone on if she had not tripped and fallen and cut her head open on a sharp stone and passed out for an instant with the loss of blood. When she came to, he was cradling her in his arms and kissing her and showering her with frantic endearments, and there was no more hope of keeping her distance. She loved him. It was simple, after all, defying all sense but true nevertheless. He asked her to marry him there and then and she accepted and that was the happiest moment. But it was only a moment. It did not last nor, really, had she expected it to. He said he had told his parents who had raged and stormed and would not hear of such a marriage; and she asked why he had ever thought they would. He had no money, none at all, and neither of course did she, and all prospect of marrying was hopeless. He said he would have to go to Canada and restore his fortunes and then return and claim her. She accepted this, it was inevitable, there was no other way. So they had their own ceremony, in the little church before he left, and she did not regret it for one minute nor pine for a real priest and a real service.

Nor did she regret the child, except for the first days of uncertainty when her mind filled unpleasantly with all the practicalities of her position. She had Hugo's address in Vancouver and she wrote to him at once, as he had instructed her to do should anything untoward occur. He had wished her to write weekly, as he would write to her, but with bowed head and hot cheeks she had been obliged to confess she was barely literate. He vowed that when he returned from Canada and they were married properly he would educate her himself. He painted a fetching picture of them both sitting side by side on the riverbank with open books on their knees and a slate and pencil at their side. She was intelligent, he said, he could tell she was and she would learn quickly. But he was relieved that she could, if with difficulty, write her name and some simple words and could copy his own name and address on to an envelope. It was fluency she lacked, the ability to pen a letter expressing her feelings and, similarly, though she could read simple sentences, a solid page of writing was a blur to her and took hours of laborious scrutinising before it made sense.

Her message, some six weeks after his departure, had been crude: 'I am well,' she wrote, 'I am with child. I am happy.' Afterwards, she wondered if she was wise to have proclaimed her happiness but she had not wanted him to think her distraught or that she was accusing him of ruining her. He had not ruined her. He had never forced her and had most conscientiously acknowledged the possible consequences of their love-making. She had told him she would take the risk if he would and that, in truth, as he could see, as he could feel, she could not hold back. How, later, could she ever convey to those who questioned her the urgency and power of that desire? It was impossible. She remembered only that it was so, that she was overwhelmed, without being able to call up the exact sensations. Where her sharp mind was at the time she did not know and did not trouble to search for the answer once it was over.

Money arrived immediately, even before his passionate, remorseful letter half of which she failed completely to decipher. Fifty guineas, in the form of a banker's order, payable on proof of identity at a bank in English Street, Carlisle. The part of his letter which she could understand, if with difficulty, said that the presentation of the ring he had given her would serve to identify her together with a sample of her signature. The ring had his initials and hers intertwined on the smooth inner surface, and he had already sent the signature on her letter to the bank for them to match it. He had thought of everything but was in an agony of apprehension on her behalf. Correctly, he envisaged she would have to leave the pub and urged her to find some lodging in the village where she would be safe and comfortable until the child was born. More money would follow, he said, and by the time she was brought to bed he would have booked his passage home and would come to claim her.

But she did not try to find lodgings in the village. She did not wish to stay there, among people who despised Hugo and who would sneer at her condition and see her as a victim of his villainy. It was her own choice to return to Carlisle, where she had been born, and she went there full of confidence, excited at the new life which was opening before her. She was very far from being a wronged woman, humble and penitent. She swept into the bank as though she was perfectly accustomed to doing so and met the eyes of the clerk to whom she presented Hugo's draft with some hauteur. She knew her signature revealed the uncertainty of her hand but she did not care. He gave her a pen and a fresh piece of paper and she saw him watch as, with immense concentration, she formed the letters of her name, making, as ever, a mess over the double 's' in Messenger – try as she did, she could never stop those letters running into each other and looking ugly. Then she had to remove her ring, which she never liked to do. She watched anxiously as it was lifted up and looked at through a magnifying glass and then, to her consternation, taken out of her sight into some back room to be checked by an invisible person. It was only then that she felt vulnerable and that her position seemed precarious. Once the ring was back on her finger she was reassured – as she was by the money, fifty guineas counted in front of her into a cloth bag with a drawstring. She pulled the string tight.

It was a fortune to her, a sum so substantial it represented absolute security and she wished everyone she had left behind in the village could know the goodness of a man they thought had no good in him. She stood for a moment on the steps of the bank surveying the busy street and thought of what all the money in her possession could buy. There were shops lining the street to which she could give her substantial patronage – dresses she could have and a fur tippet and boots of the finest leather. She smiled, amused at this absurd thought, knowing she would never be tempted. The money was for her keep to give her shelter and food, to pay for a nurse when the baby was born and see her safe until Hugo returned. Her sole concern was to use it wisely. Her first task was to trace the only person in this city whom she knew to be a member, if a distant one, of the family to which she had once belonged. Her recollection of this woman, an aunt she thought, was vague in the extreme. Mary, she was called, Mary Messenger, and she had been kind. It was this Mary who had taken her to the coach so long ago and kissed her and wept over her and hoped she would be lucky in the place to which she was going. Mary had given her food for the journey and a shawl to wrap herself in and, if she was not mistaken, it was with Mary that she had lived up to then. Where exactly she did not know and could not fathom, however hard she tried. An impression of crowds came back to her but she could not grasp what this might signify.

Leah walked past the cathedral and turned the corner at the castle to walk over Caldew Bridge. A pub in Caldewgate, the Royal Oak, had been mentioned often by her relatives at the Fox and Hound. Messengers had that pub and it was from those Messengers she had always understood she came. Occasionally, one of these Carlisle Messengers visited, on their way to or from Newcastle, and she would be paraded before them and reminded she was 'Annie's lass, poor soul'. Caldewgate was a sorry sight, full of smoke pouring from the tall chimney of Dixon's factory and from the trains shrieking their way out of the railway yards below the old wall of the city.

The people at the Royal Oak had none of that interest in her which they had begun to show during recent visits to the Fox and Hound. They looked at her belly and looked at her ring and smirked, and were disposed to draw her into the kind of questioning to which she had no intention of submitting. But they gave her Mary Messenger's address readily enough. Mary now lived in Wetheral, a village on the river Eden some five miles to the south of the city. A washerwoman, she lived by herself and was never seen in Carlisle. Leah made her way to Wetheral at once, walking briskly, her spirits lifting as the river came into view, broad and fast-flowing with the winter rains. Mary lived on The Plains, a row of houses just outside the village, beyond the pretty triangular green. These houses looked too solid and imposing for a washerwoman, but there was a short row of terraced dwellings near the end and here she knew she would find Mary. It was not the most satisfactory of reunions. Mary was in her wash-house, mangling. She stood in her clogs turning and turning the handle and forcing folded sheets through the rollers with such energy that great streams of water shot into the tub below. All around were tin baths of washing in all its various stages and the air was full of steam and dampness.

'I am Leah Messenger,' Leah said. Mary did not stop mangling. Leah repeated her name but still the mangle was turned until at last a long sequence of bed sheets had passed through and were piled on top of others waiting to be dried. There was plenty of time for Leah to observe Mary. She saw that she was old, much older than she had expected. Her hair was white and she had no teeth and her body, though it gave every indication of a surprising strength, was bowed. Leah felt a little dismayed – this was not the kindly, motherly creature of her memory. In the silence that followed the mangle's screechings and strainings she said yet again that she was Leah Messenger. Mary stared at her, no hint of welcome or recognition in her fierce face.

'What are you wanting?' she asked eventually. 'I've nothing to thank any Messenger for, I'm sure, eh?'

'Neither have I,' said Leah. She had not meant this as a challenge or an attempt in any way to cap what Mary had said, but it stopped the old woman from fussing with the washing.

She came closer to Leah and peered into her face. 'You were just a child, eh? When they sent you away.' She shook her head. 'Bad days, bad days,' she sighed. She began to trudge out of the wash-house and in through the back door of the house. Leah followed. The back kitchen was dark and not much warmer than the wash-house, but there was a kettle spluttering above the fire where it hung on a big iron hook. Mary poked the dead-looking coals and flames leapt up and the kettle boiled in seconds. She made tea, measuring one level spoonful carefully into a brown teapot, and covered it with a tea-cosy. Then she sat rocking the teapot backwards and forwards, absently. Leah sat down too, without being asked.

'Annie's girl,' Mary said at last, speaking as if to herself, all in a mutter, 'poor lass. She died of fever when you were two and then what was to become of you, eh? The Grahams next door had you for a while, their lass had died and you were of an age with her and a comfort, and then he died and she went back to her folk and they wouldn't have you, that wasn't their own. What could she do, eh? Nothing for it. "You'll have to take her back," she said to the Messengers, and they wouldn't hear of it, you were about seven then, a long time till you'd be of real use. I tried, I tried. Nearly a twelve-month I tried, begged them to let you stop with us but they wanted more work out of me than I could give with you under my feet and they fixed for you to go to Annie's uncle but they lied, said you were ten and able to help in the pub, and I don't know how you weren't sent straight back, that's the truth.'

'I was tall,' Leah said, 'and I did work.'

'Oh, Messengers always get work out of folk, eh? That's one thing, always get work, worked me to death, then I saw my chance and got away, but not from work. Oh I work, work, no end to it, but not for them, not now. I manage, that's what, I manage.'

'Can I help you manage?' Leah asked.

'Eh?'

'Can I help you manage? I've got some money, I can pay my way and I can work hard too. I need a room. I can pay rent. Look,' and she took out the little cloth bag the bank had given her and tipped the coins out on to the table.

'Honest money, eh?' Mary asked.

'Honest money. I can pay rent.' And then, in case Mary had not noticed, since she had neither let her glance at any time rest on Leah's belly nor asked any question about her condition, Leah said, 'I'm expecting, in February, I need a place to lie in.'

There was no formal agreement. Mary looked at the money steadily, until Leah pushed two of the guineas towards her, and then she grunted and got up and said that since she must return to her mangle, Leah must sort herself out. There was very little to sort out. Mary's house, if it was indeed hers, which the more Leah thought about it seemed unlikely, was small. There appeared only to be the kitchen and next to it a room with a bed; up the rickety stairs was one other room only. It, too, had a bed in it but there were no covers on it and Leah deduced Mary slept downstairs. She sat on the edge of the doubtful-looking mattress and was relieved to find it was firm and did not smell. There was no rug on the floor, which had several holes in it where the planks had split. There was a trunk in one corner which she did not yet feel up to investigating and two other boxes under the window, both open, both containing blankets and covers. It would do. It would have to do. Some of the guineas could be spent, legitimately, on making this room more comfortable. She could scrub it and distemper the walls and make a curtain for the window. She could help Mary with the washing so long as she avoided lifting heavy weights. And it was temporary, only a way of getting through the next months until Hugo came and rescued her. She would be quite content here with old Mary, waiting for her baby to be born, waiting for Hugo to return, it would work out well.

And it did work out well, very well. Leah was content in Wetheral and Mary was more than content. The difference Leah made in the house was great and, though Mary never commented on this vast improvement in her way of life, she registered it within her. Leah was tidy and neat and a hard worker. She found ways of doing things that Mary had never thought of, ways of making the heaviest work lighter. She was ingenious and saved both of them strain and, though she was four months pregnant when she came to live with

Mary, she did not let her condition hold her back from almost all the jobs to be done. There was not much communion between them at the end of each weary day but Mary grew to love Leah's very presence as she sat with her eyes closed in the rocking-chair she'd bought from a woman selling off her dead mother's furniture. She watched her rock and rock and was pleased by the sight of the young mother-to-be. She asked no questions and would not have had much interest if information had been volunteered – it was enough that Leah was with her, her arrival a piece of good fortune the like of which Mary had never known.

The baby was born in the middle of March when Leah was well past her time both by her own reckoning and that of the midwife whose services she had engaged. 'We can't leave it for ever,' this woman said after two weeks of high expectation that the birth would occur at any moment, 'I'll have to bring you on soon, my lass.' But Leah, though tired, did not want any interference. Every day she walked down the hill to the river Eden and up through the woods, lovely with all the new spring growth, and with every step over the rough ground she felt her child turn and kick and knew it would come when it was ready. Mary did not like her to walk alone in the woods in case she went into labour far from help, but Leah was sensible, she took no risks. The first strong pain came when she was indeed far from home, at the very top of the high woodland path, but she was not frightened. Slowly, slowly, she made her way down, even pausing to break off a branch full of dancing catkins, and at every subsequent pain she stopped until it was over. Her waters broke at the foot of the steep hill leading up to The Plains but she did not panic, only shifted her shawl from round her shoulders to round her waist to hide the stain and then she continued, a little faint it is true, but determined not to rush. Mary, looking out for her, as she always did now, knew from the way Leah walked that she was at last in labour and went for the midwife before ever she reached home. The birth was not as swift as this beginning had promised. All night Leah laboured and it was not until dawn that the baby was born after a great loss of blood which had alarmed the midwife. It was a girl and she was small, not the robust creature Leah was reckoned to be capable of bearing. There were many distraught tears because it was not the boy, the image of Hugo, that she had desired. But she requested pencil and paper – an envelope had been prepared long since – and wrote the news of the child's safe arrival upon it.

After that had been done, it was only a matter of waiting.

Chapter Eight

THE HABIT of obedience was so natural to Hazel that it took a mighty effort for her to query an order or instruction. This had always made her popular with teachers and much loved by her parents and relatives but, not surprisingly, except to Hazel herself, it caused problems with her siblings and contemporaries. 'Why do you always do what you're told?' they asked her angrily and were exasperated that she did not even understand the question. It was effortless for her to do what she was told since she automatically respected authority. Life to her was simple. It was governed by laws and rules which had been designed to protect her and she saw no reason to reject them. She enjoyed being obedient, and quick in her obedience, not because of the praise she earned, the frequent '*good* girl', but because of the sense this gave her of everything being controlled.

This made her pregnancy at seventeen the most astonishing and unbelievable occurrence. Her mother could not stop herself in the first instance from saying, 'Hazel, are you sure?' and she did not mean was her daughter sure of her condition but rather was she sure she had had sexual intercourse at all. She had warned Hazel of its dangers, of the horror of an unwanted pregnancy, at an early age; her daughter being such an obedient girl, she had hardly thought it necessary to go on reinforcing this warning. Hazel was only a schoolgirl and a model one at that. Her A-level results had been better than expected and both her parents were eager for her to go to university. She had not yet gone out much into the world and so far as her mother was aware knew no boys beyond her brothers and their friends whom she only ever saw in their company. It was simply extraordinary to think of Hazel having sex, and Mrs

Walmsley had to block from her mind the vision she suddenly had, of her daughter crushed under some oaf. Because, of course, it must have been some brutish oaf, whatever Hazel said to the contrary. She would have told her mother the name of her seducer but this was banned. No names were to be divulged. A university place could be deferred. And nobody, *nobody*, was to know, not even her best friends.

It was easy for Hazel to obey this order. She had no best friends, no girls with whom she had intimate conversations. She was a solitary girl, self-contained, who at her boarding school made no lasting alliances. Since she was pretty and gentle-natured she was perfectly attractive to others but she resisted all efforts to involve her in relationships. This was noted by her teachers, who would write pointed comments on her reports about her failure to mix. They concluded that Hazel's problem was twofold: she was considered a goody-goody by her peers, and she was a true loner, best left to get on with life as she wished, by herself. So far as could be judged, she was not unhappy, nor did she appear shy and reserved. She spoke to other girls quite freely and joined in games and other activities but preferred not to carry friendship any further.

By the time she was sixteen, Hazel was one of those girls frequently in demand to make up numbers. She was pretty and clever and quiet, and absolutely no threat. It was 1954 and the only way girls met boys at her school was when they were allowed, once a term, to go in an organised and supervised group to an equally illustrious boys' school with which they shared dances. There was no opportunity on these visits to pair off outside the hall where the dance took place, since hawk-eyed teachers guarded all exits. But it was impossible to prevent boys whispering invitations to girls while they danced and assignations were made accordingly. These were not dangerous on the surface. There was a small town half-way between the two schools to which sixth-formers were allowed to go on Saturdays between the hours of two o'clock and five o'clock. Here, in tea-shops, boys met girls and the thrill was tremendous. Both sexes felt that anything could happen after the obligatory tea and doughnut. Walks could be taken in the park, along the river ... Oh, there were opportunities for the bold.

Hazel was not in the least bold. She politely declined when invited to meet a boy in a tea-shop. But when she was asked by girls to please, please, go with them because they did not want to meet a particular swain alone, she could think of no objection. There were no rules about not meeting boys to have tea and, curiously for one not interested in close friendships, she liked to do favours. So she obliged. She went to the tea-shops and after ten minutes, given an agreed signal, she left. It was harmless and she derived some amusement from her role as chaperone. This was how she met George. He was always inviting girls to tea-shops and his invitations were met with alacrity. Hazel had accompanied four different girls over a year to meet George and all of them rapidly wanted to get rid of her once their first nervousness was over. 'Don't go, Hazel,' George urged, but she always went. He invited her to meet him at the schools' Easter dance but she refused, as usual, even though she thought George more interesting than anyone she had yet met. He was not good-looking – for one thing, he had red hair and the skin that went with it – but he was witty and sharp and fun to be with, far more fun than those handsome but dull boys with whom girls liked to be seen.

It turned out that George lived near Hazel in London, a few streets away in Notting Hill. She met him in a bookshop in the Christmas holidays and they stood for a while and talked about what they were buying. George suggested they go round the corner and have a cup of coffee in the new espresso bar that had just opened, but Hazel declined politely. She met him again, getting on a bus, and sat with him until Oxford Circus. He suggested she might like to go to an Ingmar Bergman film with him, in the afternoon, but she said no, thank you. 'Is it your middle name? "No thank you"?' George asked before she got off the bus. 'My middle name is Rose,' Hazel said, quite seriously and straight-faced. But she found herself wondering, as she walked down Oxford Street, why she did always say no to George when she found his company agreeable. She was a puzzle to herself as well as to him. It was somehow tiring to be with other people, she seemed always to be glad to be alone again however much she had enjoyed the conversation. But she knew she could not go through life with this attitude. She saw herself isolated by her own disinclination for friendship and it troubled her. She would have to make an effort of some sort, she thought.

So she made the effort with George. At the next dance, three months after the chance meeting on the bus, he made straight for her on the dance floor and the moment they were waltzing – waltzes and quicksteps were the preferred dances at these events – he said he knew it was no good asking her but would she meet him the following Saturday not in a tea-shop but in an art gallery where he was going to see a painting by Dante Gabriel Rossetti. She agreed. George was triumphant, wrongly assuming it was the originality of his suggestion which had made Hazel capitulate. They met, as arranged, and stood in front of Rossetti's painting of his sister, and George talked a little glibly but quite knowledgeably about it, while Hazel listened attentively. Then they went for a walk to the other side of the town and George talked all the time. She was about to say no, thank you, when he suggested meeting again the following week, but stopped herself just in time.

George passed his driving test as soon as school broke up in June and was allowed to borrow his mother's car. This was a great event in his young life and he wanted Hazel to share in his luck. His invitations to go for a drive were pressing and he could not understand why she did not share his excitement.

'A drive?' Hazel said. 'Where to?'

'Oh, anywhere,' George said. 'Does it matter?' Hazel thought for a moment. Of course it mattered, surely it did. What was the point of driving if one was not driving *to* somewhere. 'You're so literal,' George complained. Hazel did not argue. She thought she probably was literal and did not see this as a criticism. 'To Oxford, then,' George said. Hazel thought carefully again. George was hoping to go to Oxford. There was a purpose to this drive. He wanted to look round several colleges and this attracted her. She had not entertained any ambitions of Oxford for herself but was nevertheless interested enough to look round. So she agreed. She even mentioned it to her mother, though not that she was to be driven to Oxford by a young man. Her mother was distracted at the time, organising a charity ball (she was heavily involved with a great many charities and on a great many committees) and when Hazel said she was going to look round Oxford with a friend she simply said, 'Very nice, dear,' and that was that.

Hazel had no sexual experience whatsoever. She had never held a boy's hand, not even George's, and certainly never been kissed or embraced. She had heard other girls talk of being fondled and petted and there were even hints of more breathtaking contact but it had meant nothing to her. It did not worry her that she alone seemed unimpatient to be made love to: she was, as in many departments of her life, content to wait. This patience was severely jolted in Oxford.

George took her on a punt, very pleased with himself, because he had thought to bring a picnic and a rug. Dutifully, Hazel got into the punt and allowed herself to be punted as far up the river Isis as George could manage without collapsing. He moored the punt among some reeds and out of the picnic basket he produced a bottle of champagne. Hazel had had no more than a sip of champagne occasionally, at weddings, and still thought of it only as a pleasant fizzy drink. She drank half the bottle with George and was amazed at how it made her feel – she floated, she felt light-hearted and giggly. This encouraged George and for the first time he touched her. It was awkward in the punt, which rocked alarmingly, but he managed to wriggle himself down beside her and he put his arms round her and squeezed her. 'Do you mind, Hazel?' he asked anxiously. No, she said, no, she didn't mind in the least, she liked it.

George could not believe his luck but then he grew worried. He put his hand up Hazel's skirt, a very full affair with a stiff crackly petticoat underneath, and she had no objection. He slipped it inside the bodice of her dress and got it round her breast inside its wired bra, and she did not remove the hand. He kissed and kissed her and she lay there smiling and serene, while his excitement grew. 'Hazel, Hazel,' he said, 'you aren't drunk, are you? You do know what you're doing, I mean what I'm doing?' Hazel said she wasn't drunk and she knew what he was doing. So then it was up to George and he was in agony. He could tell he could go as far as he liked and it shocked him. A bit of resistance would have made him happier, the need for persuasion on his part would somehow sanction his advances. He didn't want to take advantage of Hazel but on the other hand he couldn't bear to pass up such a chance. He was too honourable and it wasn't fair. He groaned and sat up and put his head in his hands. He shouldn't have given her the champagne. She said she wasn't under the influence of the alcohol but she acted as if she were and he had a sudden image of Hazel's furious parents accusing him afterwards ...

There was no afterwards that day. Angrily, George pulled himself together, punted Hazel back, and drove home like a maniac. He lay on his bed hitting the pillow and cursing himself for his saintlike behaviour. Next time, he vowed, he would take Hazel Walmsley at her word: if she acted as if she wanted it then she'd get it. In preparation, he bought some Durex at the barber's.

He met Hazel now every day and they embraced – in Hyde Park, in all the public places they frequented – and she was as soft and yielding as she had been in Oxford, without the help of alcohol. But she was going the following week, with her family, to France, and time was short. Then they were both invited to a party by a mutual friend and George knew this would be it. Hazel knew too and was quite composed. The whole idea of finding out about sex now intrigued her and she had replaced her former willingness to wait with a curiosity all the keener for being so sudden. Not, she reassured herself, that it was so sudden. She had known George now for well over a year. For the whole of the last week since the Oxford day, they had been kissing and cuddling and Hazel was beginning to wonder at George's self-restraint. She could see he was apprehensive and she couldn't think why. She wasn't. She knew that anyone looking at her, so demure and modest, would never know how she felt. This interest she had, to understand what sex was really about, was all the more powerful the longer the discovery was delayed. She didn't love George in the least nor was she sure that she was attracted to him in the way he seemed to be to her but she liked his company. Wasn't that enough, to begin with? Wasn't George the sort of boy suitable for a first sexual experience? She hoped so.

The party was in a large house near Campden Square. There were lights in the trees in the long narrow garden and very pretty it looked. But George and Hazel were not in the garden with the other eighty-odd young guests. They were in the house in a room at the top, with the door locked and barricaded (like all the other doors on that floor). They took all their clothes off at once and George fell upon her eagerly and that was the first time, quite unsatisfactory for both of them, what with George's struggle with the wretched Durex and Hazel's impatience. Second and third attempts were better but it was not until the early hours of the morning, when mine host was hammering on doors yelling that his parents would be back soon, that the two of them caught any rhythm. 'I love you,' George murmured during their last embrace. Hazel didn't say a word. They dressed slowly, with barely the energy needed, and left the accommodating house. 'When will I see you?' George asked. She shrugged. She was relieved that she was off to France in a few days and he was going to Scotland to relatives in St Andrews. She felt she wanted a long rest from George and plenty of time to absorb and analyse what had just happened.

She never saw him again. 'Tell no one,' her mother said, and she obeyed. The moment she suspected she was pregnant she wanted George kept out of it, dreading any further involvement with him. She didn't want the baby, of course she didn't want it, but she didn't want George either. Her own foolishness maddened her. Why had she placed such faith in George's use of Durex, his confident assurance that she could not become pregnant? It seemed such an aberration, such a deformity of what she knew to be her true character. She wanted to be rid of the baby, rid, too, of all thought and memory of George. But her mother said abortion was both illegal and too dangerous and she herself had not the faintest idea how to obtain one. The idea that she would have to give birth to this consequence of her lust appalled her. Her quietness, when she was told by her mother that she would have to have the baby then give it up for adoption, was mistaken for her usual obedient reaction; but it was something else, a quietness born of shock and inner panic. She couldn't be going to have a baby, it was surely impossible. She had not a single maternal feeling nor any nurturing instinct. It filled her with disgust to think of what she was going to have to go through.

The absurdity of finding herself in Norway took some time to strike her. She could not claim to be either stunned or in a dream, but there was something automatic about everything that happened once her mother had made the arrangements. She packed her things, new things, strange garments her mother had selected for her from a maternity clothes shop, and she said goodbye to her father, who was still chortling at the idiocy of her destination, telephoned her brothers who told her not to do anything they would not do, then left London with her mother. During the journey to Bergen neither of them spoke much. Hazel closed her eyes and feigned sleep, reflecting upon what an odd person her mother was: on the surface so bright and cheerful and utterly conventional, yet secretly full of cunning, a woman whose thrill in life seemed to come from the excitement of subterfuge. She felt she was simply a plot to her mother, something complicated to be worked out as neatly as possible in the minimum time. She wasn't a girl at all.

The house she found herself in was tall and narrow, quite unlike the generously proportioned home from which she had come. She had a large attic room at the top. There was a window at either end but disappointing views from both – rooftops out of the east window, a vast wall out of the west and no greenery in sight. She smiled wanly, as she hung up her clothes, to think that her natural preference for being alone was now so completely gratified.

The two women with whom she lodged were polite and helpful but she could tell at once they were only interested in her situation and not in her. They made no attempt to mother her nor did they subject her to any kind of cross-examination. She gathered there had been other girls in her predicament staying with them before her. She feared, from the look of them, that they might be religious but if so they kept their beliefs to themselves. They took her round the house and showed her where everything was, gave her a map of the town and a timetable of meals, and then she was left to get on with her new life. She thought both women very strange but their detachment suited her. Each day she went to the library and there she followed a work plan that Miss Bøgeberg, the teacher of the two women, had made out for her. She learned the history of Norway in detail and studied its economy and of course its language, at which she became reasonably proficient after an initial struggle. She left the library shortly after three in the afternoon and walked round the town, taking care to be home before dark. She ate with Miss Bøgeberg and Miss Østervold and then retired to her room where she read or wrote to her mother. This was a laborious business because she had so little to say. She wrote a great deal about the weather every week and struggled after that to fill up the page. She wanted to ask her mother again how she knew these two odd Norwegian women, what her connection was with them, but she never did. Her mother would only be evasive.

It was autumn when she arrived but even so the first snow fell within three weeks and she was glad. Her mother had not exaggerated Hazel's passion for snow – she loved it, not for its prettiness but for the way it sealed off noise and dirt. She liked the muffled feeling that came with thick snow, that feeling of being cocooned, of time being suspended. She liked the clothes that had to be worn, the heavy coats and thick scarves and hats and gloves – beneath them she felt herself slipping away from exposure and was happy. It suited her particularly well to be garbed like this now that she was pregnant. Nobody, looking at her in her fur overcoat, could tell her condition. In the library it was so hot there was no question of keeping on her outdoor clothes, but she always waited until she was in the bay by the window, which she had made her own spot, before divesting herself of the heavier garments. Even then, she wore big sweaters and did not have to resort to the hideous maternity smocks until the last month.

The last month was hard. It was February and the snow lay thick on the ground and there was a bitter wind sweeping in from the sea which meant she could huddle inside her furs and not arouse any comment. But she did not go to the library any more. She did not go out much at all. The two women did not press her, only expressing the opinion that exercise was important and so was fresh air 'for the sake of the baby'. Hazel was unmoved. She was not interested in doing anything for the sake of this baby. Why should she be? She was not going to keep it. It was her fault that she was having it; she admitted readily to herself that it was her carelessness and greed and ignorance that had led to the baby being conceived at all, but that did not make her care what happened to it. It made her angry to think she had been denied an abortion. The baby was a mistake and should have been treated as a mistake. It should have been wiped out. She blamed her mother for not being able to procure an abortion and herself for not insisting. But she had not even tried to abort herself – no sitting in hot baths, drinking bottles of gin, no hurling herself down flights of stairs, no experimenting with knitting needles. Her obedience had been her undoing and she wished she had rebelled ferociously. The anger grew in her with the baby and every time it heaved and kicked in her stomach she punched it back.

She had been to the hospital where she was to have the baby on three occasions only and otherwise had been seen once a month by a doctor. All kinds of information was offered to her about the condition of the baby and about preparation for the birth, but she absorbed none of it. She listened and nodded but said nothing. The only thing that she wanted to know was when the child would be born, and no one could be precise about that. Her own birthday was on 1 March. Her mother must have told Miss Bøgeberg and Miss Østervold because they had made her a cake, a very nice cake with icing on it and the number 18 picked out in little pink sugar roses. Miss Bøgeberg gave her some writing paper and Miss Østervold some talcum powder, and she was suitably grateful. But she went to bed at four o'clock in the afternoon that day, suspecting her mother would telephone and not wanting to speak to her. She thought she might cry and, hearing her weep, her mother might come, which she did not want. She said she was tired and told the two women to tell her mother, if she should ring (which she did) that she would phone her the next day.

She lay in bed on this, her eighteenth birthday, and tried to imagine her mother having her. She knew the details of her own birth but they seemed sparse to her now she was poised to give birth herself. Her mother had always been matter-of-fact: she was born on a Tuesday at two in the afternoon, after a short and easy labour at home, a much welcomed girl after two boys. Her grandmother Rose had come down from the North to see her and pronounced her the image of her dead grandfather. For some reason this had not pleased her mother who, when relating this, always added, 'Nonsense, of course.' Never did her mother talk about any emotional feelings to do with motherhood, and Hazel had always been glad, but now it dismayed her to realise she didn't know how her mother had *felt*. Nothing had been passed on to her. Her mother had not acted as though she could recall any emotion. In a daze of misery and of apathy she spent her birthday going over what her mother had said when Hazel had confessed she was pregnant. Surely it was shocking, her mother's apparent lack of shock? Her first words had been, 'We must be sensible,' and her second, the instruction to tell nobody. The whole message had been delivered swiftly and coolly: this was a practical problem to be solved in a practical way. The unborn baby was never given any reality beyond being a problem to be solved. And how grateful she had been for such a mother, never once pausing to reflect until now how unlikely such a response was. 'Your life must not be ruined,' her mother had said, and she had agreed. Ruin. An illegitimate baby equalled ruin. Oh, she agreed. 'Times have changed,' her mother had gone on, 'even if not enough. Your life doesn't have to be ruined.' Quite.

She was given 16 March as the most likely date and at once made a calendar so that she could cross off the days, which she did viciously every night. The first vague pain during the night of 15 March she welcomed eagerly, and when her waters broke she was triumphant, not minding in the least the growing strength of the contractions. Getting rid of the baby was a process she so longed to have completed that she did not fight the pain but went with it, surprising the midwife and the doctor in the clinic. They told her she was very brave, for one so young, but they were mistaken, she was not brave. She wanted this *over* and was doing her best to help her body expel the intruder. The greater the pain, the nearer she felt to escape, and the problem for those attending her was to hold her back not urge her on.

She hadn't wanted to know whether it was a boy or a girl but they told her anyway, forgetting what she had requested. But they could not make her look at it. She saw the child's shadow on the wall but then closed her eyes and turned her head away. She didn't open them again until she was in a room on her own and had been assured that the baby had gone. She didn't ask where. Miss Bøgeberg and Miss Østervold took care of everything. She slept blissfully that night. It was all over, the mistake overcome, her body and life returned to her. When her mother came to take her home she was radiant with relief and the impatience to start where she had left off. People back home told her how well she looked, if pale. They asked about Norway and what on earth she had done there, but she recognised their lack of real curiosity. She had only to say a few sentences in Norwegian and they laughed and made dismissive movements with their hands. It was all too easy to return without suspicion just as her mother had known. No one inquired too closely as to what she had done in her year off.

In October, she went to University College to read law. She had always supposed she would go out of London to university, to Bristol or Exeter, or Durham, all places to which her school regularly sent people, but having left London for so long, she had developed an affection for it. Her parents were pleased. They gave her the granny flat, recently adapted out of the basement in readiness for her father's mother who was in poor health and thought unlikely to be able to manage on her own much longer. It had its own entrance and was entirely self-contained, and Hazel would be free to do whatever she liked there. There were no student parties or hordes of young people trooping in and out. There was no loud music and no crashing about. Hazel studied hard and took very little part in college activities. She was an exemplary student just as she had been a model pupil at school. Sometimes her mother looked at her and could not believe what had happened – Hazel was so unruffled, so undisturbed. A period in her young life which had been traumatic had, in fact, resulted in no trauma at all. She was the same Hazel.

But she was not. It took about a year for Hazel to appreciate that she was more unlike other young women than ever. Her original sense of being different had been to do with her desire to be self-contained, but now she was different through the nature of the experience she had undergone and because it had to remain forever secret. In the company of her contemporaries she felt so used and old that she could hardly relate to them or to their concerns (unless they were to do with work). Sex, sex, sex was the ever-prevailing subject of conversation and pregnancy the ever-present terror; and she had no patience with either. She knew about sex, she knew about pregnancy, but she could confess to neither rich knowledge. She wanted to stay away from both for a very long time. But keeping herself apart no longer came effortlessly. She could feel herself gravitating towards a certain kind of human contact, the kind she had had initially with George, and then shying away, afraid of where it would lead.

George had written to her, several times, letters forwarded to Norway which she had read with such detachment they seemed not to make sense. Who was this man, full of his undergraduate days at Magdalen? He was nothing to her. He was an ex-, and brief, first-time lover and the father of a child she had not wanted. It irritated her to be reminded of his existence, and she had no intention of acknowledging it. She worried, once she was back home, that he might turn up at her house, or attempt to contact her through their mutual school friends, but he did not. It was enough, apparently, for George to receive no response to his letters for him to decide he was rejected. He had doubtless found consolation elsewhere. He did not know, she couldn't help thinking, how very fortunate he was. In idle moments, she wondered if he would have married her. He couldn't have denied he was the father of her baby – she didn't think he would even have attempted to, not just because he was proud of being honourable but because it could be so easily proved. But he was only eighteen, with Oxford before him. How could they have married? There was part of George, she realised, which would have relished the agony of the moral dilemma to do or not to do the decent thing. Well, she had done it for him. She had borne and got rid of their mistake and saved him from any anguish at all. It made her proud of herself. Not many girls, she reckoned, would have been so unselfish. They would have wanted the boy to suffer. It was remarkable, too, that her own mother had not wanted George named and pilloried – most mothers, surely, would want the boy forced into facing up to his responsibilities and made to pay.

Gradually, though only in the vaguest way, Hazel realised her mistake had not been entirely obliterated. With time, instead of growing weaker the memory of the baby grew stronger. It was only the memory of a shadow, after all, but that shadow crept around in her subconscious and she did not know how to get rid of it.

Chapter Nine

IN JULY, Leah went back to the village, taking Evie with her. The journey, which had seemed adventurous the year before, now seemed tedious. It passed in a daze of discomfort, as she clutched the baby to her breast to cushion her fragile bones from the brutal joltings of the coach. On the way to Carlisle, all those months ago, she had not even noticed how rough the road was as it climbed over the moors. She had no interest now in her fellow passengers and they had none in her – she was just a poor young woman with a child. Choosing to get out at the crossroads and walk the mile to the Fox and Hound, she was overcome with nostalgia, seeing in her mind's eye her former braver self marching so confidently at Hugo's side. Now she trudged, dreading the mission she was on and yet knowing it had to be undertaken.

There was no other way. She had waited long enough. She had sent three other letters but none had been replied to nor had any more money been sent. Those fifty guineas, which had arrived with such speed in November, were long since finished and she had become what she had resolved never to be, a dependant on old Mary. Both of them lived on the washing they took in and though the income was regular it was pitifully small, enough for one person to live on but a struggle for three. Mary never objected. She was used to hardship and found it easy to be even more frugal than usual, but it pained and shamed Leah to witness the extent to which Mary's small comforts were gradually whittled down.

A month ago she had dressed herself as smartly as possible in the one new dress she had made after Evie's birth (believing more money was on its way), and she had gone to Carlisle and into the bank to inquire if a money order had come from Canada for her. But it had not. The clerk had stared at her insolently and smiled, and she had been unable to return his stare with a similar spirit to that which she had displayed on their first encounter. She had bowed her head and retreated hurriedly.

She knew there might be all kinds of reasons why Hugo had not replied and had not for one moment imagined herself finally deserted. He could be ill or dead. Who, after all, would have been able to inform her of this? No one knew where she had gone when she left the Fox and Hound and she had communicated with no one since she had taken refuge with Mary. The only way to find out what had happened to Hugo was to return to the village and ask. The people there would know. They always knew everything, especially if it were scandalous or tragic, about anyone whose family inhabited their village. She had only to appear with her baby, well known to be Hugo Todhunter's bastard (as Evie would be labelled), for information to be showered upon her from all sides. She was prepared for it. Whatever she learned, whatever she had to bear, no one would see her weep. She would return to Carlisle on the evening coach and so back to Wetheral and Mary and face up to whatever was to be her fate. But she had to *know* – it was unendurable to tolerate any further waiting.

She had never noticed before how the village blurred into the hillside. It was all grey houses, grey-green tiled roofs, grey-brown stone walls and the black road running through it. Even in summer, as now, the hardness of the stone was barely softened. There were few trees – the wind was too strong to allow all but the toughest to stand – and no flowers. It surprised her, but then she had grown used to Wetheral and its soft prettiness, the pink sandstone houses and white-washed cottages and the rich colours of the trees and flourishing shrubs. She thought, as she passed the church, now fallen into disrepair, where Hugo had 'married' her, that she was glad after all to have left this dour spot behind. It was no place to bring up a child, there was nothing here to lift the heart or bring joy and colour into a young life. She pulled Evie closer to her and quickened her step.

No one at the Fox and Hound was glad to see her. Her uncle Tom was changing the beer barrels and hardly looked up. 'Come back, have you?' he grunted. 'What for? Not hoping we'll take you in, are you?' She said no, she was not. Then she stood still and waited, knowing he would not be able to resist passing on whatever malicious gossip he had hold of. The silence was long and humiliating. Evie began to cry and her uncle said, 'Crying for her dad, is she? Then she'll cry a long time, she can bawl her head off all day and he'll not hear.' Leah's heart began to thud, fearing this announcement was the prelude to news of Hugo's death. 'He hasn't come home, has he?' her uncle went on. 'Disappeared, that's what, clean off the face of the earth, or Canada, any road. And in debt, as usual, owing his relatives a packet. You got yourself tied up with a rascal there, Leah, but you can't say you weren't warned.' Leah turned and began to walk out. 'Hey, where you off to without saying a word? Going to his parents? Well, they'll give you nothing, my lass, they're tired of him and his bastards, they've had enough of women knocking on their door with his babies in their arms ...'

She did not hear any more. The last jeer, she was certain, was made up and thrown at her only to hurt and worry; but she had perfect faith in Hugo. It was the kind of rumour about him there had always been and she took no heed. There was no point her staying in the village any longer, but it was some hours before the coach would return to the crossroads. There was nowhere for her to go. She had no friend to visit. She had worked, she had walked and she had gone to church to sing in the choir, but otherwise she had had no life in this bleak village. She would go to the church now, not St Kentigern's but St Mungo's, the new parish church, where she had gone every Sunday after they closed the other. She would sit quietly there and feed Evie and eat the bread she had brought with her. She might even sleep a little and the thought comforted her. There was so much to absorb. If Hugo had vanished, leaving debts again, what did it mean for her? No more money, for sure. He would be so wretched and ashamed and this would prevent him contacting her. He would imagine she would now wish to cast him off. How, then, could she reach him and tell him this was not so, that she wanted him on any terms and could forgive him sins far worse than running up debts or failing in business? Her head ached and she longed for the soothing interior of the church.

But on the way there she was bound to pass the Hall where the Todhunters lived. Her steps slowed. She stood at the gates, both standing open, and looked up the drive. It was not a long drive and the house could clearly be seen, squat and square, with its broad oak door. Hugo had told her he was afraid of his father, who was a bully, but that he loved his mother and his sister. His mother and his sister were called Evelyn, and Leah had taken that name for her baby, thinking to please him. She went on standing there, quite still. She imagined herself doing what her uncle had so untruthfully said many girls had done before her – walking up to that door, knocking, and presenting Hugo's child and claiming support from his family. She would never do such a thing, of course, not even for the sake of her baby. But it seemed hard that Evie's presence, her very existence, should remain a secret from her father's people, some of whom, the women, might be glad to know of it. She resolved that when she had Evie baptised she would send a card to Hugo's mother. A baptism card would surely not seem like a demand for help but a mere notification of fact.

She reached the church and sat inside for several hours and was bothered by no one. She did not sleep but nevertheless was refreshed and ready to face the long journey home. Mary was glad to see her, having feared she would not come back at all. Leah told her the truth, that Hugo could not be looked to any more and that she must provide for herself and her child as best she could. She believed that one day she would see him again but it was impossible to guess when that would be. Mary said nothing, only that Leah was a good worker and she was a good worker, and she was sure the child would in due course be a good worker; and they would manage. And manage they did.

Leah began to keep hens and grow flowers in their garden. She was given four hens and a cock by a farmer's wife whose washing they did and they were lucky, the hens under Leah's care were great layers. They sold the eggs and bought more hens and soon had a regular enough supply to make it worth going by cart to Carlisle market to sit at the butter women's stalls and sell their eggs there for a good price. They sold flowers, too, bunches of lavender and carnations and, in the spring, daffodils and tulips. They paid their rent on time and had food to eat, and Mary, at least, was happy. Leah was less so. It was not that her life was hard which depressed her – it had always been hard and in many ways was not actually as hard as it had once been – but thoughts of the future, hers and Evie's.

Hugo was becoming a dream from which she had woken up with feelings of bitterness she had never thought to have. She had been a fool, to trust him as she had done. She did not blame him nor did she think he had acted at the time of their loving with any deliberate deceit. She quite believed his love for her had been real and his intentions sincere, but what she ought to have seen was his inability to carry them out – *that* was where her faith had been misplaced. His own parents had had to learn the same lesson and though he had instructed her in how they had learned it, she had not heeded him. She had given way to her own strong desires and had believed in the power of love to solve all problems. And now she had to pay for her folly.

But what disturbed her most was how she seemed unable to stop herself blaming Evie. Leah had loved her unborn baby fiercely, and continued to love her while she was still sure of Hugo; but increasingly now she had come to see Evie as a constant reminder of her own stupidity and Hugo's weakness. By the time Evie was two, Leah had to force herself to hold her in her arms at all – Hugo's eyes, in Evie's face, were an affliction and his hair, framing the child's face, made her want to cut it all off and burn it. Evie was all her father – the eyes, the hair, the skin, the small ears, and it was agony to see this. It troubled Leah deeply to feel anything other than love for her child, and she hoped she never betrayed her lack of it, but she could not control her sense of a shocking alienation. It was a relief, always, when Evie was not with her. Poor Evie, poor Evie, she said to herself, the saddest of refrains running constantly through her head, but her pity combined with guilt to intensify her bitterness towards the child. Mary, old Mary, was the one who gave Evie affection. It was a touching sight to see the child on her knee, being sung to, or holding her hand and staggering (both of them) round the garden. Evie called Mary 'Grandma' and Leah did nothing to correct her. It seemed natural that Mary should regard herself as grandmother to Evie. Once, Mary told her, she had had her own little girl, her own baby, but she would not tell what had happened to her.

From the little girl's own grandmother there had been no sign, though Leah had sent Mrs Todhunter a baptismal card. In some vague attempt at continuity she had taken Evie back to Caldewgate to be christened in the same church, Holy Trinity, where she knew herself to have been christened. But she had regretted this. She ought to have taken Evie to Wetheral church, which she now attended every Sunday and where she sang (though not in the choir). Wetheral was her home now and except for the weekly trips to Carlisle market she did not suppose she would ever leave it. She was only nineteen but her life seemed mapped out for her, at least until Evie was grown up, and probably for ever.

Others did not think so. Mary saw how the men ogled Leah and knew it was only a matter of time before she was made an offer it would be absurd to refuse. She dreaded the day when Leah would capitulate and kept an eye out constantly for threatening suitors. There were plenty. Even the curate was smitten, though fortunately he realised, as Mary did, that he had no hope. Leah had not a single good word for any of them. Men fell over themselves to please her and she took no notice. Mary knew Leah believed herself no longer attractive since the birth of Evie had thickened her waist and left her heavier, but she was wrong. Her figure was all the more pleasing since it had filled out, at least to the men it was. Mary knew Leah also thought the severity of her dress and the way she wore her hair made her ugly, but it did not. The lack of adornment, the blonde hair pulled tightly into the nape of the neck, the dark brown dress – all accentuated her beautiful complexion, the translucent quality of her skin. Even her reserved manner and her lack of conversation made her appealing, gave her a quality of mystery. In the market especially, Mary noted the looks. Among the ruddy-cheeked, weather-beaten faces of the butter women, Leah's stood out, a pale flower amid the florid colour. Her composure, as she sold her eggs, contrasted with the laughing, restless energy of the other women who twisted and turned to talk to each other all day long. It would have taken a blind man not to notice Leah Messenger in that setting, and the men in Carlisle market were not blind.

Henry Arnesen, though not blind, was severely short-sighted. He had struggled for years not to give in to the wearing of the eye-glasses he hated, but it was impossible for him to follow his trade as a tailor if he could not see clearly. Twice, at fairs, he had paid good money to people who claimed to be able to cure poor sight and twice he had been made a fool of. Now he wore his spectacles – two pairs, one for close work and one for distance – with resignation, gold-rimmed ones, as light and invisible as they could be made. He was sure they made him look old and unattractive, but in this he was mistaken. The glasses did not detract from the pleasantness of Henry's features and they magnified his striking blue eyes – 'Too beautiful for a lad,' his mother had always said. He had thick brown hair and a splendid bushy moustache, and he was tall and well built – he was, without realising it, a handsome man.

But it was true, all the same, that, at the age of thirty, he was not only unmarried but had never gone courting seriously. His mother, anxious for grandchildren (Henry was her only child), complained about it. Henry's excuse was that he worked too hard to have the time for courting. This was partly true. He did work hard in his modest premises in Globe Lane. His father, also a tailor, had set him up there when he was twenty-one, and Henry had since repaid the investment many times over. When his father died Henry had taken on his regular clients too and had been supporting his mother ever since. Not only did he cut and sew clothes, made to measure, but on Saturdays he had a stall in the market selling material. Saturday was the busiest day at the market, when all the country people came in to sell their produce and, with any profit they made, might treat themselves to a length of fabric for a dress. Henry had a good eye for what these women liked and stocked his stall accordingly. Sometimes he made as good a profit on a Saturday as he had all the rest of the week. Besides, Henry liked his Saturdays. They were relaxing. He didn't have to wear his spectacles, because there was no need to see clearly. True, things were a bit hazy but he could manage perfectly with a little care.

He first saw Leah through a haze. He was standing behind his stall during a momentary lull and, staring across the sprigged cottons, he saw her pale, delicate face among the row of red ones. It seemed so still and pure among the tossing and turning of other heads, and he fumbled for the correct pair of spectacles and put them on. Leah's face sprang sharply into focus, a sad, quiet face with downcast eyes and a mouth closed and firm. But nothing could conceal the perfection of the skin, nor could the serious expression rob the face of grace and natural refinement. Henry kept his glasses on and watched Leah all the rest of the afternoon. He saw her leave with an old woman who was carrying a child. The child must be this younger woman's, which disappointed him. She was almost certainly married, then. He took his glasses off and sighed. It was always the way. Any woman who caught his attention was invariably married. Probably she was a farmer's wife, in from the country with her butter and eggs and about to be collected by the farmer in his cart. He thought he would just check to see, but his mother, who was usually on hand to look after the stall while he took a break, was indisposed that day and he was on his own.

But the following week his mother was there and so, he saw, was the woman with the pale, delicate-boned face. He waited all day, observing her closely, and when the other, old, woman arrived with the child, as before, to collect her, Henry was ready, and he followed. He saw them go out of the back entrance and down towards the sands where they got into a large cart, already full of women, and off they went. It proved nothing. All farmer's wives, all going to the same village, likely. But the absence of a particular man and his individual cart gave Henry a small scrap of hope. The following week he left his stall half an hour before the general packing-up time and went down to the sands where all the carts were waiting. He recognised the cart he had seen the week before by its extra large, muddy, red-painted wheels and approached the driver. Henry was direct, seeing no point in subterfuge. 'Where are you going to?' he asked. The driver barely looked at him. 'Wetheral and parts,' he said, 'and no room for any more, like.' Satisfied, Henry went back to the market. Wetheral wasn't far. Five miles or so. He had occasionally taken his mother there and rowed her across the river Eden to Corby. Very occasionally. So occasionally he couldn't remember the last time. She would be delighted if he suggested such an outing now.

It was foolish, of course. Henry knew this perfectly well but nevertheless he drove his mother to Wetheral in his smart little pony trap – only recently acquired and a source of great pride – and once there the two of them walked round the village green and down to the river and sat watching the salmon leap. Henry had not expected to see the woman who intrigued him parading around Wetheral for his delight, so he was quite philosophical when she did not put in an appearance. But every Saturday thereafter when he saw that pale face on the far side of the market he derived some curious pleasure from knowing she came from Wetheral. It gave him an advantage, he felt, though it took him a long time to put this to any kind of use. He noted that the woman sold flowers as well as eggs and he began to buy them from her for his mother. Every week he bought two bunches of whatever the Wetheral woman had, taking care, Carlisle-fashion, to betray not the slightest interest in her. Only when this transaction had been going on for twenty-five weeks – he had counted – did he chance any attempt at conversation and even then he limited himself to pleasantries, all of which were responded to with similar ones. After almost a year, he was quite pleased with how things were going and was working himself up to bolder action, convinced that such was his subtlety that his true interest had not been guessed at.

Mary had guessed within a month of Henry's performance what he was about and so, really, had Leah. Henry was not alone. Many market men had suddenly begun buying flowers for astonished mothers, and Leah had reaped the benefit. But where Henry was different was in his patience and extreme caution. Mostly Leah's customers could not contain their ardour beyond a couple of weeks. Then, they would buy the flowers, thrust the money into her hand and ask her if they could bring her a cup of tea or, if they were very forward, meet her behind the market after it closed. These men were amazed, even shocked, by the straight rejection they met with and the look of anger which blazed from what they had misjudged as a calm, docile face. They were frightened off and never came back. Leah began to earn a reputation as one who belied her looks, a woman who was after all a spitfire, and Henry naturally heard what was said about her. The market looked vast but it was a small world and gossip circulated easily. He heard also that Leah Messenger – it was good to know her name at last – did indeed have a child, a girl, and that, though she wore a wedding-ring, there was neither sight nor sound of a husband.

Henry thought long and hard about the child. She would be a complication, were he to proceed. Undoubtedly, Leah would cling to the child and consider her future of more importance than her own, he was sure of it. Mothers, he had observed, were like that. So the question he pondered as he stitched away all week was, did he mind the child? She looked, so far as he could tell, a quiet little thing, never giving any trouble. During the hours she was with her mother and not taken off by the old woman she seemed to sit still and keep quiet. There was no running about shrieking, as many of the children did. But was the child a product of a marriage now over, for whatever reason, or of some unfortunate liaison? Was Leah Messenger, in short, what could only be called a fallen woman, and if she was, did he mind? Henry decided he did, a little. He had always thought that any woman in whom he took a serious interest would have to be above reproach. He was honest himself and highly moral, and expected the same standards in others. His own chastity, at thirty, was not something he could say he relished – far from it – but on the other hand he was not ashamed of it. He knew what lust was and it had caused him some anguish, but he also knew how to deal with it, or to control it without hurting anyone else. But he was tired of such control and yearned to have a wife. It was time.

It became irrelevant to Henry, after the first year, whether Leah had a child or not and what the existence of that child signified. He felt hypnotised by her. With or without his glasses, he found that her face swam before him all the time and he longed for Saturdays. At Easter, he bought all the flowers Leah had with her in a sudden uncharacteristic moment of recklessness. 'All?' said Leah, startled, since, because it was Easter, she had a great many flowers – tulips, narcissi, daffodils – arranged all round her in buckets. 'All,' said Henry firmly. 'But how will you carry them?' Leah asked. Henry made a gesture to indicate this was of no concern. 'I'll come for them when you pack up,' he said, grandly. When that time came, he took an Easter egg with him and asked permission to give it to the child. This was readily granted, and so was his polite request to wait while he ferried all the flowers across the market and up Lowther Street into Globe Lane (where he intended to leave all but one bunch in his workroom). It took him three trips and as he collected the last few bunches Leah became agitated, as he had known she would, and confessed she was afraid she would miss the cart home. Addressing old Mary and not Leah herself, Henry begged to be allowed to take them home to Wetheral himself since he was the cause of the delay.

Permission was very nearly not granted and Henry's flamboyant gesture of buying all the flowers was very nearly a grave mistake. Leah had respected his slow advances and had tolerated his addresses only because they were modest, even timid and presented no threat. She had hoped she would never have to put this nice-seeming man down, but now she was not so sure. Her hesitation was marked but Henry had the sense not to try and persuade her and this swung the verdict in his favour. Elated, but struggling to seem matter-of-fact, he rushed off to deposit the last of the flowers and to get his trap and harness the pony, all of which took him far longer than he expected. When he finally came into view, down Market Street, Leah, Mary and the child looked a forlorn little group and he was touched by their evident anxiety as to whether he would turn up at all.

He tried to make the drive last as long as possible which was not difficult because although the trap was new the pony was old and rather tired. He had seated the child, Evie, beside him, between himself and her mother, and the old woman in the back. Gently, he put the reins in little Evie's hands and allowed her to hold them all by herself for a while on a straight and empty piece of road. If Evie had been older and talkative she might have given him the means to learn a great deal that he wanted to know about her mother, but since she was so very young and utterly silent she was no help. By the time Wetheral came into view Henry had gleaned no information about his passengers whatsoever. Leah volunteered nothing and he had asked nothing. She did not speak until they came to the turning off the green and then only to direct him to where she lived. The tiny terraced house did not look big enough to be home to more than the three people he delivered to its door, but he cautioned himself against optimism. He lifted Evie down and helped the old woman out and then, without hanging around, he doffed his cap and, brushing aside Leah's thanks, set off at once back to Carlisle.

Later in the same week, one evening after work, he went out to Wetheral and strolled around. He resisted the temptation to walk past Leah's house and instead passed the road end and walked along the river. From the river road, he climbed the steps which brought him out near the Crown Inn, and on a sudden impulse he went into the bar. It was fairly full and he almost walked out again but his thirst was great and he wanted a glass of beer before going home. Supping his beer at the bar he heard, as he was aware he had secretly hoped to, mention of the Messenger name. The two men standing just along the bar were talking about a rumour of some cottages being knocked down nearby and the tenants being put out into the street. A Mary Messenger was mentioned, with sad shakings of the head, and 'that young lass with the child who lives with her'.

Henry finished his beer and went up to the green to untie his pony. His mind was quite made up. He would ask Leah Messenger to marry him and he would say he was happy, of course, to accept Evie and love her as his own. His offer would surely be irresistible if it was true that Mary was to be evicted from her house. But would he take on old Mary too? He thought not. Surely that much would not be expected of a man. He would have to make it very clear that his offer did not include giving a home to old Mary. At least he could not be taken by surprise.

The surprise, when it came, had nothing to do with old Mary and was a much greater one than Henry had envisaged. It was more of a shock than a surprise. When he duly proposed to Leah, during a drive arranged with some difficulty, she said she had two conditions.

One was that he should never question her in any way about the father of her child. She would not reveal his identity, ever, nor did she wish to disclose the circumstances of how she had met him or what happened. She said so far as she knew he was in Canada and, since she had heard nothing from him in three years, she regarded him as dead. There had been no one before or since. The wedding-ring was real but did not signify a legal wedding. Henry listened carefully and said he would never, ever, mention anything to do with this episode in Leah's life. She need have no worries on that score – he would accept her as she now was, with her child. But then came the shock. Leah's second condition was so extraordinary Henry thought he could not have heard aright. He asked her to repeat what she had said and bid her wait until he had stopped the pony so that the noise of its hooves and the rattling of the trap would not interfere with his listening. 'I can't have Evie living with us,' Leah said, calmly, 'she must go with Mary. We must pay Mary to keep her. I can't marry you if I have to bring Evie. I must start afresh, that is all.'

For a long time Henry sat stock-still, wondering what kind of woman Leah was after all. It occurred to him that this might be in the nature of a test, a test perhaps of his decency. Eventually, starting to drive again, he said, 'But she is your child, she is barely more than an infant.'

'I know she is my child, but I cannot bear the pain of her. If I marry you it is to put all that pain behind me. I cannot love her as I should and would wish to. As I ought, as I have wanted to. Mary loves her. You may judge me harsh and cruel, but that is what I want, Evie to go with Mary if I am to go with you and be your wife.' This last was spoken in a whisper, with bowed head.

Henry took a quick look and saw the tears falling. 'Now then, now then,' he said, lamely and, clearing his throat, 'there's a lot to understand all of a sudden and I'm trying, but nothing alters my wanting you as my wife, I'm clear on that, if on nothing else.' They trotted a bit further until again Henry stopped the pony. 'You're the mother,' he said, 'it's for you to decide, not me. I only hope folk won't think I wouldn't stand for the child. It'd be natural for them to see it that way, whereas ...'

'Yes,' Leah said, 'you would take Evie, you made it plain.'

'To you, but it wouldn't be plain to others.'

'Would that matter?'

'I wouldn't like misunderstandings, to be thought ...'
'People forget,' Leah said. 'Hardly anyone knows me.'
'They see more than you think in the market.'
'Well, if you feel you can't ...'
'No. If that's what you want, then that's how it will be. Unless you change your mind, when it comes to the bit, and keep the child.'
'I won't,' said Leah. 'I will never change my mind. I would wish her a thousand miles away. Do you still want me as your wife?'
'Yes,' said Henry.

Chapter Ten

IT WAS a quiet but very pretty wedding, all planned for the gratification and pleasure of Hazel's mother. It was what she most wanted, and Hazel could not see how she could refuse to co-operate. Her mother had been so sad ever since the shockingly sudden death of her husband the year before – he had been only sixty-two and in good health. It was the unfairness of it which continued to grieve his widow. Hazel felt she could not add to that sense of grievance by marrying Malcolm in a register office, as she would have wished, and so she capitulated and left all the arrangements to her mother, who was quite restored to life for a while.

A pretty country wedding in Gloucestershire, where the Walmsleys had a cottage. Hazel walked from the cottage to the church, which was just down the hill and round the corner, a matter of eight hundred yards (Mrs Walmsley had the distance measured, the better to time the bride's entrance). Her eldest brother gave her away and very imposing he looked in traditional morning-dress. Hazel wore a deceptively simple-looking dress, white of course, white satin with a long, narrow skirt which made her look even more willowy than usual. She carried a spray of tiny yellow rosebuds, the colour of the bridesmaids' dresses. Four bridesmaids (her nieces) all under the age of ten and balanced in height to a most satisfying degree. Very sweet the little procession looked – 'like something out of Hardy', one of the more literary guests was heard to murmur. It was a windy day in April and the wind caught Hazel's veil and whirled it round her, though gently, and lifted up the dresses, adding an air of life and vitality to their slow progress. The church was beautifully and unusually decorated, with bowls of primroses and jugs of catkins.

Mrs Walmsley could not be completely content, since she longed for her dead husband to be at her side to witness this happy event, but she came as near as possible to perfect contentment for the duration of the service. Hazel looked absolutely beautiful. She was quite unselfconscious, lacking entirely that nervous embarrassment which afflicts so many brides, and she moved with a rare grace and composure towards the altar. Who, reflected her mother, would ever guess Hazel's past? Or guess that hidden part of her past? Things could have been so different. Mrs Walmsley felt momentarily ill when she thought how different. If she had not acted, all those years ago, with such speed and efficiency, Hazel's life would have been wrecked at eighteen. She would never have gone to university, never qualified as a solicitor, never met Malcolm McAllister, who was so exactly right for her. Her whole life would have been ruined for the sake of one mistake. And not just her life, the life of the child, that child who had now been part of another family all these years and much better off. The burden on the child would have been intolerable. Mrs Walmsley had no doubts about this. She had doubts about very few things, in fact, though she had always tried hard not to think how her husband would have reacted if he had known why Hazel was really going to Norway. He had always let his wife manage domestic matters, but perhaps her secrecy on that momentous occasion would have appalled him. Perhaps. She didn't know.

But there before her was Hazel, a beautiful bride. Her mistake was never referred to. It had not been mentioned for years. Only when Malcolm had come on the scene had Mrs Walmsley been unable to resist the merest suggestion that Hazel should perhaps think about ... Hazel had been sharply offended. 'Mother,' she had said, more angrily than was surely necessary, 'Mother, surely you don't think I would let myself get anywhere near the point of marrying without being able to trust whoever I was involved with?' Mrs Walmsley had said no, of course not, but that it would be difficult and maybe, just possibly, there was no real need ... But Hazel had been even angrier. 'No *need*?' she had almost shouted. 'Mother, how could I not tell my future husband something so important?' 'Oh,' Mrs Walmsley had been unable to stop herself saying, 'Oh, is it important now, darling, when it was so long ago and over so quickly?'

The reception was in the house, spilling over into the garden. The wind dropped during the afternoon and the sun came out, and once the lunch was over everyone went outside. It was all very relaxed and Malcolm's people, who were rather under-represented (most of them seemed to have emigrated from Scotland to live in Canada), were particularly pleased with the informality. They were shy people, socially quite timid, Mrs Walmsley was surprised to discover, since there was nothing timid about Malcolm. His parents hardly said a word, though as the afternoon wore on they looked more at ease and loosened up sufficiently to express their appreciation of Hazel. She was the daughter-in-law they had always wanted. Malcolm was so fussy and they had begun to despair that he would ever consider any woman matched up to his high ideals. Hazel, they could see, did just that. She was flawless – beautiful, clever, diligent and without a divorce or some other entanglement in her past. They could not, they said, believe Malcolm's luck.

At five o'clock Hazel changed into jeans and a sweatshirt – she didn't think that indulging her mother with a traditional wedding meant she had to dress up conventionally to 'go away' – and left with Malcolm, similarly clad, for Heathrow airport where they boarded a plane for the Algarve. They reached the villa they had rented just before midnight and went straight to bed, to sleep. They had had their first night long ago, at Malcolm's flat. It was the first sex Hazel had had in eight years. There had been no one since George, not through lack of offers but because she would not allow such intimate contact. Something in her was damaged, though she was not sure what. Several times she had been tempted. But she had deliberately held back, forcing herself to consider the consequences of her desire. It was not that she was afraid of becoming pregnant again. Contraception was no longer a problem. The game had changed. She could take the Pill and, in common with her generation, she had no qualms about this. What she had qualms about was her self and her needs. She was afraid she would want to dispense with a lover the moment she had been satisfied. Then there might be a mess and she dreaded the complications of an unsatisfactory affair. She had never met any man who seemed worth the risk.

But Malcolm seemed worth it. He didn't want to own her mind as well as her body. What had first attracted him to her was that very air of detachment she so prized. He wouldn't, he said, want her to sacrifice this in order to accommodate him. He had proved, during the two years she had known him, as good as his word, and she loved him for it. Realising she loved Malcolm was such a relief, such a blessing. It freed her from the growing conviction that she was so self-contained she was incapable of loving another person, and selfish to such a frightening extent that she would never be able to put anyone else's needs before her own. The closer they became, the more she was liberated from self-obsession until, after six months, she was ready to move in with him. Malcolm said there were a few things she should know first. He told her he had been living with someone for four years before he met her. The flat he lived in had belonged, originally, to this woman. He took it over when they split up and she went to America. This, Hazel realised, explained the ruched blinds, the white lace bedspread and shaggy carpets so uncharacteristic of Malcolm, who had never had time to change them.

Malcolm offered to tell Hazel in detail about his 'previous' as he called her, but she declined to be enlightened. She said she didn't want to know about Malcolm's past, beyond simple facts such as where he was born (St Andrews) and if he had parents alive (yes) and brothers (no) or sisters (yes, one). She wanted to know *him* but not whom he had been with. 'Ah,' he had said, smiling, teasing her, 'but can you ever really know a person without knowing who they've been with? Aren't people their past?' It had been the perfect opportunity to tell him about George and the baby, but she wasn't ready for confessions. To her relief, he made no attempt to pry into her own immediate past, though he did express surprise that she had never lived with a man before him. Once they were sure of each other and had agreed to marry, Hazel knew she could keep silent no longer. He had to know about the baby she'd given birth to and abandoned, and she had to know what he thought about this. She intended to choose her time well, but in the end didn't choose it at all. Malcolm chose it, by asking her if she wanted children. They'd been to see his sister who had two boys of six and eight, both of whom Malcolm clearly adored. He'd played all day with them in a way Hazel found extraordinary – she hadn't suspected he would like fooling around with children so much, and she'd said so on the way home.

'Oh, I like children,' he'd said, 'don't you? Don't you want children? I mean, don't you want us to have a family eventually?' Her silence went on so long he became anxious and took his eyes off the busy road long enough to shoot her a quick look. 'What's the matter, Hazel?'

'I'll tell you when we get home,' she said. She wished she'd blurted it out there and then, when he was driving, as though it was a casual bit of information she thought nothing of. Instead, by the time they did get home, this thing she had promised to tell him had built itself into something of huge significance and she was irritated by his clear expectation that she had some momentous disclosure to make. He opened a bottle of wine and she made sandwiches and they sat by the fire and, though he did not prompt her, she knew she could put it off no longer than she already had done.

'It's just,' she said abruptly, looking directly at him, 'that when I was eighteen I had a baby. It was adopted.'

He put down his glass and clasped his hands in front of him in that way he had, the way of seeming to brace himself, which she had noticed first about him. He'd been sitting in court exactly like that, hands clasped and pulled into his chest in that tense fashion. 'Adopted?' he asked, finally, and then, very carefully, much too carefully, 'Were you happy about that?'

'Yes. But I'd have preferred an abortion, if I could have found out how to get one.'

'So, obviously, you didn't want the baby.'

'Obviously,' she said, unable to keep the sarcasm out of her voice. 'Very, very obviously. I was only eighteen, seventeen, in fact, when I became so stupidly pregnant.'

'Stupid? I can't imagine you were ever stupid.'

'Well, I was. I was carried away.'

'I can't imagine that either.'

'No, you can't imagine any of it, I wouldn't expect you to. I can hardly imagine it myself now.'

There was a long silence. His face hadn't changed, the expression remained calm, but she saw a little muscle beating in his jaw. She wanted him to say something else though she couldn't think what. When he did speak, his question was exactly what she did not want from him.

'Do you know what happened to the baby?'

'No. I didn't want to. It was adopted.'

'It? Boy or girl?'

'Does it matter?'

'I'd like to know.'

'A girl.'

'Did you see her?'

'No. Only a shadow. I didn't want to see her, ever.'

'I suppose that's natural, if she was going to be adopted. They say women change their minds once they've seen the baby.'

'I wouldn't have changed my mind. I wanted to be rid of it so much.'

'No feelings for her?'

'None.'

'No guilt? No pity?'

'No. I was angry.'

'With the baby?'

'Yes, with the baby, even if it wasn't to blame.'

Malcolm nodded, and this annoyed her. He suddenly seemed complacent and smug. He was treating her professionally and she hated this.

'Well, then,' she said briskly, 'that's what I felt I should tell you.'

'I'm glad you did.'

'I'm not.'

'Oh, why not?'

'I've never told anyone, ever. Only my mother knew. My father never did and my brothers don't, and I liked it like that, secret. It isn't something I want to talk about even with you. It upsets me.'

'Pride,' Malcolm said. 'It all comes down to pride. It often does with you.'

'Does it indeed?'

'Yes. You're proud of being secretive, self-contained. It's a loss of face to have to reveal something so hidden.'

'Clever, aren't you?'

'Yes. So are you. Clever enough to know *I* know why you're upset, and it isn't anything to do with telling me about the baby. It's what I make of all this, isn't it? Whether I'll hold it against you? Whether I'll want to know who the boy was and all the other details? That's what's upsetting you, not the giving of the facts.' He refilled his glass and hers. She smiled. She liked it when he so neatly and accurately summarised her thoughts. 'Well, I do feel quite shocked,' he said. 'It *is* quite shocking, and sad, to me anyway, the thought of you, at a mere seventeen, eighteen, whatever, having to have a baby you didn't want. Awful.' He put his glass down and reached out and touched her hand, and to her own surprise she found tears welling up in her eyes, but she was determined not to let them fall. 'And I can't help thinking of that baby ... *your* child ...'

'I never think of it, the baby.'

'Is that really true?'

'Yes. I dream of its shadow sometimes, nightmares I suppose, but I never think of it growing, as a person. I don't want to, I won't allow myself to.'

'And what about having other babies, ours, and keeping them? That's how all this began, didn't it, when I said didn't you want children?'

'I don't know if I do.'

'I want them.'

'Well then.'

'Well what?'

'If you want them, I'll have them, I suppose.'

'Hazel, please, what do you think I see you as? A breeding machine? Why would I want to make you have children if you had no desire for them? It would be horrible.'

'I don't see why.'

'Then you should.'

Nothing more was said that evening, but Malcolm seemed preoccupied and distant for some days afterwards, and she felt sorry to have burdened him. She could see he was worried and struggling with the idea that he might be going to marry a woman who did not share his vision of family life. There was nothing she could do about it. He had to accept her lack of maternal instinct because it was so much a part of her that it could hardly be concealed.

*

Philip was a honeymoon baby. It was, of course, a failure of contraception, not an accident or mistake – she had not been stupid again – something to do with that tiny degree of unreliability which she knew should always be taken into account even with the Pill. But this time she could, she also knew, arrange to have an abortion if she wished – a speedy, painless operation if done at once, no more serious, they said, than having a tooth out and far less messy. Before ever she told Malcolm, she considered her options and decided she would have this baby. What she felt was not the excited satisfaction Malcolm would want her to share with him but more a sense of quiet pleasure, the pleasure of his delight. But was that enough? She remembered how she had loathed her body that first time, and how she had detested the whole process of pregnancy and birth. Was it worth going through it again on the grounds of giving Malcolm what he wanted? This time the baby would not end up a shadow. It would be hers, to nurture and love, and she wasn't sure she could fulfil this curious role. Giving birth in itself, she had cause to know, did not automatically produce instinctive maternal feelings.

She said nothing at all for three months. Every day she asked herself if she felt any growing spark of love for what was developing inside her, but came up all the time against an inability to identify her own response. It was only by isolating what she did *not* feel that she could arrive at any kind of decision. She was relieved, for example, to realise that she did not feel any hatred or resentment, that she did not feel her body had been invaded or assaulted. She did not feel, either, that she was not in control. That was the most important thing: whatever happened this time she felt in control. She could have the baby, or not have the baby. There was no need to place herself in her mother's too capable hands. Then one weekend, when they were visiting Malcolm's sister again, Hazel noticed a newly framed photograph on the mantelpiece of his nephews as babies. One of them, the younger one, was, his sister pointed out, exactly like Malcolm as a baby. Hazel picked it up and studied it carefully. A chubby, smiling little Malcolm. Her stomach gave a flutter and a sudden thrill went through her – how very odd it would be to see Malcolm, whom she loved so much, as a baby.

She didn't know if that amounted to the beginnings of maternal love or not, but she took this unexpected emotional reaction as good enough evidence of something similar, and was relieved. Her decision seemed made for her. She told Malcolm that night and his jubilation was matched by his concern for her – did she want this baby, was she sure she wasn't going ahead just to please him? She convinced him that she did want it and he actually wept with happiness. (How, she wondered, could a man want a child so much?) Her whole pregnancy was a happy time and she enjoyed it. Occasionally she would remember Norway and the misery of those months and shiver at the memory, but there were no shadow dreams during the whole of that time to haunt her. She had to tell the hospital this was not her first baby but she did so without embarrassment and did not mind the few questions she was obliged to answer. When the date of the birth grew nearer she found herself praying she would have a boy. Philip was born after a short labour and the moment he was put into her arms and she looked at him, a great weight rolled off her mind – she did love him, she did feel what she was supposed to feel. But then, during the next few days, which should have been blissfully happy, a strange anxiety came over her. It felt precisely like that, something which came over her, a fog, a muzziness, and with it an unreasonable terror that she was not in control of herself. She did mention this briefly, hesitantly – it was so hard to describe – to a doctor, before she left the hospital, but was reassured that this dizziness (but she knew she had not said she felt dizzy, that it was his word) was a common post-natal symptom. It was all to do with re-adjusting to a different balance and to the shake-up of her hormones. She accepted this but the mental distress did not go away. It increased. She struggled to conceal her agitation but then she began hallucinating, seeing in front of her that other baby, the one she had given away without in fact ever seeing properly.

Malcolm, normally acutely sensitive to her mood, noticed nothing. He was so thrilled to be a father that he failed to detect, underneath her smiles, the tremors of real fear and, though she was an expert at suppressing emotion, she found it hard. Handling Philip, changing his nappy and seeing the fragility of his tiny body, watching his head loll if it was not supported, hearing his cries – all these things unnerved her. She felt so ill at the thought of once having wilfully abandoned such a dependent creature. It was brutal to remember, especially when she was feeding Philip, when his minute hands clawed at her full breast and her milk spilled from his mouth. None for that other baby. It had been denied everything, *she* had denied it her milk, her care, her tenderness and yet it had been hers, it had belonged to her, as Philip now did.

When she began to have nightmares it was almost a relief. She woke Malcolm with her screams, but could not tell him what had made her scream. She said she had dreamed that Philip was harmed and made a performance of getting up and checking him in his cradle. Since it was so easy to understand why she had this hideous dream, always beginning with that glimpse of the dangling shadow on the white wall, the shadow of her other baby, she tried hard to rationalise the content of the nightmare. Everything she had not let herself feel then she was feeling now. The nightmare was about acknowledging not just guilt but emotion. Though during the day she worked all this out satisfactorily, she still, however, woke up screaming at night. Malcolm held her close, soothed her, put the light on, made her a calming milky drink, did everything he could think of to reassure her. But he knew, after several weeks of these shattered nights, that this was not the natural anxiety of a mother for her newborn baby.

'Come on, Hazel,' he said, stroking her hair back from her damp forehead when at last her shivering had subsided, 'what's this about? What are you dreaming of? Tell me. I want to know.' She was silent, but began to move away, out of his arms. He resisted, holding her closer still. 'Come on,' he urged, 'tell me. This is no good. You're making yourself ill. Tell me.' She murmured there was nothing to tell, it was all 'silly', the way nightmares always are. 'You wouldn't scream like that if it was just silly,' he said firmly. 'You scream because you're terrified. What terrifies you, what do you see?' She said she couldn't bear to talk about it. Depressed, he realised there was no point in pressing her. They went back to sleep. But the next time the nightmare happened and her screams began he was ready. He didn't put the light on, nor did he hold her. He stayed quite still and let her scream and saw in the half dark how she sat up and seemed to push something away, shouting, 'No! No!' Then she collapsed back on to her pillow muttering almost incoherently about babies and weeping.

Next morning, he said to her, quite calmly, 'You had your nightmare last night.'

'Did I?' She looked embarrassed. 'I don't remember.'

'No. I didn't wake you up out of it. I thought I'd watch and listen.'

'And did you learn anything interesting?' she said, smiling, but alert, knowing he had.

'Yes. You talked.' He waited. Tricks like this were well known to them both. 'You talked about babies, in the plural. And you fought something off and shouted "No", repeatedly.'

'So?'

'So tell me. Don't make me guess.'

'I'm sure you've already guessed.'

'Stop it, Hazel. Why do I have to put into words what you can say much better? Is it some kind of test? Do I have to go through this when all I want to do is understand and help?'

'You can't, you couldn't understand. And no one can help.'

'Thanks.'

'It's true. I couldn't explain so you couldn't understand. It isn't an insult. I don't understand myself. I'm quite happy.'

'So happy you wake up screaming at least three nights a week.'

'I'm sorry.'

'That's exactly what you kept saying last night. "*Sorry*, *sorry*." You don't need to apologise, not to me. But of course you weren't saying sorry to me, you were saying it to her, that other baby, right?'

He thought she might hit him, so great was her anger. But she mastered herself and sat down on the bed, looking suddenly defeated. 'Yes,' she said, voice flat, 'I dream I see the shadow of her again, growing bigger and bigger and coming towards me. Pathetic, isn't it? Ten years too late and I discover I have a conscience.'

'It's all delayed guilt, brought on by Philip's birth.'

'I *know* that.'

'Of course you do. Right. So the only way to deal with it, if you can't persuade yourself that retrospective guilt is pointless, is to be practical. Your daughter ...'

'Don't call it that, don't! I hate those words.'

'Your baby, then ...'

'The baby, that will do, the baby, *it*.'

'It will be ten. It's been brought up by whoever adopted her – I can't go on unless I can at least use the personal pronoun, Hazel – and she's happy and settled and hasn't a clue about you nor does she care.'

'You don't know that. You don't know it's either happy or settled or that it doesn't think about me and wonder what kind of woman would give away her own baby, and never try to trace it and ...'

'Is that what you really want to do? Trace her?'

'No. I dread the thought, though, of being traced, hunted, and having to give an account of myself.'

'Not very likely.'

'You don't know that either.'

'All right then, for the sake of argument, *if* you could be told the baby was happy and settled and knew nothing about you and cared less, would that help?'

'Yes. It would let me off the hook, for the moment.'

'Then let's try and find out.'

Hazel didn't ask how. Malcolm was not a solicitor for nothing. He was expert at knowing whom to approach, how to get information. And he was discreet, there was no need for her to beg him to take care that her own name and address and circumstances should not be revealed. She had to provide him with some details, of course, or he had nothing to give a researcher or detective to go on. His expression, when she told him about the two women in Norway, was curious. Pained, she thought, it pained him to hear of all the subterfuge, or was the pain she thought she saw for her, for her young self in that predicament. But all he said was, 'Your mother. My God. Your mother ...' 'She did her best,' Hazel said, quite defensively. 'Her best? My God,' Malcolm said, and left it at that.

She had no nightmares while Malcolm, or someone on his behalf, several people, she imagined, though she didn't ask, pursued inquiries. He'd promised not to mention the subject again until he had definite news, and for her part she had promised to try to wait patiently – which she did. Just knowing that frightening shadow of her dreams was to be given substance helped to calm her, and she was able to devote herself to Philip without the very sight of his fragile baby body making her shake. And at last they bought a house and moved from the fussy flat, and all her time was taken up with choosing paint and wallpaper and furnishings. It wasn't the house they had envisaged, nor was Muswell Hill an area they knew and liked, but she found that the lack of familiarity was exciting.

Once installed in the house, Hazel felt a new person. She wasn't sure who that person was, or how she related to the old Hazel, but there was an exhilaration in feeling the boundaries of her life had changed dramatically. Being Malcolm's wife and Philip's mother in this friendly north London district was completely different from being her parent's daughter in smart Holland Park, or even Malcolm's mistress in chic Canonbury. She saw how, long ago, she ought to have found her own home, her own place, and not been content to depend on others. Surroundings did matter, after all; a break with the past, that break she had wanted, did follow on from a change of scene. Who you were depended more than she had ever guessed on where you were, or at least in her case it proved to be so. She felt so much better that she wished she had never let Malcolm try to trace her shadow-baby; she was on the point of telling him to cancel any investigation, when he came home one day with the result.

If he had asked her again, at that point, whether she was still sure she wanted to know, then Hazel would have shaken her head and told him to forget it. But he didn't ask. It made her think afterwards that he had guessed she would say no, and that he had decided to force the knowledge on her, believing it was for her own good. He didn't even wait until after supper but launched straight into a matter-of-fact account, as though relating one of his cases to her.

'She lives in Scotland,' he said, reading from a single sheet of paper he'd taken from his briefcase, 'name of Shona McIndoe, father's a captain in the merchant navy, mother doesn't work. She's healthy, an only child ...'

'Why did you have to tell me her name?' She watched him put the paper down.

'Shadows don't have names. This was all about turning a shadow you were afraid of into a person you don't need to fear, a little ten-year-old girl called Shona, living in Scotland beside the sea with a daddy who's a captain and a mummy who is devoted to her. Can you see her now? Not at all threatening, is she? Bears no comparison to that huge black heavy shadow.'

She didn't reply. He'd spoken very slowly, as though to someone of limited intelligence. There had been an edge to his normally even, quiet voice which she hadn't liked. He was angry, she deduced, but whether with her, and her reaction to his information, or with himself, for caring about this Shona, she was not sure. He did care, she knew that. She only cared because she was afraid of the long-term consequences this girl might bring about, but Malcolm cared about the girl herself, about Shona as Hazel's daughter, not as an instrument of possible vengeance. He wanted her for their own, that was what it was, she felt. They ate in silence. She didn't ask him how these details had been obtained. Slowly, she was absorbing them. Shona. A pretty name, wildly Scottish. Her father a sea-captain. An image came unbidden into her mind of a seashore and a girl running along it waving to a ship ... Romantic nonsense. She half smiled at that absurdity.

'So,' Malcolm said, watching her, 'a ghost, well, a shadow, laid to rest, I hope.'

'Thank you.'

'It was for my own sake too. I don't want my wife suffering nightmares for the rest of her life.' He paused, frowned, looked worried. 'Our children,' he said, 'will you ever tell them?'

'Of course not!' she cried, shocked. 'Why would I do that?'

'To stop being secretive,' Malcolm said, 'to be open about what happened.'

'I don't want to be open. It's my business.'

He shrugged. 'Maybe when they're grown-up, you'll change your mind, maybe if we have daughters.'

But there were no daughters. There were two more sons, at almost two-yearly intervals, and they had agreed three children were enough. When Anthony, the youngest, was two they almost weakened, but Hazel was ill, with an ovarian cyst which burst, and that was that. Three much-loved sons but no daughters. Hazel felt it was a kind of judgement but she was not unhappy to have three boys. It was Malcolm who had yearned for a daughter, who had the fantasy of a golden-haired girl to call his own. Sometimes Hazel thought how pleased he'd be if the unknown Shona emerged out of the shadows to confront her – Malcolm would welcome her and be eager to take her into his family. Hazel did not have nightmares about this any longer, but there were times when she would waken in the night and be unaccountably apprehensive and then a cold feeling would creep over her and make her shiver, and she would think 'Shona'. She tried to whisper the name aloud to get rid of it but it stuck in her throat. There was not even the smallest part of her that wanted to see this girl's name made flesh – no, she blocked the reality off completely. Instead, she concentrated on thinking of her as a happy, laughing creature without a care in the world, fortunate and content with her lot, and not even knowing she was adopted – not knowing that the woman who had so carelessly conceived her wished she did not exist. That is the worst thing, Hazel thought, I still wish, however happy she may be, that she had never existed. It doesn't matter to me what she has made of her life, or what life has made of her, I do not want her to exist. She is not nothing to me, not a bit of it. She is a strong, strong presence out there in the world, and I cannot stand up against her unless I deny her right to force retribution upon me.

But these were the exaggerated, melodramatic meanderings of night-time panics and were, thankfully, rare and soon over. She never spoke of them to Malcolm. As the months went on Hazel's thoughts were so full of her sons that there was no room for other speculations about her first-born. Gradually, she relaxed into a sense of security she had never had before. Her life, her happy and successful life resumed, with Malcolm and their children at the centre, and there was neither reason nor cause to feel threatened any more.

Chapter Eleven

LEAH MARRIED Henry Arnesen in St Mary's church on a wild autumn day with the wind howling through the trees in the cathedral close, sending the brilliant-coloured leaves swirling over the heads of the bridal pair as they emerged. Leah pulled her coat tightly around her (she had been married in an elegant pale grey coat and dress made by Henry himself) and shivered. Henry put his arm protectively round her and hurried her along to the Crown and Mitre where the wedding breakfast was to be held. Her head down against the wind, Leah nevertheless saw old Mary, and Evie with her, standing well back in the shadow of the wall, and first anger, then shame, heated her before ever she reached the fire in the inn. She had asked Mary to stay at home, and had thought she had been understood, but now that she had seen her and the child, the pathos of their position was unbearable. She had made them outcasts.

Mary had not after all been evicted, not yet, nor had the knocking-down of her cottage taken place, or been mentioned again by her landlord. She was still living in Wetheral, the sole custodian now of Evie. Henry paid a weekly allowance, enough to mean Mary need no longer take in washing. She couldn't manage the hens so they had been given away and the garden soon grew wild without Leah's care. The whole arrangement worried Henry more than it did Leah. She appeared to see Evie as perfectly well placed, whereas Henry fretted about Mary's age and infirmities and wondered if it was not irresponsible, unchristian even, to leave such a young child with her. He would feel happier, he said, if Mary and Evie were nearer, in Carlisle, but Leah would not hear of it. Henry had wondered also if it might not be kind to visit Evie at regular intervals to check on her welfare and reassure her that she was not forgotten by her mother. Leah was exasperated at his failure to grasp the depth of her desire to separate her child from herself completely. 'It is not natural,' Henry kept muttering. 'No,' agreed Leah, 'it is not.'

She had asked Henry not to tell his mother the true reason why Evie was to remain in Wetheral with Mary. It should be sufficient, argued Leah, to say the child was settled there and it would be wrong to uproot her. Mrs Arnesen accepted this quite happily. She wanted, in any case, to pretend her beloved son's bride was everything she had hoped for – a virgin, a modest, sensible good girl – and not a woman with a past containing a child and an unknown man. She was not at all sure she would be able to take to Leah, pleasing to look at though she was and by all accounts a hard worker. She saw her son Henry as already under Leah's thumb – he, who had been independent and nobody's fool for so long. And she saw clearly that Henry was far more in love with Leah than she with him. It was apparent the moment she saw them together. Leah, she correctly deduced, was making the best of things and in accepting Henry she was thinking of her future, allowing her head to rule her heart.

There were only six people at the wedding breakfast, all Arnesens. It was a subdued affair, though meat and drink were plentiful. It was over within an hour and the newly wed couple set off in Henry's trap for Silloth, bundled up in thick coats and with a blanket across their knees. Henry worried that it would be too cold – he had not reckoned on September weather turning so cold – but Leah enjoyed the ride and did not suffer at all. She had never been to the seaside and was excited at the thought of visiting Silloth, the little town on the Solway coast where Carlisle folk took their holidays. They came towards it along the sea wall, from the Skinburness end, and she felt exhilarated at the sight of the great waves crashing on the shingle. There were fishing boats far out in the firth and she marvelled at the courage of the men in them as she watched the boats all but disappear in the heaving water.

They stayed at the Queen's. Henry had spared no expense. They had a room overlooking the green with the sea just visible through gaps in the trees. There was a roaring fire and supper laid out in front of it – Solway shrimps, and hot buttered toast and Cumberland ham and roast potatoes, and apple pie to follow. They ate heartily and then it was time. The food was taken away, the maid came to turn down the bed, and finally they were left alone. Leah saw Henry put his glasses away and open his arms, and she knew she must respond and walk into his embrace, however much she dreaded it. This was what marriage was about, it was all part of the bargain. It was no good remembering Hugo, no good at all. She tried to act as though she had never known the lust that had overcome her with Hugo nor the exquisite pleasure which had followed, and indeed it was not too difficult. She *felt* like a shy, untutored bride, nervous and hesitant, a young woman who would need tenderness and care to be brought to respond to any caresses, let alone to a full consummation. And Henry treated her as this woman, touching her gently, pressing her to him gently, kissing her so gently at first that she hardly felt his lips and was tickled by his moustache. Yet his caution and respect were irritating to her – she would rather he had been passionate and quick and the whole thing over and done with. It was harder to hide her distaste the longer he tried to rouse her and it was she who broke away and, going over to the bed, swiftly took off her clothes and climbed between the sheets, as a signal that he should hurry and follow. She saw well enough that he was unhappy with this abruptness of hers but eager too and unable to stop himself following her lead. He came to bed and she turned towards him and he immediately clutched her to him and penetrated her, and it was over. She felt nothing at all.

Henry never grew any more skilled as a lover and Leah did not try to teach him, holding that it was not her business. She did not want to have to tell him where she liked to be touched or positioned – that was unnatural; it filled her with revulsion to think that the passion she had instinctively felt with Hugo was now something to re-create artificially. Sometimes Henry, after he had finished, asked her if she was either 'happy' or 'comfortable' but she never replied, only squeezed his hand, which seemed to suffice and reassure him. He was triumphant when she became pregnant immediately and, without any prompting on her part, left off sleeping with her for the sake of the baby. His grief when she miscarried in the fourth month was terrible to witness – if ever she loved Henry, she knew it was then, loved him for his distress and his compassion for her. He nursed her himself, doing all manner of intimate services which no man should have had to do, recoiling not at all from the mess and blood. She was weak afterwards for several months and he never once tried to resume normal relations. It was she who, seeing him plagued with longing as he bid her goodnight, held out her arms to him and assured him she was restored enough to be his wife again. Once more she became pregnant and Henry's joy was tempered with such fear that she felt sorry for him.

They moved house before the baby was born. For a long time Henry had wanted to live somewhere a great deal more salubrious than Globe Lane. He would have liked, in fact, to live at Wetheral, but with Mary and Evie there it was impossible. He searched everywhere for a house near enough to the city for him to get to his place of work, but far enough out of it to be countrified; and eventually he hit on Rockcliffe, a village on the Eden estuary only four miles away. Leah liked the house and the village. It felt quite separate from the city, cut off from it, more so than Wetheral. It was smaller, far less prosperous, and she was not known there. They moved when she was in the sixth month of her pregnancy and she settled in well. It was a long drive for Henry each day but he swore he did not mind and was delighted at how Leah thrived in the bracing air of the estuary. His mother, whom they had been obliged to take with them, hated Rockcliffe and soon moved back to Carlisle, to her sister's home. Leah had the house to herself and was happy.

She experimented with saying this each day as she walked slowly on the marsh, watching the seagulls wheel off above the river-mouth to the open sea. 'I am happy,' she said aloud, and paused. It was, she thought, perhaps her state of pregnancy which made her feel so content and dreamy, and she did not know if it would continue once the child was born. She had an easy life suddenly after years of hardship and was constantly charmed by her luck. She had a husband who adored her and was kind and generous, and a little house all her own, a house it was a pleasure to clean and care for. She was a woman who was indulged and she never stopped marvelling at this unexpected upturn in her fortunes. Thoughts of Hugo were dim and distant and only occasionally troubled her. Sometimes, she fantasised his appearance on her doorstep and could not be sure she would greet him with rapture any longer. Perhaps, perhaps not. She would have a great deal to sacrifice now if Hugo arose and said follow me. The misery of not knowing where he was, the fever of wanting him, no longer burned within her and she supposed this meant that time had done what it was bound to do and healed her wounds.

But one still festered. Mary and Evie were in Carlisle now, in St Cuthbert's Lane. Henry paid the rent and an allowance. Leah had wanted Mary to be kept in Wetheral when at last the long-rumoured eviction (though not the demolition) took place, but Henry said Mary herself had insisted on coming into the city for the sake of the child. This struck Leah as nonsense – children were far safer and healthier out of the city and she did not know what Mary could be thinking of. 'Go and talk to her,' said Henry, but of course she refused. She knew how bitterly old Mary thought of her, and with justice, and was not brave enough. Nor did she wish to set eyes on Evie. Henry had done so. For a long time he kept it secret but she always had suspicions, though she never confronted him with them. In the end he could stand his own deceit no longer and blurted out that he had felt he must see Mary and Evie settled in their new home, it was his duty. She never asked him about them and when she saw he was on the edge of volunteering information she turned away and put her hands over her ears. Once he tried to talk to her about Evie's future, about what would happen if Mary died, as she was bound to soon. She would not discuss this eventuality, but he warned her that he could not stand by and see his step-daughter sent to the workhouse, or a charity home.

Leah hoped that when Henry had his own children he would worry about Evie less. This time she carried the baby to full term, but when labour began she knew almost at once something was wrong. The pains stopped and started and were sluggish, and she began to bleed heavily and to feel the baby as a lead weight within her, without movement. The midwife sent for the doctor at once, saying the afterbirth was coming first and was causing the bleeding. Long before he had come out from Carlisle, Leah had lost consciousness and when she revived she hardly needed to be told her baby was stillborn and that she herself had been on the edge of death. More of Henry's tears, more weary months recovering, far less heart now for trying again, and when she did and a son was born it was only to end in another tragedy. At three months, he contracted whooping-cough and did not survive.

But Leah was still young and, even if a couple of years of unsuccessful child-bearing had sapped her former robust health, she still had every hope of raising a family. The doctor said so, she said so herself, but Henry was pessimistic and despondent. She knew, after they had buried their little son, what he was going to say, long before he managed to dare her fury by putting it into words.

'There's Evie,' he said, tears in his eyes, 'there's a daughter ready-made and waiting.' 'No!' she said, and turned away from him.

They thought of moving to Newcastle, and Leah was all for it even though she loved Rockcliffe – the further away from Evie the better. There was a business opportunity for Henry which both attracted and yet alarmed him. He had expanded the Globe Lane premises and employed a workforce of five now. He saw that if he was to prosper further, as he knew he could, he needed a partner with capital. A partner presented himself, the friend of a customer, but he was a Newcastle man and wanted to stay there. Henry was tempted – the terms he was offered were good – and Leah was encouraging, but in the end his affection for Carlisle and his lack of any spirit of adventure led him to turn the proposition down. He would stay in his home-town and keep his business within his own grasp. A joint venture would not suit him, he said, he liked to be his own master. 'You're afraid,' Leah said, 'that's what it is.' Henry acknowledged perfectly cheerfully that this might indeed be so and he saw nothing wrong with it. He didn't like taking risks, he never had done, and he didn't like change. These folk who emigrated were beyond his comprehension, he added, to be reminded sarcastically by his wife that going to Newcastle, sixty miles away, was hardly the equivalent of emigrating. His last attempt at rationalising the decision was to say he couldn't desert his mother and that she was far too old and frail to move with them.

His mother died soon after the suggested move that had never taken place. Henry's mourning struck Leah as absurd and she upset him by coming as near as she could to saying so. 'She was old,' Leah pointed out, 'and ill, Henry. She had a long life, seventy-two is a fine age to have lived to. What did you expect?' 'She was my mother,' said Henry. Leah had no reply to this undoubted fact. True, Henry's mother had died. But why did her having been his mother make her death in old age so unbearable to him? He had not even liked his mother particularly. He had always been dutiful but had complained under his breath of how tedious she was, how she exasperated him with her fussiness. Now, suddenly, he was distraught. She found it embarrassing, at the funeral, to see her husband's face blotched with tears and see him sway as the coffin descended into its pit. It was ridiculous.

They cleared Mrs Arnesen's things out from her sister's home (this sister, Leah noticed, was gratified by Henry's distress) and once more Henry broke down. He handled his mother's few bits of tawdry jewellery with something like reverence and talked of passing them on to his daughters if he had any. It made Leah feel sick. But she had sufficient insight to realise that half her contempt might spring from the resentment and jealousy she felt because she had never known a mother. It was mysterious, this apparent bond between Henry and a woman to whom he had never been close, a woman sanctified by motherhood.

Soon after his mother's death, Henry came home one day feverish and was ill for nearly a month with pneumonia. Leah was terrified she would lose him, seeing her new-found easy life and contentment disappearing at a stroke, and seeing too that her affection for her husband had grown into something not so far from real love. She nursed him devotedly and when he was out of danger was so overcome with relief she could hardly leave him alone. A weak Henry, hardly able to move, kindled a strange desire in her. It shocked her, that she should find herself wanting to fondle and rouse a man lying on his bed with barely the energy to move his hand to lift a cup, but she could not conceal her agitation. She told him, for the first time, how she loved him and wanted him, and he, too, was more alarmed than captivated by the urgency of her embrace. He convalesced slowly, fretting all the time about his business, worried it would collapse without him. But he was pleasantly surprised. His assistants had managed well, the orders had been dealt with efficiently and had kept coming in. Financially he was still quite secure and the profit margin had barely dropped. The only thing that had been overlooked was the payment of the regular allowance to old Mary – and that was because nobody knew of it except himself and Leah.

He had always paid it in person, on the first of every month. But he had been taken ill on the 29 March and his illness had lasted until mid-May, which meant that Mary had been almost two months without any money. It worried him terribly to think of the consternation and indeed real hardship his failure to pay the allowance would have caused, and he hurried round to St Cuthbert's Lane as soon as he could. He still felt weak and light-headed and returning to work had tired him, but he could not return to Rockcliffe after that first day back in the city without taking money to Mary. He hoped to see Evie too, though Mary seemed to think, for some strange reason, that the child had to be kept hidden or she would be taken away from her. Sometimes, though rarely enough, Evie opened the door to him and then he did everything he could to prolong the interchange between them. His heart always went out to her – she was such an appealing elf of a child with her huge dark eyes and mass of unruly hair. There was nothing of Leah in her that he could see, but that did not detract from the fascination she had for him.

But a strange man opened the door, giving Henry a fright. He visibly started and was for a moment speechless.

'Were you wanting something?' the man said, belligerently, and made to close the door.

'Please,' said Henry, clearing his throat, 'please, where is Mary Messenger?'

'Who?' the man said. 'Mary who?'

'Messenger, Mary Messenger, who lives here with the child Evie.'

'That the old body found dead?'

'Dead?'

'Aye, a month back. Found dead.'

Henry stared at him, shocked and faint, and put out his hand to steady himself. He must have gone paler than he already was, because he heard the man say, 'Here, are you took badly?'

'No,' Henry managed to say, 'no, it was a shock, the news. Do you know what happened to the child?'

'No,' the man said, 'never heard of a child.'

All the way home Henry was rehearsing what he would do. The next day he would begin inquiries and find out where Evie was, then he would go and rescue her and bring her back with him. He would stand no nonsense from Leah. Had he not always said that when Mary died Evie must come to them? It had always been intolerable that she did not live with her mother, and this cruel and unnecessary separation must cease. But when he did reach home Leah greeted him with smiles and her own happy news, and he was not able to plunge immediately into telling her what he had decided.

She was once more expecting a child and that very day the doctor had pronounced her particularly healthy and well. She was to take things very easy, not allow anything to upset her and all would go well, he was sure. So was Leah. She said she felt confident in a way she had never done before and had only waited until he was better to tell him of this latest pregnancy. She was four months now, past the danger period, and the baby would be born close to Henry's own birthday, in September. Seeing her joy, Henry was trapped. Any mention of Evie would result in storms of argument and protest and endanger his wife's well-being. He could not tell her Mary had died nor could he find and claim Evie until after this baby was born. As it was, his quiet rather than rapturous acceptance of the news made Leah anxious once more about his health.

But he began making inquiries, secretly. He quickly discovered where Mary was buried and went to pay his respects and place a wreath on her grave. It was unmarked so he arranged for a stone cross to be made and erected with her name and dates carved upon it. Feeling furtive, he then visited the workhouse to see if Evie had been taken there but, to his relief, she had not. She must be in one of the city's homes for abandoned children, and he did not know where to start, nor was he sure if he should simply tour all the likely establishments in an effort to locate Evie. What was the point if he could not then take her back with him? And besides, a man coming to claim a little girl as his step-daughter would seem suspicious. He had no proof, no documents to brandish nor any explanation which sounded feasible as to how Evie had come to be in a Home. He needed Leah with him and he could not have her at his side until after the baby was born, if then.

Still determined to do the right thing, Henry bided his time uneasily, vowing to himself that he would make these miserable months up to Evie when finally she was with them. Leah never once asked about the welfare of either Mary or her daughter. She never mentioned them, which struck Henry as a sign that she had consigned both of them so successfully to a past she wished forgotten that in her own mind it had, in fact, been obliterated. Meanwhile, she flourished, growing happier and happier as the birth approached. This time, all went well. Leah was safely delivered of a baby girl on 14 September, Henry's own birthday. She would have preferred a son but the relief of giving birth to a fine, strong child was great enough to banish any feelings of disappointment. The baby, named Rose, thrived. She was like Leah from the beginning, with her mother's eyes and mouth and, once it began to grow, her mother's lovely golden hair. Yet gazing adoringly at her or nursing her in his ever-willing arms Henry still thought of poor Evie. When Rose was six months old he decided that at last he could safely speak.

He waited until Rose was asleep and Leah was in a visibly tranquil mood before he began and when he did he begged her first to listen to the end of what he had to say before she said a word herself. Quickly and unemotionally he told her of Mary's death and of Evie's disappearance, and then he said he would not stand for the child's abandonment. Firmly, he said it was their duty to locate and claim her as their own and that he was prepared to override any objections of hers. He understood them but they no longer carried any weight beside Evie's plight. She was only six or seven years old, a poor little thing, and would fit very neatly into their family as an elder sister for Rose. He finished by urging her to consider how there was room enough, surely, in their own happiness for a child who had done no wrong and would have been obliged to suffer much through no fault of her own.

Leah, as instructed, kept silent and did not interrupt. Even when he had stopped speaking she remained quiet. But her expression was mutinous. She turned away from him, walked to the window that overlooked the marsh and stared out of it, though it was already dark outside. He went over to her and put his hands on her shoulders, but she shook them off and moved away to poke the fire. Then she sat herself in front of it, hugging her knees and swaying slightly.

'We'll start visiting the Homes tomorrow,' Henry said. 'There aren't so many, we should be able to go round them all in a few hours. It's a simple question we'll be asking, only a yes or no needed.'

'It isn't simple,' Leah said, and smiled in a way he knew well, in that proud, sly way she could have when she was conscious of her own superiority.

'It is,' Henry said, but warily. 'All we do is ask if Evie Messenger has been brought to them.'

'Messenger isn't her name,' Leah said. 'You won't find her that way, not by giving that name.'

'But it's your name ...'

'True. But it isn't hers, not on the certificate, not in the baptism register.'

'What is her name then?'

'It is her father's.'

'But you weren't ... you weren't ...'

'Afraid to say it, Henry? We weren't married, is that what you're too kind to point out? That's true too, we weren't, but I gave her his name. I said we had been married and showed the ring, and no one queried it. I gave her his name because she was his and I thought it only a matter of time before she was entitled to it.'

'Well, then, we ask for a child of that name.'

'We? I'm doing no asking, Henry.'

'What was his name?'

'You promised never to ask.'

'I'm not asking to know about him, only so as to know the name Evie goes by.'

Leah rocked in front of the fire and said nothing.

'I can find out,' Henry said. 'I can search the baptism register for your name, Leah.'

'You won't find it. I told you. I gave his name.'

'I know her birth date, I can do it that way. I can search the records for that month, June, wasn't it?'

Leah smiled again and Henry realised he did not, in fact, know Evie's birthday. He did not know the day or month and was not even certain of the exact year, it could be 1888 or 1889, or even 1887. Nor, it now occurred to him, did he know where Evie had been baptised. Had it been in Wetheral parish church? Mary would know but Mary was dead.

'Damn it, Leah,' he said, 'you think you can make a fool of me.'

'No,' said Leah. 'You're not a fool. You're good and kind, Henry, I know that, and you want to do right by Evie, but I told you from the start how wicked I was. I cannot bear to have her near me. I wish I could. I know it is not her fault. I know I am unnatural and fail in my duty. You can damn me. But nothing has changed.'

'It has, it has,' broke in Henry excitedly, 'everything has changed. Mary is dead. Evie is suffering in a Home ...'

'You don't know she is suffering. It is a year now, or nearly. She may be settled, or she may have been given to a family. Let her have her own life.'

'Leah,' said Henry, despairingly, 'I don't know how you sleep at night with this on your conscience.'

'My conscience? What do you know about that, Henry Arnesen? My conscience is black and heavy, but I sleep. Whether *he* does I can't know and I don't want to.'

'You could make it light, you needn't have this on your mind.'

'It is not on my mind. I said my conscience was black and heavy, not my mind. My mind is as clear as it ever was. I can't bear to have that child with me and that is that. She's gone now, wherever she is. She's young, she will have no memories.'

'But you're her *mother*, Leah.'

'I am, and it means nothing beyond the word, not where Evie is concerned. To Rose, I am a mother and always will be. I cannot help it, Henry.'

'Evie will never know a mother now ...'

'She might. You cannot tell. She could be with a woman mothering her already. And I did not have a mother, you forget that, and I managed, as children do.'

'But your mother was dead.'

'As I am to Evie.'

There was nothing Henry could do, or nothing he felt able to do, but he bore great resentment against Leah. She had outwitted him and prevented him from following his own instincts. He felt how powerful his wife was in all matters emotional and it angered him. But because he was not the sort of man in whom rage could be sustained, this anger melted down into disapproval and this in turn trickled into feelings of detachment towards Leah. She was set apart somewhere within him because of Evie. Sometimes he found himself regarding her with such a sense of distance that it shocked him. He had to remind himself that this was his wife, the woman he loved greatly and to whom he had once felt joined in every respect. It worried and puzzled him, this strange awareness, but he found he had not the will to fight it. The birth of another daughter, Polly, two years after Rose made Leah into even more of a mother and, so it seemed to him, less of a wife. In a way it was a relief. He got on with his work and she got on with her mothering and he never again mentioned Evie.

The Arnesens stayed in Rockcliffe until Rose was of school-age and then Leah began to think they should move back into the city. She wished her daughters to be educated in a way she had not been and, though the village school would serve to begin with, she thought Rose and Polly ought to go on to the new Higher Grade School. Henry, whose own education, while far superior to Leah's, had not amounted to much (though he wrote a fine hand and kept excellent accounts), was in agreement. So when Rose was seven they moved back to Carlisle to a house in Stanwix with a fine view of the park and the river. It was a larger house than they had had in Rockcliffe but still a modest dwelling, though its location made it more expensive than Henry had expected. The girls went to Stanwix School, of which Leah greatly approved. The children were all from good homes and were clean and well-dressed, as of course were her own daughters, clad in the dresses and coats their father made so exquisitely. To be the wife and daughters of a tailor was a fine thing, though Henry himself did not do much of the actual tailoring any more. He was head of a regular little emporium, Arnesen & Co., with premises in Lowther Street, and supervised a staff of thirty. His own prosperity pleased him but he never took it for granted. Every year he salted away his profits in careful investments and, though he was generous to his family, he never got carried away. Leah took pride in Henry's carefulness. It was why she had married him, recognising as she had done his sound commonsense as well as his talent and willingness to work hard. Whenever Polly, who was inclined to impertinence, complained of her father's meanness Leah would admonish her sternly and declare Henry the most generous man in the world and tell Polly she did not realise how grateful she should be.

Leah was grateful. When she looked back to the horror of that period after the birth of Evie and remembered how Henry had provided the way out of the trap she had sprung on herself, she was overcome with gratitude. She thought she might have ended by murdering Evie. She had been mad inside herself while functioning perfectly on the surface – mad with grief and resentment and a terrible unjustified hatred. She'd seen her whole life wrecked by Evie, whom she would have to carry on her back for ever. At first the tiny child had been a symbol of that love she and Hugo had had for each other, and she had been precious, but gradually she had become significant in a different way, as a symbol, instead, of betrayal, of stupidity. She could no longer see Evie in her mind's eye, which was a comfort since that image had the power to torture her with its pathos, but she still felt her presence in a shadowy way from time to time, usually in occasional moments of low spirits.

She trained herself not to wonder, not ever, where Evie was, or what she was doing – that way real madness lay. Evie was gone, long since. Guilt had been kept at bay for so long that Leah considered it defeated, but never quite admitted this to herself. Five years, ten years, nearly twenty years, and now Evie would be a woman. No longer need fear of her lurk within that conscience she had once told Henry was black and heavy. Whatever had happened to Evie was now complete. The child had grown, the pathetic mite was no more and not even Henry could reproach her by trying to conjure up a vision of a poor weeping little soul searching for her mother. Evie would no longer need a mother.

But she did.

Chapter Twelve

THE WOMAN was thick-set and tall with long untidy hair tied back with an elastic band. The weight of the hair, which Hazel felt would normally have hung free, a chaotic mess, seemed to pull the skin of her face tight, giving it an unpleasantly strained appearance. She wanted to tell the warder to let the woman wear her hair loose, but that was silly since it might be so fiercely yanked back at the woman's own request. Both her hands were heavily bandaged. Hazel could see a tiny spot of blood near the wrist on the left hand though the dressings looked absolutely clean, freshly done.

'Are you the lawyer?' the woman asked. Hazel said she was, tried to say it with a pleasant smile, showing sympathy. She was aware she was not good at sympathy, or rather not good at demonstrating it. Did this make her a bad or good solicitor? She was never sure. Malcolm always said detachment was important but she felt her failing was to appear to carry this too far and it troubled her. It was not that she was afraid of being involved with clients, particularly clients of this sort, but that she did not know how to project what she felt. More was expected of women in this situation and she could tell already that this client was disappointed in her.

'Well, then,' the woman said, 'tell them they can't take my baby away. Tell them. Tell them the law says she's mine. I had her. She's mine. They've no right. Tell them.'

Hazel sat down. The warder stood leaning against the wall, near the door, and the woman, Stella Grindley, sat opposite. They were quite close. Hazel could smell the soap used to wash Stella's clothes. She thought Stella must be able to smell her perfume, faint though the scent was, and wished she had not worn any. It might seem tantalising, a reminder of the outside world and the kind of lives lived in it which

Stella could not share. She felt all her own senses heightened and this led to a tension in her which she struggled to dissipate before she began speaking. Everything she was obliged to say would be resented by Stella Grindley and though she was prepared for this, she was not prepared to deal with the rage and grief her information would surely release.

She spoke as quietly but as firmly as possible, choosing her words carefully, making them as clear and simple as she was able without being patronising. What she had to tell Stella was simple enough, after all. She could not keep her three-month-old baby, just as she had not been allowed to keep the last two. A place of safety order had been obtained and the baby was in the process of being adopted. Stella had been arrested outside King's Cross Station on charges of soliciting, stealing and common assault. She had been drunk, five months' pregnant and had a string of convictions behind her. At the age of forty her record was enough to make it out of the question that she should be allowed to keep this latest child, born while serving her sentence. She had already been told this, which was why she had cut her wrists with a piece of broken mirror glass she had managed to secrete. The cuts were not deep, her life had never been in danger, but her intention had been serious. This, she thought, was her last baby. She had had eight and kept none of them. The first four she had had with her for their first few years but then they had been taken into care. The fifth had died, apparently a cot death (though there had been some doubt at the time and suspicions of fatal neglect were raised). The last three were all taken away at birth or soon after.

When Hazel had finished the sad recital of what the law said, Stella Grindley was silent for a moment and then, with a speed which was shocking and took even the warder by surprise, she leaned forward and spat at Hazel a great gob of saliva which landed in the middle of her white blouse. 'You can fuck off,' Stella shouted, 'and so can the law. Go on, fuck off, you're useless.' The warder had already moved forward to restrain her but restraint was unnecessary. Content now, Stella sat still on her chair and folded her arms and smiled. 'Stupid little bitch you are,' she said. 'You know nothing.' She was reprimanded for language by the warder but ignored her. She was watching Hazel, who remained in her own chair, deliberately making no attempt either to inspect or mop up the patch on her blouse. She held Stella's stare and did not blink – she knew that of course she should get up and go without another word but she could not do it.

She was held by Stella Grindley's contempt and wanted to challenge it. It was unwise, but she could not resist asking, 'Do *you* think you are fit to care for a baby?'

'She's mine,' Stella said. 'I had her.'

'Nobody denies that. But you can't care for her. You have no home, no money, no job, you're always drunk and you're in and out of prison. You are not fit, are you, to care for a baby? The law is only safeguarding the child.'

'She's mine. I had her. I'm her mother and I'm not giving her away and I'm not letting them take her away and you can go fuck yourself.'

'That's enough,' the warder said. 'Time's up.'

Hazel watched Stella Grindley being taken away and then followed. It was stupid of her to have hoped for any kind of rational discussion. Stella's only argument was one of possession: she had created and given birth to the child and therefore she was hers. In her mind, simple. There had been no point after all in Hazel's sanctimonious recital. The law was right to say what it did, but Hazel recalled most vividly the cut wrists and the yearning for the child – a yearning so powerful even if it seemed based not so much on overwhelming love as on fury at being cheated – and she was uneasy in her own mind. Efforts had been made, she knew, to help Stella cope with her children. She had been helped over and over again by the social services to reform so that she might keep her babies. Places in hostels had been found for her, grants of money procured, and even work found at one stage. But always she reverted to drinking and soliciting and stealing and, when in a temper, which was often, attempting to beat people up.

This latest baby would be adopted. Lucky baby, to escape Stella Grindley as a mother? But even while thinking this, Hazel was rejecting the underlying premise, that only good, decent, clean-living sober women could be allowed to be mothers. She drove home knowing there was something wrong somewhere in this obvious truth. Stella had indeed given birth to her baby and it was *her*, as well as *hers*, an indisputable part of herself. That could not be contested, that fact could not be changed. It did not matter who adopted the baby, it was still Stella's and always would be. Caring for it was different. Stella had shown she could not care for it and any anguish she felt at having it taken away was as nothing compared to the anguish a child would suffer if left in her care.

What, then, Hazel wondered, worries me so much? Stella's passion to keep her own baby, that's what. For whatever reason. A passion that made her cut her wrists. A passion I never felt, not once, for that baby whom I allowed to be taken away from me. Stella Grindley would think me a monster, not just a bitch, if she knew.

And then there was the evidence of Stella's suffering. She was suffering because her baby was being taken away, there was no doubt about that. There was always the mother's suffering, of one sort or another, in these cases. Stella was experiencing a terrible sense of loss. And I, Hazel wondered, did I suffer? And if I did, did I have any right to?

She became obsessed, in the days that followed, with this question, to the point of several sleepless nights when she disturbed Malcolm with her feverish tossing and turning. 'What's the matter?' he asked, but she said nothing. How could she tell him she was wondering if she had had any right to be regarded as having suffered at eighteen when she had that first unwanted baby? She did not want to return to any mention of the subject. What she had suffered from, she decided, was a failure of compassion. At eighteen, she had had no acquaintance with such a sophisticated emotion. She had thought only of herself, as young people do, of her own life being wrecked. There had never been any inclination to think beyond that.

But supposing she had thought about her baby as anything but an object to be disposed of – what then? Supposing she had had the imagination as well as the compassion to think of this baby as a person who would have feelings and dreams and desires, and to whom the deliberate denial of any attachment by his or her mother, would seem a terrible thing? She tried to think of having wanted to keep her baby, of being determined to do so at any cost to herself. It seemed to her extraordinary, all these years later, that she had never once thought of saying to her mother that she wanted to have and keep the baby. What would her mother have said? The temptation to ask began to plague her. Almost eighteen years had gone by and they had never, except for that brief moment when her mother had tentatively wondered if she had told Malcolm, talked about it. It made her realise what she supposed she had always really known, that she and her mother, by the tacit agreement of both of them, never discussed anything that was distressing or difficult. It was a habit she had grown up with and kept to without ever attempting to force a different kind of communication. But now she wanted some kind of confrontation all these years too late – she wanted to know what her mother had really thought and felt, and most of all what she thought she would have done if her daughter had not fallen in so obediently with her plans.

Mrs Walmsley, at almost sixty, was busier than ever. Every day she had some charity work to do, of the organisational variety, and when she was not sitting on committees she was taking her work as a magistrate seriously – it was all action, just as she liked life to be. Then there was her role as grandmother which she relished and threw herself into. Seven grand-children, all living in or near London, so that she saw them often and had them to stay frequently. During the holidays she was much in demand, often taking her grandchildren to stay with her in her Gloucestershire cottage. She came to know the Science Museum, the Imperial War Museum, and the British Museum intimately, not to mention the Planetarium and the Zoo (though she refused to set foot in Madame Tussaud's, pronouncing it vulgar). Hazel, whenever she rang her mother, which was not as often as she felt she ought to, was treated to such a stream of approaching appointments that she felt she should get off the phone quickly. Delivering and collecting her own sons to and from their grandmother's she had only the most hurried of chats, since her mother was, if anything, busier than her busy self. It was impossible to contemplate any level of serious conversation in such circumstances. She knew she would have to wait until the next occasion when her mother came for supper and stayed the night, something she did no more than three or four times a year.

She was surprised, when the opportunity came, how hard it was to bring up the subject that troubled her. Of course, her mother never stopped talking, so it was always a strain trying to find a gap in her energetic résumé of her own activities, but when finally she paused long enough for Hazel to say anything at all, the words were slow in coming.

'Mother?' Hazel said.

'Yes, dear? But not next week, I am going to be *frantic* next week, not a spare hour ...'

'I wasn't going to ask you to do anything.'

'Oh, good, because I simply couldn't manage to take on another thing, not even for you, darling, so what was it, what was it you wanted to ask?'

'I'm not sure really,' Hazel said, faltering, before she had even begun. 'It's awkward, rather embarrassing actually ...'

'Embarrassing?' Mrs Walmsley said, astonished. 'Good heavens, Hazel, how can anything between us be embarrassing, how ridiculous. What is it? What's happened?'

Hazel heard the note of excitement in her mother's voice. Probably she thought she was going to be treated to some tale of adultery and even now was calculating who was having a fling, her daughter, or her son-in-law.

'It's about when I was young,' Hazel said.

'Oh.'

Smiling slightly at her mother's obvious disappointment, Hazel plunged into explanations but speaking in a staccato fashion quite foreign to her normal smooth speech patterns. 'When I was seventeen. Pregnant. That time. And I came to you. Told you. You took over. You organised everything. Well, what if ... I mean, what if I'd said I wanted to keep the baby ...'

'Absurd, you wouldn't have been so absurd,' burst in Mrs Walmsley. 'It never entered your head, thank God.'

'Why "thank God"?'

'Why? Really, Hazel. It would have ruined your life, of course it would, saddled with a *child* at seventeen, eighteen when you had it. What on earth would you have done with it? How could you have gone to university? An unmarried mother at eighteen – good heavens.'

'But if I had, Mother, if I'd refused to part with the baby once I'd had it, what would you have done?'

'Made you see sense.'

'So you wouldn't have helped?'

'No. What is this, Hazel? I don't understand.'

'What if I'd told Daddy ...'

'Told your father? He'd have been livid, he'd have wanted to find the boy and horsewhip him. There would have been the most fearful fuss, it makes me quite ill to imagine the scenes. No, you couldn't have told your father, impossible. It was essential the whole thing should be kept secret.' She paused, eyeing Hazel critically and with exasperation. 'You're a happily married woman, darling, with three lovely children and a good career, and here you are being silly, not like yourself at all. You're usually so sensible, you always have been except for that one bit of madness, and now you're plaguing yourself and me with all this speculation about what might have been said and done half a lifetime ago. It's so unnecessary.'

Hazel sat quietly for a few moments, watching her mother who was perched on the very edge of her chair, back rigid, head high, face flushed, a vision of righteous indignation. It was late. The boys had been in bed for ages, and Malcolm had retreated to his study a good hour ago.

'Let's stop talking about it anyway,' her mother said. 'It's bedtime, I've a long day tomorrow and so have you.'

'No.'

'What? Well, if you haven't, I have and ...'

'No, Mother, please, let's not stop. I want to understand and I don't. I've wanted to for ages.'

'*Understand?* What are you talking about? There is no mystery about what happened, it might have been kept secret but it wasn't mysterious, we behaved quite logically ...'

'That's it. All head, no heart, no thought for the baby, not from you or from me ... appalling ... I don't understand it.'

'It's perfectly easy to understand. You were a child yourself, you couldn't keep a baby, and it was thought about, it was thought about most carefully, I was most concerned it should go to good people, and I was assured it did.'

'But how could you or anyone else know? How could you know the people who adopted my baby were good?'

'Miss Østervold knew one of them. They had references, I expect, and ...'

'You didn't ask?'

'It wasn't my job, it was the responsibility of the organisation those ladies worked for.'

'No, it was ours, yours, since I just did what you said like an obedient little girl.'

'Hazel, are you accusing me of having failed in my duty?'

'No. I just want to understand how you could let me, encourage me, order me really to give my baby away.'

'You *wanted* to ...'

'Yes, yes, I did. I know, I certainly did. I wanted to get rid of it, true, quite true, but you were older and wiser, you were a mother yourself and knew what it meant ...'

'It meant doing the best for *you*, that's what it meant. It's what it always should mean, and that's all I thought about.'

'Didn't you ache for the baby, didn't it break your heart to think of the poor, motherless, rejected ...'

'Stop it!' Mrs Walmsley got up. 'I'm going to bed, I won't have this, it's unseemly and upsetting.'

'I'm sorry,' Hazel said, 'I don't want to upset you, but I'm upset myself. I thought I'd got over the guilt' – her mother clicked her tongue at this – 'a long time ago, but recently I've started thinking about what I did and it shocks me. I only wanted to know if it shocks you, when you think back.'

'I don't think back, there's no point.'

'Don't you wonder about your lost granddaughter sometimes?'

'Never. Lost granddaughter? I never think of there being such a thing. She isn't my granddaughter, wherever she is, she's the granddaughter of whichever family took her as their own.'

'And when they tell her?'

Mrs Walmsley, having gathered up her book and knitting and spectacles, and being ready now to go to bed as she had announced she would, began to leave the room, ignoring this last question. But Hazel followed her and stood in the doorway and repeated it. 'When they tell her, Mother? Tell her she was given away?'

'She may never be told. Lots of adopted children never are, and why should they be?'

'But if she were told?'

'Hazel, I'm tired, let me pass, I must go to bed.'

Hazel let her pass but went on following her, up the stairs to the spare room. She shut the door behind the two of them and stood with her back to it while her mother put her things down and picked up her nightdress and turned the bed covers down.

'What if she's the sort of girl who demanded to know everything?'

'Highly unlikely.'

'Not if she's my daughter, your granddaughter, *us*, not unlikely at all, she'll demand to know, and what then?'

'What do you mean, "What then?" I really don't see what you're getting at, Hazel, and I haven't since you started all this.'

'She has the right to make us suffer.'

'Hazel! I cannot stand this. Now let me go to the bathroom and when I come back I don't want to see you still here. Go to bed.'

Hazel went to bed. There was no point in trying to get her mother to help her nor any hope of comfort. Her mother had always been a woman of few doubts about her own behaviour. A blessing, really, to be like that, convinced that what one did was right. It made decisions simple – not the making of them so much as the bearing of the consequences. Once her baby had been 'dealt with' Hazel saw that her mother had obliterated all memory of her. Remorse was a word with which she had little acquaintance. The following morning, Hazel apologised. Her mother, smiling very brightly and at her most cheerful, stopped her and said she'd forgotten 'that little scene' already, and then she swept out to begin her deliciously hectic day.

Hazel never again assumed she might be able to form a new relationship with her mother, one based on an exchange of real feeling instead of superficial concern, which had always dictated a strange kind of wary politeness. But she knew that though seeming superficial, because it manifested itself in careful language, her mother's concern for her was not in the least shallow. She did care deeply, she did, as she had said, do everything, in her own opinion, for her daughter's good. What had angered her was that Hazel had challenged this. She had dared to suggest that what Mrs Walmsley had seen as the only course of action had not been the only course. Even more offensive had been the suggestion that she had had another duty, one she had failed to acknowledge, to the baby. Nothing hurt her mother more, as Hazel knew, than implying any dereliction of maternal duty. But she would not risk doing so again. The matter was closed.

In her own mind, it began to close again too. She did not do any more work connected with adoption. She went on dealing with Family Law, moving as time went on into Divorce Law, and specialising in cases where women had been beaten and abused. For months at a time she was untroubled by stray thoughts of that baby she had given away; and even when, for some reason, the memory was triggered, she was able to deal with it calmly. The older her sons grew and the more consuming family life became, the less she was bothered by her conscience. The little pricks of fear which had alarmed her disappeared, and she became serene and less wary.

That proved, eventually, to have been a mistake.

Part Three

Evie – Shona

Chapter Thirteen

EVIE HAD imagined Carlisle would be familiar to her but it was not. All the long way in the coach she had been remembering St Ann's, high on the hill above the river Eden, and in her mind's eye she had seen again the outline of the squat castle and the glint of the sun on the cathedral windows. She knew the bridge would be crowded as the coach left Stanwix and crossed the Eden into the city and that the streets round the market would be jammed with people and animals being driven home from the Sands. She expected to feel happy that she was back in her home town and was dismayed, when the coach stopped outside the Crown and Mitre, to discover that everything she saw looked different. The town hall market place was not the cheerful, friendly place she had remembered, full of women sitting beside makeshift stalls and with their children playing all around. It teemed with carriages and coaches and she was startled to see her first tram careering noisily along its iron rails. Her heart began to thud and she stood motionless, clasping her bag, not knowing what to do, and suddenly aware of the enormity of the decision she had made.

She had to go somewhere. She could not stand in front of the Crown and Mitre all day transfixed by the turmoil before her. But moving was difficult because of her heavy bag, which she could not carry more than a few yards without stopping. Her vague idea was to go back to the only place she knew, St Cuthbert's Lane, where she had lived with old Mary, but she knew this would be foolish. Somebody else would be living in the house where she had once lived and the sight of a girl carrying all her worldly goods in a shabby carpet bag would not appeal to them. But where could she go? She had no money for a lodging-house and the only people she knew of in Carlisle were the Messengers who ran the pub in Caldewgate and had occasionally called in at the Fox and Hound. She supposed she could claim truthfully to be of their family and therefore worthy of shelter, but she could not go to them. They would report her presence in due course to Ernest, who would come and get her. Even if he did not, and she was sure he would, she did not want Ernest and Muriel to know where she was.

She could go to the Home, to St Ann's, if she could get herself there, if she could beg a lift on a cart going in that direction. They might take her in, give her a bed in return for her labour. But that was another likely place Ernest might look, and besides she had only bad memories of the Home. Fleetingly, and she knew it was foolishly, she thought of the woman who had taken her to the house in West Walls on the day Mary had died.

Standing with her back to the wall of the hotel, her bag at her feet, Evie stared straight ahead as though having a vision. Nobody appeared to notice her. She was quite insignificant in her drab coat and the dark brown bonnet she wore had a wide rim which shaded her small face. She looked like a girl waiting to be collected, waiting with patience and resignation, and gave no hint of the inner terror she was experiencing. An hour she stood there, two hours, three hours. The crowds never seemed to diminish nor the clamour lessen. She heard the cathedral bells chime and watched the time on the Town Hall clock. It was already midday. She was lucky that the sun shone, though she was standing on the side of the main street which was now in shadow, and that there was none of that biting wind there had been earlier when she had left the Fox and Hound.

Opposite her she had been watching a scene she did not at first understand. There were a great many ladies milling about, all well dressed to Evie's untutored eye, and all pointing and talking to each other. They were pointing at girls, poor-looking girls, all of whom stood stock-still, many of them on wooden crates. The ladies walked round these crates and appeared to examine the girls, who looked downcast and mournful, then they would halt and some interchange would take place. Sometimes a girl would then step off the box and follow one of the women. Evie strained to see where they went, but could never quite make out their destination – woman and girl were both swallowed up in the crowds. It took her the whole morning to work out that what she was witnessing was the hiring of servants. There could be no other explanation. She had never known this could happen, there had been nothing like it in Moorhouse, but now it seemed blindingly obvious that this would be her salvation.

She was worried as she dragged her bag into the space in front of the Cross, where the girls were on view, that there was perhaps some system of which she was not aware. Was any girl allowed just to appear and offer herself for hire? She saw some older, rough-looking women standing a little way off, eyeing the girls, and when one of this group rushed forward and took a coin from a lady holding the arm of a girl she had selected Evie realised she was the mother. Maybe a girl had to be owned and brought for hire by her mother. Well, she had no mother and if this debarred her from trying to be hired she would soon find out. She did not have a crate to stand on either. Instead, she stood on her bag. There was nothing in it that could be damaged, it was full of soft goods. She knew she looked odd, perched on the carpet bag, and not like the other girls. There were few of them left now, the majority had been claimed, and those that remained looked pathetic specimens. They were thin and dirty with bare feet and sorry-looking clothes. Evie, in her tweed coat and felt bonnet and buttoned boots, knew she looked too grand but she could not help that. It was the one time in her life she had felt in any way superior and this only embarrassed her. She could not bear to look directly at any of the ladies inspecting her and dropped her eyes, as indeed she had seen most of the girls do.

She did not have long to wait.

'What have we here?' she heard a voice say. Evie knew the question must be directed at her but kept quiet. 'Are you for hire, girl?'

She nodded her head.

'Look at me when you're spoken to,' the sharp voice instructed, and obedient as ever Evie looked up. She disliked what she saw. This lady was not like the others she had noticed. She was tall and heavy, dressed all in black, with a fierce, red face and a cane upon which she was leaning hard. She was much older than any of the other ladies who had hired girls and she was by herself. 'Age?' she snapped, staring at Evie.

'Eighteen, ma'am.'

The lady snorted. 'Eighteen indeed! And if you are, which I doubt, too old to be hired. Did you know that? So you see you should have told the truth. You are fifteen, am I right?'

Evie stayed silent and did not move.

'Hold out your hands.'

Evie held them out. The lady touched them, turned them over. Evie knew her hands were rough with all the time they had spent doing dirty work. They were covered in keens too, where she had cut herself and some of these cuts had festered and left little scars. But the lady seemed satisfied.

'Open your mouth,' was the next command. Evie opened it. She had had four teeth pulled last winter but otherwise she had all her teeth and they were sound, the travelling dentist had said so. 'Where are you from?' the lady asked next. Evie still stayed silent. 'Are you a runaway? Have you left a situation?' Evie shook her head. 'Then how do you come to be here, miss, coming from nowhere? Were you turned off?'

'No,' Evie managed to say.

'Where is your home?' the lady said, impatiently. 'You have to have had a home. I cannot take a girl with no home. You might be anybody, a thief, a little whore, how would I know? Where is your mother?'

'Haven't got a mother,' said Evie, worrying if that was strictly true.

'Father?'

She shook her head again.

'Have you come from the workhouse?'

More head-shaking.

'No, you do not look as if you have. You've been cared for. Out of the city?'

'Yes,' said Evie.

'A long way away?'

'Yes.'

'So you are a runaway. The police will be on to you, or whoever. Unless you are eighteen and small and had the right to leave, I don't know. Get off that bag. What's in it? No stolen silver or the like?'

'No,' said Evie.

'What then?'

'My clothes and shoes.'

The lady went on staring at her for a long time. Evie tried not to flinch. She knew this person would be trying to judge her character from her face and demeanour, and she tried to put into her expression her honesty and obedience and desire to work hard and not be any trouble. She knew she had succeeded when the lady said,

'Very well, I will take the risk, but I'll be watching you and one sign of impertinence or worse and you'll be out. Now pick up that bag and follow me.'

Luckily, the lady walked so slowly because of her age and needing her stick that Evie had no difficulty making her way behind her. There was a pony trap waiting on the corner of Bank Street and the lady got into it and gestured to Evie to do the same. An old, vacant-looking man was driving the trap and as soon as both women were settled, he flicked his whip and the pony set off at the slowest of paces. Nobody spoke. They went down Bank Street and round the corner into Lowther Street and round another corner into a square. Evie saw the houses here were all very tall and set close together in terraces. The trap stopped outside a house in the middle of the terrace on the far side of the square and the lady was helped out by the driver. He did not help Evie nor did he lift down her bag. She managed to heave it on to the pavement, though the effort strained her arms. Slowly the lady mounted the stone steps and the door was opened as she reached it.

'God knows what I've brought back with me, Harris,' she muttered, 'but in an emergency beggars cannot be choosers. We'll have to watch her like hawks.'

Evie saw a very tiny woman, surely even older than the lady who had hired her, standing holding the door.

'I don't like this at all, Mrs Bewley,' the tiny woman said. 'It isn't right, going to a hiring, it isn't proper, it isn't safe, it isn't for the likes of you, it isn't ...'

'Oh, hold your tongue!' snapped Mrs Bewley. 'I know all that, for heaven's sake. But we need a strong young girl, we can't go on without Hattie and Ella. The place is going to rack and ruin. You're too old, I'm too old, and the discomfort was becoming insupportable. It was time I used my eyes and my head to see if I couldn't find better staff myself. So be silent, woman. Take her up to the attic and then bring her down and get her started.'

Afterwards, Evie did not know how she had survived the first months in Mrs Bewley's household. She had thought she knew what hard work was, brought up as she had been in the Fox and Hound, but she quickly decided that working for Muriel and Ernest had been restful compared to slaving for Mrs Bewley and Harris. They had her up at five each morning and she was never allowed to crawl to bed before midnight, with only a few minutes here and there throughout the day for her to eat and rest. She was, in the full meaning of the description, the maid of *all* work. And the work, too, was infinitely harder than it had been at the Fox and Hound. The Fox and Hound was a pub but it was not large. There were only six rooms besides the bar and all of them were small. But 10 Portland Square had twelve huge rooms on five floors and sixty-six stairs connecting them. Evie had to clean them all, take coal for fires to half of them and wait at table besides. She was drunk with exhaustion, visibly swaying on her feet by six in the evening, but if this was noticed it was never commented on. Often she thought that if the food she was given had been more substantial she would have had more strength, but she rarely had a good meal and existed mostly on bread and margarine and sometimes cheese or an egg. She had always been thin but now she saw there was hardly any flesh on her and her ribs showed through alarmingly. She could feel them with her hands as she dressed and undressed and she loathed that feeling, the evidence that she was becoming little more than a skeleton.

What sustained her was knowing she was in Carlisle, and therefore near her mother. Somewhere in this city Leah Messenger lived and, given time and opportunity, Evie would surely find her. She was allowed to go to church on Sunday, a request Mrs Bewley obviously felt bound to grant, though she was disbelieving that Evie really intended to go to church. 'A churchgoer?' she had queried, and had promptly subjected Evie to an interrogation. She had been challenged to recite the Lord's Prayer and, when this proved easy, the Creed. Only when, for good measure, she had thrown in a few Psalms, faultlessly recited (Mrs Bewley got her prayer book and checked), was Evie grudgingly believed. Mrs Bewley herself did not go to church, on account of her leg, she said, but she directed Evie to St Cuthbert's. St Paul's was nearer, but Mrs Bewley did not approve of the vicar for reasons she did not divulge.

Every Saturday night, no matter how exhausted she was, Evie felt uplifted by the approaching excitement of Sunday. She could hardly sleep for the anticipation of perhaps seeing her mother without knowing it – any one of the women in church could be her mother. She knew, after the first Sunday, that Leah was not going to be found in the choir of St Cuthbert's, since it was all male, and perhaps not in any choir, but she was sure she would be in some church on Sundays. The church she really longed to go to was Holy

Trinity, but it was twice the distance from Portland Square as St Cuthbert's, and Mrs Bewley timed her return. If she came back a minute later than the ten minutes allowed for the distance there would be trouble, and trouble was not something Evie could afford to risk. Even after she had been in Mrs Bewley's household for a year she continued to be very careful to give total satisfaction and not to cause offence. But she saw that her goodness and her tolerance of harsh treatment in itself aroused suspicion. Mrs Bewley could not believe a young woman could be so docile and hard-working if she did not have some sinister ulterior motive. Sometimes she would look at Evie and say, 'So butter doesn't melt in your mouth, it seems,' which would be followed, after a significant pause, by, 'I don't believe it, you're too good to be true, you are, Miss. I'm watching you, mind.'

Watch Evie she did, closely, continously, and Evie was fully aware of her scrutiny. She knew Mrs Bewley hauled herself up all the narrow stairs to the attic on Sunday mornings and inspected it for stolen goods, though what there was to be stolen Evie could not imagine. She supposed jewels, since Mrs Bewley wore plenty of them. She had many glittering rings to decorate her gnarled fingers, and her throat was always circled with pearls. But if none of these was missing, why, Evie wondered, did Mrs Bewley go searching for them? At least her search would be quickly over. There were three truckle beds in the attic, but of course Evie used only one and was glad she did not have to share the miserable space with the two other maids there had once been in Mrs Bewley's employment. Otherwise there was only a chest of drawers and Evie's old bag to ferret around in and that could not take long. Yet Sunday after Sunday she could tell Mrs Bewley had yet again put herself through the pointless ordeal of climbing up to the attic and Evie marvelled at such persistence. The strain made her employer even more bad-tempered than usual and, if the thought of Sunday morning made Evie happy, the thought of Sunday evening depressed her. Nothing was ever right during the rest of the Sabbath. Every service she performed was criticised and it was on Sunday nights she invariably gave way and cried herself to sleep.

She was always ashamed of this weakness. She had hardly ever cried as a child, when she had felt desolate and despairing, but now she seemed to need to. It did no harm. No one knew she cried. She rose soon after dawn on Monday mornings with no visible evidence of having wept and neither Mrs Bewley nor Harris saw her at that hour. She had fires to rake out and reset, and the kitchen range to black-lead, and all manner of gruelling jobs they were not around to see. Nobody spoke to her until noon and then only to give her orders. In that vast house there were only the two old women, and most of the cleaning and polishing Evie did was to keep unused rooms in perfect condition. Only four rooms were regularly used – the kitchen, the dining-room, the breakfast room, and Mrs Bewley's bedroom – though the drawing-room fire was lit once a week when Mrs Bewley received visitors. These were few. The vicar of St Cuthbert's came every three weeks, took a cup of tea and departed within the half hour. The doctor came once a month, took a glass of sherry and made his escape even more quickly. Otherwise there was only a lady called Miss Mawson.

Evie did not know who Miss Mawson was, or why she visited Mrs Bewley every week, staying at least an hour. 'This is my new maid,' Mrs Bewley said to Miss Mawson the first time Evie was in her presence (bringing in more coal for the fire) but she did not, of course, tell Evie who Miss Mawson was. Only Harris could have done that, but Harris never engaged in any kind of conversation with Evie. She was very deaf in any case and completely in her own world. She shuffled about the house doing little except issue orders to Evie, and when she was asked a question never replied. In the mornings Harris did the orders for the day, sitting at the kitchen table and laboriously writing lists. These lists were the same every day, but every day they were made on a fresh sheet of paper. Harris's real job was to cook, but she had told Evie she was the housekeeper and that Evie was to remember that. She had no interest in Evie at all (unlike Mrs Bewley, who was consumed with curiosity as to her background and real identity). It was easy to imagine how maids could have run rings round this old Harris without her noticing, until Mrs Bewley would have been mad with rage. In fact, she heard Miss Mawson say, 'Thank goodness you have got rid of those two wicked girls. I hope this one will be more satisfactory.' Evie longed to hear Mrs Bewley's reply, but it was not given while she was still in the room.

Miss Mawson always came at three o'clock in the afternoon and it became one of Evie's many jobs to let her in. Harris liked to receive people but her deafness meant she very often did not hear either the bell or the knocker, and Evie had been told to answer the door herself. She changed her clothes to do so, which is to say she took off the all-enveloping grey calico apron and cap she wore in the mornings to do dirty jobs, and put on an old white apron of Harris's. This was quite an attractive garment and Evie liked it. It only covered her front, exposing rather too much of her by now woefully worn once best dress, but it had frills round the shoulder straps and the bottom edge. It had been starched and kept pristine and dazzled Evie with its whiteness. Harris was no taller than she was herself, so this splendid apron fitted her and, while wearing it, she felt she had some self-respect after all. Miss Mawson was always particularly gracious to her, saying, 'Good afternoon, Evie' and 'Thank you, Evie' when her coat was taken, and 'Goodbye, Evie' as she left. Evie loved the sound of these simple pleasantries and murmured them to herself afterwards. Miss Mawson had a way of investing the unremarkable words with some real meaning and it was comforting to hear her. Also to see her. Evie did not know her age, but she thought Miss Mawson not more than forty or perhaps younger. She had lovely clothes in muted colours, dresses of lilac silk and pearl grey wool and blouses intricately embroidered round the cuffs and collars. She was, in fact, elegant in an understated way, and Evie responded to this elegance instinctively.

She wanted very much to discover where Miss Mawson lived and why such a kind lady visited the unkind Mrs Bewley so regularly and often, but she never came any nearer to doing so. But she saw Miss Mawson at church. Evie always sat near the back in an aisle seat behind a stone pillar. She crept in some five minutes before morning service began and took a prayer book and hymn book from the sidesman without looking at him. She liked to sit listening to the organ and preparing herself for the first hymn, but now and again she would look up and across the pew and watch the grander folk make their confident way down the main aisle to the family pews. They always held their heads so high, these people, and the mothers in particular were beautifully dressed in their Sunday best. There would be a good deal of subdued hissing at sulky children who were not being quiet enough and then the family group would settle down, a row of bent heads saying their prayers. Evie looked and drew her coat tighter around herself, feeling cold and tired.

Miss Mawson walked down the aisle on Sunday with such a group – a father, a mother, two young boys and an older girl – and Evie presumed she was with them. Immediately she saw her as an aunt, the father's sister surely, since she did not resemble the mother, but when the family entered their pew Miss Mawson did not after all accompany them. Instead she slipped into one of the unmarked pews where anyone could sit, and it was clear when the service had begun and nobody had joined her that she was on her own. This somehow excited Evie. Miss Mawson, like her, was alone even if their circumstances were very different. Perhaps Miss Mawson lived entirely alone and had no family. Evie longed to follow her home, but of course there was no possibility of being able to do so. After the service, she hung back behind the departing crowd instead of darting out first to avoid the embarrassment of passing the vicar when he had taken up his station at the door. She followed Miss Mawson at a distance, separated by a dozen or so people, and was out of the church in time to see her walk down St Cuthbert's Lane. Evie usually went that way back to Portland Square in any case. But coming into English Street, Miss Mawson crossed in front of the town hall and turned left down Scotch Street. Evie's way turned right and down Bank Street. Standing for a precious few minutes on the corner (she could run the rest of the way home and still arrive on time) she strained her eyes to see where Miss Mawson was going. Towards Eden Bridge, it seemed. Then she must live somewhere in Stanwix. Gratified to have learned this, Evie hurried along wondering why, in that case, Miss Mawson attended St Cuthbert's and not a church in Stanwix. Was it out of some old loyalty? Or because she was in the habit of worshipping at different churches for variety? Or even that there was something special about that Sunday's service at St Cuthbert's?

Evie enjoyed pondering on this question. The little mystery gave an additional thrill to the following Sunday – would Miss Mawson be there or not? She was not. But two Sundays later she was, and Evie had a stroke of luck, such as rarely came her way. Mrs Bewley was unwell. The doctor had been on Saturday and pronounced her feverish and possibly about to go down with shingles. Mrs Bewley had instantly beseeched him to send a properly trained nurse to her since she vowed 'that chit of a girl' as well as 'that old fool, Harris' could not adequately nurse her and she would die of neglect. The nurse had been sent and Evie and Harris banished to their more mundane duties. When Evie had gone into Mrs Bewley's bedroom to do the fire, as she did every morning, she had been told by the nurse not to disturb the patient again unless she was specifically sent for. Nervously, Evie had bobbed a curtsey at the nurse, who was a figure every bit as formidable as Mrs Bewley, and asked if it was still all right for her to go to church as she did every Sunday morning with her mistress's permission. The nurse had said of course and that nothing would be required until one o'clock at the earliest.

Normally Evie had to be back in the house by a quarter past twelve, fifteen minutes after the end of morning service. Given this unexpected bonus of another forty-five minutes, she had been planning all the way to church what she would do with it, but when she saw Miss Mawson once more her other tentative plans were abandoned. She would follow Miss Mawson home and still be back in Portland Square by one o'clock unless her quarry lived a very long way away – which was not likely, or she would have come in a cab. Evie could hardly contain herself through the service, which she was used to wishing would go on for ever. This time, knowing the direction Miss Mawson would take, she shot ahead and fairly scurried down Scotch Street, pausing only at the corner of the market to withdraw into a deep doorway. There, breathing heavily from the exertion, she waited for Miss Mawson to pass, which she did, after a time that was long enough to restore Evie's energy. She passed quite near but looked straight ahead, walking gracefully and slowly and obviously enjoying the air and exercise. Evie followed at a distance of fifty yards, her head down in case Miss Mawson turned round. On the bridge, Miss Mawson hesitated briefly, but only to look down at the swollen river and possibly admire the daffodils growing wild along its banks. Then she proceeded up Stanwix Bank and turned eventually into Etterby Street. Evie did not follow her all along the street, which fell away down a hill then went up again. She could see perfectly well from her vantage point that Miss Mawson had entered the second last house on the right, using her own key. So far as Evie could tell, this house was quite small, quite modest, a terraced house, but not in the manner of the Portland Square terraces. There was no time to go down the hill and up again to examine its interior closely, not this Sunday. Turning back towards the city, Evie rushed home. To her immense satisfaction she was inside the house at ten minutes to one and not called upon by the nurse until half past.

Mrs Bewley did have shingles and was very ill. The nurse stayed three weeks and Evie had two more Sundays of extra free time as well as a much easier life during the week. There was no Mrs

Bewley to stand over her and make her do again jobs she had already done faultlessly. She carried on methodically cleaning and polishing and performing all the tasks expected of her but, since she was not forced to do half of them twice over, she had, for the first time in over a year, hours to herself. These hours did not come all together but in separate stretches throughout the day. She still rose before six but by eleven she had done all the morning work and had two hours until dinner-time. It was the same in the afternoons, only the other way round – free until three and then busy until seven. She worried as to her rights in this situation. Might Mrs Bewley, when recovered, demand to know what had been going on? But Evie reckoned that if she had kept up her employer's standards and had always asked the nurse for permission to leave the house then she could not be accused of cheating. Doubtless Mrs Bewley would accuse her but then she was likely to do so however Evie had behaved.

So Evie went out regularly and experienced a feeling of freedom that was quite intoxicating. She roamed the market and convinced herself she remembered it well, though in truth she was disappointed to find she did not. There was something about the butter women's stalls that was vaguely familiar but that was all it was, the vaguest of recollections of sitting looking at people's feet. More daringly she ventured past the cathedral and over Caldew Bridge and into Caldewgate to Holy Trinity, passing on the way the Royal Oak, which she knew was run by Messengers. It was not a Sunday and Caldewgate was busy. Workers streamed out of Carr's biscuit factory and the place seemed as hectic as Portland Square was tranquil. Evie was apprehensive about entering the church on a weekday – she did not know if it was allowed – but her desire to see inside was so great that she went and tried the door. When it opened, she slipped inside, heart thudding and throat dry, rehearsing what she would say if challenged – 'Please sir, I was baptised here.' She went up to the font and stood touching the stone, her eyes shut. Here her mother, Leah Messenger, had stood holding her, a baby, in her arms and had given her a name. Mary had been with her, old Mary had been a witness, and it was all written down somewhere, there was proof. Evie trembled a little and wondered if this was the church, with its memories of her baptism, to which her mother still came. She could come one Sunday, while Mrs Bewley remained ill, but what good would it do? She would not recognise her mother, her mother would not recognise her. It was pointless.

The whole search was pointless and not even a proper search. Evie, walking home through Caldewgate, despaired. She needed help. She needed someone to instruct her in how a search could be made and she had no one to advise her. While she had been at Moorhouse it had seemed so hopeful – knowing her mother's name, knowing where she herself had once lived with old Mary, knowing where she had been baptised – surely, knowing all this, she could find her mother. But now she saw how she had deluded herself and even been wilfully stupid. What she knew amounted to nothing. It was nineteen years now since she had been baptised, thirteen since Mary had died. She knew no one in Carlisle, a city of thousands and thousands of people. Her mother might not be here, and if she were, her name might be different, she might be married. Entering the Portland Square house, quietly, she thought she might as well leave. It was dark in the hallway, the heavy door shutting out the light except for a few feeble rays of sun struggling through the stained glass panels at the side. She should go up to the attic and pack her bag and leave. But where would she go? To the hirings again? She shuddered. How ever she had brought herself so low she could not now imagine. There must be other ways to find employment. She had often looked at Mrs Bewley's *Cumberland News* when making it into paper sticks for the fire, and she had seen advertisements for maids of every description, but they all asked for references, and she had none. Mrs Bewley would certainly not give her one and there was no one else in Carlisle for whom she had worked, or who knew her. Except Miss Mawson. Miss Mawson could be said to know her, in a manner of speaking. Miss Mawson might vouch for her obedience and reliability and politeness and trustworthiness, unless Mrs Bewley had told lies and poisoned her mind.

Throughout the following week, the third and last of Mrs Bewley's illness, Evie turned over and over in her mind the possibility of throwing herself on Miss Mawson's mercy and asking her help. But she was intelligent enough to realise that, as Mrs Bewley's friend, Miss Mawson could not reasonably be expected to give a reference to the maid who wished to leave her friend's employment while she was ill. It would not do, and Evie saw clearly that it would not. There was no point in embarrassing, perhaps even angering, Miss Mawson and humiliating herself. But the next time

Miss Mawson visited and Evie opened the door to her she found herself trembling so violently that the visitor noticed.

'Why, Evie,' said Miss Mawson, all concern, 'you are shaking, dear, are you ill?'

Evie whispered, 'No, ma'am.'

'You are cold, then? Indeed, it is cold in this hallway, I have often thought so.' Evie nodded, relieved to be given this excuse. She stood aside to let Miss Mawson mount the stairs to Mrs Bewley's bedroom, but on the first step Miss Mawson lingered and looked over the banister at Evie. 'Are you worried, Evie? Are you afraid of what might happen to you if, God forbid, there is a tragedy?' Startled, Evie looked up. She did not know what Miss Mawson meant, but found herself nodding. 'Then do not fret, my dear, I would help you find a new situation.'

And, with that, Miss Mawson carried on up the stairs and Evie returned to the kitchen weak with gratitude. Hope had returned, stronger, promising more than ever and, though she had not yet quite worked out the implications of what Miss Mawson had said, she knew beyond any doubt that some positive reassurance had been given to her for the future. Miss Mawson had shown her a most motherly concern.

Chapter Fourteen

THE TRAIN journey from London to St Andrews was always long and tedious, but Shona quite liked the numbness that regularly overcame her after the first hundred miles. She would try at first to read but the book would fall from her hands within half an hour no matter how good it was. Train journeys, long journeys like this one, were conducive only to day-dreaming and soon she would be in a stupor, no longer aware of the eating hordes around her. She watched the endless procession of travellers coming from the buffet carrying their absurd little paper carrier bags full of disgustingly smelly food and was surprised what little impact they made on her. People, nameless people about whom she would never know anything. She felt utterly remote from them.

The woman opposite her was clearly longing to engage her in conversation but Shona had resisted all overtures. No, she had not wanted to read this stout, dry-skinned, white-haired woman's magazine and no, neither had she accepted a share of her sandwiches. To the query 'Going far?' she had said she was and promptly shut her eyes. Fatal to be polite with five hundred miles ahead. She wanted to have established herself before Watford as unfriendly, uncommunicative and very, very tired. All true, especially the last. She felt exhausted and deeply, deeply tired, a drained, dizzy feeling not at all like ordinary fatigue. The thought of Catriona's fussing over her was for once something to look forward to. Good food would be cooked, a warm bed prepared and every comfort lavished upon her. She could wallow in all this spoiling and enjoy the sensation. For a few days, at least. Then she supposed the rot would set in as it always did. She would start to feel irritable again and that unbearable sensation of wanting to escape and never return would overwhelm her.

She kept her eyes closed until Oxenholme and then she stared out of the window at the snow-covered hills of the Lake District. It was a dark afternoon. Though it was only midday, the December light was already fading fast. The white of the snow seemed fluorescent, beaming up towards the dark grey sullen sky. It felt like home though it was not. Shona was always puzzled by this strange sensation of familiarity whenever she was amid snow-covered mountains – she felt happy and comfortable yet there was no reason for this. Home was the sea, always had been. She closed her eyes again after Carlisle. She was going to Glasgow instead of Edinburgh, where usually she changed trains for St Andrews, because she was visiting her Grannie McEndrick on the way home. It was not something she wanted to do, but the suggestion, her mother's of course, was not one she felt she could turn down. She hadn't seen her grandmother for over a year and she knew fine well how a glimpse of her was fervently desired. Grannie McEndrick had been ill since the summer and was full of sudden intimations of mortality. She'd let it be known she wanted to see Shona 'for one last time'.

She got off the train at Glasgow, dreading the trail out to Cambuslang and the big stone house where her grannie lived. She had no money for a taxi – what student had? – and the buses were so slow. Lumbered with a rucksack and another heavy bag she had difficulty getting on the bus at all, and nobody helped. She looked big and strong enough to manage on her own, she supposed. And she had made no effort to look attractive, why should she? She hated girls who traded on their looks to cadge help. Her beautiful hair was bundled up inside a woollen ski hat and she was wearing her customary black ski jacket zipped right up to her chin, with black trousers and heavy boots. Who would imagine such a formidable creature might have arms that were weak and ached with the weight of her load? She was so tired by now that she felt sick. She wished she had refused to stop off at Grannie McEndrick's for a night and day. There would be no luxury in her house. It was a house that had died in the last few years. Only two rooms were in use and all the others were shut up, the cold air seeping out from them through the ill-fitting doors. A house which had once seemed warm and hospitable was now bleak and repellent, everything about it neglected and dated in a shabby rather than quaint way. There would be no delicious food. Grannie McEndrick existed on tinned soup and crackers and cheese these days.

Shona had to stop four times on the journey from the bus stop to her grandmother's squat house. She stood, bowed over, almost in tears. Tears of that kind of self-pity she found despicable but to which she had lately been succumbing more and more often. It was going to be such a strain undergoing her grannie's questioning. She knew what line this would follow: was she happy at university? Was she enjoying herself? Was the work interesting? Was it hard or easy? How was she managing in the big city? Had she been homesick? And, the most pressing question of all, 'Any romances, Shona?' She ought to be able to take it all in good part, or else lie cheerfully. No harm in joking, making up entertaining answers. But she had not the energy for it, nor for the truth. She wanted to get through the next twenty-four hours as painlessly as possible and then move on, duty done. Her one thought, as she reached her grandmother's door, was how quickly she could get to bed.

Not quickly at all. Ailsa McEndrick had had an afternoon sleep so as to be alert when Shona arrived. And she had stirred herself sufficiently out of the lethargy which seemed her new permanent condition to make a proper meal. No tinned soup. She had made a stew, the sort she used to make when all her family were at home, a stew with dumplings, and an apple pie. It had cost her a great deal of effort and she was looking forward to watching her granddaughter devour her offerings voraciously. Her first words were, 'Sit yourself down and tuck in, you'll be starving after that long journey.' Shona was indeed hungry but stared in dismay at the plate of stew plonked with triumphant speed in front of her, even before she had had time to take her jacket off.

'It's meat,' she said.

'Of course it's meat, best stewing steak, and the *price* now, it's scandalous, so you tuck in, there's plenty.'

'I don't eat meat,' Shona said. 'Grannie, I'm sorry, I really am. I should have told you. I just didn't think you made stew any more ...'

'Specially! For *you*, specially for you, you'll have to eat it.'

'I don't eat meat, I'm a vegetarian ...'

'There's plenty of vegetables in there, carrots and neeps and onion, they're all in with the meat, so you'll be all right, now eat up.'

Ailsa's face was red with exertion and fury. Such *nonsense* these children talked, no meat indeed. Silly, silly ideas. How did they think they would grow? Though by the look of her there was no need for Shona to grow any more. She was a big enough lassie already, she'd be putting the men off if she got any bigger. She'd changed. Ailsa saw the changes and grieved. All that bonny hair in knots, she could see it was all full of knots. It needed a good brushing. That long, thick, wavy head of auburn hair scragged back and tied with an elastic band, not even a ribbon. And she was pale, dreadfully pale, no roses any more in her cheeks. She sat there, picking out the delicious, expensive pieces of meat and putting them on the side of her plate as though they were tainted, and not even the dumplings seemed to meet with madam's approval. But the apple pie was given the reception it deserved, which was something. Half of it eaten at one sitting, and with relish. Mollified, Ailsa settled into her armchair and said, 'Now, tell me *all* about it, I want to hear every word, mind, every word, just you start at the beginning and tell me all about what you've been doing down there in London.'

Carefully, Shona scraped her pudding bowl clean. It was a pretty bowl, blue and white, part of a set she knew her grannie's mother had given her as a wedding present. It was never used on normal occasions. Her grannie was treating her like royalty, making her special stew and apple-pie and using her best china. Now she wanted her reward. Shona swallowed the last morsel of the pie and took a drink of water. She could delay things by requesting a cup of tea. She disliked tea but all her grannie's meals were followed by tea, and she was surprised it had not yet been offered.

'Tea?' she suggested. 'Shall I make it?'

'I don't drink it any more at this time of night,' Ailsa said, 'it makes me have to get up to go to the bathroom. It'll happen to you too when you're my age. We McKenzie women have weak bladders and you're half McKenzie. But I'll make you some if you're wanting it, except I don't believe it, you've never cared for tea, just humouring me, were you?' Shona smiled. 'Now, what have I said that's funny, miss?'

'Nothing, just you're so sharp.'

'Sharp, am I? Sharp enough to know something's amiss with you. What is it? Have you got yourself into trouble?'

'No,' said Shona.

Trouble was not what she had got herself into. A mess wasn't exactly the same as trouble. She'd got herself into a mess and she could see no way of getting out of it. From the moment she had arrived in London the search for her real mother had taken over her life to the exclusion of everything else. She went to lectures and wrote essays without any real understanding of what she was doing and was astonished that she got away with such minimum effort. She felt like a robot but nobody seemed to notice. Within a month she had moved out of the Hall of Residence and into a bed-sitter in Kilburn, a bleak little room in the basement of a dilapidated house which would appal her parents if they were ever to see it. But she preferred living there on her own to living with other girls. They all irritated her. They were so childish, so preoccupied with utterly pointless pursuits. They distracted her. Hearing them giggle, or yell, or sing enraged her. She felt the fog that seemed to surround her penetrated by a sudden harsh beam of light when she heard their noise and it disturbed her; she didn't want its illumination. She didn't want to be recalled to the life of an eighteen-year-old with an eighteen-year-old's desires. All she wanted to do was concentrate on finding her mother.

It was a point of honour not to have asked her parents a single question. They had finished the holiday in Norway in some style, the sense that something important had been achieved lifting all their spirits; and then there had only been a few months before she had gone off to London. She made phone calls and wrote dutiful regular letters, but never once did she bring up the subject of her adoption. She hugged the new knowledge to herself fiercely, telling no one, loving her secret, revelling in it. To ask questions would be to damage the constant pleasure of it. She wanted to find her real mother herself, without help, and particularly without the help of Catriona and Archie, though she knew that by excluding them she would be making her task much more difficult. But she wanted it to be difficult. She wanted to have to work hard and overcome all kinds of obstacles to discover this woman's whereabouts, this woman who had given her away immediately she had gone through the labour of giving birth to her. The searching was like a kind of labour itself to her – the pain, the struggle and then, she hoped, the joyful delivery.

She thought she would start by obtaining her birth certificate. Surely nothing could be simpler. St Catherine's House in Holborn was not far from University College and she found it without difficulty. She had imagined it as a grand building with an imposing, perhaps intimidating, entrance, but the doors, net-curtained, were like those to a block of council flats. The inside was equally unimpressive – low ceilings, grids to let light through, cheap lino strips down the middle of the shabbily carpeted floors. She wandered bewildered through the first room. Somehow she had thought the actual looking at records would be done by clerks, but no, she could handle the huge books herself – black for death, green for marriages, red for birth, yellow for adoptions.

The record books were wide and long, two inches thick, with heavy handles to pull them out of the racks where they were stored, four to each year, all arranged alphabetically. She loved the feel of these registers, the very difficulty of hauling the heavy volumes out of their nesting place and opening them, jostled on either side by other people doing the same. Such ordinary people, not scholarly as she had imagined, and all with the same intense air she had herself. There was no entry at all for Shona McIndoe's birth. The disappointment was sickening, but then she chided herself at once for her own stupidity – of course there was no entry in the records here, because she had been born in Norway. Would she have to go to Norway?

But she had been adopted in Scotland. Or had she? Had all the adoption proceedings taken place in Norway too? Was she adopted through a society? Or privately? Was that possible? She had to ask advice. She was assured by a clerk that the best way, in her case, to find out what she wanted was to consult the Norwegian records. Either that, or ask her adoptive parents for the papers they must have in their possession. Shona left the building disconsolate. No, she could not and would not ask Catriona and Archie for her birth certificate and adoption papers. If she did, they would know what she was doing and she did not want them to know – not because she feared hurting them but because she simply did not want anyone to spoil her secret quest. It *had* to remain secret. She would feel exposed and vulnerable, an object of pity, if the extent of her longing was known.

So she went to Norway. To explain her absence to her mother, who had expected her home earlier, she set up an elaborate pretence of going to stay with a girlfriend at her home in Sussex for a few days. Catriona sent her a £10 note to buy some little present for her friend's mother – 'Never go empty-handed, Shona.' It came in useful because Shona had very little money left at the end of term and had already cut down her spending on food and fares to save the amount she needed for her boat and train tickets. Even with drastic economy and no other expenditure she only just managed to raise the money and knew she'd have to stay in a youth hostel once she got there.

The journey was terrible. How easy it had been to fly from Edinburgh with her parents in the spring, how horrible to go by boat across the bucking winter sea. It seemed to take for ever and once they had docked and she was in the train she still felt herself swaying for hours. The building where the Norwegian records were kept was not like St Catherine's House, and Shona could not get the hang of how to look things up. Speaking not a word of Norwegian didn't help, though it was true everyone she asked for advice spoke English. But again she came up against the problem of not knowing her real mother's name, only her own date of birth and the place. It was no good trying to find her birth registered here – she would have to go back to the hospital in Bergen and ask to see their records. Another train, another freezing walk through icy streets to a hostel. But then, in the morning, when she went to the appropriate office in the hospital, the woman in charge was not helpful. Shona had thought up a romantic-sounding story, but it did not impress the official.

'I only want to look at the entry made for my birth,' Shona pleaded. 'I'm a student and it's part of an assignment we've been set.'

'You are from England?'

'Yes.'

'You come from England on a student assignment to look at your name in our records?'

'Yes.'

'Why, please?'

'I've told you, it's an assignment.'

'To gain what?'

'Sorry?'

'What is the point of this assignment?'

'It's history, I mean using records to verify what we know as facts, to check facts.'

'And they send students to Norway?'

'Only because I was born here. It's just that I want to be thorough ...'

'Very thorough indeed.'

'Yes, very thorough. I want to impress my teacher.'

It took several more minutes of hostile staring and questioning before this woman went off to consult some superior. She returned with a form for Shona to fill in. It asked for the father's and the mother's names of the applicant. Shona hesitated. It would be no good putting McIndoe. The hospital records would surely have her real mother's name.

'I really would like to do this the other way,' she said, trying not to sound nervous. 'I'd like just to look at a list of all the babies born here on the day I was born, without using my parents' names. It would add to ... to ... it would be more original. Please, could I not simply look at the list? Isn't a record kept of every day?'

'Yes,' said the woman, 'but the files do not work on a daily basis. This is eighteen years ago. The list for that year is under names, not times. If you do not give me your name I cannot help you.'

There was nothing to do but cry, and how Shona cried. She collapsed on to the red plastic chair in the woman's narrow little office and wept and wept, her face buried in her arms resting on her knees. There was the scraping of another chair and the sound of the woman walking round from behind her desk. But then, instead of comfort, a constantly repeated, 'Stop, please. I ask you to stop, please, stop.' There was anger, not sympathy in the voice and Shona heard it. The whole thing was ridiculous and this woman knew it was and it made her furious.

'I'm sorry,' Shona said. There was nothing to be lost now. 'I don't know my mother's or my father's name,' she said, voice thick with tears still. 'I was adopted, I want to find my real mother, that's all.'

The woman frowned. 'There are rules,' she said. 'They must be followed in such circumstances. It is a very serious matter.'

'I know,' said Shona. 'What shall I do?'

The woman told her to go home and 'ascertain some facts'. Without them, no search could proceed.

And now Shona was sitting exhausted in her grannie's Glasgow kitchen, barely able to speak of what she had been doing down in London. 'Oh,' she said, covering her face with her hands, 'I'm tired, Grannie, can we wait until the morning?'

'But you're off in the morning, you're barely going to warm the bed. And you'll be off without so much as the time of day, I know you will. Your mother's told me you have to be on that eleven-thirty train, she can't do without you a minute longer. She's missed you something cruel. Have you given any thought to that?' Shona groaned. 'No good groaning, it's the truth. Dotes on you, always has, the light of her life. It isn't healthy, never was. I knew it would end like this.'

'Like what?'

'You wanting to be away, not wanting your mother.'

'I do want my mother,' Shona whispered, hoping her Grannie would not hear and read any significance into how the words had been said.

'What? Want your mother? Never, never, you've never wanted her, independent from the word go, that was you. You're like my mother, your great-grannie, dead before you were born, but you're the image of her.'

'How very odd,' said Shona sarcastically. It was so tempting to tell her grannie the truth and smash all these silly ideas of inherited genes. But it would be cruel. Grannie McEndrick would not be able to bear having been hoodwinked. She would be outraged, not at the deceit itself but at its wholly successful accomplishment.

'It isn't odd,' she was saying, 'it's obvious. You and your mother are chalk and cheese, but you and your great-grannie are as like as two peas in a pod, so you are.'

'I'm going to bed,' Shona said, abruptly.

'Aye, you go to your bed, and I'll go to mine because there's no sense in staying up when you're in this mood. Maybe a good sleep will freshen you and sweeten the sourness. There's a bottle in your bed. I'll wake you at nine o'clock and you'll at least have some porridge and a civil tongue in your head, I hope.'

'I'm sorry,' Shona said.

'I should think so too, disappointing your poor old grannie.'

Next morning, Shona made a huge effort. She took Grannie McEndrick her tea in bed and would not allow her to get up to make the blessed porridge. She made it herself and took two bowls of it into her grannie's bedroom, and they ate it together while Shona chattered away making up every word of her lively description of her life in London. No comment was made, but her grannie seemed prepared at least to pretend she was satisfied. They parted on good terms, with Shona promising to write. 'Be kind to your mother,' were the parting words. 'Remember now, mind you're kind to her.'

Kind. Shona contemplated the word all the way to St Andrews. How was one kind to one's mother? It suggested condescension somehow, a faintly patronising attitude. Kind, as to an animal, or child. Catriona, she knew, did not want kindness. She wanted intimacy, as she always had done. Kindness was surely an insult. But she tried, when she arrived, to be affectionate and happy to be home which was, she hoped, a version of the kindness her grannie had had in mind. Christmas passed off well and so did Hogmanay. There were no arguments, no sulks. The three of them managed a rapport which convinced Archie that telling Shona she was adopted had brought her closer to them. Catriona shook her head but could not come up with any specific reasons for doubting this.

'She's trying,' she said to her husband. 'She's trying so hard, and I'm thankful. But she isn't happy, she's changed.'

'Of course she's changed,' Archie said, exasperated. 'She's eighteen, she's just left home for college, it would be unnatural if she hadn't changed.'

'I meant in herself, her nature,' Catriona persisted. 'She used to be fearless and that's gone. She's anxious, tense, underneath.'

But Archie wouldn't discuss such nonsense.

Shona took the dog for long walks on the beach and gradually felt better. The weather was stormy but she welcomed the biting wind scudding off the black sea and even the rain suited her. She felt busy struggling along the empty sands and she wanted to feel busy. It helped her to think. She began to see quite clearly that she had been deliberately foolish over the last few months – it had been absurd to try to trace her real mother in the way she had done. She had to put a stop to this idiotic stubbornness and use the resources available. If she did not want her parents to know she was trying to find this woman who had abandoned her, then the only alternative was subterfuge. The vital documents would be in the house. Her birth certificate, the original one, and the adoption papers – there would have had to be some kind of document – would be in a drawer somewhere. All she had to do was find them and copy them. Simple.

She was not sure where to start, with her mother's belongings or her father's. Archie was away so much that it was Catriona who handled all the household affairs, all the bills and so forth, but then the papers she needed did not come into that category. Her father kept their passports in his desk and she'd heard him once refer to some insurance policies in a drawer there. So she began with his desk, not even waiting until both parents were out. She waited until they were both watching television, a favourite programme lasting an hour during which they always said they would not move even to answer the telephone, and then she went into Archie's den, leaving the door wide open. His desk was neat. Three drawers either side of the kneehole and one long one running above it. Each drawer was labelled. She looked into all of them in case the labels were misleading, but they were not; insurance policies were where they were said to be and so were personal documents. But no birth certificate, no adoption papers. She sat for a moment looking at her father's passport. It had never occurred to her, when he had given her her own, that to apply for a passport a birth certificate was necessary. Archie had dealt with it and merely handed her passport to her.

She could not bring herself to search her mother's drawers until the house was empty. Catriona had no den or desk. She had a bureau in the sitting-room, which was much too public to hold secret papers, stuffed full of bills and receipts. Shona knew it was pointless but looked through these quite openly on the pretext of searching for a guarantee for her camera which she vowed she had given her mother. The only other place in which her mother kept things was her bedroom. There were photographs there, some in a box and some in albums, and all kept on a shelf in her wardrobe. But Catriona rarely went out and if she did, wanted Shona to accompany her. With only three days of her vacation left, Shona was beginning to think she would have to risk a quick raid of the wardrobe shelf while her mother was busy in the kitchen. An appointment with the dentist came just in time.

'You should come with me,' Catriona said, 'you haven't had your teeth looked at for ages. I'm sure he'd fit an inspection into the hour he's booked me for, a whole hour, I can't imagine why he thinks he's going to take that long.'

'Make me an appointment for Easter,' Shona said. 'My teeth are fine just now.'

She locked the front door the moment her mother had left. It was better to risk her unexpected return and her discovery that she was locked out than have her walk in on her daughter's spying. That is what I am, Shona thought, a spy. There is no other word for it. Spying, I am spying. She even found her palms were sweaty and her heart beating rather faster than usual, fast enough to be aware of it, as she went up to her parents' room. Such a dismal room, all creams and beiges and with the kind of candlewick bedspread she loathed.

The wardrobe was ugly but much valued by Archie. It had belonged to his mother and the solid oak appealed to him. The box of photographs was still in place and the albums on top of it. Carefully, noting their exact position, Shona lifted them down and put them on the bed. Behind where they had been was another box, smaller, oblong-shaped. She lifted that out too. But it was locked. She might have known it would be locked, of course it would be. The key would be somewhere in this room, but where? *In* something, it would be in something, in a purse or bag or some kind of holder. She ran her hands along the shelf. Nothing, nothing else there. It might be in a pocket but there were so many pockets in all the garments hanging there. No, not a pocket, the key would be somewhere more secure. Distracted, Shona looked around. Her mother had a kidney-shaped dressing-table with a flowered flounce round it. Her jewellery was in a drawer underneath it. Quickly, Shona lifted the flounce and looked in the drawer where she knew the jewellery to be, Most of it, the pearls and the gold necklace, both rarely worn, was in a white leather case. The rest, rings and bracelets of lesser value, were on an open tray, velvet-lined. Shona lifted both out. Nothing else here either. She opened the white case and looked at the pearls. Surely the key to anything important would be with other things her mother considered precious. Gently, she lifted the pearls out and experimented with the cushion upon which they had rested. Of course, it lifted out. And there was a little silver key.

There was a bundle certificates in the wooden oblong box, birth and death and marriage certificates for all kinds of people, for relatives on both sides going back a century. Catriona's sense of family was so strong, Shona realised, that she had become its archivist. But there was no mistaking the certificates to do with her. They were at the very bottom, in a white envelope marked 'Shona'. It felt like a moment of infinite importance, a moment she suddenly wanted to extend in time. She held the envelope tenderly, almost caressing it, before very slowly opening it and extracting the few sheets of paper inside. Her real mother's name leapt out before anything else, Hazel Walmsley. Then her age, eighteen. 'Eighteen,' Shona whispered aloud. Somehow she'd known it, known her mother would have been so young. Her eyes filled with tears. Eighteen. Not her fault, then. It made the adoption seem so much more understandable. Eighteen. What, after all, could she have done, this pregnant eighteen-year-old? An abortion, Shona knew, was hard to obtain in the fifties, as well as illegal. Poor kid. Then there came over her a rising sense of excitement: her mother was only thirty-six *now*. Her real mother was young, the sort of mother she wanted. Young and like her. She must be like her.

The other sheets were the adoption papers telling her what she already knew. There was no time to copy those out. She made an exact copy of the birth certificate though, dividing her sheet of paper into the same squares and taking care to print every single word that was on the original. Then she replaced the key and the boxes precisely where they had been and even wiped them with a handkerchief as though she had been a burglar and needed to erase her fingerprints. The whole operation had taken merely fifteen minutes – her whole past laid bare in quarter of an hour. Except she knew this was only another kind of beginning. She had her mother's name and age and that was absolutely all, that and the address of where she had been staying in Norway. But there was one other little detail. Her mother, young Hazel Walmsley, had been classified as a student. She was an eighteen-year-old English student who almost certainly had returned after the birth of her baby to England.

Shona could hardly wait to return to London. Hazel Walmsley, aged thirty-six. But probably married, therefore Walmsley no longer. Still, a maiden name and a date, or at least year, of birth was something. Quite a lot in fact. Those ledgers in St Catherine's House would come into their own now. She could search them for the birth of one Hazel Walmsley in 1938. Walmsley was not a common name, and neither was Hazel. Or maybe she should search for a marriage certificate. She could look up all the marriages for Walmsley for the last eighteen years. Perhaps her mother had never married, but somehow she was sure she would have done. Married and had children. At that thought Shona felt breathless – half-brothers and half-sisters to claim! The prospect dazzled her, and when Catriona returned she could hardly conceal her happiness. She wanted to dance and shout and sing, to shriek, Hazel Walmsley! Hazel Walmsley! over and over. Luckily Catriona was in such discomfort with her swollen and still frozen jaw that she did not register Shona's exuberance, only her readily offered sympathy.

When Shona left to go back to London she gave Catriona a warm hug that almost lifted her off her feet. 'Take care, Mum,' she said.

'And you take care, dear,' Catriona said, touched and emotional at such an extravagant farewell. For years and years Shona had parted from her with barely a backward look and certainly never with any embrace. 'Take care,' she said again, 'don't work too hard, and write. You'll write, won't you? And ring if you want, reverse the charges, or else I could ring you back, and ...'

'Mum,' said Shona, out of the train window, 'I'm not going to the North Pole, remember?'

'It always feels like it. You've got such a different life now, all those people I don't know.'

The train slid out of the station and Shona collapsed at the release of all the tension she'd felt for the last two days. She was not just going back to college, she was going to meet Hazel Walmsley. Tomorrow she would spend the whole day in St Catherine's House. She'd be there when it opened at 8.30. Already she fantasised the meeting with her real mother – she could see her, astonishment and joy on her face, and behind her shadowy figures, sisters and brothers (Oh, she hoped more sisters than brothers, at least one sister) who would gradually emerge and become distinct. There was another fantasy of course, but she dealt with it firmly: rejection. She did not believe for one moment that her real mother would not welcome her, and only entertained this possibility in an attempt to envisage every conceivable reaction. So, it was theoretically possible. Her mother might not want her illegitimate child to claim her. She might have a life in which the appearance of such a child would be an embarrassment. She might never have told her husband or her other children. She might recoil with horror at the appearance of her first daughter and deny her entry into her world.

Nonsense. Shona knew it was nonsense. Her real mother would be like her. She would have suffered and grieved for eighteen years and now all her sorrow would lift. She would need to be reassured that Shona bore her no ill will and had no desire to make her feel guilty. Once she realised that no retribution was sought, she would be relieved. I can tell her, Shona thought as the train sped into England, that I have had a happy life with wonderful parents and that will make her feel better. But then I can add the bit she will long to hear – I have had a happy life with a devoted and loving adoptive mother, but *she is not you and it is you I want*. Probably, this said, there would be lots of tears. Shona smiled at the prospect.

Chapter Fifteen

MRS BEWLEY died in the early hours of 15 October, but of a stroke, not of shingles. Evie was spared the sight of her employer's dead body, though she was invited to pay her last respects if she so desired. She did not desire. She had had no respect for Mrs Bewley, though she did not of course give this as the reason for declining the invitation. She implied, without saying so, that she was afraid, and this was sufficient for the nurse and Harris to leave her alone and not press her.

A man who was said to be a nephew arrived later that day and took charge. Bit by bit scraps of information drifted Evie's way as she let people in and out of the house, took tea in and out of the drawing-room for the nephew and other unknown persons, and in general went about her normal business. She picked up that the house had been left to the nephew, and its contents divided between three cousins. Some provision had been made for Harris, and she was to have a calendar month to get out. 'Where will I go?' she kept asking Evie. Evie had no idea; she was naturally more concerned that she did not know where she would go herself, though she was perfectly aware no provision would have been made for her. It was more a question of how long she would still be allowed a roof over her head and of whether she would receive a pittance when she was turned out. This seemed unlikely, since she had never received a penny from Mrs Bewley, only her keep. The nephew – she had been told his name but it was such a complicated double-barrelled name she did not absorb it – did not leave her in suspense for long. He sent for her the day before the funeral and told her she could stay until Harris departed. It was, he informed her, generous of him, some might say foolishly generous, but he was prepared to grant her virtually a month's free board and lodging in return for the fulfilling of her usual household duties. He was putting the house up for sale and wished it to be kept clean and tidy and in good order. Evie curtseyed and thanked him.

She waited meanwhile for Miss Mawson to appear. There was a funeral tea and Miss Mawson would undoubtedly have been invited back to the house, she felt, to partake of the refreshments. Evie, taking the mourners' coats, grew increasingly anxious when no Miss Mawson arrived. Had she after all not been included in the funeral party, or had she gone straight home after the burial? It was impossible to know. Evie contemplated going to her house and throwing herself on Miss Mawson's mercy, but she could not quite bring herself to do this, not yet. She had not reached such a pitch of desperation and still had shelter for three weeks. It was a strange period of time, almost enjoyable, since with Mrs Bewley dead and the nephew returned home to Manchester, and the cousins not having come to see to the furniture, for the moment she and Harris had the place to themselves. Harris surprised her. Old and deaf though she was, she knew how to take advantage. The nephew had given her money to feed herself and Evie while they maintained the house up to its usual standard. He had asked what her mistress usually allowed her and Harris had lied promptly and convincingly. The sum Mrs Bewley had actually given her each month was small enough to be in any case so unbelievable that no suspicions were aroused by her doubling of it. 'And then there will be extra for fires, sir, if you should be wanting Evie to light them to keep the terrible damp down. Mrs Bewley, sir, was very particular about fires ever since the paper came off the drawing-room wall with the damp, and pictures on the staircase were ruined by it, and ...' The nephew stopped her. Certainly, while the house was being viewed by prospective buyers he would want fires. Everywhere. He paid for coal accordingly.

Harris gave Evie only a quarter of the profit she had made, but even so it seemed a miracle to her to have this windfall. It was the first money she had had in over a year and the very sight of the coins thrilled her. When she had to leave this house she would not after all be penniless. If she had wished, she could also have increased the sum. Harris was very willing to lead the way. Every day she filched some small article and pawned or sold it. Nothing precious, nothing that had already been itemised in the inventory, made the moment the nephew arrived, but quite ordinary things which Harris knew would nevertheless raise a shilling or two. Pans disappeared and buckets, good cast-iron buckets, and an excellent carving knife and a marble slab for rolling pastry on – Harris had an eye for the right articles. Evie, invited to join in, declined. Harris told her to please herself but that the Lord helped those who helped themselves and there was not much time to do it in.

The two of them kept the house up, with Evie, as ever, doing the bulk of the work. She liked the silent house. Safe from Mrs Bewley's shouting, she appreciated the peace and, though she worried incessantly about the future, this did not prevent her from appreciating the present. If only Miss Mawson would appear, she would be quite happy. She tried to ask Harris where Miss Mawson was, yelled and yelled the name at her, but if the old woman knew, she was not going to say. Twice Evie used her now empty afternoons to walk to Stanwix and wander down Etterby Street and up to the Scaur, but she did not catch sight of Miss Mawson. She saw a strikingly attractive-looking woman coming out of the next door house with two girls, and thought about stopping her and inquiring if she knew whether her neighbour was at home, but it would have been such a foolish question. Why did she not knock at the door if she wished to ascertain whether Miss Mawson was in residence? She left the street promising herself that if Miss Mawson had not appeared by the last but one night she would spend in Portland Square, she would indeed knock on her door.

But Evie was saved from this ordeal. A week before she was due to leave Mrs Bewley's house, Miss Mawson turned up. Evie gave a little cry of delight when she opened the door to her, but this quickly turned to a gasp of consternation when she saw how very pale and thin Miss Mawson was. 'I have been ill, Evie,' Miss Mawson said as she came into the hall and immediately sat down on the upright heavy wooden chair which stood near the dining-room door. 'I am still far from strong, but I must arrange to collect what dear Mrs Bewley left to me before Mr Banningham-Carteret sells the house. Will you help me, dear?' Alert and eager, Evie went with Miss Mawson up the stairs and into Mrs Bewley's bedroom. The curtains were still drawn and the fire was set, ready to be lit the moment anyone came to view the house, but certainly not kept burning every day as the nephew supposed. It took Evie only a moment to light it and to open the curtains a fraction, as instructed.

Miss Mawson sighed. 'I have no heart for this, Evie,' she murmured, 'but it must be done.' Out of her bag she took a list and walked towards Mrs Bewley's huge double wardrobe. 'Open it, Evie, will you?' Evie opened it, opened both doors wide. There was an enormous number of clothes packed on to the rail, starting with coats at the left-hand side and working down through suits and dresses to skirts and blouses. Evie had not known her past employer had owned so many splendid clothes. In the last year she had worn virtually the same garments winter and summer, a black dress and shawl, and a black coat if she went out.

Miss Mawson consulted her list and took out first a satin evening dress with its own little cape. It was a beautiful garment of elegant design, the bodice encrusted with tiny seed pearls, each sewn on by hand. Carrying it to the bed and gently draping it there, Evie shivered at the cool, luxurious feel of the material. 'Made by Mr Arnesen,' Miss Mawson said, 'a long time ago, for Mrs Bewley's daughter who was my dearest friend.' Evie made no comment, though she was desperate to ask questions and demonstrate her avid interest. She hadn't known Mrs Bewley had a daughter. In fact, she was sure she had heard her bewail the fact that she had not and exclaim that if only she had had children she would not now be in the state she was in, dependent on an old deaf housekeeper and a chit of a maid. Next there came out of the wardrobe a riding habit, a dark red day dress with slashed sleeves, a cream-coloured woollen coat with brown velvet collar and cuffs, a short fur jacket and several white blouses, all with lace collars and very full sleeves. 'All Caroline's,' Miss Mawson said, 'and kept all these years. I do not know what is to be done with them. They are all out of fashion and I cannot wear them in any case, I am much smaller than Caroline was. Now, Evie, will you fold these garments most carefully and put them in the boxes I have arranged to be delivered? And finally, dear, will you carry them yourself into the carriage and accompany them to my house?'

Evie could not sleep for excitement. It had never occurred to her that there could ever be any circumstances in which she could actually be invited to Miss Mawson's house – it was a dream too wonderful for her ever to have had the nerve to dream. The boxes came, full of tissue paper, and the carriage waited. Evie packed the garments skilfully, folding the tissue paper between them, and carried the boxes into the carriage one by one. The driver hired by

Miss Mawson knew where to go. Sitting in state, looking out of the window, Evie could not help smiling. Her sad little face beamed with pride even if there was no one to see it, and when she saw Miss Mawson come out of her house to greet her she was so overcome with pleasure she stumbled as she alighted and was distressed at her own awkwardness. But Miss Mawson did not seem to notice. She paid the driver and then showed Evie where to stack the boxes. Once this was done, Evie was at a loss. Should she speak up? Should she remind Miss Mawson directly of her previous promise? Though it had not been a promise exactly. But Miss Mawson was speaking to her and offering her a coin.

'For your trouble, Evie,' she said.

'Oh no, ma'am,' said Evie, 'I couldn't.'

Miss Mawson looked at her closely and seemed suddenly to realise something. 'Of course,' she said, as though to herself, 'you will be leaving Portland Square without anywhere to go, and I believe I ...' She stopped, apparently coming to some decision. 'Sit down, Evie, for I must, I am still so weak, and I cannot feel comfortable talking to you if you stand before me like this. Sit, sit.' Reluctantly, perching on the very edge of the chair indicated, Evie sat. 'Now, Evie, I cannot give you a reference because you have never worked for me and I cannot employ you because I am not rich and as you see this house is very small and I have a maid in any case, but I can give you a recommendation based on my knowledge of your work and character as I observed it during my visits to Mrs Bewley, and I can besides quote what Mrs Bewley said about you. Will that be of use, dear?' Evie nodded her head vigorously. 'Very well. Stay here and I will write something at once and give it to you.'

She disappeared up the stairs and Evie was left hardly daring to move, but wanting badly to examine the photographs she could see on the nearby mantelpiece. She could see Mrs Bewley in them, with a girl. Was that girl Miss Mawson? No. Nor did she look like Mrs Bewley. Evie was sure this must be the Caroline who had been mentioned, even though there was no physical resemblance. There was another photograph of this same girl and beside her was Miss Mawson. Younger, but definitely her. Both girls were laughing, their arms around each other's waists. Evie wondered why she had never seen these photographs among those which crowded the mantelpiece and piano top in the drawing-room of Portland Square.

Miss Mawson returned, holding out an envelope to Evie. 'I have not addressed it, dear, so you can present it to whomever it may concern. And I have left it unsealed so that you may read what I have written. I wish you luck, Evie.'

Evie sprang up from her chair and took the proffered envelope eagerly. 'Thank you, Miss Mawson,' she said.

'Do you know the way back to Portland Square, dear?' Miss Mawson asked.

'Oh yes, ma'am,' said Evie, smiling to think how many times she had walked the distance.

'It must be lonely there now, in that big empty house with only poor Harris for company?'

'I like it, ma'am.'

'Do you?' Miss Mawson looked very surprised. 'What is there to like?'

'The quiet, ma'am, it is very peaceful and easier ...'

'Easier?'

Evie hesitated. She remembered that Mrs Bewley, who had destroyed all peace, was Miss Mawson's friend. She could hardly now describe how hard that woman had made her life. But Miss Mawson was not stupid.

'You never knew Mrs Bewley as she once was, Evie,' she said. 'The kindest lady imaginable. But you see she had a great shock years ago and never recovered. The pain of it made her bitter and I know she often seemed harsh, for she confessed as much to me. There is no harm, I think, now she has passed on, in telling you why she may not have been the most considerate of employers, as once you would have found her.' Miss Mawson stopped and went over to the mantelpiece where she picked up the framed photograph of Mrs Bewley and the girl. 'That was Caroline, Mrs Bewley's only daughter, her only child. She is dead now. But before she died she was greatly wronged by a man – do you understand me, Evie? – and died, in fact, in childbirth in the most miserable circumstances. I was her friend. I did all I could, but ... she ran away, you see, with this evil man and he deserted her. It was a most terrible thing.' Miss Mawson's eyes filled with tears and she turned away.

Evie did not know whether she ought to speak but her need to do so pressed hard and she could not hold back. 'And the baby, ma'am?' she asked.

'What, dear?'

'The baby, Miss Caroline's baby, I wondered ...'

'Oh, it died, fortunately, poor thing. A girl. She died, luckily, with her wretched mother, the very cause of her misery and then her death.'

Evie felt numb all the way back to Portland Square. Miss Mawson was gentle and good. She had had no doubts that it was lucky her friend's baby had died – 'the very cause of her misery'. She was so sure about the rightness of the baby's death. Evie had badly wanted to ask how anything could have been the baby's fault, but did not dare. She had to accept that in some curious way it was, as Miss Mawson had said, right that it should die. She stopped on Eden Bridge and looked down into the fast-flowing river. She had read, in Mrs Bewley's *Cumberland News*, of a woman throwing herself into this river because she was expecting a baby. She was a servant, this woman, and not married, and she did not want the baby. Slowly, Evie carried on her way. She had not died nor been murdered. Leah, her mother, had had her and looked after her, at least at first, and had seen she was baptised. Did that suggest Miss Mawson was always right in her assumption that illegitimate babies were better dead? Evie thought not and felt a little easier. Maybe she, too, had wrecked her mother Leah's life but it had not ended in death for either of them. She was motherless, but alive and in her case always with the prospect of finding her mother and making amends. But that struck Evie as strange even as she thought it – why had she thought in terms of making amends to her mother? It was as bad as Miss Mawson's kind of thinking. The amends, if they were to be made, were her mother's, for deserting her.

Muddled and tired, Evie arrived home to find Harris about to depart for good. She had found a place in the almshouses at Corby and must take the little house or lose it. The old woman was in a state of great agitation, and Evie had to help her into the trap she had hired and soothe her with repeated assurances that the Portland Square house would be properly looked after for this last week. The trap, she saw, was laden not only with Harris's belongings but with the faded curtains taken from her bedroom and a shabby counterpane from another little-used room and half the contents of what had remained in the kitchen cupboards. Alone in the big house, Evie locked and bolted all the doors and, instead of feeling lonely or afraid, found she felt exultant. A house, all to herself, if just for a week. She roamed from room to room, touching things she had never dared to touch, though respectfully and carefully, sat on every chair and looked in every mirror, and in her imagination grew and grew in stature and status.

It was a game she played all day long for the next six days. She still rose very early but now she lit a fire in the morning-room and had her meagre breakfast in comfort in front of it. She waited to see if the house was to be viewed – there was an arrangement whereby a boy came from the agency and said so before ten each day – and if not, she went out, enjoyed the town, entering shops she had never dared go into, and holding her head high. Robinson's, the new emporium in English Street, fascinated her, it was so beautiful with its plate-glass windows and carpeted floors and its mahogany counters behind which the sales assistants seemed veritable princesses they were so grand. Evie haunted that shop, happy to drift from department to department, admiring, but not of course ever spending. When she saw, in the *Cumberland News*, which was still unaccountably being delivered, that Robinson's were advertising for waitresses to serve in their Jacobean café on the first floor she knew at once this was the job for her.

But would she be suitable? She was so small and slight and might be thought not strong enough to carry trays, and she knew she had no presence and would not inspire confidence in customers. All she had in her favour was Miss Mawson's reference which she had read over and over until she knew the words by heart – 'Evelyn Messenger has been known to me for more than a year as hardworking, honest and capable. I am sure she would give satisfaction to whoever employed her as indeed she did in the household of my friend, her employer, the late Mrs Elizabeth Bewley of 10 Portland Square.' Taking this precious document with her, Evie presented herself for interview at Robinson's. She went to the back door and was directed down into the basement and through another door into a corridor. This corridor was full of girls and women, all standing patiently in line, their backs against the bare brick wall. Evie took her place, heart sinking. All the other applicants seemed so confident. They talked loudly to each other and laughed and only she was quiet and cowed. One by one they went into the room at the end of the corridor and one by one came out, some flushed and triumphant, some downcast and in a hurry, and all, as they left, seeming to Evie powerful and desirable whereas she was feeble and unattractive.

In the tiny room there was an elderly woman who sat at a rickety table with a list in front of her. She looked extremely severe with a heavy frown line etched between her eyes and she made no attempt at preliminary pleasantries. 'Name?' she snapped, and 'Age?', and 'Previous work?' and Evie replied as clearly and firmly as she could manage. When the woman looked up she said at once, 'Oh dear, you are small and thin, you'd never manage.' Evie felt her face turn red. She pushed Miss Mawson's reference towards the woman, saying, 'Please, ma'am, I'm a hard worker.' Something resembling a faint smile crossed the woman's fierce face, but she said nothing as she read, then replaced the reference. 'It isn't just a matter of hard work, it's a matter of strength, lass. Can't see you balancing a metal tray with a pot of tea for four and all the rest that goes with it on the tray. You'd be staggering. No, you won't do.' Evie's hand, as she took the reference back, shook. The woman noticed and looked at her again, properly this time. 'Want it that bad, do you?' she said, though without any discernible sympathy in her voice. 'Let's see. You're clean and tidy. Can you sew?'

'Yes,' said Evie, thankful that she had stitched things for Muriel, and had enjoyed the work.

'Well then. I know there's a vacancy for a junior in the cutting-room at Arnesen's. Fancy that?'

'Yes.'

'Here, then,' the women said, scribbling on a scrap of paper. 'Take this to Arnesen's and say I sent you, you never know, they might take you on if they haven't got someone already. It's my daughter's just left, that's how I know they need someone.'

'Thank you,' said Evie.

'Tell the next to come in,' said the woman, 'and let's hope she isn't a waste of time too.'

Evie didn't know where Arnesen's was or indeed what exactly it was, apart from some place that employed girls to sew. She stood in English Street, outside Robinson's, and looked at the bit of paper the woman had given her. 'Henry Arnesen, Tailor' it said, and then an address in Lowther Street. Was it a shop, Evie wondered, as she hurried through Globe Lane to Lowther Street, and then as she repeated the name over and over to herself she recalled Miss Mawson saying Caroline Bewley's beautiful clothes had been made by Arnesen. It was not a shop, however, in the sense Evie understood it, the Robinson's sort of shop. The address led her to a stone house, part of a terrace, with steps leading down to a basement. On the front door she could see a brass plate with the name Henry Arnesen, Tailor, on it, but she thought she ought to try the basement first. Down she went and knocked on the door there only to hear a shout of 'Push! It's open.' Stepping inside Evie saw an extraordinary sight, three rows of women all working treadle machines with fabric of every colour flying underneath the needles. None of the machinists stopped when they saw her, but the one nearest the door shouted, 'What do you want, eh?'

Feebly, Evie waved her bit of paper and said, 'I was sent about a job.' 'What?' shrieked the machinist. 'A job,' Evie repeated, though still not loudly enough. When finally she had made herself heard, she was waved towards the door and a finger was pointed upstairs.

The front door led into a quite different atmosphere. Evie entered a large vestibule, with blue and green patterned tiles on the floor, and pushed open swing doors leading into a broad hall with a staircase rising from it. She stood there, intimidated by this grandeur, and jumped when there was a sudden slam of a shutter and a woman's head poked out of a cubby-hole. 'Can I help you?' a voice said and then, scanning Evie and her clothes, a more abrupt, 'What do you want?' Evie explained. The voice made a sound of irritation but told her to wait. The shutter was slammed shut again, but the voice and face emerged to form a woman who came out from her tiny office. 'Follow me,' she said, and set off down the hall, leading Evie into a long room where there was a trestle table set up and bales of material stacked along the walls. Without speaking to Evie, the woman went to the table and picked up two pieces of cloth. She held these out, indicating that Evie should take them, and then nodded towards a chair at the far end of the table. 'Sit,' she commanded. 'Sew.' Holding the two lengths of white cambric reverentially, Evie went to the chair, sat, and saw in front of her an array of needles arranged in order of size and a box of every coloured thread. She put the cambric on the table, selected the finest needle and threaded it at the first go. She did not know whether to sew the two pieces together in a plain seam or a French seam, or whether simply to hem the slightly frayed edges of both pieces. She resolved to do both. Head bent, she sewed a straight seam and then began to hem. 'Stop,' the woman said. 'You'll do. Report to the cutting-room Monday, eight o'clock sharp, clean hands, mind, and don't expect to be fed.'

Outside again, standing in Lowther Street, Evie was dizzy with success. She had a job, a job that paid. But how much? She had not thought to ask. A wage, though, however small. She scurried back to Portland Square, arriving just in time to hand over the keys to the estate agent's representative. He was only a boy but she had grown quite used to him and no longer felt embarrassed in his presence.

'You'll have to be off in the morning,' he said, cheekily.

'I know,' Evie replied, annoyed at this insolent air.

'Where will you go?'

'That's my business.'

'Got another situation, have you?'

She did not deign to reply, but stood waiting for him to leave which, in his own time and with a lot of alternate yawning and whistling, he did. Evie rushed up to the attic and packed her battered old bag. She had washed and ironed everything that needed mending. Her most respectable outfit she was now wearing and must continue to wear until she could afford a replacement. Her other clothes were rags, all clean but rags nonetheless and not suitable for viewing unless covered by an overall or apron.

She had no idea how to find somewhere to live by the following day, but securing the job at Arnesen's had given her a new confidence. She did not despair. First thing she would take her bag to the Citadel railway station and leave it in the left luggage, reckoning that she was more presentable without it. Tomorrow was Saturday, giving her two days to find lodgings before starting work. She slept well, as she always seemed to before days of great upheaval in her life, and was out of the house, for the last time, by seven o'clock, taking care to shut the door firmly. Her bag duly deposited – it cost two pennies but was worth it – she sat for a moment on a bench in Citadel gardens and went over the advertisements she had cut from the *Cumberland News*. She proposed to begin with Warwick Road, which seemed to be full of bed and breakfast establishments and which would be near Arnesen's premises in Lowther Street. The rents quoted were for rooms with running water, which she did not need, and for hearty breakfasts which were immaterial to her. What she was looking for was an attic with any kind of bed in it, and otherwise she required nothing but access to a tap, a sink and a water closet. The money Harris had given her would pay a week in advance at the rates quoted in the newspaper, but since she was not going to pay these rates, her wants being so much more modest, she hoped to strike a bargain and manage to pay a whole month ahead.

Knocking on doors was hard to do. Evie forced herself on but cringed every time a householder appeared and stared at her. She had begun with the rehearsed little speech of 'Good morning, madam' (or sir – quite often a man answered the door) 'I am looking to rent an attic room and wondered if you would have one available?' What she had not been prepared for was incomprehension. No one seemed able to understand what she was saying. Over and over she was forced to repeat herself and then, quite often, and to her absolute consternation, the door would simply be shut in her face. Soon she had changed her approach. She discovered that if she held up the *Cumberland News* cutting and began, 'I saw your advertisement,' she was asked in. Once inside the front door it was easier to make herself understood and, though a look of irritation would cross the landlady's face, it was momentary, when Evie, after saying she did not want the actual room advertised, moved on to say she wanted only an attic and could pay in advance if the terms were reasonable. The question she was always asked was 'Are you in work, then?' and when she replied that she worked at Arnesen's the name acted like magic.

Midday Saturday found her the occupant of an attic bedroom in Warwick Road, her bag already collected and installed. The attic was small and dirty. It had no heating of any kind, no curtaining on the broken window, no carpeting on the floor and the bed was a camp-bed with a collapsed leg. She saw the landlady, a Mrs Brocklebank, watching her closely and knew that any sensible person would be expected to say no to this hovel. To say yes would signify either desperation or standards so low the dirt had not been noticed. Evie had said yes, but inquired where she might find a mop and bucket and water to prepare the room for herself. Quite amicably Mrs Brocklebank took her all the way down to the yard and showed her where she could find cleaning implements, so she could 'Please yourself if you're fussy'. She was fussy, very fussy. Not caring a bit that she was watched and, she was sure, laughed at, Evie laboured all the rest of Saturday to make the best of her miserable room. When she woke on Sunday she had never been happier. She had a place of her own, secured to her for at least a month. Nothing was required of her for an entire day and tomorrow she had a job. She lay on the uncomfortable and inadequately balanced bed and gloried in her new life. The tiny room smelled of the bleach she had been given to use, but she liked the smell and liked the look of the bare deal boards she had scrubbed so viciously. The window pane was patched over with brown paper and she had made a curtain out of her oldest and most useless skirt. All she had to do was get up and do whatever she wanted.

What she wanted most to do was eat, but food had not been included in the terms. She had a bun, one of two she had bought the day before, and she ate that and drank from the jug of water which had been standing all night. A smell of bacon began wafting through the whole house as Mrs Brocklebank prepared those hearty breakfasts she advertised and which her ten male boarders relished. Evie did not know what she was going to do about hot food. There were no cooking facilities here and she would never be able to afford to patronise even the cheapest café. She proposed to exist on cold food and water until she saw how much she was to be paid at Arnesen's. It was quite sufficient, after all; she would buy fresh bread rolls and cheese and a tomato or two in the market and an apple perhaps, and she would eke it all out carefully. Her mother, she suddenly felt sure, would be proud of her when she knew how resourceful she was being. Her happiness was overwhelming and made evident in her singing in church that morning – her lovely voice, which usually she took care to keep subdued, soared over everyone else's, and many a head turned to look at her and for once she did not mind attracting attention. She was only sorry that Miss Mawson was not in the congregation to witness her contentment.

This was diminished somewhat on Monday. She had expected to feel lost and nervous and to have to call forth her already tried and tested reserves of stamina, but nevertheless the end of her first day at Arnesen's found her exhausted and almost tearful. There had been no sitting and sewing straight seams in peaceful rooms, not a bit of it. She had never come near holding a needle in her hand. Instead, all day long she ran up and down the building, fetching and carrying and being shouted at. The place seemed to her chaotic behind its orderly façade, full of rooms where behind closed doors there was pandemonium. All orders were screamed, all instructions yelled. And, if they were not immediately understood, the language which erupted from faces red with rage was worse than any she had heard in the Fox and Hound. She trembled under this onslaught and her legs shook. Nobody was kind or gave a thought to her. She never left the building and had nothing whatsoever to eat all day. By the time she got back to her attic, without having had the opportunity to buy any of the food she planned, she was weak and sick with hunger. The remaining two-day-old bun she still had choked her with its dryness, but she forced it down and then wept and slept. She woke rigid with apprehension but determined above all else to procure fresh food. The market she knew would be open early, so she hurried straight there and bought what she needed, consuming half a hot new loaf and a huge slab of cheddar cheese cut freshly for her on the spot, and returning home with the rest. She felt better not just because of what she had eaten but for knowing she had fresh provisions waiting for her when she returned that night.

She was not quite as tired and desperate at the end of Tuesday. The racing around and being shouted at had been the same, but she had not felt quite so invisible and despised. One of the machinists had thought to offer her some tea and she had found the few mouthfuls made a huge difference. Her name was not yet known, nor had she expected it would be, but when she was greeted once in the cutting-room with, 'Oh, it's you again, look sharp with that pattern,' she felt comforted. The cutting room overawed her. Here she felt serious work was being done. It was quieter too, though roars did still split the air when something went wrong. Paper patterns were placed on beautiful-looking materials with great precision and she hardly dared to breathe in case she sent them fluttering. She heard Mr Arnesen's name mentioned frequently here – he was always being expected and his arrival half-dreaded, so much so that she built up an image of this man as some kind of ogre. When, on Thursday, he came to supervise everyone's current work, Evie was disbelieving as she heard him addressed and realised this was the great Henry Arnesen, tailor supreme, owner of this prestigious and profitable firm which he had built up, she had gleaned, entirely on his own, starting as a one-man business in Globe Lane.

He looked so gentle. Tall, though slightly stooped, and with a fine head of hair and broad shoulders, but mild-looking, his face smooth and virtually unlined and his eyes benign behind his spectacles. He did not shout. On the contrary, he spoke quietly and never raised his voice even when a disastrous mistake in the cutting of a highly expensive silk was discovered. Evie could see everyone admired him and that in spite of his apparent gentleness they thought of him as a tough taskmaster. She heard one of the machinists say, as he left the room after instructing one girl to unpick an entire garment, because her machining had very, very slightly puckered the material (a material so gauze-like it was almost impossible to work with), that she wouldn't like to be his wife. He was such a perfectionist, the girl had complained fretfully, life would be impossible married to such a man. But there was a chorus of disagreement – everyone else, it seemed, longed to be Mrs Henry Arnesen and thought her a lucky woman. 'He's been good to her,' someone said, 'everyone knows that, very good to her, worships her, and his daughters, he's a real family man, none better.' Heads had nodded. 'No philandering,' this voice of authority continued, 'not for Mr Arnesen. Content with his wife, he is, and always has been.' A current of envy seemed to pass through the room conducted silently from machine to machine. Evie, set to pick up scraps dropped all over the room, listened avidly. 'She's a looker, though, his wife,' said another voice, 'beautiful woman, with that lovely hair. Did you see her here last week? With her hair all plaited, the French way? Lovely. She's nearing forty, must be, but you'd never know it, she's kept herself well, kept her figure even if she's had two bairns and umpteen miscarriages, they say.' 'She's a good mother too, bringing those girls up well,' a voice chipped in, and another responded with, 'I'd be a good mother if I had her looks and her Henry.' The rest was lost in laughter and then Evie's job was done and she left the room and went where she was told she was needed, feeling heavy with a longing she thought she had grown out of, that wretched yearning for a mother who would never now be found. She wished she had never heard Mrs Henry Arnesen being talked of.

Chapter Sixteen

THERE WAS a queue when Shona arrived outside the Public Search Room at 8.30 am. When the double doors were unlocked, everyone moved smartly, walking straight to the counters. She went first to collect some forms. She had discovered by now that when she found her mother's marriage entered in the ledgers she would need to fill out the appropriate form and present it to a clerk who would give her a copy of the certificate for £5. She took several birth certificate forms too. Her mother was likely to have children and she could surely trace them. Then, armed with her little sheaf of papers, she went through to the room which held the marriage ledgers. Slowly, she found the year books for 1957, the year after she was born, not because she thought her mother would have married then but because it was important to be thorough. Every year from 1957 up to the present one must be searched.

Her arms ached after the first hour, in which she had looked through five years of records for Hazel Walmsley's marriage. Twenty huge heavy ledgers taken down, spread open, looked through. Not many Walmsleys at all, which made the job easier, but still she was tired from all the lifting and from the tension. The room had filled up. By the time she got to 1964 there was no space on the counter to open the ledgers and she had to lug them to other counters where a gap briefly opened up. All around she could see people finding what they wanted and scribbling details down. She carried on through another year, dully now, sullenly turning pages, hypnotised by the very writing she was scrutinising.

Nine years and still her mother hadn't married. Shona broke off and went to wash her hands. The ledgers weren't dirty exactly but many of them were dusty. Little puffs of dust swirled around the room as the big books thumped on to the counters. She found herself looking in the mirror over the washbasin and not seeing her own reflection properly at all. She stared at her face and tried to see where it would age. Around the eyes, certainly. There were faint lines at the corners already and these would deepen and so would the line between her eyebrows. Maybe her whole face would become thinner and her full cheeks disappear and the bone structure emerge. Her hair would lose its shine and colour, it would go grey and she would at last cut it – she didn't want to be middle-aged with long grey hair. Tentatively, she leaned over the wash-basin and, scraping her abundant hair right back with both hands, she thought, yes, the greatest change of all would be to have her hair grey and short, severely short. That would age her.

Back she went to the search room, hardly able to get down the ledger for the spring of 1966. January to March for that year had few Walmsleys. None were entries for Hazel Walmsley. She put it back and reached for April to June. It was missing. She looked to the right and left of her to see who was using it. A man at the end of the crowded row had it. Shona waited for him to replace it and was annoyed when he put it back in the wrong order – how careless people were. She could have asked him to pass it straight over to her, but she wanted to go through the whole ritual.

Nearly ten years now and still her mother was unmarried. What did it mean? Maybe her birth had put her mother off men for life, maybe she had remained single, an embittered spinster. Shona hated to think so. She wanted to have been a mistake from which her mother had recovered quickly, and gone on to be happy, not an accident which had had long-lasting and dire consequences. It was beginning to occur to her that instead of tracking down a woman of a mere thirty-six years of age who had settled into marriage and motherhood with such ease that the memory of her illegitimate child was shadowy, she might be discovering a woman not far off forty who had spent all these intervening years full of remorse and regret and quite unable to build any new life. Disturbed, Shona hurried to open the summer ledger for 1966. Did she want to claim such a woman as her mother? No. She would feel so guilty, to have wrecked her life, and nothing she would be able to do would make up for the sentence she had served. Her mother would become her burden and she was not looking for a burden, she was looking for the setting down of her own.

There were twenty-seven women called Walmsley who married between April and June 1966. One was Hazel. Shona was so sunk in gloom that at first the entry meant nothing to her. Then she felt excitement course right through her as she snatched a pencil to copy the details on to the correct form. Only after she had done so, and had gone to queue at the counter where certificates had to be handed in, did she allow herself to relax and even then she could hardly bear to stand still. She wanted to shove all the people in front of her aside and bang on the glass partitions and demand instant attention. It took a full forty minutes before her turn came. She paid the fee and asked to collect the certificate at the end of the day instead of having it posted. It was agony to have to wait even those few hours ahead.

Outside, she hesitated. Covent Garden was near, she could go there and buy herself a cup of coffee and hunch over it as long as possible. She walked there and went into a café, propping the piece of paper upon which she had written the details of her mother's marriage against her coffee cup. Hazel Walmsley, aged twenty-eight, had married Malcolm McAllister in April 1966 in Gloucestershire. So little she yet knew, but so much more than she had ever done. She felt such relief that her mother had married after all and to a Scot, or a man with a Scottish name. They would have children by now, she was sure they would, but of course these brothers and sisters would be very young, it wouldn't be possible to become their friend. She felt a little disappointed at the realisation, but quickly consoled herself – it didn't matter, in fact it would be better, it would mean she could be accepted as a proper sister without question. The moment she had her mother's marriage certificate she would begin the search for her children.

Shona didn't open the envelope with the precious certificate in it until she was home. All the way to Kilburn she constantly touched it inside the pocket of her jacket, feeling the thin paper between her fingers, not ever letting it alone. Once in her room she flung herself on her bed and held the envelope high, as though offering it in some kind of sacrifice before opening it. She felt her face flush and a trembling set in as she saw that Hazel Walmsley was, or had been at the time of her marriage, a lawyer. It was so unexpected and thrilling that Shona could not get over it – coincidence, yes, but surely more significant than that, surely meaning that she and her mother shared like minds just as she had hoped. Catriona didn't have a like mind, that had always been the trouble. They did not think in the same way about anything and her own analytical, critical nature had endlessly come into conflict with her adoptive mother's gentle, rambling, discursive pattern of thought. Malcolm McAllister was a lawyer too. He was thirty-two to Hazel's twenty-eight. They had married in church on 11 April 1966. Shona was sure it had been a beautiful day – she could see it all in her mind's eye, her mother at last happy, and lovely in her dress and veil.

She didn't sleep at all that night. First she cried with excitement and then she cried with self-pity, for pity of the self shut out of her mother's happiness. Around three in the morning, giving up on all hope of sleep, she dressed and made tea and then sat hugging her cup, full of new doubts. What if Malcolm McAllister had been a case of better-than-nothing, a case of her mother waiting ten long years and marrying in desperation? No reason to think so but she thought it. What if he knew nothing of his wife's illegitimate baby? Shona pondered this long and deep. Clearly, there had been great secrecy. Everything she knew pointed to it. A baby born in Norway, well out of the way. The intention was surely to have kept the event secret and go on doing so. Why tell a new husband ten years later? But *I* would have to, thought Shona, I would want to, long before the actual marriage. Of course Hazel would have told Malcolm, of course. And what would he have said? About that she could not be so sure. Would it worry him, the thought of his wife's illegitimate child out there somewhere? Maybe. But Hazel would tell him there was no need to worry, the baby had been adopted and never heard of since. Shona smiled in the darkness of her room.

The births of her three half-brothers were quickly found the next day, Philip, born in 1967, Michael in 1969, and Anthony in late 1970, such plain names and not a Scottish one among them. No sisters, though. At first this made Shona sad but then she thought how much more special it made her to be her mother's only daughter. She fantasised the birth of her last half-brother and her mother's disappointment – still no girl to replace the daughter taken so cruelly from her. I have no rival, Shona thought, and was pleased. What pleased her even more was that she now had an address (taken from Anthony's birth certificate), which was only four years old, and it was a London address. She had never been to Muswell Hill but she knew it was in north London and not so very far east of Kilburn. The telephone directory listed an M. McAllister living at the same address as was on Anthony McAllister's birth certificate – it was easy, easy: it had all been there waiting to be found.

She couldn't afford the time to go to any lectures or write any essays – such things were trivial beside the need to lay siege to the house in which her mother lived. The nearest tube station to it was Bounds Green, which meant an irritating six stops on the Bakerloo Line, then two changes for another eight stops on the Piccadilly Line. It took forever, and yet as the crow flew the distance on the map was short. She had her *A–Z of London* in her hand as she came out of the tube and was mistaken for a foreigner by an eager-to-help middle-aged woman. 'Are-you-lost-dear?' the woman asked her, and it suddenly seemed a good idea to assume the persona of an au pair girl. She nodded, said in a ridiculously heavy French-English accent that she was and that she was looking for Victoria Grove. She didn't need the woman's help, the map was perfectly clear, but she let herself be guided across the street and directed down Durnsford Road towards the golf Course and Alexandra Park. If, as she stood guard outside her mother's house when she got there, anyone approached her, she would keep up her disguise. It added to the excitement, though she needed no boost to the tension she already felt.

The house was not as imposing as she had thought it might be. It was large enough to impress but ugly, with no redeeming architectural features and built of a particularly nasty-coloured brick. The door was painted green, but the paint looked in need of renewal. The front garden had been paved over and some tubs stood on the paving stones but they had nothing much in them, only some sad-looking wallflowers. Two dustbins, both overflowing, were perched near the wrought-iron gate and there was a broken-backed garden chair to the other side of it. Why would anyone want to sit on it and look at the unattractive front of the house? Shona couldn't understand it, but then decided that once this front garden had been a pretty place and that maybe the sun shone fully on the seat on summer mornings and it was a pleasant place to sit and watch the children play. Across the road was a church. Perfect. It had a wall round it and evergreen shrubs and a porch where notices were pinned. The whole patch where the small church stood – it was actually a Methodist chapel, she soon discovered – was in shadow on this winter morning and there was no better cover than its general murkiness, no lights on, no activity within its confines. She was wearing her usual black trousers and black ski-jacket and nobody would notice her.

She took up a position behind the wall, in the corner where it met another wall dividing the chapel grounds from the next house. The shrubs were thickest here, so thick that she had to peer closely through them to see anything at all. It was cold and raining slightly, but she had thought to put several layers of clothes on and was warm enough to withstand a long vigil. In fact, she had hardly taken up her position, at seven o'clock, when the door of her mother's house opened and a man ran out. Her heart jumped a little as she watched him unlock his car, a modest Ford, and throw his bulky briefcase and thick file of papers into the back seat. He was quite a nice-looking man, this stepfather of hers, but as the very word stepfather popped into her mind she thought of Archie and recoiled from it. This man wasn't as handsome as Archie, her real father, but Archie was not her real father any more than this Malcolm. She shook her head from side to side, annoyed, not wanting any kind of father to get in the way of her real mother. For an hour nothing else happened except for a boy delivering a newspaper, she couldn't see what, and a postman unloading a hefty bundle of letters. She'd hoped, watching him approach the door, that he would ring the bell but he chose instead to shovel all the letters through the letter-box one by one. At eight the door opened again and she took a deep breath but it was only a girl coming out, a girl about her own age. This puzzled her. Who was the girl? A lodger? Would a couple like her mother and her stepfather have lodgers? Or a visitor? A relative? A babysitter who had stayed overnight? It disturbed her not to know and to have to indulge in such speculation.

At eight-thirty another girl came out, older this time and unmistakably some sort of nanny. She had the three boys with her, two in school uniform, dark blue blazers and trousers. They were all carrying bags and kicking each other and yelling, and the nanny was ignoring them as they followed her erratically to another car, a battered Volvo Estate. Shona saw one, the middle one, had her hair, short of course, but the same colour, surely their mother's colour? It made her feel strange, this sight of a half-brother with her hair, but otherwise watching the three boys walk in front of her hiding place was not the emotional experience she had imagined it would be. They were just boys, except for the hair of one of them. They were nothing to her and she felt rather ashamed of her lack of reaction.

Half an hour went by and the nanny drove back. She went into the house but was out again within minutes wearing a long thick coat, carrying a satchel under her arm. She strode off towards the tube. An au pair, Shona thought, not a nanny, an au pair off to some course at a language school in Leicester Square or somewhere central. And that first girl would have been a friend staying the night. Maybe another day she would tail her. At ten o'clock a dowdy-looking, grey-haired woman was dropped off, by a man driving a plumber's van. She opened the front door with her own key. A dog, a labrador, rushed out barking and was called back in. The cleaner? Probably. She felt pleased her mother had a dog and wondered what its name was.

By midday, Shona was frozen and tired. It had begun to rain heavily now and the shelter she had thought so adequate wasn't any more. Where was her mother? Had she left her house even earlier than her husband, earlier than seven? Or was she away on business? Either that or she was working at home. That was more likely. If so, there was no point staying here, lurking in the bushes. Better to go home and come back another day. But it was hard to tear herself away when she still had such hope that her mother would be bound, at some point, to emerge. At one o'clock she forced herself to give up and retraced her steps to Bounds Green tube. At least she had seen the house and her half-brothers, at least the six hours of observation had not been entirely wasted. All spies – she reminded herself that she was a spy – had to be prepared to spend time reconnoitring their territory, getting to know the layout in case of – in case of what? Escape? Hardly, she was getting carried away. Maybe she did need to know, all the same, where there was a café, or pub, or somewhere warm to spend half an hour or so not far from her mother's house; then she need not go home, but could thaw out on the spot and go back again. There was a lot she had to learn about detective work.

One thing that occurred to her when she reached the comfort of her bed-sitter in Kilburn was that she should take a camera with her. No one could possibly see that their picture was being taken if she shot from behind the shrubs. She wouldn't use a flash and even if the pictures came out murky they would be better than nothing. The boys had passed quite close to her and had been making such a racket, a little sound like the click of a shutter would have been completely drowned. She would take the house too and have something concrete to hold on to when she got home. Her camera was a Kodak, an eighteenth birthday present from her parents, quite a good one, she thought, certainly good enough to turn out reasonable snaps. It was tempting to put a film in and return to Victoria Grove at once, but she resisted the impulse. She must not become obsessive and spoil everything. She had resolved to be cool and objective, not get overwrought and do something silly. It was what she was most afraid of, that she would see her mother and be unable to resist running across the road and hurling herself into her arms. The very idea made her shudder.

Every day Shona made her way on the tube to Bounds Green and then to Victoria Grove, carrying her camera. No one ever came near the chapel or challenged her in any way. After three days, she was catching the first tube and still she had not seen her mother. But the inhabitants of her mother's house were by now familiar to her and their routine known. Her stepfather always left at seven, always in a hurry, but his return home was never regular. Sometimes it was around eight, sometimes nine, and on two days he had not come home by the time Shona observed her own deadline of ten o'clock. The children came home at four o'clock, though not with the nanny / au pair figure. They came home in different cars and were seen into the house by the drivers. The nanny / au pair had always returned by then from wherever she went and opened the door to them. Once an elderly woman drove them home and went in with them on a day when Shona had just begun to worry that the usual girl who looked after them was not back. It was only after this tall, elegant woman with a commanding voice – 'Philip! I shall not tell you again, get *out* of that puddle at once!' – had disappeared inside, using her own key, that Shona thought, of course, my real grandmother.

It shook her to realise this. Not Grannie McEndrick, not Grannie McIndoe, but her grandmother Walmsley. And this grandmother, the real one, must know about her; she must, no eighteen-year-old could have managed to go to Norway and have a baby all on her own. This grandmother, unlike her two Scottish grannies, had been involved. Suddenly, Shona felt afraid but could not think why. Why should she be afraid of this woman, her mother's real mother, her real grandmother, and yet not of her real mother? She didn't like the look of Grandmother Walmsley – too organised, too powerful, too immaculately dressed. She'd noticed the boys behaved well with her, that there was none of the shouting and kicking there always was with the young woman who ferried them about. Was she a Tartar, an ogre? But the little one, Anthony, had held her hand very trustingly. Sitting in the nearest café that she'd been able to locate, Shona pondered this. She had not only new relatives to meet but a whole family history to inherit. It was daunting. She would never be able to absorb all the detail, it would take years. But then she had years, she was only eighteen, nearly nineteen.

It struck her, thinking this, that her birthday would be the perfect time to make herself known to her real mother. Melodramatic, perhaps, but then how could such a meeting ever be ordinary? It was always going to be dramatic whenever it took place and however it was handled. And it made sense, to approach her mother on the very day she would surely be thinking of her. She probably woke every morning of 16 March and felt a momentary distress, however happy she really was. It would be impossible for any woman not to have carved on her heart the date she had given birth to her first child. She would always see the date approaching, the fateful Ides of March, and remember and think about that baby and feel a whole mixture of emotions. It would be appropriate to emerge out of the shadows on such a day, to present herself as fully formed and ready to be loved and to love. But her birthday was two months away still and she did not know if she could wait. It needed patience, and her patience was running out.

Her reward came at the very end of the week. It had become like a job, going every day to Victoria Grove. She sat on the tube like a commuter, not needing to look up to know she had reached King's Cross and it was time to change lines again, and knowing her way in and out of Bounds Green so well that she could carry on reading until she was out on the pavement. She had become quite fond of her hiding-place among the shrubs in front of the chapel and had made it her own. She'd taken a collapsible wooden stool with her, and every afternoon she wrapped it in a black bin liner and left it flat under a bush. Taking it out each morning and setting it up and settling down upon it pleased her. She felt professional, less furtive, just for carrying out the ritual. She had hidden an old umbrella too, a man's brolly, which sheltered her when the rain grew too heavy. And she had her own hours, times when she went to the café near the tube, twice a day, and had a cup of coffee or bowl of soup before returning to her post.

Her mother's house was by now so familiar to her that she had memorised every detail. She knew not just how many windows there were but how many window-panes and how many were curtained, how many had blinds. She had noted the Virginia creeper literally creeping from the next house, and seen where the drainpipe near the roof had a leak. At home in her bed-sitter she had rows of photographs now of the front of the house, some with Malcolm leaving, some of the boys coming hurtling through the door. They were all pinned up on a cork board along one wall, the first things she saw every morning. Best of all were four close-ups which she had had enlarged. These had been lucky shots, taken when her half-brothers had passed so near to her that she could have reached through the bush and touched them. It had been a bright, sunny morning and the car had been parked in front of the chapel. Shona had snapped quickly and the snaps had come out beautifully, three of all three boys together and one of the middle one alone, the one with her hair.

She saw, once she had had this photograph enlarged, that he also had her features. They looked odd in a young boy's face. His big eyes swallowed his thin face whereas they were in proportion in her own, and his nose – her nose – straight and sharp-tipped, with the very full mouth beneath, just like her mouth, looked far too old for a young boy's face. But that was the point, he hadn't grown into these features yet – her features – and whereas her hair – his hair, their mother's hair? – was wonderful for a girl it looked less good on a boy. The thick auburn hair had been cut very short and its natural curliness, thwarted, had a bumpy, rough look. She was sure he must hate his hair. Her mother – their mother – would tell him it was lovely hair, just like her own, but he would still wish he had hair like his brothers', like his father's plain, straight brown hair.

That was the big surprise when at last Shona, perched on her stool, saw through the screen of foliage an unknown woman coming out of the house and realised it must be her mother Hazel: *she has not got my hair.* This woman had black hair, smooth and expertly twisted into a knot at the back. Was it dyed? Shona, peering hard, did not think so. It was quite uncurled and silky, not thick-looking hair like her own. The boy's hair must come from somewhere else in the family and so must hers. Distracted by the hair, she did not feel as emotional as she had expected and noted quite calmly her mother's other characteristics. She wasn't as tall as imagined but she was thinner, very fragile-looking indeed, a ballet dancer's figure. My eyes though, Shona thought, and felt a surge of pleasure, and my nose, and oh, how clearly my mouth. But not the skin. Her mother's complexion was olive-coloured. It gave her a slightly Spanish appearance – the black hair, the olive skin, the dark eyes. Her clothes were not exactly conventionally English either. Her suit was black but it had style. The jacket was tight-fitting with a velvet collar and unusually long, turned-back cuffs. She was obviously going to work, maybe to court, and she too carried a briefcase and thick files, just as her husband did. She was frowning as she got into her car and looked preoccupied.

The moment the car had driven away, Shona left. If only she, too, had a car, she could have followed her mother and found out where she worked and then there would be two places to watch. But why watch any longer? She had achieved her objective, she had seen her mother. There was no need to spy any more. Conscious that the next phase of this discovering operation was now upon her, Shona felt almost regretful. It had been so simple just to watch, to look, and not think of acting. Her role had been passive and she had enjoyed it. The long hours of cold and discomfort sitting among the bushes had made her feel virtuous. She was suffering for a purpose and it had appealed to her. But all that was over. Working out the next strategy was tougher and far, far more important. She'd read of people at this stage employing go-betweens, neutral people who went and saw the real mother and sounded out her reaction then reported back. It was unthinkable in this case. No one else knew, there was no one else at all who could fulfil such a delicate role.

But should she write or telephone first? Would that be the best way to announce her presence? Neither seemed right. If she telephoned and got her mother she felt she would dry up. There were no words adequate for a telephone conversation, they would be wasted. How could she say, 'I am your daughter, remember, you had me nineteen years ago and I was adopted?' No, too abrupt, too shocking. A letter would be better but it was too impersonal. She wanted to be *there* when the disclosure was made, to be able to hear and see her mother. She would just have to march up to the front door and ring the bell and do it. She would ask if she could come in – 'Excuse me, you don't know me, but could I come in for a moment?' Her mother would be amazed and ask why. 'Well, I have something to tell you, about myself and you.' Then surely her mother would guess and her face would change and ... Impossible to imagine the rest.

Shona went over and over this scenario, spotting snags all the time. Her half-brothers being there, making it embarrassing and difficult, or her mother being in a hurry and closing the door, or some stranger she didn't know about answering the door. She had to be sure her mother would be on her own, she had to have seen the husband, the nanny figure, and the boys all leave the house, and be as certain as it was possible to be that no one else, not even the cleaner, and certainly not the grandmother, was in. Then maybe she could invent some sort of initial cover, be a collector for some charity or other, just to ease the door-opening. She would need a tin or box but that was easily made. Save the Children, she'd be collecting for Save the Children, and this would lead her beautifully into 'Actually, I am your child' – oh, how ridiculous. Still, she liked the collecting disguise, it made her feel she'd have more confidence. If she lost her nerve she wouldn't feel so bad, she could just mumble and flee after saying she was collecting.

What should she wear? This was hard. Not her black outfit. She knew she looked quite threatening in that and not at her best. Vanity should not come into it but it did. She wanted to look attractive, a girl of whom her mother could immediately be proud. She would wash and brush her hair and wear it loose. Everyone, men and women, always raved about her hair. But she couldn't wear a dress, simply couldn't bring herself to be false. Anyway, unless it was an unusually mild day she would be wearing a coat and she had only one, as an alternative to her black ski-jacket, a green raincoat. But she liked this coat, though it was pretty useless, not at all efficient as a raincoat and never warm enough in cold weather. She knew she looked good in it. The colour looked well with her hair and the shape flattered her. So she'd wear the flowing green coat and her black trousers and white polo-neck sweater. There wasn't much else she could wear when she thought about it. Catriona was always offering to buy her more clothes, but she had never wanted any.

There, then, it was settled. On the morning of her birthday she would greet her real mother, trying to pick a time when she would be alone, just after everyone else had left, that hour in the morning Shona had learned was the best. Then by nightfall she would be with her real mother at last. The joy of it would be the best birthday present she had ever had.

Chapter Seventeen

THEY HAD an odd way of training people in Arnesen's firm. Young men and women were taken on as Evie had been taken on, but they were not properly apprenticed until at least six months had passed. During that time they were watched closely and only when it was decided they had the right attitude were they offered a permanent position leading to a full-time career. What this right attitude was bewildered many a new worker. It seemed to have nothing to do with actual skill, because there was no opportunity to develop or demonstrate this at first. They were not let near any cutting or sewing but spent their time fetching and carrying and tidying up. Many a disgruntled youngster, turned away after the initial trial period, claimed to have been cheated. 'They didn't give me a chance to show what I could do,' was the complaint.

But Evie understood very quickly what constituted the right attitude and prospered accordingly. There was an art, in the first place, in moving about the different rooms in such a way as not to interrupt the harmony between tailor and material, or machinist and machine. You had to be able to appear at someone's elbow without jostling it and then wait for a pause in their activity to hand them what they had asked for. Making clothes, whether cutting material or stitching it, was very far from being an automatic business – it needed intense concentration at the level to which Arnesen's aspired and this concentration must not be broken. Evie was perfect. She slipped in and out of rooms quietly and carefully without ever calling attention to herself, and yet performing efficiently all the tasks she was given. Her intelligence was also noted. Tidying up at the end of each day needed an unsuspected amount of intelligence. The tools of the trade, the scissors (of many different sizes and types) and the needles and threads (of every strength and hue), all needed to be sorted and put in their respective places so that they would be ready to hand when needed. Evie had, from her very first day, loved arranging the scissors in order of size and had laid them in neat rows beginning with the shears and working down to the tiny pairs used for snipping wisps of thread after a garment had been sewed. She had a good eye, too, for colour. Matching colours was important. She'd be tossed a scrap of silk and given the command 'Thread, quick!' and have to rush to the huge open shelf where reels of every colour were stacked and choose the right shade immediately. It was astonishing how many people could not do this, could not see instantly which of fourteen pinks matched the rose silk.

It was this talent for colour-matching which brought Evie to Henry Arnesen's attention during the second half of the first year she worked in his firm. Her relief at being told she would be taken on and trained now, at the end of the initial six months, was equalled by a genuine delight in her work. She was happy at Arnesen's. She felt she fitted in, even though she had made no friends and hardly spoke a word throughout each long day. But she realised she had been accepted, she was part of what was going on and had no need any more to be nervous and worry about being thought stupid and useless. No one thought her stupid. Little compliments came her way all the time – merely a case of 'good girl' and 'that's right, that's what I wanted' but they were enough for someone who had never been praised in her life. The forewoman in the hand-sewn department took quite a fancy to her and used her most, claiming Evie had the surest eye for matching she had ever come across. Soon Evie was not only matching thread to material but having her opinion sought on the choice of colour for the material itself. She was taken by the forewoman, a Miss Minto, to the warehouse and asked to help match the colour of an artist's sketch to material. Miss Minto would hold the sketch up and say she couldn't tell whether the dress was meant to be sky blue or aquamarine and what did Evie think? Evie would timidly point to the bale she thought the best choice and Miss Minto would nod and say she was about to choose that one herself.

The customer, of course, had the last word. The fitting-room was on the first floor and Evie was overawed by its grandeur. It had a beautiful carpet and silk curtains and a fire always burning in the marble fireplace. Here Arnesen's most important customers came to consult over patterns and materials and then later to try on garments at various stages in the making of them. If the customer was very special, Henry Arnesen himself would handle the consultations, but usually Miss Minto did so. She wore different clothes on these fitting days and looked almost as grand as the customers. When she told Evie she was going to be granted the privilege of helping with the fittings she also told her she would have to smarten up before she was ever allowed in a customer's presence. 'You are shabby, I am afraid,' she said. 'You will need a decent dress, Evie.' Evie was overcome with embarrassment. She knew she was shabby, if clean and neat, but there was nothing she could do about it. Her wage was only just sufficient to support her in her Warwick Road attic and it had been a struggle to save up enough to buy something she needed (a pair of shoes) far more than a dress. But Miss Minto was not insensitive to the situation of young apprentices and went on to tell Evie to go and pick enough material to make a dress for herself. It had to be black and it had to be plain but beyond that she could please herself.

The dress was made within a day. Evie cut it out herself, given the use of the edge of a table and a standard pattern to guide her, and it was machined for her by Mabel, the kindest of the machinists. There were no fittings. Evie could not possibly have taken off her existing threadbare navy dress, because then Mabel and everyone would have seen the parlous state of the undergarments, so she pretended she had tried this new dress on when she had tacked the pieces together in another room, and that it was just right. Since she had measured herself very carefully, disaster was avoided. The dress fitted. It was plain enough even for Miss Minto who, in fact, complained it was too plain. 'You look like a mute at a funeral, Evie, for heaven's sake put some braid on the sleeves or something.' Then there was the problem of her hair, her poor, difficult, wild hair. Evie wore it in an attempt at a bun but, though she flattened it every morning with water, it would not stay flat all day long, and by the afternoon wisps were escaping all round her face. Miss Minto made her take her hairpins out so that she could look at the hair properly and ordered Evie to fetch a brush while she 'had a go' at it. Evie could have told her 'a go' would fail. 'For goodness' sake, girl, it's like a dog's hair, it must have driven your mother wild.' Evie blushed and kept silent. 'You will have to wear a cap,' Miss Minto said finally, 'there are some quite pretty lace caps about. I will get you one, it is a justified expense.'

Clad in the new black cotton dress and the white lace mob cap covering her bothersome hair, Evie was duly initiated into the rites and mysteries of the fitting-room. It was her job to assist Miss Minto in all kinds of small ways – to hold lengths of material up, to hand over tape-measures and pins, to get down on her knees and do the pinning of the hem under the watchful eye of her superior. She was told not to say a word but that was an unnecessary instruction to give Evie. The customers usually had their own maid with them, or else a friend to help them dress and disrobe in the small room off the fitting-room, but occasionally Evie was called upon to assist in the removal of garments. She found this excruciatingly intimate and dreaded her scarlet face being commented on, but these women she helped disrobe were far too self-obsessed to notice Evie's agitation. She wondered whether, if she had had a mother, the sight of mature, unclothed female bodies would have seemed quite unremarkable, but as it was they seemed peculiar to her. Her own body was not something she had studied since her first days with Mrs Bewley, when she had thought herself so horribly like a skeleton, but even now, when she saw the breasts and stomachs and bare arms of these women trying on clothes, she felt like a different species herself. Her own body, though no longer so frighteningly thin, shrank within her black dress as she surveyed the well-rounded proportions of the customers. And these women liked their bodies, they were happy to preen in front of mirrors and conscious only of admiration. There was never anything wrong with their own shape if a dress did not look good – it was always the fault of the dress or dressmaker. Evie heard such lies being spoken by Miss Minto that she could hardly credit she was hearing aright, but then after the customer had gone she would hear the truth and understand the nature of the game being played.

Henry Arnesen himself only attended fittings for coats or suits. Day dresses and skirts and blouses were left to Miss Minto, though Mr Arnesen did occasionally supervise the choice of evening dresses, if not the fitting of them, simply because the materials for these were expensive, and it was important no mistakes should be made. Miss Minto was always there too, although merely in an advisory capacity. Evie, when she was first taken to one of these special fittings, was there in no capacity at all. She was there to be 'on hand'

and to open the door. The customer on that first occasion was the Dowager Lady Lowther, a woman well past middle age who was small and exceedingly stout. To Evie's relief the dowager had brought her own maid and required no further assistance. Her maid stood behind the sofa upon which her mistress sat and stared through Evie as though she were not there, holding one end of a length of gorgeous blue satin while Miss Minto held the other and Mr Arnesen pointed out the depth of its sheen and beauty of its rich colour. The dowager was to be presented to Her Majesty the Queen at some grand function and wished to be dressed in appropriate splendour. There was a tension in the room which Evie felt most distinctly. Mr Arnesen had already spoken of the problems ahead to Miss Minto in Evie's hearing. The dowager was almost impossible to please, convinced as she was that she had grown merely a little plump when her size was gross. She would need flattering and the dress to be cut as cunningly as possible to minimise and disguise the serious imperfections of her figure. Choice of material and of colour, Mr Arnesen had stressed, were vital. The dowager must be steered away from her favourite colour, a bright fuchsia, and towards paler shades, preferably a grey-blue or dark blue-green.

The material now being displayed was neither grey-blue nor blue-green, but Mr Arnesen was working his way towards the colour he wanted his client to pick. Evie listened to his quiet, authoritative voice explaining that this blue would not highlight the delicate tones of the dowager's complexion and was more the sort of thing for a florid person who did not care about the effect. He signalled to Miss Minto and Evie to roll that bale up and bring out another. 'This may look dull, your ladyship,' he said, 'but it is very sophisticated and subtle. You can see the way the light falls upon it, how soft the blue becomes, and this is a material which drapes beautifully, there is nothing stiff about it.' Evie saw the dowager was almost won over, but to convince her another bale was unrolled, of the very pink she so desired. Her lorgnette went up and a sigh escaped her. 'Lovely, don't you think?' she said, hopeful still. Mr Arnesen shrugged. 'A pretty enough young colour but brash, I always think, though if your ladyship insists I'm sure something can be made of it. Evie, hold it up and show her ladyship how it falls.' Blushing furiously, Evie did as she was told, knowing this was all to remind the dowager she was not young and also to make the colour look only suitable for the lower classes.

The grey-blue was chosen. Next, Evie had to bring in artists' sketches of proposed styles. The dowager pored over them, with Mr Arnesen pointing out various features in each dress and steering her away from plunging necklines and nipped-in waists towards more matronly designs. When the style was chosen and material agreed, Miss Minto disappeared into the dressing-room to take measurements, and Mr Arnesen wrote down everything that had been decided while Evie removed the bales of material one by one. She was rolling up a length of the pink from the last bale, when he stopped her. 'Don't take that back to the racks, Evie. I would like my wife to see it. It would look very striking on her. I will take it home with me tonight and see what she thinks. Leave it in the front office and tell them so.' But later, when Evie had done as she was instructed and returned to the machine-room where she was being allowed to machine straight seams at last, there came another message. Mr Arnesen wanted her to take the material to his home now, where his wife was waiting to look at it, and bring it back promptly after she had made her decision. Thankful that she was wearing her fitting-room dress, and therefore looked as well as she was able, Evie obeyed orders.

The carriage stopped, to her surprise, outside the house next to the one she knew to be Miss Mawson's. Evie got out, carrying the material, wishing Miss Mawson would happen to look out and see her looking so prosperous and fine compared to that last occasion, but there was no sign of her. Instead she had been seen by Mrs Arnesen, who had sent the maid to open the door promptly and usher her in.

'You're Evie, I believe,' Mrs Arnesen said, smiling. 'A pretty name.' Evie wondered if there was something sad in Mrs Arnesen's smile as she said this or whether she had imagined it. 'It is Evie, is it?'

'Yes, ma'am.'

'And a very good worker, I'm told.'

'Thank you, ma'am.'

'This is a mad idea of Mr Arnesen's, don't you think, Evie, to suggest such a pink for a woman of my age?'

Evie said not a word. She couldn't agree that her employer was mad and she did not want to pass any comment on Mrs Arnesen's age, which in any case she did not know. But as she watched the material being held up under Mrs Arnesen's chin she saw her husband had been right. The pink did look striking.

'I've never worn pink, certainly not this shade of pink, perhaps a very pale pink once,' Mrs Arnesen was murmuring to herself, 'and I believe I am too old now and it is not suitable for a mother of two great girls. What do you think, Evie?'

If there was anything Evie dreaded most it was being asked directly what she thought, but there was no escape. 'The colour is right for you, ma'am,' she whispered.

Mrs Arnesen laughed. '*Right*, you say? Why right, Evie?'

'Your skin, ma'am, it is pale but full of warm tones.'

Mrs Arnesen stared at Evie, astonished. 'Are you an artist, Evie?'

'No, ma'am.'

'Are you from an artistic family, dear?'

'I don't know, ma'am. I have no family, not that I know of.' Evie took a deep breath. Usually, this was all she ever managed to say on the subject of her origins, but Mrs Arnesen was so very nice, nicer even than Miss Mawson, that she felt emboldened. 'I was brought up by my mother's cousin,' she offered. 'I do not know, ma'am, if my mother is alive or not. She is lost to me and always has been.' Evie hung her head. She always felt flooded with shame whenever she was compelled to reveal her lack of knowledge about her mother. She did not see Mrs Arnesen's face change in expression but when, after there had been no response to her confession (for there usually was some response, if only a word of sympathy hastily uttered), she again looked up, she marked its stillness. Mrs Arnesen, from being animated and smiling, seemed to have gone into a trance. She was standing holding the pink material still but now she turned very, very slowly to look in the mirror above the mantelpiece and stared into it so intently and as though what she saw shocked her that Evie was alarmed. She did not know whether to ask Mrs Arnesen if she had been taken suddenly ill, or to keep quiet until what was surely some kind of fit was over. As ever, she chose to keep quiet. Mrs Arnesen did not, in any case, appear to notice she was there. She touched her own face, fearfully it seemed to the watching Evie, and the pink silk hung dejectedly now from her hands. 'No,' she at last said, 'no, I think not. But thank you for bringing it, dear.'

She looked so hurt and sad. Evie could not understand why. Was it because Mrs Arnesen had seen herself as old all of a sudden? Had the pink silk made her feel this? Was this a case of vanity? But Evie could not reconcile this judgement with the manner in which Mrs Arnesen had greeted her and her animation until the moment she had held up the silk. Or was it up to that particular moment? She felt confused. But as she struggled to understand, Mrs Arnesen said, very gently, and Evie could swear with tears in her eyes, 'Take the material back, dear. Tell my husband I don't care for it.' Distressed and still wondering what had happened to change Mrs Arnesen from a smiling happy woman to this downcast creature, Evie rolled up the material and wrapped it in a piece of calico. Mrs Arnesen had already left the room and was opening the front door, but before Evie could go through it and into the waiting carriage, two girls came in, making a great deal of noise, and her way was barred.

'Mother!' shouted the older of the two girls, 'Polly deliberately tripped me and look, my skirt is torn, it is *ruined*!'

'I did not trip you, Rose!' yelled the younger of the girls. 'Do not tell such fibs!'

'Girls, girls,' said Mrs Arnesen, closing her eyes and pressing herself against the wall of the hallway, 'my head aches as it is.' She put a hand to her forehead, but to Evie's amazement the two girls simply carried on as though she had never spoken. Evie, unable to get past the still furiously arguing sisters, crouched helplessly against the wall, clutching the material, and waited for them to stop. Neither of them seemed to notice her, so intent were they on claiming their mother's attention. Finally, Mrs Arnesen herself shouted, her hands over her ears. This seemed to bring her daughters to their senses and they both flung themselves upon her, kissing and hugging her. Still Evie stood there until at last Mrs Arnesen detached herself and said, 'Let Evie through, girls. You have made such an exhibition of yourselves.' Head down, Evie edged her way out of the house and into the carriage, further confused by what she had seen and heard in the last few minutes.

In her room that evening she lay on her bed and thought how little she knew about families. Those Arnesen girls mystified her – how could they shout so and cause their mother such pain? And all over a tear in a dress, a tear that Evie with her experienced eye had seen could be mended in a trice. Big girls too, not children. Neither of them was as pretty as their mother, though Rose, the older one, had the same hair, if already several shades darker and likely quite to lose its blondness later. But she struggled to be fair. It was not fair to judge Rose and Polly Arnesen on that scene. Perhaps they were usually as charming and content as they ought to be with such a mother and had merely been caught at a bad time. She imagined them apologising to their mother after she had gone, and making up for their selfish behaviour. Mrs Arnesen would forgive them of course. She looked the sort of person kind enough to forgive anything. She was kind enough to be interested in me, Evie thought, and marvelled at this. Her own mother, wherever she was, if she was still alive, would not be a fine lady in the same situation as Mrs Arnesen. It was not realistic to think so and Evie had cured herself of romanticism. Her mother would be working hard for her living somewhere. In her bones Evie knew this. Sometimes she had visions of a woman like herself but older scrubbing floors and cleaning grates, a woman looking worn and tired, and she shuddered. Finding her mother might have been a sad business after all.

She was no nearer finding her even though she had been in Carlisle nearly two years. She'd finally seen the baptismal register in Holy Trinity church and it had told her nothing more than she already knew. She'd even plucked up the courage to ask to see the marriage register but there had been no marriage recorded for Leah Messenger. As for choirs, no church Evie attended had middle-aged women in their choirs; and if her mother were singing away in the congregation, she could not be identified. Evie despaired of herself – how could she ever have imagined that knowing her mother had a fine voice would lead her to her? She needed to know *facts* and they proved impossible to establish. She knew that she ought to go back to St Ann's and seek help from the matron, but surely the matron would have changed and would know nothing. Records must be kept, but for how long? And what sort of records? What was ever recorded about girls like her? It would be better to let go of the vision which had filled her mind for so many years and acknowledge that she was on her own and motherless. Why, after all, did it now matter? She was grown-up, not a child. She could be a mother herself if she so wished. It was too late for dreams of being mothered.

She thought about her life and her future differently, once her position at Arnesen's was confirmed. The panicky feeling that she would never belong anywhere had gone. She belonged at Arnesen's. She was known there. Every day a score of people greeted her and said her name, and she could feel recognition if not affection buoying her up. If she wanted, she could have friends – it was only her natural reticence which prevented her from exploiting the possibilities before her. She had even been asked to take a Sunday stroll by a young man, Jimmy Paterson, one of the apprentice tailors. She had said she could not and left it at that, and she could see he was hurt. Like her, Jimmy was shy and awkward. He had big, red hands which looked more suitable for butchering than tailoring, and a long narrow face to match his tall, thin body. Jimmy was nice enough but she didn't want to go walking with him or any boy. She was afraid of all men except Mr Arnesen. The best part of every week was when Mr Arnesen smiled at her as he went in and out. She felt she had made a little mark and was no longer quite so insignificant. If, after several more years, she had done well enough to be a proper seamstress, trusted by Mr Arnesen with skilled work, then she would be content.

It was harder to envisage contentment at home. Her Warwick Road attic could not be called a home, it was not at all what she needed to make her content. But it was cheap and it meant she very soon could save a little money, and that was important for any kind of happiness. Mrs Brocklebank had offered her another room, a much better one on the second floor at the back, a room with a wash-basin and running water in it, but she had declined. The rent was twice as much, even if reduced from the normal rate because Mrs Brocklebank liked her. She had made her mark in this house just as she had made it at Arnesen's and came and went quite comfortably. Her landlady was always trying to find out where she came from: she was very inquisitive, but Evie's evasions finally defeated her and she switched to inquiries about her work at Arnesen's.

It was from Mrs Brocklebank that Evie heard more about Mrs Arnesen, though she tried not to listen, knowing the teller loved gossip and was far from reliable. 'There are folk around who remember her before she married Henry Arnesen,' Mrs Brocklebank said. 'Folk in the market, they remember her. She used to come in from Wetheral on a cart, selling flowers and eggs.' Evie thought this very interesting but could not bring herself to ask questions. 'She wasn't always a fine lady,' Mrs Brocklebank went on, 'but she did well for herself, she chose the right man, though to do her justice she couldn't have known he'd prosper as he did. He only had a little place in Globe Lane and he kept a stall in the market too, at one time.'

Wandering in the market on Saturday afternoons Evie tried to imagine Mr and Mrs Arnesen there all those years ago. It was hard. She could not imagine Mrs Arnesen as one of the butter women. It was impossible to see that slim, lovely figure among all the bulky rough-looking matrons. Dreamily, Evie stood with her back against the far wall and looked through the crowds of Saturday shoppers at the benches crowded with the butter women. She screwed her eyes up, trying to create an image of Mrs Arnesen there, but all she could see was old Mary, who had looked after her. Mary had sat there once, she was sure. Mary had reminded her of it and urged her to remember Wetheral too, but she never could to any useful extent. Maybe they had come in on the same cart as Mrs Arnesen? She wished she had not been so very young and could remember more. Opening her eyes properly again, Evie began walking slowly around the stalls. Easier to imagine Mr Arnesen here. There were several stalls selling material. This market had been the place where the Arnesens met and it gave her a pleasant sensation to think of it. She thought about going to Wetheral to try to stimulate some recollection of her first three years, but didn't know how to get there. Maybe she could find a way to go there and walk about. It would be something to do on a summer evening.

Something to do, somewhere to go. She liked to try and think up treats for herself, cheap treats. Even though she was happy at work she needed to get out of her dismal attic in her free time at the weekend and it was always a problem. There was church on Sunday and market-wandering on Saturday afternoon (she worked in the morning) but otherwise her pastime was walking. She walked until her legs ached and her biggest expense was having her boots soled and heeled. Her walks often took her up Stanwix Bank and out along the Brampton Road nearly as far as St Ann's and very often she turned the other way at the top of the bank and went left and down Etterby Street and up the Scaur past the Arnesens' and Miss Mawson's houses and along the road to Rockcliffe, though she never went far enough to reach the village. She felt conspicuous walking along the country roads on her own, and preferred the streets of the city or at least its parks. Rickerby Park, Bitts Park, Linstock – she knew them all well. And the river, the river Eden, became so familiar to her she knew its every twist and turn as it meandered through the parks. No one ever spoke to her, but then why should they, since she did not know them. Once she saw Miss Minto in the distance, descending the steps beside the bridge into Rickerby Park with her arm on a man's, and she hid until they had gone past. She dreaded encounters with people from work, who would see her exposed as lonely and without family on a Sunday.

All the time she was walking she was thinking about where she could live. She did not want to stay for ever in her attic and craved a better place, somewhere she could turn into a home. It was impossible ever to buy anywhere, she had no such delusions of grandeur, but she had heard of places that could be rented for reasonable rates and even of places where preferential treatment was given to single working women. These were not in Stanwix of course, they were nowhere near Etterby Scaur, which would have been her heart's desire. Stanwix was only for the well-off. It had huge, grand houses overlooking the river and then it had streets like Etterby Street for the not quite so affluent. The places she heard about were at the other side of the city near another river, the Caldew. She had walked there, over the Viaduct and down through the industrial suburb of Denton Holme. There was a factory near the waterfall and some little houses near it, and here some of the women at Arnesen's lived and liked it. Evie thought that with time and if she were lucky, and if there were a vacancy, she might aspire to one of the houses. They were built in closes and had only two very tiny rooms in each and no bathrooms, and a shared privy in a yard, but she didn't mind that. She would be able to settle there and be her own mistress.

She thought sometimes of Ernest and Muriel and wondered if they had searched for her and how long it had taken them to give up. Twice she thought she caught sight of Ernest in the market, and on the second occasion was almost certain it had been him. What would he have done if she had walked up to him and made herself known? But it never occurred to her to do so. She was much too frightened of what he might do, even though commonsense told her he could have no hold over her now. She had been frightened when she saw him – there was a little leap of fear in her stomach – but afterwards she had felt strangely pleased. None of her foolish dreams had come true – she hadn't found her mother – but her life now was better than it ever could have been if she had stayed with Ernest and Muriel. She had found work she was good at, she had a trade, whereas stuck in the Fox and Hound she would have remained a skivvy all her life. And she had a place of her own for which she herself paid and was not dependent on charity. She had been right to escape the loveless claims of her mother's cousin, even if her true objective had not been achieved. If Ernest had stopped her she ought to have been able, she reckoned, to act with dignity. He would be impressed that she was now an apprentice seamstress at a firm like Arnesen's, she might have had the pleasure of seeing him quite shaken by such a triumph. Probably he and Muriel would have envisaged her obliged to take to the streets or reduced to the workhouse, or working as a servant in circumstances far worse than she had endured while with them. Thinking all this through, Evie quite made up her mind that next time she thought she saw Ernest she would indeed challenge him.

But it was Muriel she saw, Muriel dressed all in black and getting out of a coach in front of the Town Hall as Evie passed it on an errand for Miss Minto one Wednesday afternoon. She stopped dead in her tracks and stared, and Muriel saw her too and recognised her, and said, 'Evie!' Evie blushed and smiled hesitantly, unsure how Muriel would treat her, and ready to fly if there was any unpleasantness. But Muriel was not disposed to be the least unpleasant. On the contrary, she hailed Evie as sent by the angels to help her find her way to a firm of solicitors in Abbey Street where she said she had business before going to her brother-in-law's public house in Caldewgate. 'It is so long since I was ever in Carlisle,' Muriel said, clutching Evie's arm, 'and I am bewildered, I don't know where I am any more. You can take me, Evie.' There was not, Evie noted, a single exclamation as to the great changes wrought in her own appearance and not a single question as to her health or status. Muriel treated her as though they had just parted the day before and nothing had changed. But everything had changed, and Evie knew she must make this clear. She explained that she was not at liberty to accompany Muriel. She was working at Arnesen's and was on an errand and must return within twenty minutes. Muriel looked startled. She ran her eyes over Evie and seemed at last to notice the difference and be amazed. Across her face Evie saw the memory of what had happened more than two years ago begin to return. Muriel frowned and said, 'You ran away, you little hussy, after all we'd done for you. It was shameful, shameful. We should have set the police on you.' Firmly, Evie removed Muriel's hand from where it still rested on her sleeve and said she must go, but this changed Muriel's attitude yet again. 'Oh, Evie, don't go!' she said, half moaning and her eyes filling with tears. 'You were like a daughter to me and it is a daughter I need now. Ernest is dead – yes, dead, last week. Come back with me to the Fox and Hound. We will let bygones be bygones and you shall share the house with me and everything.'

The idea was laughable. Evie shook her head and said she was sorry but she must go at once, whereupon Muriel became excited and came up close to her and said, 'I have something you will want, Evie, in my very bag here, something that is yours and I will give it to you if you will meet me.' Not believing her but desperate to get away, Evie agreed that after work she would return to this spot and meet Muriel, and then she left her and ran to Robinson's haberdashery where she had been going. Looking back as she entered the shop she saw Muriel still standing there, motionless, in danger of being knocked down by all the hurrying people if she did not move soon, and Evie felt suddenly sorry for her. Muriel without Ernest was harmless. There was no need to be either afraid of her or unfriendly. Even if there was nothing of interest in her bag she would still go to meet her and give her a little attention. All the rest of the afternoon Evie wondered all the same what it was that Muriel might have to give her. Money? It seemed unlikely. Muriel was a widow now and in control of whatever sum Ernest had left, but she would not be inclined to give any of it to a hussy who had run away. What, then? Something she had forgotten to take when she left the Fox and Hound?

Muriel was waiting, her bag at her feet. She looked more composed and greeted Evie calmly. 'Where can we go?' she asked. Evie shrugged. She had no idea and hoped Muriel did not expect to be taken to her attic. 'Robinson's is closed and so are all the cafés,' said Muriel, 'we will just have to sit on a seat somewhere until it is time for the coach back to Moorhouse.' They walked together to the cathedral and here they sat on one of the seats in the precinct. Fortunately it was a beautiful summer's evening and there was no danger of catching cold. 'I cannot go to them,' Muriel said as soon as they were seated. 'I could not live among them.' Evie presumed she meant the Caldewgate Messengers and murmured her sympathies. 'They are not even my own family. I never liked them. They were cruel to your mother and cruel to old Mary.' Evie held her breath, remembering vividly how she had done so every time Muriel started on one of these rambling trains of thought. 'Cruel people, and greedy. No, I couldn't live with them, but I can't live on my own and there's no one will come and run the pub, and I can't manage and so there's no help for it, I will have to go back to Newcastle and live with my sister and be useful, but I don't want to, I don't want to at all.' She took out a handkerchief and wiped her eyes. 'Oh dear, Evie, it is an awful thing to be widowed and no children to do all the managing and caring, no daughters to take me in.' Evie bowed her head respectfully but said nothing. 'But I have got something for you, Evie, and I must give it to you before I go for that coach. Oh, it is a long ride and no welcome at the other end, but I shan't come here again. I brought all Ernest's papers here, to the solicitors, and they are all in order and thank the Lord I am provided for and there is no trouble, but this was among them, and it is yours by rights, I suppose, Evie. It was given to us at the Home when we came and rescued you and took you away. Here, it might mean something to you.'

Shuffling among all the belongings in her capacious bag, Muriel came up with an envelope and handed it to Evie with an air of someone bestowing great wealth. Evie recognised the envelope at once. 'Thank you,' she said, and put it into the pocket of her jacket immediately.

'Aren't you going to look inside it?' asked Muriel indignantly.

'No,' said Evie, 'I know what is inside it. I remember it. It was in my ribbon box and Mary gave it to me. Shall I carry your bag to the coach stop for you?'

Quite put out, Muriel nevertheless accepted the offer and the two of them walked to where the coach was already standing, and Evie helped Muriel board it. She did not look at Evie once she was seated. Evie felt relieved to be spared any false emotion and walked rapidly home. Only then did she take the certificate out and smooth it lovingly with her hands until the creased and worn piece of paper seemed real again and not the figment of her imagination she had almost come to believe it was. There was her mother's name and date of birth, and there was her own name and date of birth, and there were the official signatures and marks. And this time she knew what to do.

Next day she went straight to Mr Arnesen, bold as never before, and asked to speak to him. She chose her time well, knowing exactly when he would be there, in his own office, and not preoccupied. He smiled to see her. He was fond of her, she knew that and had always rejoiced at his approval.

'Well, Evie, and what can I do for you?' he asked.

'Please, sir, will you look at this and help me? I want to find my mother and don't know how, and I have this, sir, and believe it might be used to find her if only I knew how.' She placed the certificate on Mr Arnesen's desk with an unusual confidence which he noticed and was amused by.

'Well now, Evie,' he started to say, and then he looked at the certificate and stopped. Evie saw him go quite still. He put a hand either side of the piece of paper before him and went on staring at it for a long time. Then he looked up at Evie and she saw how intent his stare had become. 'Your name is Messenger?' he asked.

'Yes, sir.'

'Why did I not know that?'

'Sir?'

'You are Evelyn Messenger?'

'Yes, sir.'

'Good God. I knew you only as Evie. Good God. I never thought to ask ... I ought to know the names of all my staff ... I thought I did ... but I knew you only as "little Evie".'

Uncomfortable now, Evie went on standing there, pleased that Mr Arnesen seemed so unaccountably impressed, but confused as to why. He got up from his chair and came round to her and put his hands on her shoulders. 'Evie, look at me.' But it was he who needed, it seemed, to look at her. He searched and searched her face until she started to tremble and then he sighed and said he could recognise nothing, and then he went and sat down again, this time holding his head as though it hurt.

'Evie,' he said, 'you must give me time to think.'

Part Four

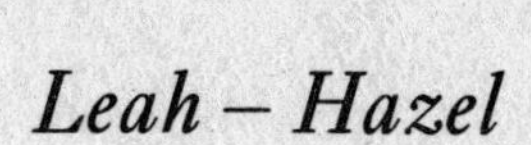

Leah – Hazel

Chapter Eighteen

LONG BEFORE Henry came home with his dreadful news, Leah had felt full of foreboding. She felt heavy and dull and could not seem to concentrate on the simplest of matters. Her abstracted air had already worried her husband, who had asked if she was still plagued with that violent headache which had come upon her the day he had sent the pink silk home. She was not. Her head did not so much ache as feel like a weight too heavy for her neck to carry. And all around her she saw ominous signs which made her heart thud. Nobody else could see them. The mirror above the parlour mantelpiece turned black overnight and frightened her when she came down in the morning. She pointed a trembling finger at it and said, 'Look!' but Henry, when he looked, said he'd noticed clouding occurring earlier and that the mirror must always have been faulty, and he would never buy anything at Hope's auction again. The clock which had always kept perfect time stopped, the crystal vase that had been her mother-in-law's shattered of its own accord, and the camellia outside the back door shrivelled and died – but Henry found rational explanations for all these untoward happenings.

Leah knew it was all to do with the girl. That scrawny young girl had disturbed her peace of mind. And, though she pretended to herself that she did not understand why this should be, she knew that, in truth, she was simply refusing to acknowledge the possible reasons. She did not want to think about them. The girl, Evie, had come into her house, all innocent and welcomed, and had poisoned the atmosphere. Leah never wanted to see her again. She never wanted to look at that humble figure or see her pale, pale face with its huge dark eyes that never seemed to blink and had so little expression in them. Evie made her shudder. A ghost had crossed before her inner vision, a shadow engulfed her happiness. She struggled to be sensible but failed. She told herself that time would restore her normal buoyancy, as time had done before. Perhaps she was unwell without knowing it, she was not after all far off forty and things happened to women at forty. She forced herself to eat properly and to carry out all her daily tasks, and when she did not sleep at night she recited hymns in her head and did not allow her thoughts to meander down dangerous routes.

But when Henry came home, with his face tight and anxious, she knew. He tried to speak to her and she would not let him – she put a hand lightly over his mouth when he began to say he had discovered something incredible which he must tell her, and she told him she did not wish to know. He frowned and pushed her hand away and said, 'But I *must* tell you, Leah.'

'You must not.'

He stared at her and shook his head and said, 'I have no choice, it is too important, I must tell you that ...'

'No! You do have a choice. You will make me ill. I cannot bear it, Henry, you must *not* tell me.'

He sighed, walked about the room, poked the fire, and then suddenly wheeled round and said, 'There are other people to consider, there is what is due to them, to her ...'

She gave a little scream and tried to run from the room, but he stopped her. He put his arms round her struggling body and asked her what she was afraid of. 'There is nothing to be afraid of,' he assured her, 'she is only a girl, and a good girl.'

'No!' Leah shouted. 'No! No!'

'She is a good girl who will make no trouble, she will understand and ...'

'No!'

'Leah, I have to do something. She has asked for my help ...'

'*I* am asking for your help, I am begging for it, and I am your wife.'

'I have given it to you, all these years I have given it to you, have I not? I have kept silent when I should have spoken out, and I have given no thought to the help she needs and now she has come and asked me for it, knowing nothing, and I cannot refuse.'

'You *can*!'

'Listen. You have not even heard the circumstances, you have jumped to conclusions. Evie Messenger ...'

'No! Do not speak her name, for God's sake, I never, never want to hear it.'

'... came to me with her birth certificate which she has only lately been given, following the death of a cousin, and she asked me to help her use it to trace her mother ...'

'Henry! Please, Henry!'

'... whom she has never known, and I looked at this document and I saw well enough who she was, and I had never recognised her nor even known her name was Messenger, and I felt such *shame* ...'

'*You* felt shame?' Leah laughed in the middle of weeping and became hysterical, rocking backwards and forwards, repeating the word 'shame' over and over until Henry became angry.

'Is this what it is about?' he asked, releasing her so suddenly she stumbled as he moved to stand in front of her with his back to the door. 'Shame? You are too ashamed to recognise her as your daughter? Then that is as it should be, yes, as it should be. I wanted to take her ...'

'Oh, you are so *good*.'

'... and you would not hear of it and when I wanted to go in search of the child you would not help me, you said her name was not Messenger, you lied to me ...'

'Yes, I lied, and I am glad I lied, and I would lie again.'

'You thought only of yourself and this strange, unnatural aversion to your own child ...'

'Yes, I did, I had to.'

'And now, now when you have the chance to redeem yourself ...'

'I do not wish to redeem myself.'

'You said you were ashamed.'

'No! *You* said I must be ashamed. I am not ashamed, not then, not now. I did what I thought right and best ...'

'For whom? Best for whom? And right? How *right*?'

'Best for us.'

'Oh now, Leah, I was not party to this, I was not, you know I was not ...'

'We were to be married, then later when Mary died we were already married and our marriage could not have survived with her as part of it.'

'Such nonsense, wicked nonsense, how you can say these things ...'

'I say them because you force me and they are true. I am wicked.

Say it if you will, say it again, and I will agree, I am wicked and evil, an unnatural woman, a woman who did not and cannot love her own child and hated the sight of her and still does …'

The rest was lost in sobbing so wild and loud Henry expected the girls to come running from their beds to see what terror had seized their mother, but they stayed mercifully asleep upstairs. Leah was on her knees, her face buried in her arms, which rested prettily on the seat of the yellow velvet-covered armchair. He did not want to touch her. Always, deeply hidden inside himself, he had known there was a part of Leah of which he was afraid and over which he had no control. He doubted if she had any control herself. This hatred, her terrifying rejection of what had been a frail vulnerable child and was now a poor, gentle good young woman, was uncontrollable. But it was time to control and tame it. His duty this time was clear. He must tell Evie Messenger who her mother was even if at the same time he had to tell her her mother did not want ever to see her and could not bear the mere mention of her name. He would have to attempt explaining the inexplicable as best he could and trust to Evie's goodness to understand and accept the unacceptable.

'You can cry, Leah,' he said after a while, when the ugly noise of violent sobs had quietened down, 'but it makes no difference. I must tell Evie Messenger the truth.'

Leah pulled away from the chair and lifted her blotched face up and said, 'If you do, I will leave you. I cannot stay here to be found and haunted by her. I will leave.'

'Don't say such things,' Henry said angrily. 'You are not yourself, talking like that, in that way.'

'I will leave,' Leah repeated. 'I will take the girls and leave.'

'You will *not* take my girls,' Henry said, as firmly as his alarm could allow him. 'I will not allow it and I will not allow this kind of talk. You are upset, I know that, of course you are, it is understandable, but this is *mad* talk and you are doing yourself no good. Stop. Stop it. Let us be sensible and reasonable for heaven's sake, Leah.'

But the crying began again and all he could think of to say was that he would send for the doctor if Leah did not control herself. It proved an effective threat. She slumped on the chair once more, her hands threaded through the mass of her hair which had come unpinned and cascaded over her shoulders, but she was quiet at last.

'Come, Leah,' he said, daring to touch her now, going down on his knees beside her and embracing her awkwardly, 'come to bed. Things will look different in the morning.' He had to half carry her upstairs and undress her and tuck her up like a child in their bed, where to his surprise and relief she slept immediately. But he himself did not. He lay awake most of the night, worrying. She couldn't leave him, of course. She had no money of her own and no family, no mother to run to, and nowhere to go, and she cared far too much about Rose and Polly to risk exposing them to the life of some kind of wandering exile. No, she could not and would not leave, but there were other dangers all too real. She could make herself ill. She could cry herself into a state day after day until she collapsed. She could make scenes, shout and scream and wear him down. She could decide not to speak to him, could decide to turn away from him in every sense, and such was her strength of will there was no guarantee that she could not keep it up. All these things Leah could do and make their life miserable; but he was resolved and that was that.

Leah, in the morning, sensed this. She woke to find a cup of tea steaming on the little table beside her, and Henry, fully dressed for work, standing looking down at her. 'You slept,' he said. She raised herself on her elbow and sipped the tea gratefully. Her head felt sore and her face ached. She felt her eyes had disappeared altogether and the skin seemed stretched too tight across her cheeks. 'The girls have gone to school,' Henry said. 'I would not let them disturb you.' She nodded. Henry was such a good husband and father, there was none better. It made her feel tearful to acknowledge this to herself, but there were no tears left, she had cried herself out. 'Stay in bed and rest,' Henry urged, 'I will come back later, in an hour or so.' She shook her head to indicate he did not need to but said nothing, afraid to speak for fear of what might come out. He kissed her lightly on her hot cheek and left. She lay back, listening to young Clara, their maid, who had just arrived and was clattering about downstairs, doing the fires. She had slept but she felt so tired, so weary. It was an effort to finish her tea and when she had done so she closed her eyes and lay back on her pillow. Tonight, when Henry came home, it would all have to be gone through again. She would have to force Henry somehow into weakening and holding his peace. It exhausted her to think of the arguments ahead, the hours of quarelling there would have to be. Then there was the threat she had made. It ought to have been saved as the ultimate threat and she had made it already. She had to prepare herself to make it again and show this time that she would carry it out.

She was lying there, trying and failing to think out a plan of action, when Henry returned within the hour as promised. He brought her tea again and she assumed he had come to check she was well and about to get up. 'Thank you, Henry dear,' she murmured, 'but there is no need to disrupt your work. I am not ill. You do not need to treat me like an invalid. Go back and we will talk again after supper, and I will try to stay calm, though it is very hard.' Here a little sob escaped her but she stifled it with a cough and reached for a handkerchief. This was pressed to her mouth when Henry said, 'I have told her. It is done and over.' The scrap of lace in her hand, pressed still to her mouth, was all that prevented her from screaming. He had no need to explain. She understood at once. Her eyes widened as Henry walked over to the window and peered through the net curtains saying, 'She took it well. No tears or hysterics. I told her to sit down, but she would not. She was solemn when I told her you did not wish to have anything to do with her and that you could not help your feelings.' He turned and came to their bed and sat upon it and looked at her, his eyes meeting hers, but his gaze far from steady. 'So, Leah, it is done. She knows and that is that. I am going to provide for her. It is the least we can do. I am going to bank a sum of money for her and in return she has agreed that what has been a secret for so long will remain one. She will tell no one. She has been very good, Leah, very good.'

'And I have been very bad,' Leah whispered, 'and now I must suffer and pay for my badness.'

'There is no suffering except hers,' Henry said. 'She suffers.' He said this sternly enough to astonish himself, but was glad at the tone he had managed even if it would bring forth the full violence of his wife's anger and grief. But she gave vent to neither. She stayed perfectly still and quiet, shocked, he judged, into calm. 'I should have acted years ago,' he said, getting up again. 'Years ago, when she was little, when we married. Everything would have been different, it would not have been too late.'

'I can never come to Arnesen's again,' Leah said. 'I can never walk the streets of this city and feel secure again.'

'Secure?'

'I might come face to face with her now I have seen her and I would die.'

'This is fanciful talk, Leah. You exaggerate foolishly. She is a poor, sweet ...'

'Sweet?'

'She has worked for me for over a year and everyone is fond of her.'

'They will hate me.'

'No one will know. She has no desire to tell a soul.'

'You believe her?'

'Certainly I believe her. Why should I not? She has shown herself truthful in every way. She is to be trusted.'

'And I am not.'

'What are you saying now?'

'You do not trust me.'

'Of course I trust you. You are my wife. I do not understand why on earth ...'

'You do not understand.'

'No. I said I do not. How can you think I do not trust you, my own wife? It is absurd.'

'You do not understand, so you do not trust me.'

'Oh *Leah*! Talking in riddles helps no one.'

'It is no riddle to me. You do not understand my feelings and therefore you do not trust my instincts. You do not know what this – this *telling* you have done does to me, how afraid I am ...'

'There is nothing to be afraid of, it is all over ...'

'... of myself, of what I have done, of what she knows I have done. She will come and claim me.'

'No, no, I have told you, she will not. I am settling a sum of money ...'

'Money? It has nothing to do with money, neither for her nor for me. She will not be able to resist coming now that she knows.'

'She will not come, though if she did it might prove the best thing that could happen. You would see for yourself what a ...'

'You forget. You sent her with the pink silk. I have already seen her.'

'There, then. What did I tell you? She is harmless, just a poor young working girl, an apprentice seamstress ...'

'In your employment. Sack her, Henry, give her money to leave Carlisle, find her a place elsewhere, *please*!'

Later, when he had at last returned to work, Leah felt some new hope. She had seen that Henry was at least turning over her suggestion in his mind and had not dismissed it out of hand. He would puzzle over the fairness of it all day, maybe even longer, and then it would be time to use more persuasion. Honour, his honour, was after all satisfied. He had owned up and told Evie Messenger the truth and now, to help further ease his conscience, he was going to tell her he would give her money. There was no moral problem about suggesting she should move to another establishment in another city. If he could find her a good situation, perhaps a better one – Henry had excellent contacts throughout the north of England – and somewhere pleasant to live, then he might convince himself he was doing the girl a favour. And the girl herself might see it this way too and be pleased and agree. But when Henry did come home at the end of that day he said nothing, and she curbed her impatience and held her tongue for another week before she could restrain herself no longer.

'Henry,' she said on Sunday night, after church, after the girls were in bed and Clara had left, 'Henry, have you thought of what I suggested, about the girl?' She could hardly say the word 'girl' and blushed nervously.

'Yes.'

'And?'

'It seems possible. I made inquiries. I could find a place for her in Halifax and see she was looked after.'

'So it is settled?' She knew, as she asked, it was not and she knew why, but he must say it.

'No. I spoke to Evie and she does not wish to leave this city, she is afraid of moving.'

'But she has hardly been here! Only a year ...'

'More than a year now, nearly two. She was in service a year.'

'Very well, two, only two. Why, it is nothing for a young woman, nothing at all, it is not as though she has lived here all her life ...'

'She says her only happy memories are here, of her early childhood, before she found Mary dead and was put into a Home ...'

'Henry, please.'

'It is what she said. She is going to rent a little house near Holme Head. It is a kind of settlement where ...'

'I do not wish to hear anything about settlements or houses.'

'You asked.'

'I asked only why she will not do the sensible thing and move.'

'And I was telling you, she is settled here and afraid to move, and attached to her childhood memories, though God knows it is pitiful enough what she has to remember.'

'She is cunning.'

'There is no cunning about Evie. She ...'

'How fond of her you have become.'

'Fond? I told you, everyone is fond of her, because ...'

'She is cunning.'

'Leah, you are being ridiculous.'

'She wormed her way into your employment knowing what she knew – that was cunning ... and now ...'

'Stop! She knew nothing when she came to work for me.'

'So she says.'

'Why would she say otherwise? How could she have known I had any connection with her? Tell me that. If she knew, which she could not have done, that my wife was her mother, why did she not come here, to confront you?'

'Because she is cunning.'

Henry left the house. It was dark, but he left the house and walked rapidly up the Scaur and out along the road to Rockcliffe, furious with his wife. He had hardly been able to look at her during the last few minutes – her beautiful face so contorted with malice, her eyes glinting and cruel. Was she ill? Fear gripped him, as he walked and walked, that she was suffering from some mental condition he had occasionally suspected. It was not normal, it had never been normal, for her to feel this revulsion towards her first child. Perhaps she needed some kind of treatment, but he could not bear to contemplate such a thing – his head was full of frightening visions of Leah in a strait-jacket, and he moaned as he turned back at last. She must be made to see she was poisoning her own mind with absurd fantasies in which, it was clear to him, she expected some form of revenge. She thought of little Evie Messenger as an instrument of vengeance about to be let loose upon her for her rejection of the girl. She could not forgive herself for what she had done and did not expect Evie to do so. But was that right? Had he got it right? Or did he not understand, as Leah alleged, was he incapable of understanding the strangeness of her attitude to Evie? The fact was, he had never been able to believe Leah. It had not, and was not, a matter of understanding but of belief. He, a man, could not believe that any woman could not bear the sight of a child, and a daughter too, whom she had borne. It was unbelievable, especially when such a woman was the good and kind and intelligent Leah he had known now for eighteen years and seen as the perfect mother to his own two daughters.

He re-entered his own house quietly. The lamps were out in the parlour. Leah had gone to bed. Thankfully, he sank into the chair nearest to the fire and wondered if he dared to think about other reasons for his wife's detestation of Evie Messenger, her own flesh and blood. He had trained himself from the very beginning not to think about the man before him, the man she said she had loved yet whose name he had been forbidden to ask. There was no real cruelty in Leah's past, he was sure of it. She might have been cheated and tricked, though even that he could not be sure of since he knew no details and had accepted that he never would, but he was convinced there had been no violence. Evie, he was almost certain, had been a love child. Somewhere there was a man, her father, whom Leah at a most tender age had loved and been loved by. Since it upset him to think this and he had recognised his own envy, Henry had banished the awkward knowledge from his head, but now he regretted doing so. In his fear of losing Leah he had acquiesced too readily to her conditions and he ought not to have done so. If he knew now who Evie's father was and what had become of him then perhaps he would be nearer to that understanding which Leah accused him of lacking.

It had been an awful thing he had had to do. Sending for Evie first thing he had felt as faint as any woman with apprehension. She was such a frail, pathetic sort of girl, though he had already come to suspect that there was a strength of character about her which was not apparent. She was not an empty-headed, silly girl and, though she rarely looked him in the eye, he had seen enough to rate her intelligent beyond her education. When she appeared and stood obediently before him, a quiver of anxiety about her clasped hands, he could not at first find the heart to proceed. He cleared his throat then cleared it again and made a performance of finding a strong mint to suck. He could not speak with such a thing in his mouth and felt foolish when he was obliged to extract it and wrap it in a piece of paper and throw it away. All the time, during this fussing, Evie had stood patiently, declining to sit on the stool he had waved her towards. Her very patience distressed him. He was going to hurt her and it was like hurting a dumb and defenceless creature. But she had surprised him with the dignity she showed. 'Evie,' he had said, 'I have some news for you.' She said nothing, there was no start of expectation, no eager looking-up. 'It will come as a shock and not a pleasant one.' Still no response. 'It is complicated.' He hesitated. 'There is no easy way to tell you, but I believe, in fact I know, who your mother is.' Now, at last, there was a reaction. She smiled, a small tremulous smile, the first he ever recalled seeing on her wary little face. The smile made everything far worse. 'It is not necessarily happy news, Evie,' he had said, 'and I wonder if it might be better for you to remain in ignorance.' She looked alarmed and he hurried on. 'Oh, your mother is perfectly respectable, my dear, it is nothing like that, don't think the worst, it is only that your mother prefers not to open up wounds, which is to say, it is to say ...' He had floundered and stopped and sighed and started again. '... Which is to say, you will understand, she is married and has her own family now and she, well, she is reluctant to meet you.' He had been sweating by this time and felt red in the face. 'Would it not be better to know nothing, Evie?'

She had stared at him long and hard, her smile now quite faded. He waited, trying to encourage her by nodding his head. Her silence went on so long he was compelled to repeat his suggestion. 'Evie, would it not be better to remain in ignorance?' At this she shook her head. It was like dealing with a mute. He could not have this settled by a shake of the head. 'Evie,' he said, as solemnly as possible, giving her name as much gravitas as he was able and deepening his voice to do so. 'Evie, you must tell me properly. Are you prepared to take the consequences of knowing who your mother is? Do you understand those consequences?' She nodded. 'It is not enough to nod or shake your head, Evie. You must speak clearly, or I cannot be sure you do understand.'

'I understand,' she said.

'And what precisely do you understand?'

'My ... she, she does not want to know me.'

After that, what else could he have done? Climbing the stairs to bed, Henry could hardly bear to remember the painful dialogue that had ensued. Colour had flooded Evie's face when he had revealed the identity of her mother – he had been frightened by the sight of such pallor changing in a second to such a violent hue. She had looked about to faint and he had rushed to support her, but she had pushed him away and retreated to the door where she seemed to cower against it as though afraid of him. He had felt such disgust to have done this to her and had said over and over how sorry he was. Then there had been the ugly business of the money. He did not want to sound as though he were buying her silence and yet he could not let her go without offering her some token of his sincerity and sense of responsibility. He had wanted so badly to tell her how he had been willing and eager to bring her up as his own daughter, but he had thought it unwise to launch into what would sound like a defence of himself and an attack on his wife. He had wanted also to reminisce, to recall Evie as a baby, to tell her he remembered old Mary and the house in Wetheral and the place in St Cuthbert's Lane, and glimpses of herself as a child even if she did not remember him. But it was unseemly, in the circumstances. Instead he had tried to be business-like, though the atmosphere had been too emotional for a business transaction. When he told her the sum of money he was settling upon her he had been afraid she would reject the offer, but she made no sign of either rejection or acceptance. She had let him talk without interrupting, showing neither pleasure nor disgust. But when he had begged her not to speak of any of this to anyone, she had shown some spirit, and he had been glad of it. 'I only wanted to know,' she said, 'not to tell.'

There had been no cunning. Slipping into bed beside his wife, who if not asleep feigned it very well, Henry knew such an accusation was unfounded. In fact, he was agreeably surprised at how little cunning Evie Messenger had shown. She had been in a position of great advantage for a while in his office and yet she had not exploited it. She could have bargained and there had been no hint of her doing so. She could have threatened all manner of things, but instead had appeared to accept his proposal without opposition. There had been not one word of resentment against her mother, and Henry had prepared himself to endure the hate for Leah he felt Evie was entitled to express. If only Leah could be brought to see how well, how nobly Evie Messenger had behaved, she might be less afraid and soften towards her. Meanwhile, she would carry on her campaign to get rid of the girl and he would have to withstand her selfish efforts. He was the one who would see Evie virtually every day, see her and know her story. Leah had not thought of the embarrassment he would have to endure. Tucked away at home she was protected, whereas he was not.

Henry slept badly and was glad to get up. Leah did not speak to him over breakfast and he did not speak to her, but the girls chattered enough to make their parents' silence unnoticeable. He ate his kipper and ran his eye over his daughters in a way he had never done before, searching their features for signs of their sister, Evie Messenger. There was none, no comparison to be made. Evie must be like her unknown father. He wondered how Rose and Polly would absorb the news that they had an older half-sister if he were to tell them. But he would not. He would not dare, and he found he had no desire to tell them after all. It was too shocking. They would think less of their irreproachable mother and that would be dreadful. But later in life, if they were to find out? Would they be kind? Kind to Evie? He was full of doubt on that score. Evie was a working girl, she belonged near the bottom of the social scale, whereas Rose and Polly were in the middle and quite likely to look down upon her without thinking this at all cruel. They would be embarrassed by a half-sister like Evie and there was little chance of their clasping her to their bosoms. No, on this he stood with Leah, though the matter had not been discussed. Rose and Polly were better left in the dark. The sad facts of their mother's early experience should not be thrown in their faces, ruining their happiness and endangering their sense of security. His duty to Evie, he decided, did not extend to spoiling his young daughters' happiness.

Leah, presiding over the breakfast table, seemed calm if quiet. She was wearing a dress he had made for her a long time ago and he wondered if there was some significance in this choice. It was a very pale green cotton day dress with a high collar and leg-of-mutton sleeves and he had edged all the seams with dark green piping. It was an old dress, fit only for mornings at home, but it was unusual and pretty, and he had always liked it. The cotton was very fine and creased easily, the one fault of the dress. He remembered giving it to Leah soon after Polly was born, and his dismay because it did not then fit her. 'I am a matron now, Henry,' she had laughed, 'the mother of two big babies and not the slim sylph you married. Childbirth changes women, Henry, have you not noticed?' She had teased him and he had loved her lack of vanity. When, after six months, her measurements had changed back again and the dress fitted he had been delighted. 'See,' he had said, 'childbirth did not change you for ever. You are still my slim and lovely sylph.' And now she was wearing it again and though the material across the bust looked a little strained to his expert eye and he suspected the waist was uncomfortably tight, the dress still looked very well on her. He thought he would risk stating the obvious and in doing so break their silence in a harmless way.

'You are wearing that old green dress, I see,' he said. 'It looks as pretty as ever.'

'It is not pretty and neither am I. It is old and worn out.'

'I like it, Mama,' Rose said.

'Thank you, dear.'

'And so do I,' said Henry. 'I am very fond of it, old or not.'

'You would be. You are always devoted to what you have made.'

There seemed no reply to that. Kissing the girls and then her – she did not avoid his kiss, but nor did she kiss in return as usual – Henry went to work.

The moment he and then the girls had gone, Leah locked and bolted both the front and back doors, explaining to Clara that there had been robbers about and that from now on the doors were to be made secure at all times even though people were in the house.

Chapter Nineteen

MARCH, BUT more like January this year. The weather had played its usual trick. Glorious sun the first week, all the daffodils in bloom and the magnolia buds thickening and opening against the bluest of skies, but now there was sleet and stingingly cold rain and a general murk hanging over everything. Hazel hated March for its fickleness.

Everyone except her had left the house by nine o'clock, even Conchita, their Spanish au pair. Hazel was in her study, a little room on the first floor, working her way through the dreary details of a wife-beating case. She'd stayed up until after midnight and been back at her desk by 6 am, before either Malcolm or the boys were up. They knew not to disturb her though she could hear the howl of protest from Anthony when Conchita told him he could not, this morning, see his mother, because she was working very hard on a case that was coming to court next day. The boys were used to it, these occasions when she shut herself up late and early every now and again, but they never stopped resenting them. She often thought she might as well come out and see what Anthony or the others needed her for, because while they were yelling she could not concentrate anyway and simply sat staring out of the window until the commotion was over.

But it had been quiet now, the whole house, for nearly an hour. She liked the feeling, the bulk of the house behind her silent and somehow reassuring. In front of her she could see the road through the as yet bare branches of the big old pear tree which bore rotten fruit but magnificent white blossom. It was not exactly a striking or uplifting view but it was faintly rural in a satisfying way – the fruit tree, the shrubs, the chapel roof through them and the general air of peace. Few cars passed, fewer still pedestrians. She gathered up all her papers and began stuffing them into different files and was on her feet doing this when she saw a girl turn into the gate. She stopped and stared, curious to know who could be visiting at this time on a weekday morning. One of Conchita's many friends? No, they were all at their language school and this girl did not look Spanish with her auburn hair, quite lovely hair, long and curly. She was carrying a tin but Hazel couldn't make out what was written on the side. Collecting, though, she was collecting for something, and since she was a girl there was no need to be suspicious.

Hazel was not suspicious. She suspected nothing, there was no need to. On the way down the stairs she picked up some change from the hall shelf and had it in her hand as she opened the door. It was the girl who was startled, not she. She jumped and Hazel smiled and said, 'I saw you from my window upstairs. Here you are, will that do?' The girl didn't even hold out the tin. Hazel had to reach out for it and force her three coins through the slot. 'Save the Children – a good cause. I hope you're doing well,' she said and made to close the door again. 'Wait,' the girl said. Hazel paused, politely. She was a very attractive girl, what with the beautiful hair and very clear, light blue eyes, but she seemed to be in some kind of trance. She was staring so hard it was faintly alarming, even worrying. 'Was there something you wanted to say? To ask me?' Hazel said. A spiel, probably. Collectors were meant to convert you to their cause. Well, she had no time for that, she had to get to the office. 'I'm afraid I must go and get ready,' she said. 'Good morning to you, good luck with the collecting,' and once more she tried to close the front door.

'No!' the girl said, and blushed, and then said, 'Could I come in for a moment, please?'

'I'm afraid not,' Hazel said, and looked pointedly at her watch. 'I'm about to go to work. What is it you want?'

'You.'

'I beg your pardon?'

'I mean, to talk to you.'

'About?'

'Me. And you.'

There had been enough of them in her working experience, women who looked normal but were unhinged. Police stations were full of them and she'd dealt with her share in the past. The thing to do was to be polite and simply side-step them. 'Look,' Hazel said, 'I really must go,' and she began to push the heavy door shut. But the girl was leaning against it and she was strong. Irritated rather than afraid, Hazel told her to stop being so silly and said she would have to call the police if this nuisance went on.

'Please,' the girl said, 'I don't want to be a nuisance, I just want to tell you something and I can't do it on the doorstep, it's too personal. I'm not mad or anything, I promise. It's just, you know me. You don't know you do, but you do, and I want to explain and tell you who I am. I haven't come to make trouble, I promise.'

There was nothing to do but let the girl in. Hazel, walking stiffly, and not looking back, led the way not into the living-room but into the kitchen. She had to be occupied, do some small mechanical tasks. She prepared to make coffee, without asking the girl if she wanted any. She would grind beans, a good, loud noise. She filled the pot with water, another hearty sound as she turned the tap on. Clatter the cups, tinkle the teaspoons, fill the silence. She did not speak. Her back to the girl, she busied herself and tried to think. She had always said it was bound to happen. She could hear herself later on, when Malcolm came home, saying she had always known it would happen. But not like this, she hadn't thought it would happen like this, without warning. She'd imagined a letter or a phone call and could have dealt with those. Most of all, she hated being taken by surprise. It was an affront to all that was organised and efficient and prepared about her.

She had to turn eventually and put the steaming coffee pot on the table. 'Milk?' she asked, pleased at her steady, flat voice, 'Sugar?' The girl nodded. She seemed overcome now that she was actually inside the house. Hazel poured two cups, added milk to her own, pushed milk jug and sugar bowl across the table to the girl. She was not going to help her by telling her she knew now who she was. Let her do the telling since it was she who wanted to. She sipped the coffee and waited, imagining the girl as a client. Patience, that was the secret, and a relaxed atmosphere. But the girl across the table was far from relaxed. She was tense and nervous, biting her lip constantly, playing with the rings, little silver things, on her hands and not ever raising her eyes from the table. Nothing like me, Hazel thought, and felt unaccountably relieved.

'It's difficult,' the girl said. 'My name is Shona, Shona McIndoe. I'm a student, a law student at UCL.' Hazel noted how she did look up quickly at this point, checking to see if there was any reaction and, failing to see it, being disappointed. 'I don't know how to get to the point without maybe shocking you.' She paused, but Hazel kept silent, interested, in spite of the turmoil in her head, to see how this child of hers would go on. 'I've no wish to distress you, none at all.' Another pause and since no help was forthcoming the plunge had to be taken. 'I was born in Norway, in 1956,' she said. After that, it would have been stupid to pretend to be still unenlightened. 'So you are my daughter,' Hazel said, calmly, 'I see.' Not another word. Instead, she found she had to get up and do something. She walked to the telephone, back to Shona, and dialled her office number, her finger steady. She spoke to her secretary and said something important had come up and she would not be in for a while, she didn't know how long. Then she said, 'Let's move somewhere more comfortable.'

The living-room was messy, not yet cleaned up by Mrs Hedley. The boys had left Lego all over the floor and comics covered the battered sofa. Hazel swept them into a bundle and then opened the still drawn curtains. 'What a day,' she said, standing looking into the sodden, gale-buffeted garden.

'My birthday,' Shona said.

'Is it? 16 March, yes.'

'I thought maybe you always ...'

'No. I didn't, never. I promised myself I wouldn't and I didn't. It seemed – mawkish, somehow. I didn't want to do it for ever. I deliberately blanked out the date very successfully.'

'I suppose you were too unhappy, you just wanted to forget me and all about it.'

Hazel turned, unable any longer to avoid looking at the girl. There she stood, her hands in the pockets of her green cape-like raincoat, uneasy but also defiant, clearly bracing herself to face whatever was to come, bravely coming out with the theory she wanted to believe was true. Carefully, Hazel said, 'Unhappy? Yes, I was, of course. And I did want to forget but it took a long time. Forgetting the date you were born was nothing, but forgetting the rest, it was difficult. Impossible, really. But I tried very hard.'

'I'm sorry.'

Hazel allowed herself a little laugh. 'Shall we sit down?' she said, and sat herself, on the only straight-backed chair, leaving the girl with the choice of sofa or easy-chairs. She chose the sofa, but only perched on its arm. 'You have nothing to be sorry for. I'm the one who ought to be.'

'But you're not,' the girl said quickly, without a hint of a query in the words.

Hazel said nothing for a moment, studying her face. It was so hard to measure the degree of distress which might be under the controlled surface calm. 'It's complicated,' she said finally, 'as you might expect. I'm sorry, or I was sorry, about a lot of things. But nineteen years is a long time.' She wanted to say as little as possible. That was surely the right decision. She knew perfectly well that every word she said, every expression that crossed her features, would be analysed and reflected upon. It was cruel, perhaps, to make the girl take the lead, it would be kinder to help her by launching into a string of lively questions, but she did not intend to. And as for the gestures that would be even kinder, the warm embrace or tender kiss, she was incapable of them, which the girl would already have sensed.

'I shouldn't have come,' the girl said, and stood up again.

'Please,' Hazel said, surprised at herself as she stood too, and not knowing quite what she meant by this plea. The girl took it to mean that she had no need to apologise. 'No, really,' she said, 'I see now it was stupid. You've got your own life. It was just I couldn't resist it, I had silly ideas. But I'll go now and I won't trouble you again.' She was on the edge of tears, trying, Hazel could see, to contain them for a few more minutes until she was out of the house.

'Please,' Hazel repeated, 'you're upset. Sit down. I don't want you to leave like this. You'll go away with all the wrong conclusions. Give yourself time. And me, give me time. I'm more shocked than I perhaps look.'

'You don't look shocked at all. You don't even look surprised,' the girl said, and Hazel was relieved to hear at last the resentment.

'No,' she agreed, 'but then you don't know me, so you wouldn't be able to tell, would you?'

'I thought there would be some reaction. There's none. I could have been telling you what time it was for all the notice you took.'

'Oh, I took notice. I was thinking, but you can't see thinking, can you? I was thinking that I had always expected this, but I didn't know how it would happen.'

'Not like this.'

'Not like this, no.'

'But you dreaded it, you've always dreaded it.'

'No. What I've dreaded is not knowing what to do, or how you would be, whether you'd come full of hate or merely in a spirit of curiosity, and I suppose I hoped for curiosity.' She had said far more than she had meant to, but felt herself pleased with what had come out.

The girl was not pleased, though. She had flushed and was biting her lip quite savagely enough to draw blood if she continued. 'I don't hate you,' the girl said, 'and I don't blame you, but you aren't what I thought you'd be, I mean you aren't how I imagined my mother to be.' She stammered over the word 'mother'. Hazel knew she was expected to ask in what way she was different but was determined not to fall into that trap. 'I thought,' the girl was saying, 'I thought it would actually be a relief to you to find I'd been so well brought up and happy.'

'It is,' Hazel said quickly.

'It isn't. You just don't care. I'm nothing to you and the sooner I accept that the better.'

She picked up the shoulder bag she'd dropped and rushed to the door in a whirl of green coat, hair pushed angrily back but Hazel was as quick and reached the door at the same time. She would have to use the girl's name, but it was a struggle to do so. 'Shona,' she said, 'don't leave like this.' She couldn't let her go with so much unresolved and this feeling had nothing to do with concern for Shona. It was all to do with concern for herself and a sense of another solution being possible which would free both of them from each other. 'No, don't go,' she said again, 'not like this. You will only regret it and the disappointment will get worse.'

'It isn't disappointment. I knew that you'd probably ...'

'It is disappointment, only deeper. I'm letting you down, of course.'

'You can't help it, I told you, I know, I can see, I can feel. I mean nothing to you.'

'Oh, you mean something.' Hazel smiled, tried to look ironically at the girl and pull her into a shared sense of amusement. But the eyes were swimming and there was no possibility of irony being recognised. 'Sit down again,' she urged, 'at least let me satisfy your curiosity and wait until you're more in control.'

'I am in control. I'm not really crying. I'm not at all an emotional person, this isn't *me*.'

'No, I'm sure it isn't. And this isn't me either, but what could we expect? In the circumstances. As I said, we need time.'

'But you obviously don't want me here, I was wrong to think you might.'

'Yes, you were wrong, but you are here and that changes everything. I can't ever feel the same again and I don't know that I would want to. I'm going to go and take these clothes off and ring my office again and then maybe we could go for a walk, do you think? It's strange sitting like this. It would feel more natural, well, comfortable, to be outside and ...'

'Yes, it would to me too.'

All the time she was changing and telephoning Hazel found herself worrying about the imminent arrival of her mother, who was coming over to drop in what she referred to as 'real country eggs' brought back specially from her weekend in Gloucestershire. She had her own key and would just march in, expecting nobody at home, to put the eggs in the kitchen. It would be appalling to have her arrive while Shona was here. Hazel hurried, aware too that she was somehow hoping, even expecting, to hear the click of the front door, the sound of Shona running away, but it never came. She'd given the girl her opportunity to escape but she had not taken it, so that was that. Or maybe, thought Hazel, that wasn't what I was doing at all, maybe I was doing the running away and it hasn't worked, and now I must face up to the consequences and act appropriately. She came back downstairs, wearing trousers and a sweater, determined to do that. She would go through what had happened all those years ago and invite questions and then with a clearer conscience she would bid Shona goodbye. It was no good thinking she could, or ought to, pretend affection and gladness. She couldn't. She would have to be honest and get this over.

They walked down the road, Hazel relieved to have escaped her mother's arrival, their long strides matching and the dog straining at the leash in front of them, without talking. The flurries of sleet had stopped, but it was still a grey, ugly day, the sky heavy and murky.

'Are you warm enough?' she said to Shona as they entered the park. 'That coat looks quite thin for this weather.'

'This weather is nothing,' Shona said, 'I was brought up in Scotland, on the north-east coast.'

'Yes, I know.'

'You knew? How?'

Hazel was silent for a good stretch. She could sense Shona waiting. This, she thought, is going to please her, it will give her some satisfaction. 'Oh, some years ago, a long time ago, in fact, I can't remember exactly when, I had nightmares about you. They got worse and worse. You as a baby, though I never actually saw you, I didn't want to. And anyway, Malcolm, my husband, thought if he could find out that you were well and happy the nightmares might stop. They did, actually. I haven't had them since.'

'What happened in the nightmares?'

'Nothing in particular. Just a baby, you, or a baby I knew to be you, crying, howling.'

'How did he trace me, your husband?'

'I don't know. He's a lawyer too, he has access to various ways of finding things out. I didn't ask him.' There was a long silence. The dog bounded about and Hazel watched him, thinking what a hopeless park this was, not at all a substitute for real country as Hampstead Heath could be on such a weekday morning. She knew perfectly well that Shona would be working out the significance of what she had told her and she waited with interest rather than apprehension to see what she would say. But the girl said nothing at all. Stealing a sidelong look, to check if she was perhaps weeping again, she saw no sign of tears. 'Were there things, questions, you wanted to ask me?' she said.

'Yes.'

'Ask, then. I suppose you want to know who your father was and why I ...'

'No, I don't. I don't want to know about any father, he doesn't matter.'

'Well, if you say so, but his part is surely relevant. He was a schoolboy, no, between school and university ...'

'I don't want to know, I said.'

'Fine. But I want you to know he never knew, about you, I mean. Maybe one day you *will* want to know about him and that's what you should get clear.'

'It's the other bit.'

'Why I gave you up?'

'Yes. I mean, I know you were very young, younger than I am now, and I know abortion was illegal ...'

'I hardly even thought of abortion, it was something other girls had to do in back streets, that kind of thing, too dangerous and impossible. I would have been too frightened even if I'd known how.'

'Yes, I realise. And you were only eighteen, so how could you keep a baby?'

Hazel listened to the tone of sympathy. It was tempting to allow the girl to paint the attractively pathetic picture she was conjuring up. 'I didn't want to keep you,' she said, 'that's the truth.'

'You hated me?'

'No, not hate. I just wanted you cancelled out. I wanted to get home, back to my real life. Those months in Norway were, well ... they were ... I can't seem to think of a word to describe them.'

'Hell.'

'Near to hell, I thought. But that's too violent. It was the numbness, being suspended in time, it was more an in-limbo feeling, and that scared me.'

'But then you came home and you were happy ever after, so that was all right.'

The hint of sarcasm is my own, Hazel thought, it is precisely how I deal with hurt. Either I am sarcastic or contemptuous and she is only a girl and can't risk open contempt. But she suddenly felt less constrained, the girl's sarcasm helped. 'I wasn't happy for a very long time afterwards,' she said. 'I was lonely, though I'd always been quite a lonely sort of person, I mean a person who preferred to be on her own, not the same at all. And I just became more and more like that. Cynical, I was a little cynic too. I felt I'd learned my lesson. I was better on my own. I'd tried relationships, I'd tried one, that is, and it had messed up my life. I concentrated on working hard and keeping myself more and more to myself.'

'How sad.'

More sarcasm and now also that hint of contempt. Hazel smiled slightly. 'Yes, a little sad.'

'But you didn't think about me.'

'No. I was easily convinced you were happy somewhere and even if you weren't it wasn't my fault. I was told you'd go to a couple who desperately wanted a baby and I thought that would be a lucky thing, for you to be wanted so much. You can call it a hard attitude, if you want, but that's how it was.'

'Hard.'

'Yes, hard then.'

'But then you had nightmares.'

'My punishment, you mean? Later, I told you, a very long time afterwards.'

'When you really were happy, married to Malcolm, on 11 April, in a pretty Gloucestershire church.'

Hazel didn't bother asking how the girl knew such a detail. She could imagine the visit to St Catherine's House and the excitement of locating the entry in the ledger and getting the certificate. 'I remember now,' she said, 'it was after I'd had Philip, my first baby ...'

'Second.'

'Second. My first son.'

'You must have been so glad he was a boy.'

'I was.'

'And the third and fourth, both sons.'

'Not so glad with Anthony. Malcolm wanted a daughter.'

'But not *your* daughter.'

'That never arose. You were adopted and settled, and ...'

'And a secret.'

'Not from Malcolm.'

'You did the decent thing, of course, and confessed. So noble. How did he take it?'

She wants me to rise to this sarcasm, Hazel thought, but I will not. 'Well, he said the past was past.'

'Original. Not bygones will be bygones too?'

'Not quite.'

'And he didn't think any less of you for your disgraceful secret?'

'He didn't think it was disgraceful. He understood.'

'What did he understand?'

'That I hadn't intended to get pregnant, that I was very young, that adoption had been the only solution, that ...'

'Best.'

'What?'

'Best solution, not only. Adoption wasn't the only solution. You weren't a poor, penniless waif out of some nineteenth-century novel who'd been done wrong.'

'No, I wasn't. I didn't pretend I was.'

'But Malcolm, dear Malcolm, understood and forgave you and bore you not the slightest grudge.'

'Not a grudge, no. But something. It disturbed him to think of a child of mine out in the world somewhere, however well looked after. He has always felt it wasn't right, which I haven't felt myself.'

'Except in nightmares.'

'Did they mean that? Not necessarily.'

Everything had changed. The girl walking beside her was no longer just an attractive but somehow neutral person – her very voice, young and light though it was, had become charged with menace, but even though Hazel found her stomach tightening with nerves, she also found the real emerging Shona exhilarating. She liked being challenged, she wanted to be. Defence was a way of life to her and she excelled at it. Others might feel that having their backs against a wall was an uncomfortable position to be in, but she didn't. If this girl had one unassailable right it was to attack, so she must be encouraged.

'You're imagining, of course, what you would do,' Hazel said, 'in the position I was in.'

'I'd have an abortion.'

'So would I, if I were eighteen and pregnant now.'

'But if I'd been you and couldn't because it was illegal or too difficult to arrange, then I would have to keep it.'

'Easier said than done.'

'No, not easy, but for me there wouldn't be any choice, I couldn't give away my own baby.'

'Not even for the sake of the baby?'

'That's just trickery, that sort of 'tis-a-far-far-better-thing-I-do sort of argument, it's despicable.'

'There's no point in discussing it ...'

'I don't want *discussions*.'

'What do you want, then? Remind me.'

'I wanted you, that's what I wanted. My mother. It's natural, isn't it?'

'Yes.'

They turned and began to walk back. This had gone on long enough. Hazel longed to get home and go through the awkward business of saying goodbye. It wouldn't be over, of course. She realised that. This girl might part with her believing she would never return, but she undoubtedly would. She'd go home, in a state of fury and misery and crushing disappointment, and then the resentment would build up inside her and she'd be unable to prevent herself returning. She would have to feed on that sense of being cheated which she was so transparently suffering from now. Hazel saw how it would be and was resigned to her own prognosis.

'Have you always known you were adopted?' she suddenly asked.

'No. I only found out last year, on my eighteenth birthday, well, almost on it.'

'That's interesting. Why tell you at all if it had been kept so secret, I wonder?'

'Dad thought it was time. He hadn't thought it should be secret, but Mum was ill when she had me, I mean *got* me, and she made him promise. They pretended to everyone, even my grandmothers.'

'True deception, then. And you grew up perfectly happy and without suspicions. No harm done, after all.'

'So, applause for you, you mean, with your far-far-better-thing stuff.'

'No applause for me, but relief.'

'But the point is you couldn't have *known*. You gave me away without being able to know I'd have good parents. Anyway, I don't care about that even if it sounds as if I do. I really don't, whatever I've said. What gets me is that you didn't *think* of me at all. I didn't haunt you except for those nightmares, which didn't last long. That's what's so awful. To have a child growing in your body and going through giving birth and knowing it is yours, your flesh and blood, and then *just giving it away*. It's obscene, that's what it is. And even now, I turn up, and you're not fussed, not really, just a little thrown but you can't wait to get rid of me when you think you've been *reasonable* and *civilised* enough. It isn't right, it isn't – oh, I can't think what ...'

'Understandable?'

'Yes. It isn't possible to understand the mentality of women who give their babies away when they don't have to and then when they've done it they don't *suffer*.'

'You want me to have suffered the tortures of the damned, to be still suffering them.'

'Don't mock. I didn't say anything about tortures. I just – I just want to have meant something to you and then I could forgive.'

'This is getting a little heated, you're shouting ...'

'Certainly I'm heated, I'm shouting, why shouldn't I? We're in a bloody empty park ...'

'It doesn't matter where we are, I don't respond to shouting.'

'You don't respond to anything, you're cold and unfeeling.'

'Maybe. You see what you escaped. You could have been brought up by a cold and unfeeling woman instead of your mother. I'm sure she is neither.'

'She isn't. She's warm and kind ...'

'There you are, then.'

'No, I am not, I'm not anywhere, you miss the point again. I thought you were a lawyer, but any lawyer would see the point. It doesn't matter about Catriona being warm and kind and all that, or about your being cold and unfeeling, or whatever. The point is, *you* are my real mother and that makes the difference. I'm looking for myself and I never could find me in Catriona.'

'Lots of girls are totally unlike their mothers. I'm unlike my own. We have nothing in common.'

'I've seen her.'

'When?'

'Bringing your sons home. I watched, I've been watching your house, just to see. Spying, I've been spying. Shocking, isn't it? And pathetic.'

It was both, but Hazel knew she must not agree with the girl. She was touched in the strangest way by this confession – hiding somewhere, watching, spying, and all to see her own mother. She thought of all the scheming and planning that must have been involved, and then she recalled how bitterly cold and wet it had been recently and imagined this girl shivering as she stood concealed behind some tree, or building. She couldn't just say goodbye to her. It was becoming more and more inevitable that she would have to invite her to meet Malcolm, but she couldn't bear the idea. Malcolm would love the girl. He would be fascinated by her and be eager to get to know her. And the boys, what would the boys think? They would take their lead from their father and, besides, they were too young to have the desire to make judgements of their own, they would not understand all the implications implicit in the sudden introduction into their lives of a fully grown half-sister.

They came out of the park and back on to the road. Hazel put the dog back on to his lead and caught up with the girl, who had not waited while she did so. She disliked the feeling of running after her, even if only for a few yards. Neither of them spoke all the way back to the house and as they neared it the girl said she was going straight to the tube.

'I'll drive you wherever you want to go,' Hazel said, 'I'll be driving to work anyway.'

'No need. The tube's only a few minutes away.'

'Where are you going?'

'I don't know, I can't think. Home, I suppose. You don't care, anyway, so why pretend you do?'

'I do care. I don't want you to be so upset ...'

'It's a bit late to worry about upsetting me.'

'It wasn't my intention to upset you.'

'Listen to yourself – "it wasn't my intention" – and you're talking to your own daughter. But I forgot, I'm a stranger and you like it that way.'

'Neither of us has any choice about that. We are strangers. The question is whether we're going to remain so.'

'Well, of course we are – you've made it quite plain that that's what you want.'

'I don't think I have. I might not be able to give you what you want, but I don't think I've said anything to indicate ...'

' "To indicate"! Listen!'

'... that I want to remain a stranger.'

'But you do. You don't want to be disturbed. You don't want your lovely life disrupted.'

'Would you disrupt it?'

'What do you mean?'

'You were the one who used the word disrupted.'

'I meant messed up. If I came into your life properly, it would mess everything up.'

'Not necessarily. You, your life, might be the one messed up. You'd find me wanting. You'd be quite likely to find everything about me and my family and my life wanting. And what about Catriona, it was Catriona, wasn't it? That's her name, what about her?'

'She doesn't know. She doesn't need to.'

'But she would if we became close.'

'Close? Who said anything about close? With you? I can't imagine that, there would be no danger of that.'

Hazel found she had walked right past her own house even though the dog had tried to turn in the gate. They were at the end of her own quiet road and near the noisy main road, standing now on the corner of it.

'I'm off,' the girl said, 'I won't be back, don't worry.'

'Give me your address,' Hazel found herself asking without crediting that she could be doing so. 'I ought at least to have your address.'

'Why?'

'I don't want you just to vanish.'

'Worried about nightmares coming back?'

'No. That was unnecessary.'

'Yes, it was. I've said a lot of unnecessary stuff. Well, goodbye.'

A car was turning from the main road into Victoria Grove. Its horn tooted and it came to a halt beside the two women before Shona had had time to set off.

'Hazel!' a voice shouted, and, turning, Hazel saw her mother leaning out of the window. She ought to have seen it was her car.

'Who's that?' Shona said.

There was a single moment to make the choice. Hazel knew her mother could not hear her. She was in the car and just out of range of any interchange. And the girl had obviously not recognised her, she hadn't associated her with the elderly woman bringing the boys home whom she'd identified as their grandmother. She could lie or easily practise evasion. But she did neither. 'It's my mother, your grandmother,' she said. 'Come back with me and meet her.'

Chapter Twenty

HENRY WANTED no more secrets. He wished all his dealings with Evie Messenger to be above board and to be known to his wife. However resistant she was to this knowledge and to any kind of involvement, even at second-hand, he was determined to force it upon her. But it was difficult. The moment he started to speak to Leah about anything to do with Evie she left the room or put her hands over her ears in a thoroughly childish way which angered him. If he tried to talk about the girl without using her name it made little difference – Leah still tried not to hear. He managed, nevertheless, to make it clear that he visited his step-daughter.

She was living now near Holme Head in a little house above the river Caldew. The money he had given her was banked and she had used it to rent this property and furnish it modestly. He had advised her to buy a house, which made far more sense than renting, but she would not hear of it. Money in the bank, and a substantial sum at that, pleased her more. She said she did not like spending and was averse to all extravagance. But as well as equipping her two rooms and kitchen with basic items she did have some clothes made for herself out of his money and this gratified him. He would have liked to have made them for her himself, as an additional contribution to her welfare, but she would not allow this, saying she did not want to give people any reason to talk. The idea of being the subject of gossip worried her continually, and he was surprised at the great care she took not to seem in any way familiar to him. At work, she was deferential in precisely the way she had always been, and outside work she was most reluctant to be in contact with him if an obvious reason was not readily available.

These reasons were hard to find. He, after all, was the head of a prosperous tailoring establishment and she was a mere apprentice. Out of the Arnesen building what possible reason had they to meet? Only Evie's widely acknowledged usefulness provided Henry with excuses to take her out with him and, at her insistence, he used them sparingly. When he travelled to markets or to factories to buy cloth she went with him. There was nothing unusual in this. He had always been in the habit of taking an apprentice partly as a treat, partly to involve them in the business, and partly to run errands for him, to fetch and carry and procure all kinds of haberdashery as well as the material he had come for. When they returned from these trips – to Newcastle, to Halifax, to Rochdale – it was only natural that Henry should see Evie into her house since it was invariably dark by the time they reached Carlisle.

These expeditions were exciting. Every apprentice he had ever taken had been excited by the long journey and the experience of visiting a new and much bigger town. But Evie's excitement was well contained. There was no bouncing about on the seat beside him and no high-pitched stream of talk. She always sat, grave and composed, and said nothing unless directly questioned. He decided she was merely nervous and made allowances for this, but then, after their third trip in six months, he knew she was not nervous at all. This reticence was simply her. He saw in it, and in her unnerving steadiness, how life had treated her. She had had only herself to rely on and had never known the love of a mother. Henry reasoned that Evie could not open up to affection because she had never received any, and trust was quite unknown to her. It saddened and depressed him to discover how she was moulded and he spent many an hour on these trips, Evie utterly still and silent beside him, speculating on how different she would have been if Leah had kept her. She would surely have been like Rose and Polly, noisily secure and confident. But there was no way of being sure. Evie had been motherless and whether or not this unfortunate state had made her as inscrutable as she was could never be known.

She was unhappy about allowing him to enter her house when he duly delivered her home, but he insisted it was his duty to see her safely inside and said so loudly enough for anyone listening to hear. He left the door open, pointedly, and merely stood just inside while she lit her lamps. The room was very small but she had it nicely arranged. She had a round table with a fringed cloth, two old armchairs for which she had embroidered antimacassars, and a hook rag rug of many colours she had worked herself. 'Very cosy, Evie,' he said, 'you are quite the housewife.' He had to stop himself adding, 'Just like your mother.' She never said anything in reply, never showed pleasure in his admiration. Reluctant to go, he was always obliged to say goodnight very quickly and leave her. His own house, when he entered it a quarter of an hour later, always seemed overfurnished and lavishly decorated and overwhelmed him with its evidence of prosperity. He reminded himself that Evie had been here and seen all this and it made him uncomfortable to know she had witnessed the thriving and comfortable home-life she had been denied.

On one trip to Newcastle they passed through the very village, Moorhouse, where Evie, though reluctant to answer questions, had recently told him she had been raised. He wondered how she would react to passing through it and was watching her closely as the coach breasted the hill above Moorhouse and began its descent. She looked straight ahead, not a flicker of recognition on her face, and made no comment. He was the one who could not keep silent. As they came level with the public house she had named, the Fox and Hound, he said, 'Would you like to stop, Evie, and step inside for a moment?' She shook her head, but violently, not in her usual unresponsive way. 'I thought you might like to show people how well you are looking in your fine clothes.' She kept quiet until the pub was behind them and said, 'I know no one there now. My mother's cousin's wife has left. She has gone to Newcastle.'

'Ah,' Henry said, seizing eagerly on the slender prospect of any kind of conversation and not wanting to let it go. 'Of course, I forgot. Your uncle, if I can call him that, died recently. Were you fond of him?'

'No.'

'Was he unkind?'

'No.'

'Were you fonder, perhaps, of your aunt?'

'No.'

'Was she unkind?'

'No. She was kind sometimes, I think.'

'You think?'

'She did not beat me or starve me. She fed me well and bought me clothes, but I worked hard for it.'

'You are a hard worker, I know.'

Then they passed the school and the two churches, one ruined, and finally he saw Evie was not untouched by the sight of them. 'You went to church?' he asked.

'Yes. If I was allowed to. It was somewhere to go and I knew my mother used to go to church, in that ruined place.'

Henry tensed and sharpened his concentration upon her. Were her hands trembling ever so slightly? It was the first time she had ever referred to her mother. 'How did you know?' he said, gently.

'I was told. By my mother's cousin. He was not my uncle. She sang, my mother, in that church, when there was a choir there. I have her voice.'

Astonished, Henry let the coach rattle several miles while he absorbed this detail – so Evie had her mother's voice, Leah's singing voice, which neither Rose nor Polly had. She had told him this so proudly, the words 'my mother' coming out of her mouth so full and rounded this time and the statement 'I have her voice' so authoritative.

It was extraordinary, he reflected, that Evie made so little comment about her mother's outright and total rejection of her. He wished she would protest, that she would beg him to explain this cruelty to her, beg him to intercede. But she never did. She seemed quite fatalistic, accepting what was surely the most severe blow she had ever received with equanimity. It was not normal. He could hardly bear her acceptance and longed for it to fade away and for resentment, with which he could cope more easily, to take its place. All the time there grew within him the desire to break this deadlock, this intransigence of Leah's and this acquiescence of Evie's. He wanted the two women to come together even if only to clash resoundingly, and yet with neither of them could he make any progress. What he could not be sure of was how real, how sincere, was this attitude of Evie's? He could not claim to know her, or to be able to fathom her mind, whereas, though Leah's feelings were a mystery to him, he was certain enough of their genuine passion. Was Evie pretending? Did she dissemble for some purpose he could not guess at?

It made him uneasy to think so, but then he chided himself for becoming as fanciful as Leah, who was still afraid of Evie. It at first puzzled and then exasperated him that his wife insisted now on locking the doors when he was out at work and called out to know who was there before she would open them. The girls could not understand it – they came home from school and were locked out, and explanations of robbers being about frightened them.

'This is absurd, Leah,' he was finally moved to say. 'What is it you are locking our doors against in the daytime?'

Her reply was, 'You know.'

'But I do not know.' He must, he felt, force her to give voice to her ridiculous idea.

'You do. She will come, one day, and I do not want to be taken unawares.'

'She will never come. What makes you think she will? Nearly a whole year has passed since she was told the truth and she has come nowhere near you, nor made the slightest attempt to contact you. Admit it, Leah, you have no grounds for fearing her.'

'I have grounds.'

'You do *not*.'

'She is biding her time. I would do the same, bide my time then strike.'

'Strike? Are you mad? What is it you imagine? She is only a young woman without an ounce of hatred in her and ...'

'You do not know what is in her.'

'I know enough. I have got to know her as much as anyone does, whereas you know her not at all, and yet can make these senseless allegations.'

'I made no allegations. I merely said you do not know what is in her.'

'And you do?'

'She has me in her, whether I like it or not.'

'And so, because of that, you imagine her capable of coming here and striking you?'

'I did not mean actually strike ...'

'Thank God for that.'

'... so much as arrive and accuse me and claim ...'

'Claim what?'

'I do not know, how can I? What she thinks is due to her.'

'And all this, this imagined rigmarole in her head, is because *you* would do this and you see her as like you?'

'Of me, she is of me.'

'She is nothing like you, nothing. I can see nothing of you in her whatsoever, even if she does have your voice.'

'My voice?'

'Your singing voice, apparently. She told me as we passed a ruined church on the Moorhouse road where, she was told by your cousin at the Fox and Hound, you used to sing in the choir.'

Henry carried on, describing the trip to Newcastle, but Leah heard no more. She was back in that little church and singing her heart out, and Hugo was coming home soon to claim her and the baby she had just written to say she was carrying. So many years since that happy time – then she caught herself, astonished. A happy time? It was now that she was happy, surely, and that other time belonged to dark days, when she was lost and abandoned and a fool. Singing in that church she had been foolish and only in that sense 'happy', meaning vacant, stupid. It made her feel hot just to remember her trust and faith in Hugo Todhunter who, compared to Henry, her Henry, was weak and faithless, and had not known the meaning of the word love. She hated him. It had taken years for the hatred to build up – Oh, how forgiving she had been, it made her sick to think of it now: such excuses she had made for him, such blind understanding of his position she had shown. And he had left her with evidence of his betrayal, that crying scrap of a baby – and she could not bear it.

So the child had grown up to have her voice. It surprised her. She had not the build to have a good voice. She was too thin, with hardly any chest, and looked as if she could have no power. It was a useless gift in any case. Singing had never helped her get on in life and it had not helped this girl, this daughter of Hugo's.

Henry had finished his recital. 'We came back the same road,' he was saying, 'but the village was all in darkness.'

'It would be,' she said, 'nights start early in Moorhouse. I dreaded the winter, dark by three in the afternoon on bad days.' She paused. Henry was giving her such a strange, pitying look. She turned away from him and said, 'She passed her father's house too, on that road, but you know nothing of him.' Henry cleared his throat. 'Do you wish to, Henry? Do you wish to?'

'Not if it distresses you. I haven't known, or asked, all these years, and I can manage.'

'But do you wish to know?'

'If you wish to tell me, at last.'

Leah went and stood by the fire and, leaning on the mantelpiece and staring into the flames, she said, speaking rapidly and in an irritated tone, 'His name was Hugo Todhunter. I vowed I'd never say it again. He was well-to-do. His family had the only big house in the village, on the edge, outside it. He went off and got into trouble and came home only when it was made a condition of his debts being paid. He met me on the road, he on his horse. You know the rest.' She turned round so suddenly that her dress was in danger of catching alight and Henry cried a warning. 'She is his daughter,' Leah said, 'she should go in search of him.'

'She has no interest in him. She does not even wish to know who he was and made that plain.'

'But she ought to know, it is her right. It is he who is responsible for her lack of a mother.'

'That does not make sense, Leah.'

'It does to me. It ought to make sense to her. Let her go to Moorhouse, to the Todhunters. I wrote to them, to the mother and the sister, and told them I had baptized their son's daughter and given her their name, Evelyn. Does she know that? Tell her that, tell her to go to Moorhouse and present herself.'

Henry did tell her. He told Evie the very next day, but he could see at once that she still had no interest. 'Of course,' Henry said, carefully, 'my wife does not know what happened to him after he went to Canada and left her. He may have returned, or he may be dead. There is no way of knowing. But if you were to visit the Todhunters and explain ...' Evie shook her head and stood still with an air of waiting to be dismissed. She was looking prettier lately, though that was not so very pretty. Her better clothes helped. She was wearing a deep royal blue dress with darker blue trimmings and it gave a brightness to her pale face. She had a more confident posture too. She stood with her thin shoulders back and her head lifted whereas formerly she had seemed hunched and her eyes were always on the ground. It was pleasing to see this improvement and he was sure others would have noticed it. He wondered, as he sent her back to work, if Evie might now attract a suitor, but it was not something he could ask her. He wished some young man would come along and take an interest in her and make her happy, but then while wishing this he had to remind himself that nothing would apparently make Evie happy except acknowledgement by her mother, or so she believed.

Since nothing could be done about this, Henry learned to put it out of his mind for longer and longer stretches of time. Evie seemed settled. She had her house, she was doing well at work. And Leah, though still bolting the door when she was alone, had settled down too. She was not quite her old self, not quite as carefree and cheerful, but there were no more tearful outbursts nor any overt signs of irrational behaviour. He hoped that she had come to believe that what he had told her was true – Evie Messenger would not make any trouble. If she could not have her mother's love she was now apparently prepared to forget about it and resign herself to being motherless. Perhaps she had decided it did not matter so much after all. What was a mother? An accident of nature, no more than that, and a father even more so. Only when one was young was a mother important and he reasoned that Evie had worked this out and accepted her loss. She might have found her mother, but she could not put the clock back and therefore rejection by her was all simply part of a tragedy that was over. It had become a fuss about nothing.

Henry was all the more surprised, having rationalised the situation to his satisfaction, when one afternoon two years later he returned to his house to find Leah refusing at first to unlock the door for him. He had to bang and shout before he saw her face pressed up against the stained glass, peering through it to check that it was indeed him. Then when the bolt was drawn and he gained entry it was only to see his wife run up the stairs and into their bedroom without a word of explanation. He called after her but she would not answer and he was obliged to follow her, highly irritated at the disruption to his usually soothing homecoming.

'Well, Leah?' he said, rather more sharply than he had intended. 'This nonsense again, after all this time?' She lay on the bed looking, he suddenly saw, so truly ill that for the first time he was concerned. 'Leah? What has happened? Are the girls ...?'

'The girls are out, at Maisie Hawthorne's, they are fine.'

'Well, then?'

'She came. I always knew she would.'

'Who? Evie Messenger?'

'Yes. Her.'

He was stunned, and sat down on the edge of the bed. 'Good God. When?'

'This afternoon.'

'But she would be at work.'

'It is Thursday. She works Saturday and has Thursday afternoon free now. You told me yourself of this change for your staff.'

'What did she say?'
'Nothing. I closed the door.'
'In her face?'
'Yes.'
'Was that necessary, Leah? After all this time ...'
'Time? What has time to do with it? She is allowed to do anything simply because two years or so have gone by in which she has done nothing? I knew she was biding her time, I knew she would come one day.'

Henry sighed and held his head in his hands. 'I am tired and hungry,' he said.

'There is food prepared for you. I cannot eat.'

Henry went slowly downstairs and into the dining-room where there were several plates laid out with covers over them. He went first to the cupboard and poured himself a whisky, which he had taken to drinking recently. Then he ate his way through the cold meats and the potato salad and the cheese, and afterwards got up and defiantly had another whisky which left him feeling sick. There had been no sound meanwhile from upstairs. He wished his daughters would come back to liven the place up and distract him. If Leah did not come down he would have to go up again to her. It was more tempting to go to Evie and find out from her why on earth she had come here, but his pony and trap were put away and, though trams ran into town now, it would mean walking to the top of the bank to catch one and then changing at the Town Hall. He would have to wait until tomorrow to see Evie and straighten this out. There was no point in talking to Leah before he had seen Evie. If she had shut the door in the face of her unexpected and dreaded visitor without allowing her to speak, then she could not possibly know anything.

It was an uncomfortable night. Leah wept, though quietly, and Henry slept only fitfully. Any sympathy he had previously had for his wife had disappeared. Her behaviour was inexcusable now and his main feeling was one of profound annoyance. They had been through all this and it was exceedingly tiresome to be faced with the prospect of having to go through it all again. He rose early and saw to his own breakfast and left without taking Leah any tea – she could make of that what she liked. The moment he arrived at work, he sent for Evie only to be told she was in attendance at a fitting, helping Miss Minto. Since he could hardly drag her out of it without arousing intense curiosity, he had to wait a whole hour, by which time he could hardly conceal his very real impatience. It was not a sensible state of mind to be in and he tried hard to seem calm when Evie at last appeared.

He asked first about the fitting at which she had just been present, nodding his way through her report without taking in a word. Only when he was sure his tone of voice would emerge as quite even, did he say, 'I believe you called at my house yesterday afternoon, Evie.'

'Yes, sir.' She did not add that the door had been shut in her face. Evie, he well knew, never added anything unnecessary.

'I am sorry my wife was indisposed,' Henry said, 'and had to close the door without hearing you – she was taken ill with such suddenness – but might I ask the reason for your visit?'

'I am getting married, sir, Mr Arnesen.'

Henry was so startled he dropped the pair of scissors with which he had been fiddling, and had to cover his confusion by making a performance of picking them up again. 'Married, Evie?' he finally said.

'Yes, sir. Next month.'

'May I ask to whom?'

'James Paterson, sir.'

'Jimmy? Good heavens, I did not know he was courting you. Has it been a long engagement?'

'There has been no engagement, sir. James has no money for an engagement ring and since we know our own minds there is no sense in an engagement.'

'I am very happy for you, Evie.'

'Thank you, sir.'

'So you came to my home to tell me?' Henry put into his voice his surprise that she should do this, since she must have known perfectly well he was at work, but Evie was not perturbed.

'No, sir. I came to tell my mother and to ask her to be at my wedding and sign as witness to it. She is my mother, after all. It would not cause comment. James does not know, nobody does. It would be a favour, and your being my employer and my mother your wife, and you have been very good, and at other people's weddings, sir, you have graced other occasions and are known for it, for the kindness and compliment. Otherwise, I have no one. It will be very quiet and simple and quick. Half an hour, sir, and that is all, and no breakfast or formalities.'

It was a veritable speech, and Henry recognised the effort it had cost Evie to make it. She had rehearsed the words over and over, he was sure, and thought about them long and carefully. But what she could not have calculated was the effect. Henry felt moved to tears and at the same time disturbed. There was in Evie's voice an element he could not quite identify and it worried him – there seemed a note of warning in it, but of what was she warning him? And yet she had now gone back to looking as harmless and demure as usual, the sort of person who would not have the strength of character to issue warnings to her employer.

'Well, Evie,' Henry said, eventually, 'I must discuss this with Mrs Arnesen, but I fear she will not be well enough to attend any wedding.' Evie hung her head, but whether in disbelief or disappointment he could not tell. 'When are you to marry, exactly?'

'Saturday week, sir.'

'At which church?'

'Holy Trinity, sir, in Caldewgate, where my mother had me baptised.'

Again, Henry heard the same subtle message: take note, this is significant. 'Ah yes,' he said, pointlessly. 'And will you carry on living at Holme Head?'

'No, sir. Those houses are for single women. We have bought a house.'

Henry raised his eyebrows. There could be no 'we' about it. Jimmy Paterson could not possibly have any money. His money, the money he had settled on Evie which up to now she had refused to invest in a house, was the only identifiable source of the revenue needed for purchasing property. 'I am pleased,' he said, 'it is a wise move. Where is the house, might I ask?'

'Etterby Terrace, sir.'

Henry looked up sharply. Etterby Terrace was a tiny row of terraced houses running off to the left of Etterby Street, at the top of which, on Etterby Scaur, the Arnesens lived. Evie's expression was free of anything remotely resembling triumph, but he was quite sure she had understood the impact of this news. 'I did not know those Etterby Terrace houses could be got so cheap,' he said.

'It is in bad condition, sir, very bad.'

'Is it wise then, to take on such a burden when neither of you are yet earning anything substantial?'

'James's brothers are builders, sir, and his father a carpenter, and they will see us all right. And we mean the house to work for us, to be a lodging house.'

'You are full of plans, then.'

'Yes, sir.'

'I wish you luck.'

'Thank you, sir. So you will come to my wedding, sir?' There was the faintest emphasis on the word 'you' and once more the hint of threat.

'I will let you know, Evie,' Henry said, 'but with my wife ill I cannot promise.'

He did no work for the rest of that day. His concentration had entirely gone and he could not settle to anything nor bear to be in the same building as Evie. But neither could he bear to go home where Leah languished so dispiritedly and would go into hysterics when informed of the reason for Evie's visit and when told where Evie and her husband were to live. In Etterby Terrace, Evie would be their neighbour. She would walk down the same street as her mother, stand at the same tram stops, use the same shops. Her presence would be insupportable to Leah, who would wish to move house at once. Well, this was not an impossibility. Henry had quite often contemplated buying a better house, a house more in keeping with the affluence that had come his way, and it was Leah who had demurred and asserted herself very fond of her present house. They could move. Stanwix was not the only place in Carlisle to live, even if still reckoned by everyone to be the choicest area. They could have a new house, a house built to their specifications, in some other pleasant part of town. There were building plots for sale on the other side of the river where there would be attractive views of Rickerby Park. It would distract Leah wonderfully to have meetings with an architect and then to have rooms to decorate.

But to leave Etterby Street for those reasons would be folly. Henry knew he would be foolish and cowardly to suggest such a solution. If Evie was set on making herself visible to her mother, then nothing would stop her. It grieved him to have to admit to himself that Leah had perhaps been right, or that at least she had had some correct inkling of how, given time, Evie would respond. Leah was a very determined, odd woman; Evie, it seemed, was equally determined and strange. They were after all, in spite of the external evidence against it, two of a kind. And neither would yield. Leah would not accept Evie as her daughter, and Evie had resolved to force her to do so. And he was caught between them, seeing the rights and wrongs on both sides and obliged to arbitrate.

Without being aware of where he was heading, Henry had walked down Lowther Street and down to the river, and now he was striding distractedly along the bank presenting the false picture of a man who had an urgent appointment. His mind was full of wild schemes to each of which he gave only a moment's consideration before rejecting them all as absurd. Most of these wild ideas hinged in one way or another upon engineering a meeting between Leah and Evie, locking them in a room together and making it impossible for them to escape until some kind of compromise had been hammered out. Evie would be all in favour of such confrontation, he was sure, but it would drive Leah mad and he was afraid of that madness.

Concern as to how to tell his wife about Evie's approaching marriage made him far more weary than all the walking he had done. His footsteps slowed as he neared home and he wondered if he would ever again enter it quite as eagerly and happily as he had once done. Leah was still in her bedroom, the girls once more out, and Clara nowhere to be seen. He felt brutal but could not abide the thought of a long drawn-out performance and so marched upstairs and announced straight away what Evie had told him – all of it – without pause. There was silence from the prostrate figure on the bed. No screams or sobs. Relieved, he went and sat beside Leah and took her hand. It lay in his own, limp and unresisting. Her eyes were closed but no tears coursed down her pale cheeks. She seemed more composed than he had thought could reasonably be expected. He was pleased with her and bent over her and kissed her lightly. 'She can do nothing to us, love,' he said, 'remember that. She is a troubled soul who wants what she cannot have, because you cannot give it and she will come to realise this. When she has children of her own all this need of hers will fade, you will see. Be brave, no more shrinking from the sight of her, it will not serve.'

Leah, listening, knew he thought his words very fine but to her they were entirely empty. She let him pontificate and by her silence think she agreed with him. There was nothing else she could do. But next day, when he had gone to work, she bolted the door, once Clara had come, and again when she had gone. Clara left at five, since it was Saturday. Rose and Polly were at dancing class. She had hardly locked and bolted the door before there was a knock upon it. She went into the hall and saw the shadow and was not in the least surprised. She stood still until it had gone. Every Saturday after Arnesen's had closed, it would be like this – the knock, the shadow, the disappearance. They would have to move. It was intolerable to live like this, equally intolerable the thought of facing Evie Messenger out and telling her to go away and never return. She had thought of one of those speeches Henry delighted in – she had framed words of explanation in which she asked this woman for forgiveness, but begged an end to this haunting. It would never be made. Her punishment was to endure these visitations and the woman who was punishing her knew it. Nor was Henry right to imagine that, once children had been born to her, she would understand and desist. On the contrary, once she had given birth it would become more inexplicable, more monstrous that her own mother had first abandoned and now denied her. The anger would grow, not subside, and the hate intensify. And all the time Leah asked herself: in her position, would I have haunted my mother as she haunts me? She struggled to think not, but all the time Evie's right to persecute her seemed stronger and more frightening than ever.

Chapter Twenty-One

THERE HAD been malice in her sudden decision, but Hazel was unsure at whom she had directed it, at the girl or at her mother, nor could she fathom the reason for it. But standing on the corner of Victoria Grove, with the girl about to depart, and hearing her mother call from her car, she had felt a sudden and violent urge to do harm – inexcusable and horrifying. She saw in the girl's eyes a sort of hope, quite naked and somehow touching and, as she guided her towards where her mother was now parking her car, she realised it was the first time she had actually made any physical contact with her. Only a hand on an arm, but it made the girl seem vulnerable and needy, to feel the skin on the wrist where it pulled free of the sleeve of her coat.

They walked together back to the house not quite arm in arm – Hazel's hand rested on Shona's rather than linked it – to where Mrs Walmsley stood holding a box she had taken out of her car. 'Hello, darling,' she said. 'I've brought you the eggs I promised. I didn't expect to find you at home – I was just going to use my key and pop them in.' All the time she was speaking Hazel and Shona were coming towards her and she had a bright, inquiring expression already on her face. 'Mother,' said Hazel, 'this is Shona McIndoe. Shall we go in and have some lunch? It's nearly lunchtime. We can make an omelette out of your eggs.' The three of them went inside, Mrs Walmsley talking all the time, very loudly, about her drive back from Gloucestershire and the horror of the traffic and there being no such thing these days as a quiet time on the roads unless one was prepared to drive in the early hours of the morning which, at her age, she certainly was not . . . Neither Hazel nor Shona spoke. Hazel was busy breaking and whisking the eggs and heating the pan, and

Shona stood uncomfortably to one side while Mrs Walmsley laid the table.

'I don't think I've met you, my dear?' she finally said to Shona, her smile wide and forced. She wasn't sure she ought to say even that, but Hazel, rather rudely, had made no more than a sketchy attempt at introductions. It was impossible to know if this stranger was a friend or a new au pair, or a friend of the au pair's, or even a client, though that seemed unlikely, and she wished very much to be given some guidance before she tried to engage her in any kind of conversation.

'No, mother,' Hazel said quickly, 'you haven't met Shona. Sit down, this omelette is nearly ready. There's some wine open over on the dresser ...'

'Good heavens, dear, you know I don't drink in the middle of the day and never when I'm driving.'

'Water, then, put a jug of water on the table. Do you want salad with it, or bread?'

'Just the omelette will be very nice, though I had no intention of eating my own eggs.'

They sat down, Shona first removing her coat. Hazel noted how shapely her figure was now that she could see it undisguised by the loose coat. Not my figure either, she thought. More my mother's, that small waist and full bosom, more hers when she was young.

'Mother,' she said, as Mrs Walmsley took a mouthful of omelette and daintily dabbed at her lips with a napkin, 'Mother, this is Shona's birthday.'

'Oh, how nice. How old are you, dear?'

'She's nineteen,' Hazel said, before the girl could reply. 'She was born in Norway nineteen years ago today and adopted by a Scottish couple.'

There was an absolute silence. Mrs Walmsley put down her fork with extreme care, so extreme that the metal prongs touched the wooden table with no whisper of a sound. Her face delighted Hazel. It was so rare ever to see her mother confounded, and now she was. It took several seconds before signs of life returned to the frozen features and when it did the mouth tightened, a frown contorted the forehead and a flush slowly spread across the cheeks. Shona, Hazel saw, was smiling, a bitter smile acknowledging that here, too, there had been no exclamations of joy, no rush to embrace her. She was on her feet again, omelette untouched, struggling back into her coat.

'Don't go,' Hazel said.

'What a way to tell me,' Mrs Walmsley croaked, 'the shock, Oh dear.'

'I'm sorry to be a shock,' Shona said, grabbing her bag, 'it's all I ever seem to be to your family. But I'm off. I won't bother you again.'

Hazel pushed her chair back and followed her to the front door, but she was not quick enough, Shona was out of it and off. When she returned to the kitchen her mother was still sitting there transfixed. 'What a way to tell me,' she repeated, this time with the beginnings of anger in her tone. 'And how embarrassing. Did you not think of that?'

'Embarrassment? No.'

'Well, you should have done. You embarrassed me and embarrassed that poor girl. There was no need for it.'

'So what should I have said?'

'You shouldn't have said it at all, not in these circumstances. You should have told me quietly, when we were alone.'

'Secretively.'

'What?'

'Secretively. You want me to have kept it all secret still, as we did from the beginning.'

'To confront me with that girl, to put her in such a position ...'

'She put herself in it by coming here.'

'When did she come?'

'An hour or so ago.'

'She just turned up and announced herself?'

'Yes.'

'I can't believe it.' Mrs Walmsley pushed the half-eaten omelette away and got up. 'After all this time, who would have thought it ...'

'Anyone with any imagination.'

'She seemed a nice girl too. Is she a nice girl?'

'I've no idea.'

'What did she want exactly? What was her idea?'

'To satisfy her curiosity, but more than that really.'

'More?'

'I think so.'

'What kind of more? Will she make trouble?'

Hazel smiled. She could see how worried her mother now was – she craved reassurance, wanted to be told that Shona was a nice girl who would do the decent thing and, having made herself known, would also realise she was as unwanted as she had ever been and disappear. She might fleetingly have referred to Shona as 'poor', but there was no genuine sympathy there, nor any desire to know what had been the fate of the girl. A smooth, orderly life, that was what her mother wanted, as she had always wanted and invariably succeeded in getting.

'What kind of trouble did you envisage?' she asked her mother, taking pleasure in how cool she must appear.

'Well, I don't know, be unpleasant, want some sort of recompense ...'

'Compensation for being given away? What would that be, do you think? What form could such a thing take?'

'I don't know. You're the lawyer. Money, I suppose.'

'Money? Hardly, Mother. The law doesn't say adoption is a crime, the law sanctions it. Everything you did was perfectly legal and above board. You couldn't be sued for a penny.'

'Me? Why would I be sued? I didn't mean that, that's silly. I meant – oh, you know perfectly well what I meant. Is this girl going to hang around you, has she some axe to grind?'

'Would you call your mother giving you away an axe to grind?'

'But presumably she knows what the situation was, surely she understands ...'

'No, that is precisely the point. She finds it impossible to understand. It hurts even to try to understand when she feels, as she does, that nothing and no one would ever be able to force her to give up any child she ever had.'

'Oh, that's just romantic.'

'Maybe. At nineteen, you're entitled to be idealistic or romantic. I just wish I had been.'

Round and round the kitchen Mrs Walmsley went, putting straight objects that were perfectly straight, fussing with the kettle, first putting it on and then off, and displaying without seeming to realise it her agitation. Hazel watched her, never moving from her seat, and thought that if she had believed all this pacing about was evidence of emotional distress she might have felt sorry for her mother. But what she was seeing here, she was convinced, was resentment alone. Her mother resented Shona having had the impertinence to turn up, she resented Hazel for confronting her with Shona, and now, most of all, she was resenting what she would be labelling her daughter's obtuseness. She wanted Hazel to agree with her that something quite unacceptable had happened and that it must be dealt with firmly. And I am giving no sign of that, Hazel reflected, I am not showing either willingness to be organised by my mother or any eagerness to defer to her judgement and conspire with her to deal with 'trouble'.

But Hazel was wrong. Mrs Walmsley's thoughts were not at all along these predictable lines, and the loss of composure was indeed caused by her being far more distressed than Hazel could possibly appreciate. She was remembering and in remembering she evoked a deep-felt shame which had been her own. She was unable to turn to her only daughter and explain why she was as she was – it was too difficult, too much in the nature of confessional, and she was not in the habit of making confessions. All her life she'd striven to rise above the temptation to unload her fears and worries on to others and this had been at some considerable cost. She was labelled hard and unfeeling, was thought to care only about being efficient and respectable and keeping a masculine stiff upper lip. Her lip now felt very weak and quavering, but Hazel was so unsympathetic, it was impossible to break down in front of her and expect comfort. They did not, as mother and daughter, behave in that way. They were cerebral women who prided themselves on putting heads before hearts. Everything had to be talked about, reasoned. It was how their relationship operated.

And now it was not operating at all. Hazel was sitting there looking aloof and detached, whether because she had taught herself to be so – or been taught (and if so, by whom?) – or because this was her. There was no reaching her.

'I'd better go,' Mrs Walmsley said. 'I didn't intend to stay in any case.' She picked up her car keys and without looking at Hazel, and struggling to seem more like her usual self, said, 'I expect you'll tell Malcolm.'

'Of course.'

'Very wise, in case she turns up again. Will you get in touch with her, do you think?'

'I haven't her address or telephone number.'

'Poor girl. If I hadn't been so terribly shocked ...'

'Yes?'

'I should have said something. It wasn't kind.'

'No. Neither of us was kind.'

'Hazel, do you feel anything for her, for the girl?'
'Meaning?'
'Oh, are you upset? It's impossible to tell, and I feel so upset myself, it must be the shock, there's really nothing to be upset about.'

The rest of the day seemed very long. Hazel went to work and was busy, but still the hours dragged. She realised she both dreaded telling, and yet was eager to tell, Malcolm about the extraordinary visit she had been paid. His reaction was easy to predict. He would be desperate to meet the girl and would not be able to credit that she had been allowed to leave without revealing her address or phone number. But that would present no problems to Malcolm – he could track the girl down in no time given her name and age and the single fact that she was a law student at UCL. Then what? Would he go and see her? Would he persuade her to come again, to meet the family? And what of the family, their boys? Malcolm would insist upon telling them. He would enjoy it, the explaining, and because they were so young what he had to tell them about their mother would simply seem a story having nothing to do with pain or distress. It might even be salutary for her to be present while Malcolm did the explaining – it would make everything seem comfortingly ordinary after all.

Yet it was not as simple and straightforward as she had imagined, to acquaint Malcolm with the facts about her daughter's reappearance. There seemed no way into the subject. Evenings were so chaotic and exhausting in their house, with all three boys demanding and noisy, food to be made, and the next day's work hanging over both her and Malcolm. It was usually eleven o'clock before they had time to exchange any but the most perfunctory news. At midnight she made some cocoa and took it up to his study where he was still poring over documents, head in hands, looking grey and tired. He barely murmured his thanks before turning another page and did not even glance at her. Only the fact that she went on standing there caught his attention after a while and finally he looked up and said, 'Mm?'

'Come down to the sitting-room,' she said.
'I can't. I'm in court tomorrow, have to be, on this one.'
'Come down for a break.'
'I'd never get back to it, I'm nearly asleep anyway.'
'How much longer will you be?'

'An hour, I don't know, you go to bed.'

She stood, sipping her own cocoa, watching him. Whisky would have been better, she didn't know why she'd made this sickly milk drink. He was drinking his quite greedily though, in great gulps. But she was annoying him by hanging about.

'What is it?' he said, irritated. 'What's wrong?'

'Nothing.'

'Good. Go to bed then.'

She did. She went downstairs and washed her mug out and put all the lights off, but didn't tidy up, that could be done in the morning, it was what Mrs Hedley was paid for. She quite liked the look of the house at the end of the evening, the evidence there of living going on. Her mother's house had always seemed dead, with none of the debris of family life littering the place. Then she went upstairs and looked in on each of the boys, more mess, more things strewn everywhere on the floors, so that she had to take care not to trip in the half dark. She put her bedside lamp on and propped herself up to read, but she hardly took in a word. She liked her bedroom. Everything in it was her choice. Malcolm had views about the rest of the house, but not about their bedroom. It was mainly a green room – pale green carpet, dark green linen blinds, a white and green cover on the bed. It always soothed her. In spite of her tiredness she felt a little refreshed after she'd lain there a while. Malcolm would be too exhausted when he came to bed; it wasn't fair to tell him anything important, but if she waited he would be angry with her later and vow that he was always ready to be told vital things whatever his state, whatever the hour. It was no good thinking she would tell him in the morning, the mornings were hopeless, as disorderly as the evenings with the added pressure of everyone needing to depart on time. She would have to tell him now, here, peacefully.

He didn't come to bed until two o'clock and was startled to see her still sitting up with the light on. 'Why on earth are you awake?' he said. She put her book aside and watched him as he undressed. He was putting on weight. In his suit this was hardly noticeable but naked she could see the flab beginning. His whole life was stressful and unhealthy, but he loved his work and could not be persuaded to take time off for leisure. 'I hope you're not going to keep that light on when I get into bed,' he said, 'I can't sleep with the light on, you know that, and I'm dead-tired.' It crossed her mind that he was imagining she might have been staying awake to make love and that he was warning her of disappointment. That made her laugh – she had so little interest in sex these days – and so it was with a smile of amusement and a little derision that she said, as soon as he had got into bed, 'I'm sorry, it won't take a minute, there hasn't been a good time all evening, but even if you're shattered, I can't let you go to sleep without telling you what happened this morning.'

She told him as quickly as possible, managing to reduce the whole trauma of these hours to a few succinct sentences. Malcolm became alert immediately. He jumped out of bed and came round to her side to face her and put back on the light which she had just switched off. Then he scrutinised her face for what seemed ages before saying: 'So you're not upset?'

'Not really, no. Disturbed but, no, not upset in the way you mean.'

'You haven't said what she looks like.'

'Not like me. She has beautiful auburn hair, she's tall, and her figure is like my mother's used to be.'

'Attractive, then.'

'Yes. Oh, she's attractive.'

'But what is she *like*?'

'I don't know. It was impossible to tell. She was very strung up and nervous and then she became quite defiant and sarcastic ...'

'Hardly surprising.'

'No.'

Malcolm put the light off and got back into bed and lay with his hands behind his head, as she was doing, both of them staring into the dark. 'Well,' he said, 'let's get some sleep. I can't think straight, I can't think what we should do.'

'We don't have to do anything. It's been done. It's still up to her.'

Malcolm groaned and repeated that they must get some sleep and promptly turned over and began breathing deeply.

They were both very quiet and polite in the morning, holding themselves clear of all the confusion. It was a day when both of them left the house together, an unusual occurrence. Hazel found herself automatically scanning the bushes in front of the chapel, remembering the girl's reference to herself lurking there. Abruptly, she told Malcolm this as they got into his car and he was horrified, and she wished she had never mentioned it. 'Pathetic,' he said, over and over again. Pathetic. All day, fully occupied though she was, she heard that word thumping in her brain, its rhythm insistent and strong. She fought it, not wanting to associate pathos with the girl, wanting to admit that it was only the spying and not the person who spied to whom the description pathetic could be applied. She told herself the girl wasn't a waif, she was an intelligent, able law student with a good home and loving parents who on her own admission could not have been more fortunate in life. That was not pathetic. That was lucky. It all came down to whether being mothered by your actual mother mattered – no, it all came down to whether being disposed of by her mattered – no, it all came down to whether being rejected by her when you had found her at last mattered.

Yes. By the time Hazel went home her analysis was complete. It mattered. This was what was crucial, how the girl was treated *now*, by her mother. She had not behaved well when the girl – oh, this must stop, when *Shona* – came to claim her. A great deal of her treatment yesterday was excusable but not all of it. It was perfectly excusable not to have pretended delight where she had felt none. It might be sad that she had not been able to fling her arms round her daughter's neck and embrace her passionately, but it was excusable. She had merely been true to her normal self and could not be blamed by Shona or anyone else for that. But she had not tried to empathise with this newly discovered daughter of hers. She had been wary and distant and from the first, she knew, had given off strong messages that she did not want any involvement. She had not really given Shona a chance to explore her own feelings, but had more or less dictated terms to her. And that was not excusable. She owed her some kind of welcome even if it could not be effusive. It was cowardly to freeze her out. The result could be that she would go through the rest of her life far more damaged by her mother's disinterest than she had ever been by her original rejection. It was not the adoption which hurt but the discovery of it, the sickening realisation that she, Shona, was valued even less as a fully grown person than she had been as a characterless baby. A baby was nobody, Shona was somebody. A mother who, face to face with her own creation as a *person*, turned away could not be excused.

Before Malcolm came home, Hazel had done her own detective work. Shona's name made looking for her easy – one phone call and it was located on the student list and her address and phone number given more freely than Hazel thought right, even if her voice, as a middle-aged, middle-class woman, could be said to arouse no suspicions. She thought that if she telephoned she might do more harm than good and if she wrote she would be ignored. The only thing to do was what Shona had done to her, turn up, unannounced, and plead. The moment she had decided this, she could not bear to wait. She asked Conchita to wait until Malcolm came home before going out to meet her friend. Then she dashed out to her car. Shona's street in Kilburn wasn't far away, but the traffic was heavy and it took her forty-five minutes. Then, when she had parked in the street and found the house she suddenly felt she should not be empty-handed. Did Shona drink? All students drank, surely. She found an off-licence and bought a bottle of the best champagne they had.

It was good for her, she conceded, to have to wait on Shona's doorstep as Shona had waited on hers the day before. Humbling, that is what it was. She was the supplicant now, unsure and uncertain of her reception, afraid of having doors slammed in her face, nervous as to how she should proceed, what she should say. Yet still, compared to Shona, she had the advantage. She was secure and had nothing to resolve, whereas she had seen how Shona felt: she could not know herself without knowing her true mother. She was wrong, Hazel was convinced, but was it up to her to demonstrate that? She was still debating this with herself. What she must do was give Shona reassurance, the sort of reassurance which would come only from being made to feel valued if not loved.

It was a mighty mission and Hazel half smiled at herself as she stood on the doorstep. She was no crusader. Neither in her personal life nor in her work – where it would have been welcomed – had she ever shown any sense of mission about anything. She had never felt inspired, she had always followed rather than led, or else stood quite apart. Now she felt that she was engaged on a conversion of great importance and that only she could manage it. It was crucial to get Shona to see *I do not, after all, matter*, thought Hazel, and neither does my lack of love for her.

The door was opened by an elderly man, which surprised her. She told him she was here to visit Shona McIndoe and he directed her down the stairs to the second door on the left in the basement. She realised she should have gone down the outside steps to Shona's own door and apologised. 'Happens all the time,' the man said, 'not that she has any visitors, she's no trouble, it's the other one, hordes of them coming to see her.' The window beside the basement door had wooden shutters barring it. Probably wise, given the area, but how dark it must make the room. Hazel knocked on the door but there was no sound from within, though she waited and repeated her knock several times. Maybe Shona was not back from college yet, maybe she had gone out. Leaving the champagne on the doorstep was not a good idea and yet she wanted to do that. In her bag she had a pen and paper and now she leaned against the door and scribbled a note – 'I came to drink this with you. *Please* get in touch – Hazel.' She thought about signing it 'Your mother' but that would have been outrageous. Then she laid the champagne sideways on the doorstep with the three empty milk bottles that were there in front of it. It was dark, nobody would see it unless they came and looked. She felt curiously elated after she had done this, as though something had been achieved, though it had not.

Malcolm was home early, for him. He was sharp with the boys, ordering them to bed before nine o'clock and allowing no television programmes. And he did not go to his study. He was in one of his rare clearing-up moods and rushed around tidying like a demented housewife, saying, as he always did in this mood, that his mother would have a fit if she saw this place. Hazel let him carry on. This was all too obviously a prelude to the kind of serious-talk sessions Malcolm loved to set up. Sometimes she was amused when he started his staging, sometimes so deeply irritated, she withdrew. Tonight she was neither. Malcolm's fussing was part of him, the lesser known part. It had to be endured just as her own detachment had to be when it was carried to similar extremes and used as a weapon. She watched him plump up cushions and straighten chairs and let him make and bring coffee.

'There,' he said, 'that's better.'

'Everything ready?' she asked, brightly.

He didn't ask her what she meant. He settled himself in his chair and drank some coffee and cleared his throat. 'I've been thinking of nothing else all day,' he said.

'Of course.'

'Same as you?'

'Of course.'

'And what conclusion did you come to?'

'Oh, Malcolm, for heaven's sake, conclusions?'

'Decisions, then.'

'None.'

'So you're not going to try to find her and do something about her?' His face grew red with indignation. It made her despair. How could he be such a good lawyer when he took so little care to establish facts, and assumed those that had never been stated?

'I've found her,' she said, with the deepest satisfaction, only with difficulty holding back from open gloating.

'Good,' he said, and nodded. 'Good, I'm glad.'

'Aren't you going to ask how?'

'No. It's easy enough. I'm not interested in how. Have you rung her, spoken to her?'

'No.'

'Why not?'

'I've been to her house, to the bed-sitter she has in a house in Kilburn.' Now she had him truly surprised. 'She wasn't in. I've left a note.' But she said nothing about the champagne.

'That's good,' he said, nodding again in that infuriating way. 'I didn't think you would act so quickly.'

'You didn't think I would act at all.'

'True. I thought …'

'That you would do it. You were looking forward to all the persuasion, weren't you, Malcolm? To marshalling the arguments and guiding me towards my duty as a decent human being. I've spoiled your fun.'

'It wasn't going to be fun. I was dreading it.'

'Liar.'

'I was, I was absolutely dreading it. You can be so …'

'Difficult?'

'Difficult, stubborn, and …'

'Cold?'

'No, not cold, that's what you always think people, even me, see you as. Not cold. Remote. *Apparently* unmoved even when you are moved. And anyway, I know it isn't really my business.'

'But you're pleased with me for seeing the light all on my own.'

'Yes. Don't be so mocking. What now, though?'

'She might ring.'

'You don't sound too sure.'

'Of course I don't, how can I be? She might, she might not.'

'What if she doesn't, how long will we give her?'

'It's "we" now, is it?'

'I hope so. I'm in this too, come on, and so are the boys. It's our family she'll be coming into. We'll all have to welcome her.'

'What a horrible thought.'

'But I thought you ...'

Hazel got up and went through to the kitchen. There was nothing to wash in the sink, but she turned the cold tap on until the basin was full. If Malcolm came through she would scream but he didn't, he knew her well enough. Calmer, she filled a glass of water and went back to him. 'It isn't going to be a party,' she said, 'that is when, if, she comes.'

'I know it isn't.'

'You talk as though it would be a jolly little celebration – here is our long-lost daughter and sister, let's all dance.'

'I didn't say that, I said ...'

'I know what you *said*, it was how you made it sound.'

'No, it was how *you* made it sound. All I meant was that this is something we all have to cope with and it will take some doing, knowing how to act, what to say, striking the right tone ...'

'Acting.'

'What?'

'Acting, that's what it will be. We will all be acting parts.'

'The boys won't. When shall I tell them? What would you like me to say? How shall I explain things?'

'I don't want anything explained yet. If she comes, I'd rather she came just as a new friend and then later the boys can be told, when they know her a bit.'

'I'm not sure that's wise.'

'I'm not trying to be wise. I'm thinking of what she can handle and what I can handle. You've too much of a taste for drama, Malcolm. I don't want any drama. I want, I need everything to be as quiet and ordinary – well it can't be ordinary or natural – but as quiet and unemphasised as possible. It's too tense, the whole thing. I don't know her, I don't know what she's capable of, what could happen.'

'You mean you don't know what she wants, what she's after?'

'I don't think she knows herself. She thinks she's just satisfying some deep urge to find me, but I don't know. We'll see.'

'You haven't told me enough about her adoptive parents and how she was brought up.'

'She seems to love them, she thinks they were good parents, and she's been happy.'

'Well, that's significant, surely. She isn't looking for a happiness denied her, or anything like that. She can't be motivated by resentment.'

'Can't she?'

'Doesn't sound like it. Why should she want to make you suffer, or want to barge her way into your family, if she hasn't suffered herself and has had her own perfectly happy family? Why should she think you owe her, given this background of hers?'

'Oh, she'll think I owe her.'

'Why?'

'Because ...'

And then the telephone rang and even before Hazel picked it up she knew who it would be. 'Shona?' she said.

Chapter Twenty-two

HENRY WENT to Evie Messenger's wedding. It was not an occasion that could in truth be called a wedding, in his opinion. It was a marriage ceremony and that was different. Evie, however, to his surprise, did wear white and she had a veil and a bouquet. She looked quite transformed. The word that came unbidden into his mind was 'proud': she looked proud, and he saw that all the members of the small party present were aware of this even if unable to give a name to the change in her. Henry told himself that long white dresses and veils were renowned for making the most humble and unlikely girls seem queens for a day, but he did not think it was only, as in Evie's case, a matter of disguise. She was proud, proud to be having a wedding, such a proper wedding, all decent and above board and public. It was only a pity her bridegroom had not similarly risen above himself. Jimmy was in a new suit, very smart, as befitted a tailor, but he looked uncomfortable in it.

It had crossed Henry's mind that Evie might ask him to give her away, but to his great relief she had asked nothing more of him than that he should sign the register as witness afterwards. Jimmy's uncle gave her away, though Henry was extremely doubtful about his right to do this. Presumably Evie had let it be known to the vicar what the circumstances were and he had sanctioned the bridegroom's uncle playing this role. Henry himself had consulted the vicar about his own proposed signing of the register and had been assured this was permissible. He had been rather startled, however, to hear from the vicar that Evie had told him she regarded Mr Arnesen as (the vicar's phrase, this, naturally) in *loco parentis*, because he had been like a father to her at work, although she had not wished to presume by asking him to give her away.

Miss Minto was present too. Henry was glad of this. He could not decide whether Evie had invited Miss Minto in order to make his own presence less obvious or because she truly wanted her. But Miss Minto was delighted to have been asked and sat with Henry on the bride's side of the church with obvious pleasure. There were only the two of them and not many more either on the bridegroom's side. Jimmy's mother was dead and the male members of his family were not church folk. His father and one of his three brothers had turned up and there was a male friend of his from Arnesen's and another young man Henry did not recognise, and one solitary elderly woman who might be a grandmother, Henry supposed, or an aged aunt. The church felt vast with only nine people and the vicar within it, and Henry could not help thinking how Leah and Rose and Polly would not only have swelled this pitifully small congregation but would also have given it the grace and charm and colour so conspicuously lacking.

'Doesn't she look lovely, bless her,' Miss Minto murmured to Henry, as Evie came down the aisle. 'I feel like a mother to her, I do, Mr Arnesen, God love her.' Henry could not think of what to say and was glad the organ had ceased and the vicar had begun to speak the familiar words, so that conversation was no longer permissible. He was glad to leave Miss Minto behind when it was time to go, as he had promised, into the vestry to sign the register. 'You are good to indulge her,' she whispered, apparently already apprised of what he was about to do. 'After all, you have been like a father to her and taken her under your wing, Mr Arnesen.' This irritated Henry profoundly and he entered the vestry looking unlike his usual calm self. He had not acted as a father. This was not true. He was good to all his employees, he hoped, especially the young apprentices, and there was nothing fatherly or even avuncular in his attitude, surely. It was merely good business practice to be fair and concerned and provide the best working conditions he could within the limits dictated by economic factors. And here he was, branded as acting like a father to a young woman to whom he should have been a real father.

He left as soon as he had witnessed the marriage, having made it plain he could not go to the married couple's new home – where there was no wedding-breakfast but a drink had been promised – because he must hasten back to his sick wife. He wondered, as he made his way home, if he should have kissed the bride. All the other men had done so and it would have been quite acceptable – indeed, not to have done so was perhaps too marked a departure from normal custom – but he could not bring himself to touch Evie. Instead he had shaken Jimmy's hand and told him he was a lucky man, and then he had smiled and nodded at Evie and wished her luck and he had gone. He was still feeling rather shamefaced about this as he entered his house and it made him less than understanding when Rose greeted him with the news that her mother had taken to her bed and had the blinds and curtains drawn and she did not know what to do. 'Shall you go for the doctor, father?' she asked.

'Doctor?' said Henry, curtly. 'It isn't a doctor she wants, Rose. At least, not in the ordinary way.'

Rose looked mystified and Henry sighed. 'Leave her be,' he said, 'she will recover herself presently.' He had wanted to go and remove his best suit, but now he decided only to take off the jacket and loosen his collar, so great was his reluctance to enter his own bedroom.

'You look very smart, father,' Rose said. 'Where have you been?'

It was such an innocent question, innocently asked, but it caused Henry such consternation he had to pretend to have a coughing fit, and Rose rushed to get a glass of water and thumped him on the back. He was such a poor liar. The simplest lie would do in this case: he had only to say he had been dining with a business client and Rose would be satisfied, but he could not bring himself to say this. If she repeated her query he did not know what he would do but fortunately she did not. She began asking instead if she could safely go and collect Polly from her friend's house and whether they might then go as usual on a Saturday to their dancing class, or should she stay here since her mother was unwell? Relieved, Henry sent her off, glad that she was neither as sharp-witted nor as sensitive as her mother, who would certainly have divined there was something amiss with him.

Leah knew where he had been. She knew today was the day Evie was to be married. He had told her that, since she herself refused to contemplate attending the ceremony in any capacity whatsoever, he felt he must do as her daughter had asked. His conscience, he had told her, would not let him rest if he denied Evie this mark of respect when she had been denied so much else. Leah had said nothing. He had dreaded some form of blackmail, threats that if he went to Evie's wedding she would never speak to him again, but no, none was forthcoming. But he knew she would neither ask him about the ceremony nor want to hear any spontaneous description of it which he might offer. Silence, that is what Leah wanted. And, as he had anticipated, to move house, to the other side of the river, or, better still, to one of the outlying villages, preferably to Dalston, on quite the other side of the city. He had not entirely dismissed this idea, in spite of his feeling that it would be a mistake to run away so obviously, but had prevaricated, pointing out that Rose still had a year to go at the Higher Grade School and Polly had just begun there. There was no other school of its kind in Carlisle, and Dalston was far too far away for it to be practical that the girls should go on attending it. Leah had conceded that for the next three years they must stay in the city but had pleaded to move, then, within its boundaries but out of Stanwix and the proximity of Evie.

That was how matters stood, Leah determined and Henry letting himself seem open to persuasion but, as ever, hoping matters would resolve themselves. One matter he had already resolved to act upon, however. On Monday he was giving Jimmy notice. He hated the thought of this, loathed the image of himself as hard and unjust which might be the interpretation put upon his behaviour. His employees would be shocked. Miss Minto would be most shocked of all – how could he have attended this young couple's wedding and done them the honour of signing the register knowing that he intended to dismiss the bridegroom the next week? It was not what Henry Arnesen was famous for and would be taken badly by everyone. But Henry had decided it must be done. He had to disassociate himself from Evie and this was the only way he knew to do it. This dreadful situation between his wife and her unwanted daughter must be ended and a stand taken. It might not be the kind of stand he would have chosen, but it was the only one he could think of. Evie, by coming to live cheek-by-jowl, had forced upon him this decision. Or that was how it felt. She, as a married woman, could not keep her job as an apprentice, but her husband, too, must go and the separation be complete.

He took the precaution, before he did anything at all, of checking to see if there were vacancies at Studholmes and in Bulloughs and was pleased to hear that skilled workers were needed in both establishments. Bulloughs even paid a slightly higher rate than he did himself, which surprised him, though their firm was smaller. There only remained the problem of how to put it to Jimmy and he pondered this long and hard. The thing to do was to present the case to him as one in which he had his best interests at heart. He would say how talented he was and he would tell him that these talents deserved more scope than he could give them and that he had heard Bulloughs were looking for people like him and that they paid a better wage. Then he would flourish the references he had already written and give him a month's pay. All very well, so far, but the smoothness of the operation in Henry's head stopped when he envisaged Evie's one-word reaction: why? There would inevitably be a 'why'. Even Jimmy, not half as bright as Evie, would think himself entitled to a 'why'. Henry felt ill thinking of this moment. Good God, he felt like swearing, do you not think I ask myself that and never know the answer? 'Because', that is the answer to your 'why', and I wish it were not. Or he could answer their one word with one word of his own: Leah. Leah is your answer. Leah, the woman I love, my wife, that is your answer, and if I understood her I would be a genius.

When Rose and Polly came home, late that afternoon, Leah was still in her bedroom with the blinds drawn and their father still sitting in his armchair as though in a trance. Polly was desperate to show off how she had mastered the latest dance steps and by her very enthusiasm roused Henry from his torpor. Rose, standing by the window so as deliberately to turn her back on her boisterous sister's showing off, said, 'Father, such an odd thing. Look, come and look do, there is a bride in our street.' Polly stopped dancing immediately and rushed to join her sister at the window where the two of them began an unseemly jostling for position and the lace curtain was almost dragged apart.

'Stop it!' snapped Henry. 'Come away from the window. It is rude to stare, come away at once.'

'But father,' Polly squeaked, 'she is coming here, she is!'

'I'm sure I've seen her before,' Rose was saying. 'I'm sure I have, I'm sure, but I can't think ...'

Henry had seized both of them by the arm and wrenched them away from the window with such violence that they both cried out at the same time as there was a knock on the door. 'Quiet!' he hissed, and went on holding their arms with both of them whimpering at the hurt of it. Another, louder knock came, but Henry shook his head and made them keep quite still. Their terror by this time was so great that both were near to tears and neither had any inclination to disobey a father who had suddenly changed character entirely. There was a third knock and then a different sound, a muffled, soft sound, and then footsteps retreating, and silence.

Henry let go of the girls and went to the window himself, where he stood behind the thick side curtain and peered out. He saw Evie, retreating down the street, alone. She was still in her wedding-dress, as Rose had reported. As he watched her, his eye was caught by something bright in the very corner of his line of vision. A ribbon, a yellow ribbon, trailing from his doorstep. Something had been left on his doorstep, left by Evie. 'Stay here,' he ordered the girls, both now huddled in a chair rubbing their arms where he had gripped them. Quietly, dreading that Leah would choose this moment of all moments to come down, he opened the door. Evie's bouquet lay on the doorstep. A bunch of yellow roses tied with a rather faded and shabby-looking length of yellow ribbon. He bent to pick it up and heard as he did so the girls tip-toeing into the hall. 'I told you to stay still!' he shouted at them, but not before both had seen the bouquet. Rose burst into tears and Polly promptly ran upstairs screaming for her mother.

It was the end of their happy life, but then Leah had plenty of time to reflect that their happiness had ended some time ago, though they had both been reluctant to acknowledge this. Henry had been the more reluctant but now he, rather than she, was the more unhappy. She was fatalistic. She had always expected to pay and now she was paying, whereas Henry, who had done nothing wrong except in his own opinion, had always thought what he called commonsense would prevail. Evie had them both caught. Every day she walked down their street at least twice, every day she stood and looked at their house from the other side of the street. Only for a few moments, and never at the same time, but it was enough. Leah kept her blinds drawn at the front as well as her door locked. Clara had given notice, alarmed by the change in the household and not willing to clean in half-darkness, and no one else had been taken on. Leah said she would manage on her own, without a maid, and that she preferred the work to having to provide explanations for her odd habits.

Henry had talked of consulting the police and getting them to give Evie some kind of warning, but Leah had begged him not to. What could the police do? Evie was within her rights as a citizen, there was no reason on earth why she should not walk along their street whenever she chose, nor was there anything wrong in looking at their house. She offered no threat except in their own minds and even knocking at their door did not constitute a crime. She always went away when her knocks were unanswered, and who knew what she would say if asked by some policeman why she knocked at all? 'I am come to call upon my mother,' she would say, and what was wrong with that? No, it was no case for the police, surely Henry could see that. And he could. He saw it too clearly. Not only was Evie doing no harm, not only was she not disturbing any peace except theirs, but she had behaved well upon Jimmy's dismissal and Henry felt, yet again, in her debt. There had been no scenes, no complaints, not even a 'why?' Jimmy had taken his money and gone, not to Bulloughs, but to a new firm just setting up, a branch of a Newcastle firm that Henry could tell would soon rival his own.

All that was left for them to do was to give in or run away. Leah would not give in. Henry had exhausted that option and now no longer considered it. Leah was as obdurate as ever and he had wasted enough time and energy trying to change her. So they would run away. There was no time to wait for a house to be built, which is what he would have liked. Instead, they looked all round the city, everywhere except Stanwix. Finally they lit upon a house on the Dalston Road, but still within the city boundary. It was a double-fronted affair, built of local stone, and had some pleasant features – a conservatory, a spacious hall and a south-facing walled garden. The countryside was very near – once past the nearby cemetery open fields began and stretched all the way to Dalston itself – but the city centre was only a twenty-minute brisk walk away. The area was not smart, however, and that was a drawback. Coming from Stanwix, so high above the river Eden and therefore salubrious as well as green, Dalston Road was low-lying and too near the industrial suburb of Denton Holme with its many factories.

Rose and Polly were appalled when told that they would be moving house. They wept at the stigma of living near to Bucks factory and within sight of Dixon's chimney belching out its filthy smoke. It was useless to point out how much larger and prettier the garden was compared to the tiny one they would be leaving, or to list the merits of the conservatory about which they cared not one jot. They asked again and again the reason for leaving the home they loved and were told it was not their business to inquire into their parents' decision. But they could see for themselves that neither parent seemed any happier about moving than they did. Their father was more irritable than he had ever been and their mother quiet and withdrawn. It was all a mystery and an unpleasant one.

But Rose and Polly knew it was something to do with that bride who had placed her bouquet on their doorstep and thrown their father into such an uncharacteristic rage by doing so. No explanations as to why the flowers had to be thrown into the dustbin (though they were perfectly fresh) was ever forthcoming. The girls vied with each other in imagining who the bride had been and, though their interpretations of her gesture differed wildly, they both agreed it was all something to do with Father and that was why Mother was so upset. Neither of them knew about Evie walking down the street or standing outside the house or knocking on the door, and Henry privately thanked God for it. He could not face dragging his daughters into this mess and dreaded more than anything the possibility of Evie switching her unwanted attentions to them. But Leah said she only came when the girls were sure to be at school and as for them meeting her walking down their street, this would mean nothing to them since they were unlikely to identify her. One glimpse, so long ago, in the hall of their house and another as she retreated from their doorstep, her face partially concealed by her veil, was not sufficient for them to recognise her again.

In any case, Evie had changed. She was no longer so very thin. She had filled out to such an extent Henry thought she might be expecting, but as the months went by and she grew no fatter and no baby appeared in her arms, he had deduced he was mistaken. It was married life that had changed Evie's shape. It must suit her. Not only was she pleasantly rounded after six months but her complexion was quite rosy (unless she was using rouge). She walked with a bounce in her step which had been entirely lacking before and she was always well dressed. Henry heard that Jimmy flourished, as did the new firm for which he had risked working when he could so easily have played safe and gone to an established rival. Henry never had occasion to go down Etterby Terrace, which led nowhere, but, drawn to the street, he saw how the young couple's house was coming on by leaps and bounds and would soon, once painted, be as good as any in the humble little row.

It was this, Evie's prosperity, which made it so much harder to work out why the battle to win her mother over still mattered to her. 'I cannot think why she persists,' Henry said, when just before the move to Dalston Road Evie came and did one of her knocking turns, leaving Leah as usual depressed and nervous. 'She has a husband now and her own home and every reason to be content.'

'It has nothing to do with contentment,' Leah sighed. 'It is stronger than that. She cannot help herself.'

'Well, Leah, if you think that, then you should pity her and want to aid her.'

'Pity her? Oh, I pity her, I always have, but I hate her more. And as for coming to her aid, I could only do that by harming myself, it would be my undoing.'

'We are not far from being undone in any case,' said Henry, 'moving from a home where we are happy all on account of your unreasonableness.'

'Her unreasonableness.'

'No, you are equally unreasoning, you are in no healthier frame of mind than she is, frankly. When will it stop is the point? Moving may solve very little. Have you thought ...'

'Of course I have thought.'

'You realise she may ...'

'Yes, I realise. I expect it.'

'You expect it? Then why in God's name are we moving if you expect it?' exploded Henry.

'She will not be able to come so often,' Leah said, 'and I will not meet her in the street. Dalston Road is too far away for her to wander there every day. And she will not have been in the new house as she has been in this one. It is not tainted by her.' Henry made a small sound of disgust. 'Little things to you, Henry, but not to me. Even the distance of the front door from the street will help. Here, I am so vulnerable, opening as we do on to the street. In Dalston Road we will be set back comfortably and we have a porch and she cannot stand and look at that house as she can at this one. And there is a fence and a gate at the front and the gate can be locked, and it will be impossible for her to get near.'

'A fortress,' Henry said. 'You wish us to live in a fortress.'

'I wish to be safe.'

'And will the girls tolerate this? Is it not hard enough for them to be moved without locking them up?'

'They will not be locked up. I will not lock the gate when you and they are at home. She will not come then, she never does. You may shake your head, Henry, but I know her movements. She will only come when she can be certain I am alone.'

'Then one day, however careful you are with your locking of gates and however much you cower within this new house, she will catch you. You will be forced to speak with her and it may achieve in a few minutes more than all these years of hiding have done, and if I had had my way ...'

'Yes, Henry, I know.'

Those were their last words on the subject before the move to Dalston Road, which proved every bit as painful as had been anticipated. The new house seemed vast and cold, and their furniture lost in it, and in spite of the many new attractive wallpapers and carpets it was not cheerful. Left alone there all day while Henry was at work and the girls at school, Leah felt thoroughly displaced, though she forced herself to be active and set herself daily tasks in an effort to settle in quickly. She was always busy arranging and organising the house and had taken on two girls, Amy and Dora, who came in the morning to help her. While they were with her she made a supreme effort and left both gate and doors unlocked, though closed, but the moment they departed she made herself secure. It puzzled her neighbours, some of whom came to call and were astonished to find their way barred by locks. The vicar of St James, the nearby parish church, was perturbed enough to send a note by post expressing his concern and asking if perhaps he had merely been unfortunate enough to call on a day when for some particular reason the front gate had a padlock on it. Leah replied, saying that the gate had to be secured for a short time in the afternoons without offering any explanation as to why. She knew this would fuel local gossip but she did not care.

In arranging the rooms in the new house she took pains to make sure her life was lived at the back. Her bedroom overlooked the garden now, whereas in Stanwix their best bedroom had overlooked the street, and she chose two rooms at the back to be both the morning-room and the drawing-room. The rooms at the front became the dining-room, rarely used and almost never during the day, and a smoking-room which was also Henry's workroom where sometimes he did some cutting. It was delightful the way she never needed to look out of any of the windows facing the road and even more delightful that she had discovered a side entry into an adjacent unmade-up new road which she could use when she went out. She thought it most unlikely that Evie would ever realise this other door existed. It was covered in ivy and looked unused. Leah saw that it was kept in this state, resisting all suggestions from the gardener whom she had hired that it should be cleared and made accessible.

It took Evie a long time to come at all, so long that Henry wondered if the move had been more successful than he had ever hoped. She came late morning, as the maids were leaving, which made Leah suspect she had called before in the afternoon and found the gate locked. To come in the morning was perhaps more difficult and had taken time to arrange. The girls let her in and when one of them came to tell Mrs Arnesen she had a visitor Leah knew at once. 'Give me the key, Amy,' she said, 'and go, leave the gate today.' Then Leah backed inside and shut and bolted the front door, to the astonishment of Amy, who knew Mrs Arnesen must have seen the young woman who had come to call, already walking up the path. But she obeyed her orders, dodging past Evie in an embarrassed way, and catching up with Dora who had gone ahead.

Leah hardly heard Evie knock. She was in her bedroom at the back and instead of the sound of the knocker vibrating through the house as it had done in Etterby Street it barely travelled this far. But the next time she was not so fortunate. Once more Evie chose late morning, having clearly learned by now when Amy and Dora left, and she persuaded them to let her through the gate before they locked it. They were not happy about doing this, since they recognised this woman as the one who had made Mrs Arnesen act so strangely, but Evie seemed so gentle and harmless that they let her through. Then they carried out the instructions they had been given to the letter: once Evie was through, they locked the gate, as they had been told to do, and went round to the side entry to slip the key under the old door, as they did daily. Why they did this they had no idea, but ignorance did not bother them.

Leah, coming out into the walled garden, as she did every day when her maids left, saw the front gate key lying in its usual place, pushed through by Amy, and collected it. She stayed in the garden a moment, cutting some roses, and then she walked back into her house and went looking for a favourite jug into which she liked to put these pink roses. The knock caught her entirely unawares.

She stood still, half-way across the broad hall to the dining-room door. She could see the shadow as she had not seen it for months now, the distinct shape looming through the stained glass. Head bowed, roses falling from her hands and scattering petals at her feet, she waited, eyes now closed. Three knocks of course. Then the pause, then the retreat, somehow, past or over the locked gate. Leah did not move for several minutes and when she did it was to climb the stairs, slowly, and go into the spare room at the front to look out. Evie was there, but so far away she did not seem as threatening as she had done formerly. Leah did not wait to see her leave. She went into her own bedroom to lie down.

Henry, coming home before his daughters that day, had no inkling of the visitation. Since the weather was fine he had thought to take Leah for a drive to Dalston and Bridge End and for a walk by the river. But, as soon as he entered the house, he sensed a change of atmosphere and, calling for his wife and hearing her faint response from their bedroom, he suspected the truth. He found Leah lying down on her bed.

'But how did she get back through the gate?' he asked when she had told him the story. Leah said she supposed Evie had climbed over it, which presented to Henry's imagination such a distressing picture that he was shocked – the gate was solid and high, and a woman, with her long skirts, was not equipped to do such an unseemly and ungainly thing as climb over it. What would anyone witnessing this have thought? 'You must not lock the gate again,' he said, 'it is pointless now. She has found you and she is determined and no locked gate will keep her out. You must be satisfied with your locked door, Leah.' He took the lack of reply as unspoken assent.

The gate became an unlocked gate, as it had always used to be. Henry removed the padlock. Leah took back the key from Amy. Nothing was said. More months went by and Evie did not reappear. Henry wondered if finally she was expecting. He had such faith that a child of her own would reconcile Evie to being rejected by her mother that he looked to this event as a complete solution in spite of Leah's warnings. What Leah envisaged, as the weeks and weeks went by, was that Evie had indeed become pregnant, but that she was ill. Perhaps she was following her own mother's tendency to miscarry.

Then, one day, there was a knock at the door. Leah was alone in the house. When she heard it, she knew it was Evie, returned at last. But louder knocks, impatient, several taps one after the other, told her it could not be. Evie's pattern of knocking never varied. Going hesitantly to the front door, Leah saw through the glass panels a shadow far removed from that of Evie, saw the outline of a woman wearing a magnificent hat, and was reassured. She opened the door with something close to pleasure, ready with apologies for having no maid in the afternoons, and without the faintest idea as to the identity of her visitor.

Chapter Twenty-three

EVERYTHING HAPPENED so very gradually. After the drama of that first shock, it was extraordinary how slowly and calmly events unfolded (except that, since nothing so solid as actual events took place, it was more a matter of a kind of emotional progress). Hazel marvelled at the apparent ease with which Shona made her way into their family. She had never, the day of that first meeting, thought her capable of such control and nor had she guessed how astute she could be. All the time, all the remaining time, that Shona was at UCL studying for her degree, Hazel felt she was the one suddenly marginalised. Shona was the centre, the one around whom Malcolm and the boys revolved and she had managed all this with the greatest of charm.

Malcolm had been the easiest to charm. His capitulation was no surprise to Hazel – that, at least, she had anticipated. Malcolm, after all, was a man of forty, and men of forty fall easily at the feet of beautiful nineteen-year-old girls. Since Shona was his step-daughter he had no need to hide his adoration of her, but what amused Hazel was his assumption that in praising her daughter he praised her. 'She's so lovely,' he said, and 'She's so clever' and 'She has such personality,' and then he seemed to wait, Hazel thought, for her to look pleased and show she felt personally complimented to be this girl's mother. But she did not feel complimented in the least. She felt wary, suspicious, and never more so than when Malcolm was at his most effusive. He wanted to introduce Shona as his step-daughter right away and in doing so already thought nothing of telling the tale of the adoption as though it was a mere anecdote, quickly, hardly pausing before relegating it to an unimportant part in their family history. It escaped him entirely that people's astonishment – 'what, *Hazel* had an illegitimate baby at eighteen, *Hazel*?' – might offend his wife.

She saw it on everyone's face, this incredulity. People could not believe it of her. She saw them looking at her as though they had never seen her before, as though she was another and quite strange person. They were trying to imagine her reckless and daring, trying to place her in the past as having been the very opposite of what she had grown into, a serious, quiet, dependable woman to whom acts of carefree abandon were, in their experience of her, quite unknown. She felt angered by this and wanted to proclaim her own steadiness, wanted to tell them she had always been as she was now and that no essential element in her had changed. But it was impossible to launch into such a defence; instead, she smiled and by her silence – though she hoped it was noted there was nothing apologetic or defensive about it – tried to show she was above the sort of idle speculation in which they were indulging.

Shona, she saw, went along with Malcolm's delight in introducing her as his newly discovered step-daughter. She was proud of her status in his eyes. She knew she had filled a place which had been waiting to be filled for a long time – she was Malcolm's longed-for daughter. But she was faithful to her adoptive father all the same, never referring to Malcolm as Dad, even when nudged in that direction. Archie McIndoe was her father and no other. Once, when they were alone, soon after Shona had moved in with them – it was Malcolm, of course, who had insisisted she should give up that horrid little bed-sitter and come and live on their top floor without any question of rent or contribution to bills – Hazel had been stung, by something carelessly said, into asking Shona why she did not want to know who her real father had been.

'It isn't the same,' Shona said.

'But it takes two to make a baby. I didn't create you on my own.'

'No, but you gave me away on your own.'

Hazel smiled. She liked Shona's sharpness. 'True, but you could argue it was your father's fault I had you at all and needed to give you away. It's just strange that all the blame ...'

'Blame? I never mentioned blame. I don't blame you, not for the accident of having me, only for what you did afterwards and he had nothing to do with that. You said yourself you never even told him you were pregnant.'

'I would still have thought you'd want to know who he is.'

'Well, I don't, even if you're determined to tell me.'

Little spitting scenes, that is what these interchanges always were. Nothing very terrible was said but the tension was there, unrelieved at the end. They would part, each leave whatever room they were in and take care to come together again only when others were present. Hazel wondered for a while whether she was suffering from nothing more complicated than jealousy, but dismissed this as ridiculous. She was not jealous of Shona, neither of her youth nor her looks, nor, more to the point, her success as a step-daughter and half-sister. It made life easier that her daughter got on so well with everyone and that her presence, far from arousing resentment, or feelings of awkwardness, seemed on the contrary to breed a greater harmony. The boys were fascinated by her and saw her as some kind of fairy-tale princess who had come at last to claim her kingdom. She was like a present given to them and their attitude was their father's. When Shona left them to go back to Scotland for holidays they were furious with her and moped until she returned.

Hazel spoke to Catriona McIndoe once on the telephone. She had asked Shona what her adoptive parents had said when she had told them, as she was bound to do, of what had happened, and how she was now living with her real mother. Shona had shrugged and turned red before admitting the great distress this had caused Catriona. 'I'm not surprised,' Hazel had said. 'Poor woman, all that love and devotion thrown in her face.'

'I haven't thrown it in her face,' Shona protested. 'It hasn't altered anything. I still love both of them.'

'I shouldn't think it feels like it to them, especially her,' Hazel said carefully.

'You haven't a clue about her so don't think you have. You're not a bit like her, you can't possibly understand her. She'd *never* have given her baby away, never, she'd rather have died first.'

So when Catriona did ring Hazel was prepared. The voice was soft, hesitant. 'Mrs McAllister?' it said, and Hazel guessed, the Scottish accent and the worry in the voice identifying Catriona at once.

'Mrs McIndoe?' she said, trying to change her own tone of voice from the customary clipped one she always found herself using. 'How nice to talk to you.'

This seemed to take the caller back. 'Oh,' she said. 'Oh yes, and nice to talk to you too. I would not be bothering you, but I was wondering about the train Shona is catching ...'

'Hasn't she let you know?'

'No. Well, it's been a wee while since she wrote and the last letter just said the seventeenth and as it's the sixteenth today I ... well ... I don't want to bother you, but I'd like to meet her train and ...'

'I'll get her to ring you when she comes home.' The moment she'd said the emotive word 'home', Hazel knew she should not have done so, but to apologise for it would double the hurt. 'Mrs McIndoe?' she said quickly. 'I *am* glad to talk to you. I've often thought about it but I imagined you wouldn't want to hear from me.'

'Och no, not at all. We can't carry on like that, now can we? It wouldn't do Shona any good. What's done is done and we must all just adapt.' The words were sensible but the voice shook.

Hazel knew the phone would be put down with a polite goodbye any moment. 'Mrs McIndoe?' she said again.

'Catriona, please.'

'Catriona, perhaps we could keep in touch now we've talked?'

'Yes, of course, for Shona's sake.'

Not at all for Shona's sake, Hazel thought, as she replaced the receiver. Not for her sake, for our own, for my sake in particular, and then she could not think why she was so sure of this.

'How nice Catriona sounds,' she said to Shona that evening and was somehow indecently gratified when she saw the effect of her innocent-sounding comment. 'She rang, to find out which train you're going to catch.'

'She'd no need to do that, she knew I'd ring tonight,' said Shona angrily.

'Well, maybe she wanted to speak to me.'

'What? Why on earth would she want to do that? She hates you.'

'She didn't sound as if she did.' Hazel knew beyond any doubt that Catriona McIndoe had never passed any opinion about her whatsoever. It was a foolish lie of Shona's and she followed it up with another.

'Well, she does. She told me she never wanted to speak to you, ever, or know anything about you.'

'Odd, then, that she should telephone my house.'

'She'd think you'd be out during the day.'

'She'd think you would be out too, surely. Who would she be hoping to get, do you think?'

'Some servant, to leave a message with for me.'

'But we don't have servants. Have you said we do?'

'Conchita and Mrs Hedley are servants.'

'Hardly.'

'To my mother they are.'

'I'm your mother.'

Hazel said it quite deliberately. She wanted to claim to be Shona's mother precisely at the moment her identity was confused. It was a crude but effective way of reminding Shona that motherhood had nothing to do with blood and everything to do with nurturing. Catriona was her mother and all Hazel's efforts were towards forcing her to acknowledge this at last. But Shona wouldn't, not then. She corrected herself and refused to receive the message. She rang Catriona there and then with Hazel still in hearing and in giving her the necessary information about the train was so curt it sounded offensive.

'Is that how you always talk to your mother?' Hazel asked.

'No, it's how I talk to Catriona,' snapped Shona.

'Why do you do it? Why do you hurt her?'

'You wouldn't understand.'

'I've just admitted that. I don't understand but I'd like to.'

'I don't think you're capable.'

'God, you're insolent, Shona,' but Hazel laughed even as she objected. 'Very, very insolent, and childish, for one so clever. You've been spoiled, grossly overindulged. You think Catriona loving you so completely gives you some sort of licence to insult.'

'No, I don't. I think she understands, whatever I say or do, so I don't have to watch my step. That's different.'

'I can't think why you ever wanted to leave this saint and claim me as your mother.'

'I haven't left her ...'

'Home to her once, in months, for forty-eight hours? A scrappy letter once every six weeks? And if you telephone, which I doubt, it hasn't been from here since you moved in. I think she thinks you've left her. You've deserted her, abandoned this mother who loves you so much, for me.'

There hadn't been any reply to that. Hazel realised she was always pushing Shona towards a quarrel so violent she would feel compelled to leave, hurling words of hate as she went. But the moment never came and it was in Shona's abrupt departures, her lack of retaliation at the crucial time, that Hazel saw herself. Cutting off, in the midst of what seemed unstoppable fury, was their technique. It could never be mistaken for defeat or associated with giving in – it was too strong, too deliberate, this absenting of oneself, this ostentatious rising above taunts. So Shona had left the room in which they had been sitting and had gone off into the garden where Malcolm was making a half-hearted stab at weeding. She went and helped him and Hazel saw how Malcolm became instantly alert, how his previously languid movements changed to a vigorous bending and digging with his trowel. They weeded together for half an hour and then Malcolm went to collect the boys from the swimming baths and Shona went with him, though there was no need to and it would mean Conchita squashing up with the children in the back seat. Clever, Hazel reflected, she's clever, she is making herself indispensable in the most subtle way, vital to this family's, my family's, sense of well-being.

When Shona was away in Scotland Hazel felt liberated. She had her home to herself again. Her mother appreciated this. She had refused to be drawn into the admiring McAllister throng round Shona, and once the girl had moved in (which had naturally horrified Mrs Walmsley) she had taken care always to check she was not expected to be there before she herself came round. Hazel had told her how foolish this was.

'Shona can't be ignored any more, Mother,' she had said, very early on, just as Mrs Walmsley's attitude was becoming marked.

'I am not ignoring her,' her mother had said, 'I'm simply keeping out of it.'

'That's the same.'

'No, it isn't.'

'Well, whatever your interpretation, it's still silly, cutting yourself off from us because of Shona. You're hardly seeing the boys at all, you're cheating yourself and they miss you.'

'They don't miss me. They've got her.'

'Oh, Mother, really. She's just a novelty, they're excited. They're so young none of the implications occur to them. They can't work out why you don't want to be with Shona too, when she's so lively and such fun.'

'I know all that, but I can't help it. She alarms me.'

'Shona? Oh, and what is alarming about her?'

'You know.'

'Do I?'

'Yes, you do. I'm sure she alarms you too, she must.'

'Must? In what way "must"?'

'The way she's taken over your family.'

'It's hers, her family, that's what you're missing. She doesn't see herself taking over, she thinks she's fitting in, she's just slipping into a gap she sees as always having been there.'

'Well, it wasn't there. That's her mistake. There wasn't any gap. You know that, I know that. You should tell her so.'

'I'm not going to tell her anything. It would be fatal. Let her work it out eventually.'

'But she won't, she's determined. You've got her for life now.'

She'd told her mother not to be so melodramatic, but Hazel privately thought those words prophetic. Inviting Shona to move in to their house had been the first step along the for-life road. Malcolm, in suggesting it, had, she knew, expected resistance from her and she had been very careful not to offer it. Instead, she had gone to great lengths to make their tiny attic flat as attractive as possible. They had had tenants there before, students who baby-sat and did some cleaning in return for a very low rent, but once au pairs had come into their household, the attic rooms had been kept empty, for visitors only. Now Hazel had them decorated and graciously asked Shona to choose the colours for paint and a new carpet. Malcolm was pleased. It felt right to him that Hazel should prepare a nest for her daughter and make her feel truly wanted. It was a significant gesture, recognised as such by all parties. Then there was the matter of holidays. The McAllisters had good holidays. They both worked very hard indeed and holidays were not just for pleasure but for recouping lost energies and preparing them for the rigours always ahead.

'I was wondering,' Malcolm had said, that first year, as the time for booking flights and villas approached, 'about Shona. She'll want to come, won't she, as one of the family? So we won't need Conchita. She can go home for that month.' Hazel had raised her eyebrows. 'What? You don't think Conchita will like that? Surely she will.'

'Oh, I'm sure Conchita will, but what about Shona? Will she see herself as an au pair for a month?'

'She won't be an au pair, don't be silly.'

'If we haven't got Conchita, she'll have to be. How else will we cope? What about all that time to ourselves we get, with Conchita looking after the boys?'

'I didn't mean Shona won't want to be with the boys, but that won't make her an au pair, she's their sister, it's different.'

'Very different, different enough for her not to feel the least obliged to spend all day on a beach with three young boys if she doesn't want to.'

'But she *will* want to, she loves them, she plays with them for hours as it is.'

'That's her choice, her whim. Once she's expected to, she'll think differently. The point is, Malcolm, you won't be able to depend on her doing it, and if she doesn't, you have no way of making her.'

'So you don't want her to come?'

'I don't care either way. All I care about is you and me having free time really to relax.'

'I'll discuss it with her.'

'You do that.'

Shona came on their summer holiday with them, but so did Conchita. Malcolm paid for Shona of course, though with a good deal of secret swearing about the ruinous extravagance. It was not a success. Even Malcolm acknowledged this. The boys were normally quite happy with Conchita, but not if Shona was there. They wanted their half-sister all the time and when she grew tired of them, which she did quite quickly, within a week, they took their disappointment out on poor Conchita, who began to say she wanted to go home for good and thought she had been with the McAllister family long enough. Then Malcolm thought it not fair to treat Shona like Conchita and so in the evenings Shona came with them when they went out to restaurants. They were suddenly a threesome at the only time they could count on being just a couple. Hazel grew quieter and quieter, Shona more and more animated. She loved Italian night life – they had rented a villa near Sorrento – and her enthusiasm was so touching to Malcolm that he reacted by making sure they went out far more than usual. Shona was dictating the pace.

It had, some time soon, to come to an end, Hazel reasoned. Shona was a student. At the end of her three-year course she would have decisions to make, and by the end of her second year was already doubting whether she would carry on with law. Malcolm wanted her to. He told her she'd make an excellent defence lawyer and urged her to come and work as a legal clerk in his firm in her vacation. This would give her an idea of what legal aid work was about and he was sure would inspire her to try for articles. But Shona demurred. She said she felt she had made a mistake and should have done something with languages. She wanted to travel first, whatever she decided to do after her degree; and at the word 'travel' Hazel felt hopeful. But there was no sign of any travelling meanwhile. It struck Hazel as odd how much Shona stayed at home. She was twenty, twenty-one nearly, but she behaved like a middle-aged person, seeming uninterested in any of the social pursuits common to her age group. And where were her friends? There were none to be seen. No one came home with her or visited. Even Malcolm, so happy that Shona liked to be with them at weekends, thought this unusual. 'She's so attractive,' he said, 'I can't understand it. The men in her college must be blind.'

No, they were not blind, Hazel could sense that. They were not so much blind, these unknown men, as struck dumb by Shona's single-mindedness which would manifest itself in all kinds of off-putting ways. Shona had her studies – she seemed a serious student whatever her doubts about law as a career – and she had her new family and nothing and no one else was allowed to interfere. She would not be able, Hazel reckoned, to take on any relationship even if one were offered, not while she had this sense of mission to become one of the McAllisters. It was like a job to her and one at which she worked hard. Hours and hours had to be devoted to becoming part of the very fabric of this family of her mother's, and only when belonging had become effortless would she have room for anything else. It must exhaust her: watching Shona, observing her ever more closely, Hazel was sure of this. And all for what? What was she getting out of the struggle that made it worthwhile?

Sometimes Hazel envisaged how things would have been if she had kept Shona. Never, during all the lost years before Shona appeared on her doorstep, had Hazel ever fantasised about being a single parent, but then that dignified term had not existed. In the fifties there had been only 'unmarried mothers'. It had never occurred to her to wonder how she would have made out alone with a child. But now she grew fascinated by the possibilities and saw herself in retrospect exercising great ingenuity in doing what she had done while being a single mother. It was possible, she told herself, that her father, had he been told the truth, would have supported her; possible she could still have taken a degree and worked; possible that when she met Malcolm she would have had an eight-year-old daughter. This would not have put Malcolm off. He would have accepted and loved Shona. She would have been his ready-made daughter, they would have been a family from the beginning. And that was when her fantasy became interesting to Hazel – imagining Shona not desperate to become part of a family from which she had been excluded, but on the contrary desperate, in the normal adolescent and young adult way, to *escape* family ties. Especially maternal ones. Running from them, Hazel envisaged, running away, not towards, doing the rejecting herself.

She wished, often, that she could have proper discussions of this sort with Shona, but there was no chance of those. By the time Shona had lived with them for almost two years, Hazel knew her well enough to realise there never would be such an opportunity. But what was somehow comforting was the far deeper realisation that there never would have been either – even if Shona had been with her from birth, there would have been this reluctance on her part to engage in emotional encounters in which the unsayable might be said. Shona was her grandmother all over again. There never would have been any true connection. Hazel saw herself as stranded between the two of them, her mother unable to give and Shona to receive. The link, the link motherhood was supposed to give, was believed by Shona to give, was not there. She could not love Shona and Shona could not love her, but this lack of love had, in Hazel's opinion, little to do with what had happened in the past. Brought together now, as two adults, it was clear that with the exception of certain traits of mind and personality they were not alike and shared no common interests or attitudes. They would always have been destined to grow apart if, through the circumstances of intimate family life, they had been forced for many years to be close. Shona might have been denied her true mother but that mother would not have been true in any meaningful sense at all.

Hazel felt better. The more convinced she became that Shona and she would never have fused together, just as she herself and her own mother had never done so, the less guilty and anguished she felt about having given her daughter away. The shadow lifted and with it her resentment at Shona's very existence. She felt quite tender towards Shona and was able to demonstrate this in new ways. From being always on the alert and watchful, she felt she could afford to turn away and let the new family mixture settle down. It was settling in any case. The boys were growing up. Philip was mature for his age and in the two years he had known his half-sister he had naturally changed dramatically. At first he had admired and been fascinated by her, but gradually he began challenging her, competing with her, and in his arguments with her Hazel heard a determination not to let Shona dominate either him or his family. He got to a position where he had very nearly moved on to the attack, and it gave Hazel the opportunity to defend Shona and demonstrate sympathy. Philip was furious with her.

'I don't know why you stick up for her,' he would say. 'She can look after herself, she always does, she's so *selfish*.'

'She was an only child,' Hazel said, mildly.

'What's that supposed to mean?'

'Well, when you're an only child you do have everything your own way and it's hard to learn how to share properly.'

'But she's grown up, she's not a child, Mum.'

'Doesn't make any difference, she goes on learning, she still feels an outsider in groups.'

'She is.'

'Just because you've had a quarrel, Philip ...'

'It isn't just because of any row. She *is* an outsider. She doesn't fit in.'

'She's fitted in very well these last two years, amazingly well, considering she had to take on three brothers.'

'Half-brothers.'

'That's mean.'

'What is?'

'Stressing the half bit. You didn't used to be so mean. You used to hate it when Shona first came if anyone called her less than your sister.'

'I hardly knew what it meant.'

'Oh, Philip, you did, of course you did.'

'I knew the facts, but I was too young, I didn't really think about what they meant.'

'And now, that you're so grown up, you do.'

'Yeah, I do. I do. I've thought about it a lot and it's weird, her turning up, coming here like that and then just latching herself on to us.'

'Not weird at all, quite understandable really.'

'I wouldn't do it. If you'd given me away and I'd been adopted, I wouldn't have done it. If I'd only found out when I was eighteen, like she did, and if I'd had lovely parents, like she says she has, I wouldn't have done it. I wouldn't have wanted anything to do with you, ever.'

'You can't know what you would have done, and anyway, you are you, Shona is Shona, and you can't judge other people by yourself.'

'Shona does. She wants us so we are supposed to want her.'

'You *have* wanted her, up to now, and you still do really, you're only fighting with her the way I fought with my brothers, it's all to do with age, it'll pass.'

'You're always saying that, about everything. Dad loves her anyway, she's his favourite. He always wanted a daughter, didn't he?'

'Yes, but ...'

'So we were all disappointments.'

'No, don't be silly, you weren't anything of the sort. And I only wanted boys, every time.'

'That's because you'd had a girl already.'

'No, it isn't. I hadn't "had" her in any real way, I'd given her away. I just didn't want daughters.'

'Why?'

'They're too difficult for a woman.'

'Mum, that doesn't make sense.'

He laughed and that was how that particular session ended. Philip called them that, 'sessions', and it amused her. More and more he wanted sessions in which he was looking for an argument or trying out some theory, and he would follow her round the house, whatever she was doing, haranguing her and pleading for a response. Witnessing this, Shona's envy was obvious and yet Hazel was not quite sure what exactly was being envied – Philip's confidence that his mother would want to hear him, or her own clearly happy involvement with him. Once, when he had had her pinned against the airing cupboard door, with her arms full of clean towels, while he ranted on for all of twenty minutes about the injustice of his not being allowed to go to the cinema on his own and had only been stopped by Shona yelling that there was a phone call for him, Hazel had tried to draw Shona into mocking him.

'My God,' Hazel had said, 'if he is like this before he's actually a teenager, what are we in for?'

'You like it,' Shona said, her face dark, brows furrowed. 'You love him like that.'

'Well, yes, I do,' said Hazel, carefully, towels at last deposited, but the bathroom door now blocked by Shona leaning against the frame. 'But I can still see he's going to be a pain.'

'I was a pain.'

'Were you? Yes, I can see you might have been like Philip at his age.'

'I wasn't like Philip. He's got you. He's a pain and you know he is and you don't care. I was a pain and my mother was terrified of me.'

'I expect she did her best and who ...'

'Of course she did her best. God, sometimes ...' And she went off, downstairs, to Hazel's relief. She knew she mustn't let this go and yet if Shona had chosen to go upstairs, to her rooms, it would have been so much more difficult to follow her.

As it was, she ran downstairs too and into the kitchen where Shona was taking something from the fridge. 'Shona,' she said, and went to her and, greatly daring, touched her on the shoulder, a light touch she hoped would be interpreted as affectionate. 'Shona, I take your point, I do see what you mean, about your mother being afraid because she didn't know who was in you, that's it, isn't it, that's what you meant? That she was always afraid because of your being adopted and so she couldn't ever know what you were made of?'

'Something like that,' Shona said, offhand now, but grudgingly willing to continue.

'And you, without knowing why, felt alien to her, and then when you found you were adopted you thought that was why, didn't you? That you'd been a cuckoo in a nest and if you could find the right nest – Oh my God, nests and cuckoos ...' and she began to laugh. For an awful moment she thought Shona was going to do the opposite, to cry, but she smiled too, and then began to giggle and they both collapsed. 'Not that funny,' Hazel said weakly after a while. 'I was just trying so hard.'

'You do try hard.'

'Is it that obvious?'

'Yes.'

'Oh dear.'

'No, it was a compliment, I meant it as a compliment. I know you try. I try too. It's stupid, really.'

'What, two people trying hard to understand and love each other?'

'Well, not the understanding, that's not stupid, but to try to love is, isn't it? It should be natural, it isn't worth anything, it doesn't work otherwise.'

'I do love you,' Hazel lied. 'I don't have to try any more.'

'But I don't love you,' Shona said, 'that's the point. I always wanted to and expected to, but I don't. I admire you, but that's no good, and I envy you, and that's terrible, to envy your own mother for what she's got.'

'I've got nothing you can't also have one day.'

'I doubt it,' said Shona, 'but it won't be your fault, I won't blame you.'

'That's good. I've done a lot of blaming myself and it isn't good, it isn't a good idea at all. I blamed my mother and it was wrong.'

'I don't know her. She doesn't want anything to do with me, does she? That's why she never comes if she knows I'll be around, and she gets all embarrassed if I catch her here. She hates me, she thinks I'm a threat to you.'

'She doesn't hate you, she just goes on wanting to pretend what happened all those years ago never happened, that's all.' Hazel paused. It felt odd to want to defend her mother. 'She's getting old now and she's stubborn, it's hard to change her. But she'll come round eventually, she'll have to. Everyone is so used to you now, you're so accepted, the shock value has worn off. Well, for everyone else. There's only her left and she doesn't really matter, her attitude needn't hurt you.'

'But it does. I've done nothing wrong, but she acts as if I had. I suppose she thinks it wrong to have come here at all. Does she call it "raking up the past"? I bet she does.'

'I expect she does too, but to herself, not to me. She knows how I feel.' Hazel hesitated. It seemed a terrible betrayal to want to go on to tell Shona how much she had always disliked her mother. It was not something it seemed right to do. 'She's quite an interesting person really, your grandmother,' she finally said. 'She had a hard life when she was a child, but she hardly ever talks about it. Her father was killed in the war, the First World War, and her mother was widowed before she was born. It wasn't really till she met my father, your grandfather, that she had any life of her own. Her mother clung to her, she was the centre of her universe, literally, and it made her want me to feel free of that kind of thing. But I wasn't free, of course.' Hazel paused again, trying to gauge Shona's reaction. Was she bored with this potted maternal history? Did she think it superfluous to the circumstances now? Did she see it as an attempt to make her grandmother a more sympathetic character? It was so hard to know. 'Anyway,' she finished, lamely, 'she's not such a bad woman. She still thinks what she did was for the best.'

'For you.'

'Yes, I suppose so, but then I was real, I existed, I was her daughter. You were unreal, at the time.'

'And now I'm real. Definitely.'

'And she's afraid of you.'

'Well, she doesn't need to be. I'm not staying. The moment I've graduated, I'm off. I've decided. And I might never come back, so she needn't worry.'

'You're free to do what you like,' Hazel said. 'You can leave, you can come back.'

Neither of them could think what to say after that.

Chapter Twenty-four

THEY WERE sitting in the drawing-room. Leah had offered tea, her offer prefaced with further apologies for the absence of the maid. Tea had been declined, but Leah wished it had been accepted. Making tea, even if it meant leaving her visitor alone for a few minutes, would have helped ease the awkwardness she felt. Her visitor was in some way distressed. The distress was controlled, but since she had often been in such a state herself Leah spotted the signs. She could not think how this woman's nervousness might relate to herself but waited with growing curiosity for the reason to emerge. The woman was in mourning so someone had died, which could account for her unhappiness but not for her visit.

Leah was glad her drawing-room was looking attractive. She had chosen what she thought a daring colour for the new carpet, a strangely green blue which had made Henry raise his eyebrows at the impossibility of matching anything else with it. But Leah had not tried to match it. The carpet had a cream diagonal stripe in it and it was this cream she had matched, in curtains and chair covers, except for cushions which were turquoise. The whole effect was fresh and cool, quite unlike the overheated tones of the parlour they had left behind in Etterby Street. The room had hardly been used. It was a room in which to receive company and they had received none. Everything was pristine and Leah was proud of it. She saw that her visitor was impressed and was evaluating her accordingly, before she spoke.

'You do not know me,' she said. Leah inclined her head, apologetically. 'My name is Evelyn Fletcher, but that will mean nothing to you either. Fletcher is my married name.' She paused, but there was no reaction from Leah. 'It is all a long time ago,' she sighed, 'and I have no wish to upset you. I could have written, once I discovered your whereabouts – that has taken time and it felt wrong to delay further.' She stopped and a small sob escaped her.

'Please,' said Leah, 'please, do not upset yourself on my behalf. I had much rather have a visitor than a letter.' It was graciously said, and the woman, Mrs Fletcher, managed to smile slightly.

'You are very kind, very understanding, but then we should have known that.' Another sigh, and then the straightening of her back. 'My maiden name was Todhunter. I am Evelyn Todhunter.' She observed Leah carefully. 'Now you begin to see?'

Leah said nothing. Her lips felt dry and she delicately ran her tongue round them. She could only nod. Her sudden lack of composure was not equal to any other response.

'It is a sad tale,' Mrs Fletcher said, 'and it has been sad for you, too, for many years, I know.' She looked round the room and gestured at the framed photographs of the family and added, 'But you found happiness after the sorrow.' Leah flushed, a little spark of resentment starting to ignite inside her. 'I am not excusing my brother,' Mrs Fletcher said, 'never think that. What he did, how he behaved to you, to us, was inexcusable, and he knew it. At the end he begged forgiveness and that is why I am here.' A great rush of relief overwhelmed Leah, but Mrs Fletcher mistook her cry for anguish and rose out of her chair and came towards her, holding out her arms, and saying in a curiously affected and high-pitched sing-song voice which grated on Leah's nerves, 'My dear, I am sorry, I am sorry, it is a dreadful shock, shocking, I know, and after so long, when you did not expect it. I will stop if you cannot bear to hear more, only say the word and I will go and never bother you again, you have every right to tell me to go!'

It took a while for both of them to regain their equilibrium. Leah recovered first, but needed badly to escape from this woman's suddenly cloying presence. 'You must excuse me, Mrs Fletcher,' she said, abruptly. 'I need some tea.' She went into her kitchen and set a tray with two of her best cups and saucers, and the silver teapot and water jug and sugar bowl and milk jug, and a plate of shortbread biscuits, but at the last moment before carrying the tray through, she removed the biscuits. Without asking Mrs Fletcher if she would not after all now change her mind, she poured two cups. Her own she drank in a moment, not caring how this might seem, and refilled her cup immediately. Mrs Fletcher sipped from hers hesitantly and eyed

Leah anxiously from over the rim of the cup. 'Do you want to hear?' she asked.

'Yes,' Leah said, 'if you can bear to tell me.' She wanted to add 'and tell me quietly and sensibly', but did not.

'I do not know where to begin. He, Hugo, I can hardly say his name, it was banned for so long in our house, it is unfamiliar on my tongue, he died six weeks ago. He came home and died within a month. He knew he was dying, you see, and he came back, to Moorhouse, not knowing our father had died long ago and only my mother was left, ill herself. My father had forbidden her to reply when Hugo at last wrote, years after he had disappeared in Canada, he had said he would not even acknowledge Hugo as his son and she was to cut him out of her heart. But my father was dead and he came back and, of course, my mother took him in, though in no fit state to nurse anyone and needing a nurse herself. And I was sent for. I could not go immediately and nor did I wish to. I had suffered. I was at home during that dreadful time, dreadful, and I saw my mother weep and heard my father curse, and I suffered too. But I could not leave my poor mother to manage him on her own, so eventually I went. I wish I had not.' Here, there was a break in Mrs Fletcher's account, all of which had been delivered in a new low and monotonous voice, much preferable to the previous tone, but Leah had difficulty catching every word. She gave her no direct encouragement to continue beyond showing she was concentrating. 'Oh, he was a terrible sight, quite wasted away with disease, thin beyond belief and lined beyond his years and altogether a wreck of a man. Everything he touched went wrong, all his life. I cannot accurately recall the sequence of evils which befell him, and to tell the truth I do not want to. He was feverish with pain much of the time and rambling, and many things he came out with made no sense. But he spoke of you quite sensibly. He wept for shame at how he had treated you and begged me over and over to find you and beg you to forgive him, or he could never rest in peace. And he spoke of his child whom ...'

'More tea?' Leah said.

Interrupted, Mrs Fletcher was thrown. She had warmed to the drama of her description and her voice had become louder and excited, and now that she was stopped she could not quite pitch it correctly. 'The child,' she repeated, 'he thought of his child at the end ...'

'But not at the beginning,' Leah said, curtly.

'I beg your pardon?'

'He did not think of his child at the beginning. And neither did you nor your mother.' Mrs Fletcher's mouth opened and her expression was one of such consternation it was horribly comic. Impatiently, Leah said, 'You cannot believe, Mrs Fletcher, that I am not touched and moved to tears at hearing of your brother's affecting deathbed speech, but I have no feeling for him, dead or alive, beyond contempt. And contempt for your mother too.'

'What did my mother ever do to you?'

'How did you find me?'

'We employed a detective. Forgive me if that seems sordid. He began with an old address. There was an address, you wrote to Hugo, and ...'

'I wrote to your mother, after Hugo's child was born. I told her Hugo had a daughter and I had named her after her, Evelyn, after her and after you, Mrs Fletcher. I asked for nothing, but I hoped, and my hopes were not answered. Your mother had my address as well as Hugo, if it ever reached him.'

'It would be my father ...'

'I did not write to your father. I wrote to your mother, woman to woman.'

'My father would have found out and ...'

'She could have found a way, but she did not want to extend help to her son's whore and his bastard child.' Leah was sorry to have come out with such ugly words. They defiled her and she felt besmirched and ugly herself, because of having uttered them.

Mrs Fletcher sank back in her chair and wept for real, and, though at first the sight left Leah unmoved, she said at last how sorry she was and that she regretted her vulgar outburst. They were both silent for some considerable time before Mrs Fletcher pulled herself together and said, 'My mother is still alive. She is old and ill and has not long to live. You make me afraid to tell you this but she wishes to give Hugo's child some money, a gift, if she will accept, though if she is of like mind with yourself ...'

'I have nothing to do with her,' Leah said.

'Your daughter?'

'Hugo's daughter. I have nothing to do with her. It pained me too much even to look at her and she was given into someone else's care from an early age.' Leah saw Mrs Fletcher's eyes stray to the photographs of Rose and Polly. 'They are my own daughters, my husband's and my girls.' She put a certain emphasis on 'husband' which was not missed by Mrs Fletcher.

'So you do not know where my brother's child is now?'

'Oh, I know,' Leah said. She got up and went to the bureau Henry had recently bought, and opened the lid and sat down and wrote, not caring about her poor penmanship, Evie's name and address on a piece of the pretty blue writing-paper she had taken such pleasure in choosing, though there was no one to whom she wrote regular letters. 'There,' she said, 'I am sure his daughter will be glad to hear of her father and this late gift.' She wished Mrs Fletcher would leave. Her mission was accomplished. She should leave, quickly. But still she sat on, seemingly rooted to the spot.

'I did not know of your letter to my mother,' she said. 'I would not like you to think I did and that I, too ...'

'I do not think that,' Leah said, as carelessly as possible. 'I have little interest, frankly, in what you did or did not know. But you lived in that house, your parents' house, your family home, with him, your brother, at the time. You lived in Moorhouse. I think you were well acquainted, as everyone was bound to be, in such a place, with my condition. I think you knew of me.'

Mrs Fletcher bowed her head and took refuge behind her handkerchief with which she patted her eyes over and over again. 'What could I do?' she whispered. 'It was such a ... it was spoken of in such ... when I did hear of it ...'

'It was a scandal,' Leah said. 'I will say it for you. And I was blamed for it, not he. I believed in him, I trusted him, and the result ... well, the result we know.'

'The poor child,' Mrs Fletcher said, 'when I think of it, that poor child. It breaks my heart.'

Leah laughed, a dry, short, hard sound with little mirth in it. 'It broke mine too,' she said.

'But you ... I thought I heard you to say ...'

'I said I could not bear to see his child and never have been able to. I did not mention my own heart. But it is mended. It has been mended a long time and now you will seal the last crack for me, the crack which threatens to open up now and again, under certain circumstances, when a certain person tries to prise it open. You will do more than you know to mend my heart if I am fortunate at last.'

Mrs Fletcher was mystified, but Leah let her remain so. She had no desire to confide in the woman. Let her make her way as soon as possible to Evie's home and acquaint her with the tidings she had brought. Leah could imagine the scene easily. Evie might always have vowed she had no interest in her unknown father, but presented with the glory of his deathbed cry for forgiveness and to have this capped by recognition from a grandmother who was now making her a substantial gift – it would thrill her. Leah was sure of it. Mrs Fletcher, in spite of her weeping, was an imposing figure and she was *family*, she represented a family now claiming Evie as its own. Evie would return to Moorhouse with Mrs Fletcher to see this grandmother, Leah was convinced of it. And what might come from that meeting? Satisfaction, she hoped, Evie's satisfaction to have at last a mother of sorts. And something more practical even: a move. Evie might be persuaded to return to Moorhouse to be with her grandmother and she might inherit the house and ... Leah stopped herself. There was Jimmy. There would be no work for Jimmy in Moorhouse. He would not wish to move. It was absurd to imagine such a solution. Nothing would change. Evie would still persist in haunting her.

For reasons she did not want to work out, Leah did not tell Henry of Mrs Fletcher's visit. She thought of it often in the following weeks, but she never spoke of it. It was a secret she hugged to herself and she relished the sensation. When Evie had failed to appear outside the house for some months she longed to know if she had gone to see her grandmother, but there was no way she could find out. It was tempting to inquire at Jimmy's place of work if he was still employed by them, but she was too embarrassed to ask and neither did she want to make such a direct inquiry. She wanted to find out naturally, having some superstitious belief that this would bring her luck. She began to go into the city centre with unusual frequency, merely so that she could search faces, looking for Evie or Jimmy – or rather, search in the hope of noting their absence. She was convinced that if she went often enough at the most popular times to the most popular places she would be bound to see Evie if she were still in Carlisle. The market seemed to her the most obvious meeting-place – every Carlisle housewife sooner or later went into the market, and Evie had always been fond of it if Henry was to be believed – so Leah haunted the market. She drifted from stall to stall with a half-full basket, scanning face after face, searching and searching for Evie, at ten in the morning, at two in the afternoon, at closing time on Saturdays, at every time of day. Then she grew bolder. She took a tram to Stanwix and with pounding heart walked down the little terrace where Evie lived, back and forth, briskly, then loitering, watching the houses and trying to decide if the Patersons lived there still.

It was foolish behaviour and she knew it, but she could not stop herself. She walked the city centre streets, she prowled round the shops, she visited Stanwix and now she was out of the house as much as once she had hidden herself within it. Henry complained she was never there when he popped home unexpectedly, as he often did, and could not understand this new mania for shopping. Leah said there were still so many things she must buy for the house and was careful always to return with some trifling purchase. It had become an urgent necessity to find out where Evie was, and after six months of this searching she yearned for some final confirmation. It came by chance, just as she had wanted it to. Turning out of Etterby Terrace, Evie's road, which she had walked for the hundredth time, she proceeded up Etterby Street, her own old street, towards the Scaur, and met Miss Mawson leaving her house.

'Why, Mrs Arnesen!' cried Miss Mawson.

'Miss Mawson,' Leah murmured faintly, highly embarrassed.

'I am so glad to see you, my dear,' said Miss Mawson, her eyes positively shining with pleasure. 'I miss you all so much, I cannot tell you.'

'I miss you too.'

'It was a black day for me when you moved and I have never felt comfortable since without my dear neighbours. Now tell me, are you settled and happy in your splendid new home? Thank you for your card. Did I thank you at the time? I do hope so. I intended to call but I have not been well … now, why don't you step inside and let me give you some refreshment?'

'Oh no,' Leah protested, 'you are on your way out, I can see that, I would not on any account …'

'Where I was going can wait. Come, I insist. For old times' sake. This is too good an opportunity to miss. Come, I will not take no for an answer.' And before Leah could think of an excuse Miss Mawson had opened her door and was ushering her in.

It dismayed her to find herself in this position. She had lived next door to Miss Mawson for more than a decade and yet she knew her so little. They were pleasant to each other but there was no exchange of hospitality, and Leah had always felt Miss Mawson had in some way looked down upon her, because she was able to tell she was not a natural born lady, nor Henry a gentleman. This, Henry had always said, was her imagination and gradually she had conceded it might well be. After her cat had been run over and Henry had had the unhappy task of telling Miss Mawson (for it was he who saw the accident and arranged for the burial), the relationship between the two households had perceptibly changed. Miss Mawson became quite effusively neighbourly and invitations to take tea had been exchanged.

But with the arrival of Evie nearby, the friendship which had blossomed began to wither. Leah knew that Miss Mawson was acquainted with Evie. She was, if not Evie's friend, to some extent her patron and Leah always feared might be brought into the troubled situation between them. She was sure she had hurt gentle Miss Mawson by declining, under plea of headaches and general debility, all her offers of hospitality from then on. And there was always the worry that Miss Mawson had noticed Evie in the street peering at the Arnesens' house and might have inquired the reason for this of her.

But now, sitting in Miss Mawson's pretty little parlour, Leah realised she had been presented with the perfect opportunity to establish Evie's whereabouts. If Evie had moved, Miss Mawson would surely know, taking as she did an interest in the young woman. So eager was Leah to question Miss Mawson on this point that she grew bold. She no longer cared whether Evie had taken Miss Mawson into her confidence, but only that she should find out the truth. 'Has much changed in our old area here, Miss Mawson?' she queried. 'Or are we the only family to have moved lately?'

'Oh, indeed no,' said Miss Mawson, 'there has been quite an upheaval locally, all kinds of people taking it into their heads, for their own very good reasons, I am sure, to leave Etterby and find other accommodation. Those who are young seem to be the very people moving. Take the Patersons. You remember Evie? Who worked for your husband and married James Paterson? She came to live nearby in Etterby Terrace, you know, but has left already.'

'Really?' Leah murmured, hoping she masked her dreadful desire to know by seeming not unduly interested.

Miss Mawson was animated, delighting in such gossip. 'She has been fortunate at last, the most extraordinary thing. She has found her family. It seems they are a good family of some means and a son has died who turns out to have been Evie's father ... And now the grandmother has sent an aunt to find her and Evie and James have gone off to some grand house near Newcastle to be made much of. It quite took my breath away on hearing of it.'

Omitting to comment that it took hers away too, Leah asked, 'And did you hear this from Mrs Paterson herself?'

'Oh no, from her husband who was making a costume for me and ...' Miss Mawson stopped and blushed deeply. Henry had always made her costumes. To leave him for Jimmy Paterson, working in a rival establishment, was a betrayal of the first order and she gazed at Leah in horror. Leah made a little gesture of dismissal with her hands to indicate she thought nothing of this inadvertent confession and pressed Miss Mawson to continue with her enthralling tale. 'Well,' said Miss Mawson, taking courage, though unable quite to recapture her former zest in the telling, 'Mr Paterson said he would finish my costume before they left, but that would be that in Carlisle for him. I asked where exactly this grand house was and he said in a village, in fact quite some distance from Newcastle, but that there were plans already to move there. The grandmother is old and ill and there is another house owned in Newcastle itself and the plan is for the three of them to move there and for Mr Paterson to set up on his own account as a tailor there. I am so glad for Evie, all this, after her troubles lately, some fortune and happiness at last.'

'Troubles?' echoed Leah, suddenly alarmed, thinking that after all Miss Mawson was not as innocent as she seemed.

Miss Mawson dropped her voice, though there was no one else in the room but the two of them. 'She miscarried, twice. Poor Evie. She so wishes to be a mother. I had it from Mrs Batey who lives next door.'

Leah's eyes filled with tears. Seeing this, Miss Mawson, she knew, would assume she was affected in the way any tender-hearted woman would be, and would not expect her to explain the sudden tears. She wanted to leave Miss Mawson quickly, to get right away from her so that these foolish tears could be shed and she could then rejoice in safety, but it was impossible to extricate herself for another quarter of an hour. When she did depart, she was weak with suppressed euphoria and reached Stanwix Bank and the tram station in a daze. Evie had gone. She was to live a long way away. She had separated herself from the mother who would not acknowledge her. She had given up, at last.

Later, Leah was able to assess the chances of this being true in a more sober fashion. She saw that it was only safe to assume that Evie had left for the time being. Nothing could be certain about the future. If the Patersons did not make a go of it in Newcastle, they could well return to Carlisle, and Evie could start again where she had left off. But distance would work as much of a change in her as time might. Leah realised that once Evie had found her it was her proximity which had proved so tantalising – to have her mother round the corner and accessible was too tempting for her craving to be denied. Now that she was many miles away the constant pull to visit her mother would be weakened and lose its magnetic strength. Evie would be likely to be absorbed in building a new and better life around herself, and her old life and old obsessions would have the chance to fade. The abrupt nature of her departure from Carlisle also seemed to Leah to augur well – there had been no final visit to her mother's house. From the moment Mrs Fletcher had called, Evie had never reappeared.

It took a full year for Leah to feel that Evie must be settled in Newcastle and was not going to return, and another before she felt that the shadow cast by her had truly lifted. Miss Mawson told her, when she came to tea, that she had had a Christmas card. The Patersons were doing well. The grandmother had died and left them the house, and business was also good. 'But no mention,' Miss Mawson said, face composed into a suitably concerned expression, 'no mention of little ones, too sad. Time is running out for her, I fear.' Leah wondered. She calculated Evie's age now as – surely she was still only in her twenties, not too old at all. Miss Mawson must think her older. 'Her husband,' Miss Mawson was saying, 'has fears that if war breaks out he will be conscripted before long and is training Evie to be in charge while he is away.' Leah nodded. Henry was talking in a similar fashion, though he was too old to be in any danger, and in his careful way was also making preparations. Leah had no interest in rumours of war.

It was of more concern to her that Rose, very strong-willed these days, was not at all the amenable child she had once been. She had declined to stay a lady of leisure at home for ever and had insisted on having a career. Now she was threatening to marry. She was twenty years old and thought it time in spite of her excellent job in the

Town Hall. Neither Leah nor Henry approved of her intended, one Joseph Butler, a butcher whose family owned three stalls in the market. Joseph had been courting Rose for a year, long enough for her parents to have marked him down as unsteady and far too interested in pleasure. Rose, when she was with him, became giddy and quite unlike herself. Henry had begun to mutter that marriage might be the best option, considering the way things were going, by which Leah knew he feared Rose would give way to Joseph and land herself in trouble. Leah, who could not bear the mere mention, however obliquely, of such a disaster, found herself hoping war might actually break out and carry Joseph out of the way for long enough for Rose to forget him.

The opposite happened. War was declared in August 1914, and Joseph joined up immediately. Rose burst into tears and announced she would marry him at once. She loved him and could wait no longer. No amount of pleading would make her change her mind, but since, in spite of her determination to marry with all speed, she wanted a proper wedding, she agreed to wait six weeks until Joseph had completed his basic training. The marriage would take place before, as was anticipated, he was sent abroad. Leah was thrown into a frenzy of preparations for the white wedding, and Henry too, of course, since naturally he was making Rose's dress and those of the four bridesmaids. But two days before the great day Joseph's regiment was ordered to France. The wedding had to be postponed since Joseph was not allowed home at all and Rose was unable to bid him a proper farewell. She dissolved into hysterical weeping and was inconsolable. The wedding dress was carefully wrapped up and put away and a new date fixed for Joseph's first leave.

Afterwards, Rose blamed Leah, quite openly and bitterly, for preventing her marriage. She said everyone knew she had wanted to marry Joseph Butler for months and that if it had not been for the opposition of her mother the wedding would have taken place in the summer. Leah did not try to counter this. However true, Rose would also have to admit, if reminded, that it was she who had delayed those fatal few weeks in order to have a splendid wedding instead of a hole-in-corner affair. But Leah was not going to remind her. Rose was too broken. No tears now, when real tragedy had struck. Once she had been told of Joseph's death in his first week of action she seemed to seize up. She sat pale and motionless hour after hour and it was Leah who did the weeping. When Rose fainted on the way downstairs one morning no one was surprised – she had hardly eaten a thing in the last month, since Joseph was killed. But Leah sent for the doctor, hoping he would give orders to eat which Rose would heed. He issued the orders, but for a reason Leah had never suspected.

Rose had known perfectly well that she was pregnant. The child was conceived the day Joseph joined up, when Rose could resist him no longer and believed herself certain to be married so soon that a little anticipation did not matter. If the marriage had taken place, Leah was aware, Rose's plight now would have been miserable and serious enough – a widow, at twenty-one – but without that seal of respectability Rose was ruined. Ruined more disastrously than she herself had been ruined, since Rose had far more to lose. Henry raged and damned the dead Joseph but Leah wasted no time on pointless ranting. Her mind was full of schemes, schemes to whisk Rose away in a manner no one would suspect and have her looked after until the baby was born and could be adopted. It was essential to act quickly, to put the word about that the doctor had pronounced Rose ill with a wasting disease which necessitated a move to a sanatorium at once. Lies must be honed until perfect and then the telling of them practised until they were all word- and expression-perfect.

But Rose proved intractable. She would not co-operate in any secrecy. She said if her parents cast her out she would not be surprised. She had brought, or was about to bring, shame and disgrace upon them and her punishment would be to take herself off to a Home for Fallen Girls – what else did she deserve? But she would not give up her child. Never. The child was all she had left of Joseph. Never, never could she part with that child and if keeping the child branded her as a whore, then so be it. Leah wept, Henry wept, Polly (who had to know) wept, but Rose did not. Her mind was quite made up. And, of course, they loved her and could not turn her out and so she stayed at home and was looked after; and the tongues wagged as viciously as Leah had dreaded. Rose insisted on calling herself Mrs Butler which worried Henry greatly, so much so that he paid to have her surname changed by deed poll, thereby ensuring she had a legal entitlement to the 'Butler' if not the 'Mrs'.

The baby was a girl. Rose called her Josephine and was from the first devoted to her. Leah watched her carefully, remembering her own initial devotion to Evie, and how frighteningly this had been replaced with revulsion. But Rose's passionate love for her daughter grew rather than abated. She told Leah she had a reason to live now and that Josephine was a constant comfort to her, a living reminder of Joseph whom she had loved so much. She carried her proudly in her arms with no hint of shame, though there were plenty who tried to make her feel ashamed. Joseph's own family, from whom she had hoped much, would not acknowledge her as their dead son's wife-in-all-but-name. They were angry that she called herself Mrs Butler and wanted nothing to do with their grandchild. Rose endured this hostility with fortitude, merely commenting that Joseph would have despised their attitude.

It was one of the Butlers, a daughter of Joseph's sister, who, when Josephine was eight, taunted her at school with the word 'bastard'. She sang it under her breath whenever Josephine was near her, neither of them knowing what it meant. Rose, when asked by her daughter what it did mean, went white and compressed her lips tightly, saying only, 'Nothing. It is not a word for young girls.' But she went straight away to see Joseph's sister and warned her to put a civil tongue in her daughter's head, or there would be trouble. She did not know what she meant by her threat, but the violence and conviction with which she uttered it were effective. The Butler child desisted from then onwards.

Until, that is, Josephine was fourteen and long past complaining to her mother about taunts or teasing. Her one desire by then was to distance herself from a mother who enveloped her in such a squeeze of love that she felt she would suffocate. She longed for a father and for brothers and sisters, and for a normal family life instead of this claustrophobic existence, just herself and her mother, living now in a little house Henry had bought for Rose. She was so used to telling friends that her father had been killed in the war soon after marrying her mother that it came as a shock to her when first this version of events was challenged. It was the same Butler girl, grown insolent and daring enough to flout her own mother's order. 'They were never married,' the Butler girl said, hearing Josephine's patter to a new girl in the class. 'She's a bastard.' Josephine stared at her. She had an inkling now what a bastard was and, though not entirely sure, was more sure than she had been at eight that to be called a bastard was a terrible thing. She was afraid to speak and the Butler girl saw that she was. 'She's a bastard,' she repeated. 'Her mother was a slut who led my uncle on and maybe she led others on too and isn't even his bastard, whatever name she has.' 'Liar,' Josephine managed to whisper, but quick as a flash the Butler girl said, 'Prove it, then,' and all there was left for her to do was turn away and leave the classroom.

She ought to have confronted her mother then but the thought horrified her. So she kept silent. Half the class had heard, of course, and gave her strange looks for a while. She held her head high and retreated further into herself and eventually the other girls lost interest. She worked hard and did well in examinations and decided she wanted to be a teacher. Her grandparents were delighted, but her mother worried aloud that it would mean her going away to training college and that such a separation would be torture. She did not want Josephine to leave her as Joseph had done and said so. Out came the story of her romantic but brief marriage and the retelling of it, in this context, snapped Josephine's patience. 'I'm leaving, Mother,' she said, 'I want my own life.' She longed to add that she knew this love-story was a sham, or at least the wedding part, but she held her peace.

Her own former restraint made it all the harder to endure her mother's decision to tell her the truth on her eighteenth birthday, before she left for teacher training college.

'I have something to tell you, Josephine dear,' Rose said, smiling tremulously, her eyes yearning for sympathy.

Josephine knew at once what it was. 'No,' she said, sharply, 'there is no need to tell me anything. I know.'

'What do you know?' whispered Rose, looking frightened.

'I know you were never married. That's all. And I don't want to hear about it. It doesn't matter.'

'Oh, but it does!' wailed Rose, and then there was no stopping her. Out came a catalogue of excuses and justifications, and Josephine could hardly keep still from agitation as her mother went on and on. 'I have never regretted what I did for a single hour,' Rose declared at the end of her recital, 'except for a moment or two when I saw the pain it caused your grandmother.' Leah was still alive, in her mid-sixties, and Josephine looked up to her and regarded her with the greatest respect. She could imagine easily her grandmother's horror. 'Your grandmother,' said Rose, 'wanted me to have you adopted but the thought never even crossed my mind. She tried to persuade me, she said I would have no life of my own, with a baby at my age and unmarried. She said you would be far happier adopted by a respectable couple. She said I was sacrificing my whole life for a baby who would never know the difference.' Then Rose sat back and looked hopefully to Josephine for gratitude.

But Josephine felt far from grateful. What she felt most strongly was embarrassment and resentment. Her mother need never have told her this story. It had been kept secret for eighteen years and it was monstrous of her to foist such a painful truth on her daughter. Josephine hated to think of Rose behaving so improperly and saw no romance in her parents' hurried passion. She resolved to tell no one, ever. Her mother had pretended and she would pretend. It was such a little lie in any case. But the knowledge that she was in fact illegitimate changed her attitude to her mother significantly and her attitude to sex was formed by it. She had always been made uncomfortable by her mother's intensity, her total devotion and had longed to be free of it. Now, she started to free herself, absolving herself from guilt. In spite of Rose's tears, once she had qualified as a teacher she promptly moved into a room of her own near the school where she taught and then, when she had taken up a situation in a London school, she never returned to live in Carlisle after she met and married Gerald Walmsley.

She never told Gerald she was illegitimate. Why should she? Gerald's family was socially superior to hers and she was afraid of them. Gerald himself had not the least interest in her background. She had to take him home, of course, to meet Rose and the rest of her family, but once that was done he had no contact with them except when they came to stay for the rare, very rare, visit. Rose was quite overawed by Gerald's profession and hardly spoke in his presence. She once tried to ask Josephine, after she had been Gerald's fiancée for a year, if she and Gerald had ... well ... if they had ... which she would, of all people, understand if – but Josephine silenced her, saying furiously that she and Gerald were only engaged, and he respected her and there was time for 'that sort of thing' when they were married.

Josephine wrote her father's name boldly in the church register and her mother kept the secret of her illegitimacy because she did not dare do anything else. She had used Joseph's surname for so long now it did not seem to matter (but she had a miserable feeling that it did, to Josephine at least). Josephine was glad to settle in London and begin her new, her very new, life. Her first son was born ten months after his parents' marriage, to Josephine's great satisfaction. Nothing could have been more respectable, and even though times were changing and morals with them, this mattered to her. Sex did not. It appalled her to remember that it was for *this* that her mother had risked her good name. It was absurd. Why could she not have waited? Why could she not have made *him* wait? Gerald had waited. There had been no question of his not doing so. He had not even pressed her too hard and once they were married his demands were modest, to her great relief. Gerald loved her and she loved him and sex was something quite different. When, after two sons, she gave birth to her daughter Hazel, she hoped to be able to bring her up to understand this.

Then mistakes would not be made.

Epilogue

It was a strange, lost feeling to have her dead. All hope gone. Hope ought to have left her long, long ago, but it never quite had. It should have departed with her when she left Carlisle but always, at the back of her mind, there had been the image of herself, carrying her baby, approaching her mother's door once more and finding it open, and seeing all the hostility on her mother's face fade, replaced by joy as she opened her arms to welcome her grandchild as she had not been able to welcome her child. Such a pretty picture it was. It kept Evie happy. All she needed was to give birth and she could give life to this fantasy, the transformation could take place.

Only twice was a doctor called for. They could afford doctors, it was not the expense which prevented her. It was the pointlessness and then the humiliation. They were impatient, these men, with her expectations. What did she expect them to be able to do? They told her to be glad she was miscarrying for there must have been something malformed about the foetus to cause its rejection. She lay and thought about this, in the dark, with the blood seeping steadily out of her. Malformed or not, she wanted to become its mother. Her tenderness, her loving care, would compensate. But no amount of lying still could keep any of her babies inside her. They left her, as her own mother had left her, and she was helpless with grief.

Once, the child was far enough along for its sex to be plainly seen. A girl, five months in gestation. She wished to keep her, in her bed, wrapped in the shawl she had crocheted, the shawl she would be buried in, but the midwife would not allow this. Her daughter was taken away and Evie screamed and screamed and was threatened with the madhouse if she did not stop. It would be the right place for her. She felt mad. But then there was Jimmy, patient and devoted, proving himself time after time, poor Jimmy forced to bear the brunt of her brutal distress. He gave up hope long before she did but pretended he had not. He indulged her fantasies and she was grateful to him. Seven miscarriages she suffered and all except two were dealt with by Jimmy, who took away the liver-like scraps which came from her and burned them. Blood became her familiar. The sight of it haunted her even when she was not bleeding and her aversion to all things red grew. She felt many a time that she was floating on oceans of blood and there was not a sheet in the house unmarked by the stains however long the linen had been soaked and scrubbed, soaked and scrubbed.

She wondered, as she lay in the midst of this blood when she was miscarrying, what her mother would think if she saw her now. Would her heart melt at last? When she saw the pain and misery and then the futility of it all? Evie talked to her, when the pain was at its worst, and was considered delirious. 'Is her mother at hand?' the doctor asked Jimmy and was told Evie had no mother, which was what he believed. The Arnesens' secret was safe with Evie and if he had suspicions (for where could his wife ever have found the money for them to buy a house?) they were of a different nature and all to do with Henry, but not Leah, Arnesen. Evie told him, when first she agreed to walk out with him, that she had no mother and that was that. Jimmy was an innocent in every way, a man who accepted and never questioned. His own mother was long since dead and he thought nothing of mothers. His wife's passion to become a mother completely baffled him.

Jimmy brought the *Cumberland News* home from Carlisle especially for Evie to see the announcement – *Leah Arnesen, devoted wife of Henry and much loved mother of Rose and Polly, and grandmother of Charles and Josephine, on* 11 *April, at home, suddenly.* Jimmy, who went on business to Carlisle often, had connections still with friends who continued to work at Arnesen's and was told it had been a heart attack. The funeral was in three days' time. At once, Evie determined to go. She had not been out of the house since her last miscarriage some two months since (a miscarriage which at her age of forty was indeed likely to be her last) and was still weak, but she never hesitated. Jimmy was aghast. He could not believe she truly intended to make the tiring journey and saw no alternative, when he realised she was in earnest, but to take her himself, though there was no reason for him to go again so soon to Carlisle.

Evie dressed in heavy mourning, as though a principal mourner, and Jimmy privately wondered what the Arnesen family would think of such presumption. The church was almost full, because Henry Arnesen was a respected figure who had been mayor the year before. Entering the church, Jimmy saw Evie was taken aback at the size of the congregation. He indicated a row at the back still virtually unoccupied, but to his consternation she began marching down the centre aisle. He followed, because there was nothing else he could do but be loyal. She went right to the front, to the first row where Henry Arnesen and his two daughters and one son-in-law and two small grandchildren were all seated. Evie stood, waiting. Jimmy clutched her sleeve, but she shook him off, and at the same time Henry Arnesen stood up and motioned his family to do likewise and they all moved along, to make room for Evie and Jimmy.

The coffin was smothered with flowers, most of them camellias, white camellias, Leah's favourite flower. Everyone wept, except Evie. She looked through her veil at the coffin and the beautiful flowers and could not weep for the mother who had never loved her. She wanted to weep for herself, but the tears would not come. Instead, a sense of rage began to grow in her and her face behind its veil burned and she wondered the veil was not set alight by this heat. She hardly heard the words of the service and did not sing the hymn. When the coffin was taken out she was first to follow it, brushing Jimmy aside as he hesitated and cowered before the Arnesens. She knew everyone was staring at her, appalled by her impertinence and doubtless expecting Henry Arnesen to deal with her appropriately. But he handed her into the first car and got in beside her, with the two daughters whose expressions could not be seen but could easily be guessed at. No one spoke in the car. At the cemetery, Evie stood with Henry, and when the coffin had been lowered into its trench he turned to her and in everyone's hearing said, 'Will you come to the house?' She nodded. Jimmy was nowhere to be seen.

She found herself to be perfectly composed once inside the house she had never been allowed to enter. There was quite a spread laid out in the dining-room with glasses of whisky for the men and sherry for the women. Evie neither ate nor drank. She stood to one side, near the window and, looking out, thought of herself once always looking in. She was aware that Rose and Polly were engaged in whispered debate with their father and knew it was about her. He would tell them. He must tell them. It was why she had come. If he did not tell them she would have to do so herself and quite looked forward to this. But now, though she had, unlike all the other women, not lifted her veil, Miss Mawson had recognised her. 'Why, Evie, it is Evie, is it not? My dear, how good of you to come.' Evie inclined her head but said not a word. She saw that Miss Mawson positively vibrated with curiosity and the sense that something dramatic was about to happen if, with Evie's behaviour in the church, it had not already done so. 'So sad,' Miss Mawson was saying, 'so sudden, a heart attack, you know, though she had never had anything wrong with her heart.' Miss Mawson lowered her voice even further. 'It may have been weakened by the shock, of course. Years ago now but still a dreadful, dreadful blow at the time.' Evie had no idea what she was talking about. 'Rose, you know, and her intended killed in action, and then ... She is a pretty little thing, Josephine.'

Henry Arnesen came between them. He bowed to Miss Mawson and accepted her sincere condolences. Then he asked Evie to come with him a moment and, watched by the entire room, the two of them went out and into the study across the hall. Henry shut the door. 'Why did you come to the funeral?' he asked.

'I am her daughter,' Evie said, proudly. She knew what he was going to say.

'She has passed on,' Henry said. 'All that is finished. Do you wish to distress Rose and Polly more than they are already distressed? Do you wish to ruin their mother in their eyes now she is gone from them?'

Evie put up her veil. She looked long and steadily at Henry and smiled. 'Yes,' she said, 'I wish to tell my sisters I am their mother's daughter too and then I will go and never bother them again.'

'It is cruel,' Henry said.

'It is she who was cruel,' Evie said, 'and made me suffer all my life. And your girls are mothers themselves, they should understand, one of them especially, I am told.'

Rose and Polly slipped into the study nervously and stood either side of their father with Evie facing all three of them. They had changed greatly since she had last seen them. Rose in particular she would not have recognised. The pretty girl had given way to a sombre matron, pale of face and dull-looking, where once she had sparkled. Polly had merely lost weight and grown tall. They looked frightened, and their father did nothing to reassure them. 'This is Mrs Paterson,' he said. 'She has something she wishes you to know.' Rose gave a little moan. All three stared at Evie and waited. 'I am her daughter too,' she said. There was no reaction, so she repeated the words and for good measure added, 'I am your mother's daughter too, her first-born, before ever she married your father.' The two women both looked up at Henry. 'Father,' whispered Rose, 'can this be true?' He nodded, unable to speak. Nobody moved. Evie waited and waited, and then she said, 'I must go home now.' They parted and she went out into the hall and the front door was opened for her and outside Jimmy was waiting. She made him take her back to the cemetery and there she looked again at the mound under which her mother rested, and she felt it was over at last. 'I have no mother,' she said, 'I never had a mother, and I never shall be one.' Jimmy, standing at a little distance away, on her instructions, heard only an indistinct murmur and thought a prayer was being said. He was in a hurry to get Evie home. She did not look well and whatever this attendance at Leah Arnesen's funeral was about he wanted it over.

Evie went with him docilely enough. She had no more miscarriages. At forty-five she had an abrupt menopause and this was said to account for her unbalanced behaviour afterwards. She took to wandering the streets, knocking on doors and asking for her mother. And in the end Jimmy was forced to agree she needed treatment. Before it could begin, she died in a state mental institution, of a heart attack, quite unexpectedly.

*

It was in the middle of Australia that Shona suddenly felt homesick. Predictable, it was so predictable it made her smile in the midst of her melancholic turn of mind – the intense heat, the dust, the reds and browns, all so different from the Scottish coast. She sent a postcard to Catriona and Archie, saying she was missing St Andrews and would give anything for a blow along the beach in the rain and mist. At the bottom she wrote 'and missing you both too'. It was true. All the time she'd been at university in London she hadn't been back to St Andrews more than half a dozen times, for ever shorter periods, and yet now she was so far away she craved the place. She sat with her eyes shut on a bench outside the post office, her T-shirt and shorts damp with the perspiration which drenched her by midday every day and only seemed to leave her when she was actually standing under a cold water shower. She felt not just hot but sick. She had neither the skin nor the colouring, nor indeed, she thought, the metabolism to survive this kind of climate. The two girls she had teamed up with did far better. They were dark-haired Mediterranean types who soaked up the sun and came to life in its heat.

She wanted to go home. There was no reason why not. She could begin the long journey back any time she wanted. There was nothing to hold her here. Sixteen months she'd been away and it was enough – it was time, definitely time, to halt this roaming and think what she wanted to do with her life. But she felt sick and weak and lacked the energy to leave her companions and about-turn on her own. Maybe she was ill, maybe the bug she had picked up in India hadn't really left her stomach. She wished her mother was near, a babyish thing to wish, and she wouldn't say it aloud or the other two would laugh. She wanted to be looked after, fussed over and, still with her eyes shut, soothed herself with a vision of Catriona applying a cold compress to her burning forehead and ushering her into a cool and darkened room. It made her feel cheap, to think of her mother only as someone useful who would care for her. Perturbed, she opened her eyes and tried to pull herself together. Some effort was needed. They'd left their rucksacks in the hostel, but now she said she was going to go back and collect hers and get a bus to Darwin and fly to Sydney and then home. 'I'm not up to this,' she said, and the other two accepted her verdict cheerfully. They'd only been together three weeks.

In Sydney she debated whether to telephone her mother but decided not to, a surprise would be best. Catriona would be saved the worry of knowing she was flying and fearing she might crash, the kind of worry to which she had always been irritatingly prone. It was harder to decide whether to let Hazel know she was to pass through London. She'd sent postcards to the boys from every country she'd visited and kept in touch that easy way. They'd given her a great send-off when she left, all of them coming to Heathrow and waving her through into the departure lounge, with little Anthony crying. She had felt quite tearful herself and had been proud to know she had such feelings. Hazel, unexpectedly, had embraced her warmly, but she had wondered if that warmth was because she was leaving. Now, if she returned, maybe it would not be evident and she was surprised to realise she did not much care. She admired Hazel but she had never been sure that she had learned to understand her. She could not decide, either, whether she actually liked her. What was there to like? Her composure? Her cleverness? Her ability to distance herself from emotion? Her organisational skills? The harder she tried to list in her mind why she might like Hazel the less convinced she was that she did. And she did not love her. There was at least no doubt about that. But when she thought of Catriona, reasons for liking her tumbled into her head. She was so kind, so unselfish, so gentle, so anxious to help in every way possible – and in any case reasons were irrelevant because she saw now that the feelings she had for this mother of hers amounted to love. Catriona and she had virtually nothing in common but they were nevertheless part of each other. All her life she had been exasperated by Catriona and she probably always would feel some measure of irritation. But there was a connection between them which she now had no pressing need to deny. She'd stopped looking for a mirror image of herself in the woman who had conceived and given birth to her. She was glad to have got something straight, at whatever cost.

Going home was not as traumatic as she had feared. The welcome was just as she had anticipated and she basked in it and thought how lucky she was to be assured of it whenever she returned. And she felt well again for the first time in months, really well, not a trace of nausea. She shed the inertia which had weighed her down and became her old energetic self – a lesson learned, she told herself, and never to be forgotten. But she didn't stay in St Andrews. She went to Edinburgh and took a job in the university's administrative department. She'd feared it would be deadly dull and had only taken it to make a start somewhere while she sorted out in which direction she really wished to go, but she found she liked it and was rapidly promoted. She had enough money to rent a flat and buy a second-hand car, and every other weekend she went home to St Andrews, to the delight of her parents. They were ageing and she was anxious about them and liked to make regular visits to see that all was well.

They wanted to see her married, naturally. They were conventional and had no time for any other kind of liaison. She took all the inquiries about 'romances' in good part, and made jokes about their expectations, but when she did have her first affair she kept it secret. She was old, she thought, at twenty-four, to be having a first love-affair, but then she had had other things on her mind and had shut herself off from men. His name was Lachlan, and she was very happy with him for six months until she discovered he was married. The disappointment was worse than the shock, and the sense of rage at being hoodwinked greater than the humiliation.

She was more careful after that. She checked men out. From the beginning, she knew Gregory Bates was divorced and had a child of three. His honesty was heartening and so was his concern for his child. She met the child, saddled with the ridiculous name of China, very early in her relationship with Gregory. It might even, she considered later, have been a kind of test – if she didn't get on with China then there was no hope of any future with Gregory. After a year, he asked her to marry him and was most upset when she turned him down. 'I'd like to be your wife, Greg,' she said, 'but I don't want to be China's second mother.' So that was that, another relationship over.

She never intended to become involved with Jeremy Atkinson – by this time she felt liberated enough to think only in terms of an affair and nothing else – which was why, perhaps, she had such fun. Jeremy believed in having a good time. He was not her type and yet she was more attracted to him than she had ever been to any man. He made her feel lighthearted and irresponsible when she knew herself to be serious and conscientious, and she liked the strangeness of this. Jeremy was an accountant but gave the lie to the image of accountants as stuffy and dreary. He made a lot of money and spent it on holidays and entertainment and meals out. She hardly knew herself as she jetted off to the Caribbean with Jeremy and went out with him night after night to theatres and concerts. But when she found she was pregnant she had no hesitation.

She almost didn't tell Jeremy – there was no need for him to know – but in the end she did. He was vastly relieved at her attitude, her 'healthy' attitude as he called it, and insisted on paying for the abortion. It was simple enough to arrange, if costly (so she was glad of Jeremy's money) and she felt no after-effects, physical or psychological. But, naturally, during her one day in the private clinic she thought again about Hazel pregnant with her all those years ago, in the dark ages. She had always made it clear to Hazel – well, she hoped she had – that if an abortion had been possible in 1956 she would never have blamed any woman for having one. An abortion was far preferable to giving a child away after bearing it with resentment. She felt moved to write to Hazel afterwards, though not to Catriona – she would never tell her mother – and received in reply the kind of compassionate response she had hoped for. The abortion at least served the useful purpose of drawing her closer to Hazel.

She married Jeremy, but not for another three years, by which time she had decided she didn't want children, ever. She thought Jeremy might mind but he didn't: he said he had no desire whatsoever to be a father and was only surprised Shona had none to be a mother, because he assumed all women did, it being their biological destiny. The decision made, she had herself sterilised, an operation far more difficult to organise than an abortion, which amazed her. She had it before the wedding but told nobody, except Jeremy, that is. Doubtless their respective mothers would drive them crazy in the years ahead waiting for grandchildren, but that could not be helped. She would make it clear, as time went on, that she simply didn't want to be a mother without hurting them by revealing she no longer could be in any case.

She was a very beautiful bride, but what everyone remarked on was not Shona's beauty but her serenity. She seemed so happy with herself in a way she had never been, and Archie could not resist saying to Catriona, 'Everything turned out all right in the end. You were a perfect mother to her, that's why.' Catriona did not reply. She knew there was no such thing. Archie was only trying to reassure her with his compliment but she no longer needed such reassurance. Shona had come back to them. She had stayed close. That was what mattered, that was what every mother wanted.